DORA VERSUS PICASSO

DORA VERSUS PICASSO

CECIL JENKINS

Matador
9 Priory Business Park
Kibworth Beauchamp
Leicestershire LE8 0RX, UK
Tel: (+44) 116 279 2299
Fax: (+44) 116 279 2277
Email: books@troubador.co.uk
Web: www.troubador.co.uk/matador

ISBN 978-1783062-577

British Library Cataloguing in Publication Data.
A catalogue record for this book is available from the British Library.

Typeset in Aldine by Troubador Publishing Ltd
Printed and bound in the UK by TJ International, Padstow, Cornwall

Matador is an imprint of Troubador Publishing Ltd

1

'Sorry about this little hold-up, Assia.'

A chilly November day in 1935 and Dora Maar, in her studio at 29 Rue d'Astorg, was in the middle of a photo-shoot with the model Assia. Who was now sitting naked with a black fur coat over her shoulders and a Balto cigarette in her hand, describing what it was like growing up in the Ukraine while Dora was replacing a broken bulb, adjusting the lighting and changing the slide.

'So' she asked Assia a little distractedly, 'there was anti-Jewish repression even after the Bolshevik Revolution?'

'Yes, that's why we got out.'

'Oh God, it's everywhere this anti-Semitism, isn't it?'

'Yes, it's not just Hitler in Germany, is it? There's plenty of it here.'

'Yes, well, with that attack on the National Assembly by those far-right groups last year…'

'My mother is convinced there'll be a Fascist takeover.'

'Well, let's hope it won't come to that' said Dora, preoccupied with checking the lighting. 'So when did you come to Paris then?'

'In 1921. When I was ten.'

'So you're still only twenty-four? You've done terribly well, Assia.'

And so she had. For she was already a favourite nude model of artists and photographers from Maillol to the American Man Ray. Not excluding Dora herself, who had shown her masked and nude hanging one-handed from an iron ring, lying in a dreamily sensuous pose with her hair mingling indistinguishably with the luxuriant pile of a rich rug and, most technically memorable perhaps, as a standing nude with side lighting not only subtly sculpting her body with light and shade but casting an almost monstrously erotic shadow on the wall behind her. She was very natural and charming, of course, but above all she had the perfect body for the work, not simply the fresh unblemished skin, the neat high breasts and smooth young stomach, but the strong healthy look that went with the outdoor myth of the moment. Out there in the real world women aged, had babies, developed heavier breasts and stomach folds, but in the rarefied world of artistic fashion and erotica the virginal was queen. Just one of the contradictions the photographer had to work with.

'I haven't done quite as well as you, Dora!' Assia was saying with a grin. 'A grand studio in a chic district in Paris…?!'

'Oh well, I've been lucky, I have to admit. And not just because my father financed me, but because I studied at the Académie Julien of the Ecole des Beaux Arts – the only place in the country, did you know, where women students were treated on an equal basis with the men?'

'Really? So what were the others afraid of?'

'Well, can you imagine? Well-bred young ladies drawing naked bodies alongside young men! And it was bad enough when it was a female model, but imagine the horror of them looking at a naked male model – seeing things proper young ladies weren't supposed to see! The breakdown of society…!'

'And God help the poor male model' laughed Assia. 'Who might have got excited at seeing these blushing young ladies and mightn't have been able to…er, keep down his feelings. It could have been hard on him.'

'Yes, it could have been embarrassingly hard on him!' said Dora, laughing in response. 'And that really would have been the end of civilization! Even so, it was still terribly difficult for the women students when they finished the course.'

'With this economic slump that's still going on?'

'Yes, you just couldn't get exhibited commercially – which is why I turned to photography.'

'And you've done extremely well at it, Dora, haven't you? Working on set with film directors, exhibiting in Surrealist exhibitions and all that...'

'Yes, and I'm enjoying it all. So we both seem to have survived quite well.'

'I suppose so' said Assia with a wry smile. 'But it's still a funny old way to make a living, isn't it? Taking your clothes off for anybody and everybody to look you over.'

'Which makes it even stranger for me to make a living by photographing you taking your clothes off!' said Dora with a laugh. 'But that's the game we're in, Assia. And perhaps this little contretemps is a blessing in disguise, perhaps it's telling us something...'

'It's not telling *me* anything, Dora! What is it telling you?'

'To try something different. But I'll need the extra camera and the mirror, so I'll have to set up again. You're not in a great rush?'

'No, not really.'

'We'll keep the fur coat on.'

'Good, it's only just warm enough in here.'

'But you'll need to light a fresh cigarette – when I tell you. Can you look bored?'

'Watch me!'

It took some time to set up the extra camera and adjust the angle, but the end result was a naked Assia, with the fur coat over her shoulders and the fresh cigarette in her hand, rolling her eyes in boredom as Dora directed the camera – the whole scene being doubled in the slightly angled mirror behind.

'I'll see how that develops' said Dora, as Assia started to dress.

'It might just work as a take-off of erotica – or maybe not. So how's life – apart from the modelling?'

'So-so. Not much love life these days, for a start. I'm sort of in-between.'

'Well you're not alone, as it happens.'

'But I heard you were with Georges Bataille.'

'God no, that was a year ago. And between you and me it was a nightmare.'

'Yes, I've had one or two of those myself. I just don't seem to attract the right men somehow.'

'Well, you know what your problem is?' said Dora with a grin. 'You're too beautiful. You frighten all the good guys away.'

'And it's worse for you' laughed Assia. 'You're all glamorous with your purple nail lacquer and brainy as well. And a tough cookie, they all say.'

'Do they indeed?! So the trick is to be not too goodlooking, not too bright and sweetly submissive, is it? We'll have to work on that! But look, Assia' she said, in a more serious tone as she saw her to the door, 'I hope you're not too worried about being Jewish, are you?'

'Oh, just sometimes I feel a little uneasy.'

They kissed each other on both cheeks and Dora watched her proudly elegant form disappear gradually into the darkening November dusk towards the Place Saint-Augustin, before turning back towards the dark room. Thinking that many of those in the circles she moved in could well be Jewish in origin and might be feeling a similar unease. In one way or another, Paris in this dreary, dank November was beginning to feel a little eerie. And it was a political atmosphere that led you to take a rather critical look at your work as a photographer.

For much of her output was inevitably bread-and-butter commercial stuff where there was little room for self-expression. With a commission from *Magazine Beauté* or *Madame Figaro* to present the forthcoming season's fashions – in effect for middle class

4

ladies – you showed refined-looking models in refined-looking dresses either in a refined upper middle-class salon or, more aspirationally perhaps, beside a Renoir or a Degas or even a stained glass window. There might be some room for irony in presenting top fashion in a really upmarket art magazine, where a higher level of cultural sophistication was assumed – you could use modest surreal effects, a mask or two and, rather than fall back on some tired old standby like Versailles or Venice, hit them with an implausible background such as a boneyard. And in an ad for a well-known apéritif or beauty product, rather than simply associate the brand with a celebrity or a prestigious place, you could treat it more strikingly by making it the centre of some apparently unresolved conflict or mystery.

But of course you were limited by the need to sell the product. And there were ambiguities everywhere, especially in the erotic photography, where it already lay in the different motivation of the viewers and whether they were male or female. It was a risk to attempt a take-off of the erotic genre of the kind she was trying with Assia. If the sophisticated viewer could appreciate the irony of a 'Model Resting' shot, what would a randy young man – who might after all see a standard stylized nude shot of Assia as beautiful and even inspiring – think on seeing her naked and looking bored with a fur coat around her shoulders and a Balto cigarette in her hand? You could go round and round in circles in this business.

As indeed she found when developing and reviewing the gelatine silver prints of the day's work in the dark room. On coming finally to the last print, of the bored Assia sitting nude and smoking with the fur coat over her shoulders, she decided it was over-contrived and vulgar and dropped it immediately into the bin. Before moving into the studio to light a cigarette and sit brooding on that remark she had made to Assia about photography. It was almost, disconcertingly, as though she was saying it was a sleazy or fraudulent occupation that no serious person should be engaged in – that she ought to give the whole thing up…!

After a minute or two she got up impatiently and went to check her appearance in the mirror for the journey home.

Images, images – and self-images… She had been intrigued by them ever since she played as a child in her mother's hat shop in faraway Buenos Aires, redefining herself in front of the mirror with each hat she tried on – sun bonnet, flat hat, angled hat, toque or cloche hat, not to mention hats with feathers, birds, roses or whatever fashion dictated. Each hat conferred a change of image, of mood, of identity. And if she was known for her distinctive hats as much as for her colourful nail varnish, it was not just because she acquired them through her fashion work, but because she felt them to be suggestive of other possible versions of herself.

She brushed the long arched eyebrows with a forefinger, re-defined the lips with a lip pencil and lightly touched up the rouge on her cheeks. She put on her thick burgundy check coat, threw her alphabet scarf around her neck, fixed the jaunty Albouis hat at an appropriate angle over the short dark chestnut hair, and observed the young woman looking back at her with blue-green eyes from the mirror: Dora Maar, the public and professional persona of Theodora Markovitch…

'So you're thinking of giving up photography, are you?' she said.

'It's a thought' said the Dora in the mirror.

'And how would you make a living?'

'That's also a thought' said the Dora in the mirror.

It was almost two o'clock in the morning and Dora, in a thick paisley dressing gown over her nightdress, was huddled over a small electric fire, drinking camomile tea.

It was doubtless all because of that conversation with Assia about the qualities that attracted men and above all, of course, of that mention of Bataille – would they ever stop reminding her of that so-called affair with Georges Bataille…?!

She had woken up with a start, with no more than a vague feeling that something was wrong. She wasn't sure at first that it was the nightmare – which she hadn't had for months and which in any case wasn't even her own nightmare, being rather a nightmare about a nightmare. But gradually the memories had come floating back of the spiders, large black spiders, crawling over the dead white eyes of Georges Bataille. And now she was huddled over an electric fire at two o'clock in the morning, drinking camomile tea.

It was that war again, wasn't it? That awful Great War that had left millions dead in the mud and disturbed a whole generation of writers and artists – Georges more than most. In fact the whole Surrealist movement came out of that war. Many of its prominent figures, like her close friend the poet Paul Eluard or André Breton, the leader of the movement, had experienced it directly. Paul, before being invalided out after being gassed, had served at the front as a medical orderly and, like Breton, who had been a medical student tending to shell-shocked soldiers, had seen horrors which he found unforgettable. There was an uneasy sense that Europe had committed a kind of moral suicide, that the values of reason and progress that it had seen itself as representing were an illusion. If many in the frenzy of the Gay Paree of the Twenties had been dancing in relief, others – including some who committed suicide – had felt that they were dancing in despair on the grave of a dead society.

Among the writers and artists, of course, there had been two different responses. If the Surrealists were in search of a higher sense of reality that would raise human experience to a new level, others were embracing the Communist Party or other left-wing groups in order to change society. But among the Surrealists themselves there was a sharp division, between the idealists around Breton and the dissidents loosely grouped around Bataille, with their extremist views on life and death and sex.

She had met him the previous year at a meeting of the left-wing group Masses and at a time of great political tension following the attack on parliament by the far-right groups. In the midst of all this she had found Georges, with his pale eyes, strangely intriguing. He had a research post at the Bibliothèque Nationale, he was an expert on heraldry and wrote on all sorts of subjects. Also he was handsome, polite, a little shy in manner and, if he fell into mild sarcasm on occasion, it was doubtless because he felt vulnerable, the more so since his actress wife had just left him. He was said to write stories about women sticking hard-boiled eggs up their vagina or having a fork suddenly stuck into their thigh, yet there was something boyish, even innocent about him that was oddly winning. And he had charm.

'You have the most beautiful hands I have ever seen' he had told her.

'Thank you, Georges.'

'But you don't do them justice with that purple nail lacquer.'

'No?'

'No, your nails should have different colours – every colour of the rainbow.'

It quickly became apparent that he and his friends were mainly interested in carrying forward the Surrealist revolution by breaking taboos and exploring extremes. They were enthusiastic about Spanish bullfighting, admired the style of the toreador in facing up to the risk of death, and dreamt of somehow building this attitude into everyday life. They were thrilled by pictures of the Chinese man being cut into a hundred pieces, while apparently maintaining an ecstatic smile on his face. They read works by the eighteenth century nobleman the Marquis de Sade, who broke all taboos including brutalizing women and eating excrement. And they were promoting the myth of the fabled Minotaur, the ferocious creature with the head of a bull and the body of a man, through a new art magazine duly called *Minotaure,* with its cover by that ardent devotee of Spanish bullfighting Picasso. In all this they seemed to be seeing sex not in terms of love, but in the perspective of rage, violence, suffering and death.

If Dora was sceptical about many of these ideas – partly because with Georges it was suspiciously like talk about sex rather than sex itself – she felt them to be in line with the general disorder of the times. And she did not express shock – especially since she felt that he was trying to shock her – when he suggested casually that she should do a photo-reportage of a brothel.

'I don't imagine, Georges' she laughed, 'that they would welcome a camera!'

'I think I could talk them into it in a place I know in the Rue Quincampoix.'

'Where's that? Near the Bois de Boulogne?'

'No, it's on the other side of the Boulevard de Sébastopol. About as low-class a joint as you can get' he said with a challenging smirk. 'It's my favourite.'

So, unconvinced but accepting the challenge, she went along with him the following evening to that place in the Rue Quincampoix. They negotiated their way past the swarthy man at the entrance, who argued for extra money for the camera, and proceeded to the end of a dingy corridor to meet Jeannette, who apparently did 'specials'. She was a rather bony, heavily made-up, dark-haired woman in her forties, whose domain was a small, strictly functional room with a divan, a bidet, a lavatory bowl and a wall mirror with rubber tubing on a shelf beneath it. And Dora prepared herself not to be shocked.

But she was shocked. She was shocked when, after some conventional preliminaries, Georges lay naked on the floor and, with penis in hand, asked Jeannette to piss on his face. She was shocked when he went on to ask her to excrete on his face, shocked when the woman apologised that she wasn't sure that she could because she had already serviced other clients, but she would let him do it the other way round. And shocked because it dawned on her that, for Georges, shocking her in this fashion was an indirect way of having a sort of sex with herself.

She started angrily to leave, but was stopped by the swarthy man at the entrance, who wanted to know what was going on and dragged her back protesting towards the room where Georges was hastily putting on his clothes again. And after further wrangling with the man, they found themselves arguing hotly in the street, with Dora saying it was degrading, Georges saying she was a bourgeoise and a prude, her slapping his face, him protesting that he had the right to degrade himself if he wished, her saying he hadn't the right to degrade that woman, him saying angrily and then pleadingly that she just didn't understand, until he was crying in frustration and, with this couple stopping to stare at them, she was hesitating and beginning to console him – and they ended up in a bar on the Boulevard de Sébastopol staring at each other across two glasses of *gros rouge*.

And it was then that the she really began to feel shocked. She already knew that he was yet another one who had been through the war, having in his case developed tuberculosis and been discharged as a result. She now learned, in this dingy bar, that he had been brought up in a non-religious family, but had converted to Catholicism at seventeen and had trained as a priest, only to lose his faith suddenly at twenty-six, become an atheist and be treated for acute depression.

'So you weren't happy being an atheist?'

'How could I be?!' he said, with the pale eyes staring at her intently. 'I was like a mystic without God.'

Was he not more like a mystic against God, she wondered, troubled by his extraordinary intensity.

'Georges, I don't quite see' she said gently, 'how all this relates to sex.'

'But it's central. It's the meeting point of life and death, Dora – isn't that why they call the orgasm *la petite mort*, the little death? It's where you confront the nightmare.'

She sat looking at him for a moment. There was no mention of the other person in all this. Was he afraid of sex in the end? It was as though with those strange pale eyes he was challenging her, yet appealing to her, to find out.

'What's the 'nightmare', Georges?' she asked finally. 'Do you mean just the fact of being alive?'

10

'The fact of being alive in a violent world with no meaning or purpose' he said harshly, then laughed in his mildly sarcastic, dismissive way. 'But then that's just everybody's nightmare, isn't it?'

Not everybody was worried about it, she thought, watching him play slightly self-consciously with his glass of red wine.

'Of course there are also more personal nightmares' he went on. 'Everybody has them as well.'

Dora, sensing uneasily that he wanted to tell her something she might not wish to hear, sat back and looked around for the waiter as though it was time to go.

'Actually, Dora' said Georges suddenly, forcing her attention with his intense, demanding pale eyes. 'I do have a personal nightmare. A recurrent one.'

And he began chillingly to describe his family background: a mother who kept trying to commit suicide, a father with blank white eyes as he became blind, paralysed, incontinent and eventually mad from syphilis – and whom they had guiltily abandoned to his fate when they fled before the advancing Germans at the start of the war. And the nightmare was of his father with those dead white eyes carrying him down when he was only three or four years old to the cellar.

'I was very small and I was very scared, you see' he was saying, his voice thickening. 'There were rats in the cellar and these awful spiders, large spiders that my father couldn't even see and he was laughing and I was so frightened...'

'Oh God...!'

'And he had me on his knees and he was cackling away with these dead eyes and he was handling my little cock and doing things to me I didn't understand, at least I think he was...'

'You *think* he was?'

'Well, I might even have imagined it, so that I'll never know, you see, what's true and what's not true, and that's what's so terrible, that I can never even know, which is why I have this nightmare, I think, so that I can go back to that terrible rat-ridden cellar and see those big spiders and try to find out something I can never, ever find out…'

Ever since that evening, without fuss and a little guiltily, Dora had avoided seeing Bataille and was relieved to hear that he might have found a partner of his own persuasion.

But how on earth, she wondered, as she got up to look for a biscuit, had she let herself be sucked into that situation? Bataille was doubtless more extreme in his views than those others around him who shared his interest in martyrdom and bull-fighting and breaking taboos, but there didn't seem to be too much room for women in all this, except perhaps as victims or just part of the furniture.

Since the biscuit tin turned out to be empty, she decided to make herself a *tartine beurrée* and to stay up long enough to shake off all thoughts of those dead white eyes and rats and big spiders in that cellar. And to think instead about what she had heard herself saying to Assia about giving up photography.

For there could clearly be no question of giving it up. Not just because it was her livelihood, but because there was plenty of room for self-expression in her more personal work. It was there, beyond the compromises of the commercial commissions, that you really entered the realm of ambiguity and mystery that you found in art. Even in her documentary work, as in those takes she had done in London – like that of the immaculately dressed businessman bankrupted by the recession begging with great dignity in the street– there was pathos and irony beyond mere social commentary. Indeed her general tendency, for whatever reason, was to use long or plunging or angled or night-time shots to bring out the oddity, the loneliness, even perhaps the tragedy of life in cities.

With that type of work, of course, you still had the recognizable reality of the city to play off. It was when you moved into stranger territory in your Surrealist photo-montages, when you were imagining a different world – perhaps your own deeper world – that darker and harder questions began to arise. In portraying a present-day young man in shorts carrying a dead body in an obviously mediaeval setting you could seem, beyond the mystery of his action, to be raising a question about the mystery of time. And in showing an elegant female hand with lacquered nails emerging from a beautiful shell to finger the sand on a beach that might be on this or another world, with a great burst of light breaking the darkness above, you might even be questioning the mystery of life itself.

Not that you set out consciously to do that at the time, the thrill was in not really knowing where the work was leading you – and sometimes it could lead you frighteningly farther than you would want to go. You were pursuing the question rather than the answer, but not only might there be no answer, but there might be questions beyond the question, which meant there would never be an answer.

Questions, indeed, even beyond the nightmare in Georges Bataille's cellar...

Picasso sat up in bed, panting. The great dark eyes still staring at the flesh being torn off the faces in the heaving canvas, at the screaming women running this way and at the blood, all that swirling blood... A nightmare culminating terrifyingly in the dark figure lit starkly from behind in the doorway...

'Are you all right?'

'What..!?'

'It's me, Pablo – Jaume!'

It was indeed Sabartés. A strange, if now not so frightening sight in a blue dressing gown and a beret. Saying I thought you called out...

'Called out? Why would I call out...!?'

'No reason. I just thought...'

'What time is it?' asked Picasso, breathing more easily as the nightmare faded back into the darkness somewhere.

'I don't know, around three o'clock perhaps...'

'So, Jaume' said Picasso, trying to recover his poise, 'you wear your beret at three o'clock in the morning, do you?'

'Well I don't have as much hair as you, Pablo' said Sabartés, drawn reluctantly into the old Barcelona banter of thirty years before. 'And I find the Paris winter cold after Uruguay. But, look, if it was just a bad dream…'

'All dreams are bad, Jaume.'

'Yes, well…'

'They can do any bloody thing to you when you're dreaming.'

'And I suppose you can do anything to them.'

'Yes, I may have strangled Olga a few times in my dreams recently.'

'So long as it was only in your dreams. But, look…'

'Not that I would ever seriously think of strangling Olga. I merely dragged her by the hair around the apartment one day.'

'Well if that was all.'

'How in God's name could I have married a hysteric like Olga?'

'I doubt if you did it in God's name. But if you're all right, Pablo…'

'She understood nothing about what I was doing. Do you know what she said whenever I did her portrait?'

'Don't tell me!'

'That it would be nice if I tried to do a proper portrait. One that she and her friends could recognise!'

'Unbelievable!'

Sabartés smiled thinly. Olga was not alone in failing to understand that in his recent work Picasso had been trying to capture not the appearance of the person, but the essence or *idea* of the person, using signs or 'emblems' as he called them.

'I think they might recognise her better than she thinks!'

They might or might not, thought Sabartés, to judge by a couple of the small canvases propped up against the wall. Ferocious cartoon-like faces of a screeching Olga reduced to the gaping mouth, spiked tongue and sharp teeth of the vagina dentata, the vagina with teeth, the castrating female. Not exactly the work of a happy husband.

'Do you know what's so awful, Jaume?' asked Picasso. 'I realised the other day that at fifty-four I'm already a year older than my father was when he died. And I'm ending up just like him.'

'But that's absurd, Pablo, you're world famous, you live in this damned great apartment off the Champs Elysées, you've got a château in the country – Boisgeloup, is it called…?'

'That's not the point, is it?'

'Well, what is the point?'

'The point is that I'm being dragged down in the exact same way as he was. By women.'

Sabartés stared at him. It was true that Don José had been stuck with supporting two sisters and a mother-in-law as well as his wife and Pablo's two sisters – at least until little Conchita died…

'But your father was forced through lack of money to give up painting. It's hardly the same thing, Pablo.'

'It's always the same thing, Jaume.'

'Well…, look…, I'd better not stand too long here in the cold. Are you all right then?'

'Yes yes. Of course.'

Sabartés paused briefly in the doorway, hesitating. Pablo looked far from all right with the dark eyes gone dull and the strands of greying hair falling over his forehead.

'Are you sure?'

'Yes I'm sure.'

Sabartés left, the door closed, the darkness slowly established itself again.

'No I'm not sure' said Picasso to the thickening emptiness of the room. 'And I'm not sure that I'm ever going to be sure…'

For how could he have done it? Let himself be seduced by the *beau monde* around Diaghilev to the point of marrying a talentless minor aristocrat of a Russian ballerina that he hadn't even slept with? It wasn't even as though she had any money – though she certainly knew how to spend his. On the liveried servants and the tight-arsed English nanny and the champagne parties in that stuck-up little château at Fontainebleau. What did he think he was doing swanning around in evening dress at the Savoy in London or playing the celebrity painter with all those countesses and duchesses and cigar-smoking prats talking bollocks about 'high art'? Was it any wonder that Braque and Matisse had been writing him off as a poncey playactor?

And it wasn't so easy now to get out of this. For Olga was in a position to do him real harm – and not just by keeping their fourteen-year-old son Paolo from him and turning him against his father. She was in a position, whether she had discovered it yet or not, to do serious damage to him and to his reputation – in more ways than one.

And Olga was only half of it.

'Well?' said the dark figure in the bed.

'It's all right, Mercedes. Go to sleep' said Sabartés, getting in beside her.

'It's not all right with all that shouting going on, is it? I'm beginning to wonder if coming here was a good idea. Especially since I can see he doesn't like me. I think he wants you all to himself.'

'What nonsense! Go to sleep.'

But as he lay staring like Picasso into the darkness Sabartés too was wondering what they were letting themselves in for. It had seemed a good idea at the time. Since there was no money in poetry and little enough from his novel, he had been making a living as a journalist in South America, but after an enforced return to Barcelona life seemed a little tame. So he was pleased and flattered when the now celebrated Picasso – who always familiarly called him Jaume, the Catalan version of Jaime – asked him, as an old friend and the only one he could trust, to come and act as his secretary at a very difficult time. The emphasis, of course, was on the 'secret' in secret-ary and indeed he recognised that he had the same taste for mystification as Picasso, who occasionally quoted his mother's dictum – which admittedly might make social intercourse unduly difficult – that you should never mention a proper name and never say anything to anybody about anything. Nevertheless, he was uneasy.

For one thing, Paris approaching the end of this year of 1935 was not only cold – it was edgy. There was an odd sense that, beneath the everyday surface of life on the boulevards or in the Metro, disquieting developments might be stirring. And this even seemed to be affecting the non-political Pablo. For not only was he abandoning his expensive lounge suits in favour of woollen jerseys beneath a casual jacket or simply a waistcoat, but he was beginning to be courted, now that Olga was gone, by left-leaning figures like the poet Eluard and the leader of the Surrealist group André Breton.

Not that this seemed to make him any happier. And there was something difficult to fathom about all this. It was true that the Olga fiasco had been made the more humiliating by the fact that his mother had warned Olga in advance that he could never make her happy. And it was true that he had lost a good few people over the years, especially with the death of his lover Eva in 1915 and that of his poet friend Apollinaire in 1918. All that apart from the shock when he was fourteen of the death from diphtheria of the little sister Conchita, which always seemed to have left him permanently with a superstitious fear of illness and death. But there was something else lurking behind that nightmare of his…

It doubtless had something to do with this other woman whom he hadn't yet introduced to Mercedes and himself, this Marie-Thérèse whom he had clearly kept hidden away for years, but whose portraits – some propped up along with those of Olga, if rather more realistic in style – revealed her to be a big, plumply voluptuous young blonde with a classical Greco-Roman profile who, when she wasn't innocently dreaming in the nude or playing with a ball on the beach, was being ravaged by a bearded antique figure with wild eyes. Olga, of course, had been suspicious for several years, but the whole story had been forced into the open earlier in the year by

Marie-Thérèse's pregnancy and then the birth of the baby in September. Pablo had promised to get a divorce, but there had apparently been all sorts of legal delays, largely to do with the fact that they were both non-French residents – not to mention the fact that Olga had suffered a breakdown to the point of going berserk and striking a policeman with her umbrella in the Tuileries Gardens, and had now moved into the Hôtel California in the nearby Rue de Berri in order to spy on his comings and goings. Was that why he now appeared to be giving up on the divorce? But what then of Marie-Thérèse…?

'What are you doing?' he said sharply, as he felt a hand sliding down his stomach.

'Well if we're going to be kept awake by all that shouting…'

'I'm not in the mood, Mercedes.'

'Yeah, 'not in the mood', you're not often in the mood…'

'Go to sleep!'

'That's what I was trying to do! But I'll tell you one thing.'

'What?'

'For a millionaire he's not exactly free with his money. I can't run the housekeeping on what he's giving us.'

'Don't worry. he'll probably paint your portrait and make your fortune.'

'Not if he paints me like the ones I've seen in that bedroom, he won't!'

Sabartés, dressed neatly from head to foot in his habitual black, drummed his fingers on the carefully ordered work table, consulted his watch once more, only to confirm that it was 1.21p.m and therefore late – very late. So late that he could think of little to do other than to remove his spectacles, blink a little, wipe very carefully each of the thick lenses in turn, put the spectacles back on again, adjust them as he looked across the room – and sigh.

He had been here now as 'secret-ary' for ten days and still had no control over the correspondence. When he had asked about it,

Pablo had waved vaguely and said that he would deal with it himself 'for the moment', but since he had not bothered to look at any of the mail, it was piling up unopened. Sabartés had fallen back on the discreet stratagem of taking up the mail to the bedroom once Mercedes had taken up the breakfast, but there was as yet no indication that this was working. Even though – at 1.22 – there was still no sign of Pablo emerging.

For a man of order, as Sabartés prided himself on being, it was not easy to regulate the affairs of this apartment in the Rue La Boétie. Especially since it consisted in fact of two apartments, corresponding to the double life that Pablo had lived in this place. The original apartment, which had in some sense been the official residence of the fashionable couple Monsieur and Madame Picasso, was still – give or take the coating of dust which had accumulated on the gleaming parquet floors and which Mercedes had been complaining about – a perfect example of the orthodox good taste of the wealthy denizens of the *beaux quartiers*. From the drawing room to the master bedroom with its cool twin beds, it was immaculately furnished throughout, while the pictures included a Cézanne, a Renoir or two and a Corot. There were some *respectable* Picasso pictures of the Cubist period, but even the orderly Sabartés felt that Pablo might have had to don evening dress and cross himself once or twice before entering the place.

If that apartment was a high bourgeois heaven, the apartment above – which Picasso had taken over since Olga could not accept his messy activity in the flat – was a Bohemian hell. The rooms had been cleared of furniture and turned into store rooms filled with piled up canvases, moulds of statues, packing cases, frames and bric-a-brac of every description, down to the broken pens and empty cigarette packets that Pablo, notoriously, could never let go. And it was a corner of the hopelessly cluttered south-facing room he had used as a studio that now served as his bedroom – if you could call it that, since he almost seemed to have withdrawn from the world and to be living like a tramp inside his own pictures and his own nightmares. And it was there that he presumably still was, at 1.28. Which meant it was time to go up and see what was happening.

'Ah, Jaume' said Picasso brightly from the bed as he entered the room. 'Just the man I was thinking of!'

'I believe you!'

'Yes, you've been bringing it all back to me. Remember those good old Spanish Sundays in Barcelona?'

'A thousand years ago? When we were young?'

'Mass in the morning, the bullfight in the afternoon…'

'And the whorehouse at night.'

'Ah yes. There's Catholic Spain for you!'

It was a relief to find him in this bantering, playacting mode, however defensive. But the breakfast tray was largely untouched and he had left unopened both the newspaper and the several days of mail that had accumulated.

'It's half past one, Pablo.'

'It's often half past one.'

'Twice a day, they tell me. You haven't looked at the mail?'

'Rubbishy art catalogues, nonsensical newspaper clippings from the agency, shysters trying to screw something out of me – what's the point? Anyway, as you and I know, it's safer to leave well alone.'

'But there might be unpaid bills there.'

'You see what I mean?!'

'But they could be cutting off the phone and the electricity for all we know.'

'They would too, the bastards!'

'Well I suppose, Pablo' said Sabartés with an exasperated laugh, 'that we could always barricade the front door to keep them out.'

'Sounds like a hint, Jaume. All right, you had better take over all of this, just in case. I trust your discretion.'

'Good. But there are at least three letters in there that you might want to look at' said Sabartés, starting to rummage through the disordered pile. 'One is a perfumed one with the address in large careful writing that I guessed might be from your Marie-Thérèse.'

'No need to open that one. Just leave it here.'

'And there are two others from Olga.'

'How do you know they're from Olga?'

'Well. as you see, they're not stamped' said Sabartés, handing them over.

'And they're addressed to *Monsieur Cochon Picasso,* I see. Picasso the pig, charming!'

He grimaced, opened the letters and skimmed through them in turn, shaking his head in frustration.

'I'm afraid also' said Sabartés after a moment, 'that she has been entertaining the populace outside in the street again this morning. Wearing appropriately outlandish clothes – a fur coat over a pink nightdress, it looked like.'

'And shouting equally outlandish things about me, was she?'

'In both French and Russian. Should I ask the police to move her on?'

'God no, no police! That would be absolutely bloody disastrous!'

Sabartés, taken aback at the strength of that reply, hesitated, then began to gather up the letters into a manageable pile for removal.

'So where did you buy it then?' said Picasso in a startling change of subject.

'Buy what?'

'That black beret. In Uruguay?'

'I bought it in the Galeries Lafayette.'

'Where else?! All right, Jaume, tell me the worst. What was she shouting?'

'Oh, you know' said Sabartés reluctantly, 'much the same as yesterday…'

'What was she shouting?' Picasso insisted.

'Well… that it's going to cost you 'all those paintings you've got stashed away in bank vaults'. That sort of thing.'

'What else?'

'Oh look, Pablo…'

'What else?!'

'That she knows all about 'that young whore of yours – and 'the little bastard'…'

'Anything else?'

'Well, something about telling the police…'

'Oh God! *What* about telling the police?'

'It really wasn't all that clear, Pablo. Honestly…'

'Bugger that woman, bugger that woman! I'd better get up.'

He heaved himself up, smiled sardonically at Sabartés. 'Trust you, Jaume, to buy your beret at the Galeries Lafayette!'

'I'm sorry, Pablo. If only I'd known' said Sabartés with a similar smile.

'For that's where I first saw her, Marie-Thérèse. In front of the Galeries Lafayette. Straight out of a classical landscape she was. So plump, pulpy and innocent. And now Olga has found out and is trying to discover where I keep her, I'm sure of it.'

'And you think she might try to harm Marie-Thérèse and the baby?'

'She might, I suppose, but that's not the point.'

Sabartés was beginning to feel rather lost in all this, especially now that Pablo seemed to be abandoning any hope of a divorce. But he could see that he was worried.

'It would have simplified life, wouldn't it' he said diffidently, 'if you had been able to go ahead with the divorce from Olga?'

'It would have simplified life with a vengeance, Jaume! Especially since as a non-citizen I had to be married under Spanish community property law, so she would be entitled to half of everything I've got – paintings and all.'

'I see…'

'Can you imagine what she would do with all those paintings?'

'Sell them?'

'Or burn them! You can see what she's like.'

'But, Pablo' said Sabartés almost apologetically, 'since you don't want to divorce and since Olga already knows about Marie Thérèse and the baby anyway…'

22

'But there's something she mightn't know that she could use against me. I have to go on keeping Marie-Thérèse hidden in case she finds out. She could destroy me.'

'I see' said Sabartés.

But he could see only that there was indeed something else that was weighing down Pablo in a way that he hadn't seen before. Some worry about the police, by the sound of it. Enough to make him feel uneasy himself.

'What day is this?' asked Picasso,

'Wednesday.'

'I'd better go to see Marie-Thérèse on Friday. Can you look surreptitious?'

'I always look surreptitious – so Mercedes tells me'

'Good. If Olga's outside you try to draw her up the street while I slip down to the Champs-Elysées. We'll get Marcel to park the car there.'

'All right, Pablo. Just one last thing though. There have been a couple of telephone inquiries from dealers.'

'So?'

'So what do I tell them?'

'Tell them I've given up painting. For good.'

'Are you sure you're not going to burst?'

Dora was lunching on Friday with her friend Jacqueline in a little restaurant on the Place Blanche. Since it was close to the apartment Jacqueline shared with André Breton in the Rue Pierre Fontaine, she had not had to brave the Metro in her heavily pregnant state.

'You do realise' Dora continued, laughing, 'that you're now having a second dollop of ice cream with raspberry coulis on top of that heavy cheesecake?'

'I know!' said Jacqueline with a helpless giggle. 'This is a ridiculous condition to be in, but I'm still hungry, believe it or not. And this is after all our annual birthday lunch, isn't it?'

That was indeed what it had become, ever since they were art students together and discovered that they had birthdays in November within a few days of each other – though their earlier celebrations had generally been more exuberant than this quiet lunch in the Place Blanche.

'Yes, it has become a tradition' smiled Dora.

'I'm not sure I like that word.'

'You mean it makes us seem too respectable?'

'I mean it makes us seem old.'

'Nonsense, we're just bright young things – though my mother did hint the other day that a twenty-eighth birthday was not entirely a cause for celebration. But honestly, Jacqueline, you're looking better than ever.'

It was true, she thought. Fair-haired and as elegantly pretty as before, she had a new glow about her that was doubtless due to the pregnancy. It must be quite special to be pregnant. Almost enough to make a girl jealous…

'And you look more like a bright butterfly than ever' said Jacqueline, placing her hand over hers as though reassuringly. 'But somehow I can't quite believe it all.'

'Believe what?'

'Well, any of it, really. I'm sort of surprised! I'm surprised that I'm sitting here dressed like a blown up blue balloon, I'm surprised that it's almost Christmas, and I'm surprised to see us swanning around among these Surrealists and left-wing intellectuals as though we were born to it. I mean we were both outsiders, weren't we?'

Certainly, if Dora and the then Jacqueline Lamba had become such close friends at the Beaux Arts, it was doubtless partly because there were certain similarities in their backgrounds. While Dora had spent her childhood and teenage years in Argentina, Jacqueline's early years had been spent in Cairo. And while Dora had made the mistake of being left-handed and been forced to change, Jacqueline had made the more radical mistake of being a girl – a mistake which her disappointed parents corrected by considering her a boy, dressing her as a boy and referring to her as a boy as long as anybody would believe she was a boy. And of course, while they had both aspired to be painters, they had to face not only the recession, but the difficulty for women of getting their work shown unless they happened to be the 'Muse' – and therefore the almost automatic subject – of a known male painter.

'I suppose that's what made us both a bit bolshie' said Jacqueline. 'Feeling like an outsider.'

'But then we weren't the only outsiders' said Dora, smiling as Jacqueline wolfed down another spoonful of ice cream. 'Perhaps that's why we could fit in. Everybody seemed to feel like an outsider because of that big war. Except that now, I fancy, with this threat of Fascism, it's maybe time for the outsiders to become insiders in order to try to avoid a repetition…' She stopped suddenly. 'Are you all right, Jacqueline?'

'No, I'm not, actually…'

'What is it?' ask Dora in alarm.

'I'm afraid you were right about the ice cream.'

'Oh God. Had you better…?'

'Yes, I really had better…'

Dora helped her to get to the *toilettes*, waving away the concerned elderly waiter in the process, and waited outside as Jacqueline made lengthy retching noises in the cubicle. Until eventually she emerged, with her face pale and strained, smiling a little desperately.

'Poor you!' said Dora, taking out her handkerchief, running it under the tap and starting to wipe Jacqueline's face. 'Are you all right?'

'Yes, but I think I'd better sit down.'

They went back to their table and Dora asked the waiter to bring some more water for Jacqueline, plus a *café filtre* for herself. After which, as Jacqueline's colour started to come back, they sat smiling at each other.

'Of course this is all your fault, isn't it, Dora?'

'Only indirectly' said Dora with a grin.

25

But it was true that it was she who had brought Jacqueline and Breton together early in the spring of the previous year. Which was ironical since she herself was just then finishing that nightmarish relationship with Bataille – quite apart from the other irony that Bataille was the sworn enemy of Breton and had led the breakaway movement from the Surrealists some years earlier. And it was perhaps a little odd in retrospect that she had involved herself in matchmaking for someone three years younger than herself.

But she had been glad to help Jacqueline. For while Dora had been assisted financially by her father, Jacqueline had found it much harder to make her way. When her father died in Cairo in an accident and she returned with her mother to France, the family was poor, her mother developed tuberculosis and Jacqueline had to look after her for some years until her death. So while she was passionate about painting and produced interesting and colourful work, she was forced to take various odd jobs – teaching French in Cardiff, working as an interior designer at the Trois Quartiers and, most recently, performing as a nude water dancer at the Coliseum night club in Pigalle. Not an obvious launch pad for a glittering future, yet that is precisely what it turned out to be.

And the story of the meeting had become quite famous. Of how this tall, slim attractive blonde Jacqueline Lamba was sitting in the Café Cyrano in the Place Blanche one fine evening, having a break before her act at the nearby Coliseum, when André Breton noticed her, found her 'scandalously beautiful' and immediately recognised her as the woman he had always been destined for. And what followed looked like turning Jacqueline into one of the legends of the century, the living embodiment of the Surrealist view of *l'amour fou,* that mad, irresistible, obsessional love – the real love – that cut through everyday rationality, liberated the unconscious and led to a higher truth.

And indeed it was a truly magical story. For what would transpire would correspond uncannily to what Breton had imagined in a poem of eleven years before. So it was as though driven mysteriously by his unconscious mind to realise this long-forgotten dream that he watched her, observed that she was writing and somehow knew that, as though imprisoned in the same dream, she was writing to him. He left the café, waited outside, approached her discreetly as she left and persuaded her to meet him at midnight after the show.

So there followed the famous enchanted walk through a balmy night-time Paris. From the garish lights of Pigalle, down to the Place St-Georges with its carnival figures on the base of the Gavarni statue, on again along the Boulevard Montmartre, then past the dark forbidding stock exchange and on towards the markets at the Halles, where late revellers in evening dress sat at café terraces over steaming onion soup while exchanging pleasantries with market porters bustling about carrying on their shoulders crates filled with every conceivable vegetable or fruit. And on again, down the Boulevard Sébastopol towards the Tour St-Jacques, that tower that Breton had imagined swaying like a sunflower, and finally across the Ile de la Cité to the perfect culmination in the miraculously named Rue Gît le Coeur – the resting place of the heart. They were married less than three months later, the witnesses were Paul Eluard and the sculptor Giacometti, and the wedding photograph by Dora was a tribute to Manet's famous *Luncheon on the Grass*, with the slim and beautiful Jacqueline posing nude with the three perfectly dressed men. Magic from start to finish.

But not quite. For the dark secret of this magic was that Jacqueline had been reading a novel by Breton, had been deeply impressed and had asked Dora, who moved among these people, where the Surrealists hung out. When she heard that they often met at the Café Cyrano, up the street from Breton's flat and conveniently close to the Coliseum where she did her water sprite act, she made a point of spending time there, looking not only beautiful but suitably mysterious and inspired with pen in hand. Breton duly turned up, the walk was indeed magical – even if Jacqueline, in her performer's high heels, had to smile though her feet were killing her – and the rest was Surrealist history.

Had André – or for that matter Eluard or Giacometti – ever glimpsed the truth? Dora and Jacqueline, on puzzling over this, decided that they had not.

'Do you think it's because they're intellectuals?' Jacqueline had asked with a grin.

'Well, for men so intelligent, they do seem oddly innocent' Dora remembered saying.

'Or perhaps it's simply because they're men?' Jacqueline had said with a giggle. 'But it's strange, isn't it?' she had added memorably, 'I mean, they're not just following their cock around, are they? They're men in their forties who need attractive women in their twenties not just to screw but to look up to and almost worship.'

'You're on a pedestal.' Dora had said with a laugh. 'You've become a Muse.'

'Is that what I am? A Muse?'

'I'm wildly jealous' Dora remembered saying with a smile. 'You're a Muse!'

She might have said it smilingly, she reflected, but she had perhaps been rather more jealous than she had realised. And she was embarrassed to realise that she was feeling rather confusedly jealous now. However, her coffee had now arrived and Jacqueline, seeming livelier, was staring at it and then looking questioningly after the departing waiter.

'I'm sorry' said Dora. 'I didn't think you would want coffee.'

'No no, I don't want coffee.'

'Would you like tea, or a *tisane* of some kind?'

'No no. Actually, Dora...'

'Yes...?'

'Well, the fact is, to be quite frank, I'm beginning, if you'd believe it, to feel...'

'To feel what?!' asked Dora in alarm. 'You don't mean it's beginning...?!'

'No no!' said Jacqueline, laughing. 'It's just that I'm feeling hungry, desperately hungry.'

It was a moment or two before Dora heard her own musical laughter echoing through the restaurant.

'But my God, Jacqueline, don't you realise you're supposed to behave like a Muse…?!'

It was quite some time before she saw Jacqueline home, dropping her off by taxi before continuing with it through the darkening streets to her own place in the Rue de Savoie.

Of course the whole Muse saga had been an innocent deception and, while the new *Luncheon on the Grass* had been a sophisticated joke, it was still the woman who was naked rather than the men. Even so, the idea of a Muse implied a favourable, even an elevated view of women. And though the Surrealists talked a lot about free love, it was noticeable that both Breton and her old and close friend Paul Eluard, whose new wife was Nusch, had married their Muse. Which contrasted sharply with the more unconventional approaches to love and sex of some of those around Bataille.

If it was a choice between being a victim or a 'Muse', it might be preferable to be the 'Muse'.

But was that the only choice…?

2

The chauffeur Marcel, parked as arranged on the Champs-Elysées close to the end of the Rue La Boétie, dropped his paper as soon as he saw Picasso coming, stepped out of the car and prepared to open the passenger door. He was proud of the big luxurious Hispano-Suiza and of his smart maroon uniform, which contrasted not only with the short, chunky Picasso's less tailored appearance in his old *canadienne* or anorak, but with his slightly disconcerting habit of sitting beside Marcel on the wide front seat and chatting to him as to a workmate.

'*Bonjour, Monsieur*' said Marcel, with the requisite balance of formality and friendliness.

'*Bonjour, Marcel*' replied Picasso in his thick, almost whistling Spanish accent.

There were two snags to having Marcel as chauffeur. One was that, since he was plump, swarthy and had the unfortunate name of Boudin, it was hard not to think of him as a black pudding. The other, more serious, was that he sang. And sang and sang. And if he could hardly be blamed for singing badly, he could at least be blamed for his constant choice of Maurice Chevalier, whose latest leering hit was *Donnez-moi la main, Mam-zelle*. You could arrest the performance by clearing your throat in a certain threatening fashion, but that only led him to switch to humming Maurice Chevalier or, upon a further warning clearing of the throat, to whistling Maurice Chevalier, which was only a marginal improvement. However, since the superstitious Picasso's overriding concern was to avoid death or injury, and since he believed Marcel to be a safe driver – even if he had not been entirely reassured by his assertion that they would emerge unscathed from any collision since their car was bigger and heavier than everybody else's – he accommodated to Maurice Chevalier as the lesser of two evils.

'Maisons-Alfort is it, Monsieur?'

'Yes, but go up the Champs-Elysées first, drive two or three times around the Arc de Triomphe and then down the Avenue Marceau to the quays.'

Since Maisons-Alfort was an outer suburb on the other side of the city, such a perverse instruction left Marcel unable even to think of singing, humming or whistling. But Picasso feared that Olga might have seen through Sabartés's surreptitious act and already be jumping hysterically into a taxi to follow them.

'There's a chance I may have been spotted' he explained.

'You don't think, Monsieur' said Marcel gently, 'that you're more likely to be spotted by driving round and round the Arc de Triomphe in a great shiny six-cylinder Hispano-Suiza?'

'What?! Oh, all right then. But keep your eyes open.'

'Évidemment, Monsieur' said Marcel and celebrated with a brief burst of Chevalier.

But he fell into a respectful slight humming as Picasso beside him lapsed into a long brooding reverie while other cars passed them and warmly-dressed people on the pavements hurried along or stared into shop windows – going about their lives. None of them, perhaps, in quite the pickle he was in…

It was particularly awkward having to go to Maisons-Alfort, since the mother would doubtless be there, and possibly the sister Geneviève. Obviously it was sensible to go back to her mother's for the birth in September, but she should have been able by now to come back to the secret little apartment he had found for her along the street in Rue La Boétie. Except, of course, for the spying and screaming of Olga. There seemed to be no end to the relentless jealousy and thirst for Russian revenge of Olga…

It was not as though he hadn't been careful – he had for years now been meticulously careful. For you could never rely on people to understand, and they always condemned what they didn't understand. If they only knew how low he was feeling at the time, how depressed at the way his life was going. And it was as though Marie-Thérèse came as an illumination, as a predestined answer, as though she had somehow wafted in from the old classical world to land on the pavement outside the Galeries Lafayette in Paris. To buy, in all her teenage innocence, a *col Claudine*, or Peter Pan collar with matching cuffs.

She was with her older sister, but he had eyes only for the young one with the classical profile. He heard the older one say something laughingly about 'that weird old man' staring at them, but he followed them at a distance as they strolled towards the Gare Saint-Lazare. When they went into the station and stood talking beneath the departures board, he watched them furtively through a pinhole he had made with a match in his newspaper. As the older girl turned away to leave the station and the younger one moved towards a train waiting on the platform, he rushed forward in a state of high excitement, told her he was Picasso, and said he must speak to her. Since the name clearly meant nothing to her, she was turning impatiently away from this apparent 'dirty old man' when – all too aware that passengers were looking curiously at them – he seized her arm and said 'Mademoiselle, I'll wait for you here every evening at 6 o'clock until I see you again. I must see you again!'

And whether the mother did know who Picasso was and thought there might be some advantage from it, or whether the two girls simply did it for a lark, they did eventually turn up together at the appointed time and place several days later, when he explained that he was a painter who was looking for younger models and might be able to help them in other ways. And gradually, aided by the fact that the mother was unmarried and there was therefore no father around to contend with, he became something of a father figure himself, picking up Marie-Thérèse in the car and taking her to the cinema or skating or boating on the Marne. He was already sketching her, of course, but was soon suggesting using the old shed at the bottom of the garden as a makeshift studio. This produced a few flutters of respectable reticence from the mother, but it was not long before he and Marie-Thérèse were left alone to their own increasingly interesting devices in that half-hidden shed.

'*Puisque l'amour nous appelle...*' Marcel was crooning as they approached the Pont Neuf and the Ile de la Cité.

No, they wouldn't understand. Not the authorities, who would see only that the girl had been under eighteen, that in law this was the abduction of a minor and that, on top of that, it had been perpetrated by an individual who was not only a foreigner abusing his presence in France but a painter of questionable reputation who should be thrown out of the country. Even if he escaped arrest or trial, his reputation could be mangled, Olga could use it triumphantly against him in any separation settlement – and the already tricky situation with Marie-Thérèse and her mother could become impossible. No, people just wouldn't understand – and must never be allowed to be in a position where they could even try to understand.

Nor indeed would they understand – not even smirking, ogling Maurice Chevalier would understand – how meticulous he had been for all these years, the smooth inevitability with which he had managed the relationship. Soon she was coming almost every day to his studio in Rue La Boétie, while telling her mother first that she was visiting a girlfriend and then that she was working as an assistant in that art shop. But even while she was exploding into his work, he was careful to present her as an allegorical figure or even to disguise her in a bowl of fruit or, most satisfyingly, as a guitar waiting almost longingly to be plucked.

Could they even appreciate how careful and considerate he had been of her developing sensuality? True, the seduction had taken less than a week in that garden shed, but it was only very gradually, months later, that he had introduced her to the erotic images in the old albums and then to the writings, with their period illustrations, of the Marquis de Sade – she was so innocent that at first she just laughed in astonishment at those pictures of women being sodomized or old men being serviced by little girls. Even though she enjoyed the secrecy of the relationship, she had found this quite shocking and intimidating at first. And it was probably several years, after he had secretly kept her on hand in that holiday camp for girls while on holiday at Dinard with Olga, and then kept her cheekily just along the street in the Rue La Boétie, before she achieved the full range of her own sensuality.

But once he acquired Boisgeloup in 1930, perfect for sculpting in the outbuildings and perfect for keeping Olga away since it was forty miles from Paris in Normandy and only accessible by car, he could have Marie-Thérèse conveniently to himself at weekends. And all that work with her – paintings, engravings and the sculptures that began to people the grounds of the château – had exploded until he felt that, if Marie-Thérèse had appeared providentially to save him as an artist, he had enshrined her image for posterity and turned her into a work of art herself. But then, of course, it was too good to last.

For that all too successful exhibition of his in 1932 exposed her to everybody else – including Olga, although it was a year before she fully realised just how far their marriage had deteriorated. Which, in its turn, increased the vague dissatisfaction that Marie-Thérèse was starting to express – wondering if the relationship had any future and all that, and even beginning to hint alarmingly at 'doing something drastic'. Since the obvious cure for dissatisfaction in a woman was to give her a child, he had given her a child. And she was a wonderful child, this little girl whom they had named after his own little dead sister Maria de la Concepción, shortened to Concita as they now shortened the new baby's name to Maya. He had somehow always tended vaguely to associate Marie-Thérèse herself with his innocent little sister, and now that this new little girl had turned up it was like a miraculous renewal – so much so that he had even kneeled before Marie-Thérèse, asked for her forgiveness, and thanked her for the gift of Maya. All very fine and theatrical, but now things were falling apart and he was going to have to try to pull them together again…

'I doubt if I'll be staying over, Marcel. Could you wait around till six, in case?'

'*Mais absolument, Monsieur,*'

'Where the hell are we, by the way?'

'Not be long now, Monsieur. We're in Charenton.'

Charenton? Just the place! Where the Marquis de Sade ended his days in a lunatic asylum…

'There's no hurry, Marcel. No hurry at all…'

The door bell seemed to be ringing for longer than usual. Were they in?

It was a perfectly good suburban house, Picasso reflected. The absent father, a Frenchman of Swedish extraction – whence Marie-Thérèse's blonde look – was apparently quite a wealthy businessman so that the girls, however irregular their situation, had never been in want. For their mother, a still goodlooking but careworn woman who had been the businessman's secretary as well as his mistress, life might well have been more difficult.

And it was she who eventually opened the door, looking flustered.

'*Bonjour, Madame. Vous allez bien?*'

'*Bonjour, Monsieur Pablo*' she said in a strained, almost curt manner – not calling him 'Pic' as he was usually known to the family – before calling up the stairs for Marie-Thérèse and then disappearing into the kitchen. As though to wash her hands of the whole business.

He took off his *canadienne*, left it on a chair and waited until Marie-Thérèse appeared on the stairs in a loose pink top and dark red skirt. Flushed and saying she had just managed to get Maya down after her feed, she must look awful.

'Of course you don't, Marie-Thérèse, you look wonderful.'

'So you came?'

'Yes, of course I came!'

He kissed her and embraced her tightly until she grimaced apologetically and released herself slowly.

'Sorry, but they're still very tender just now. I'm breast-feeding.'

'Oh yes, how is she?'

'She's wonderful. Do you want to see her?'

She led him upstairs and they tiptoed into the bedroom, to stand gazing into the cot at the sleeping Maya, observing her tiny unconscious movements.

'She's so good I can't believe it. Isn't she lovely?'

'Yes, she's lovely – just like her mother.' He smiled and stroked the slightly untidy blonde hair.

'It was such a sweet idea to name her after your little dead sister, Pic.' Her voice was trembling a little. 'It brings the two families together.'

'Yes, but we'd better not wake her. Perhaps we should go downstairs again.'

Once below in the drearily conventional living room, enlivened only by a couple of very straightforward framed drawings by himself, he picked up an open box of chocolates from a side table and asked her teasingly if she was still eating chocolates.

'Well, a friend brought them – and you know me and chocolates!'

'You shouldn't, you know. You'll be too fat to play tennis.'

'I think it will be a good while before I play tennis. But Pic' she said a little shakily as they sat down, 'I've been waiting for you all this past week, you know.'

'I know, I know' he said, putting an arm around her, 'but it's been difficult.'

'Wasn't it supposed to be easier now that you've got your friend Sabartés there?'

'Yes, he's keeping the wolves at bay and things should soon settle down. But I must say you really are looking wonderful, Marie-Thérèse, absolutely blooming. You must be so much happier now that little Maya is here. Didn't I say that you would be?'

'Yes you did, Pic, but ...'

'But you're still reading your romantic stories' he interrupted with a laugh, reaching across to pick up a novelette lying open beside the chocolates. '*La Princesse d'Arabie,* well now! So what happens to our Arabian princess?'

'Oh well, she's not a real princess – at least not at first. She's the daughter of a famous explorer who got lost in the desert. But look, Pic, I don't want to nag or anything...'

'You never nag, Marie-Thérèse.'

'Except that *Maman* has been going on at me about Maya's birth certificate, where it says the father is 'unknown'.'

'But the birth certificate is only a piece of paper, my love. *We* know who the father is.'

'But she's still saying I'm ending up in the same position as her. That it makes little Maya a bastard. And that it could tell against her when she goes to school.'

'But the child is still in her cradle, Marie-Thérèse!' he said, laughing and planting little tender kisses on her cheeks, her forehead, her neck. 'Anyway, all this is only temporary, isn't it?'

'Well *is* it, Pic? This whole divorce business just seems to drag on and on.'

'But you know what these lawyers are like. And with Olga being Russian and me being Spanish, it's been hellishly slow getting the papers together in the first place.'

'But I still don't see' she said, freeing herself from the arm around her shoulders, 'why you still have to keep me hidden away all the time.'

'Because Olga is on the lookout for arguments that she can use to grind out of me all she can in a settlement.'

'Are you sure this isn't just an excuse? I mean, I'm not a

youngster any more, Pic. I'm grown up now and I've got Maya to think of. And she's ours, isn't she, and I love you and I just want us all to be together…'

She got up suddenly and stood facing him, the blue eyes challenging. Crying, panting, face and neck flushed, distressed – desirable…

'If you must know, Pic, I feel even lonelier since Maya's been born. It's been almost ten years, do you realise, ten years..?!'

'Of course I realise, but that's just the point, isn't it? That's the whole trouble…'

'What do you mean? What are you saying…?'

'Just that you were under-age when we met' he said, getting up with his arms towards her as she backed away from him. 'so Olga could use that to create a big scandal, go to the police, damage both of us…'

'But that was years ago, Pic! It's just another excuse, isn't it? There's always something… You just don't want us, do you? You never loved me, you just wanted to paint and fuck me…'

'That's outrageous, Marie-Thérèse, how dare you say that?!' he shouted, moving forward and holding her struggling and crying in his arms. 'Of course I love you, you know that! I'm just saying it's safer to go on as we are – for the moment…'

'Well I can't go on as we are, and I just don't want to go on as we are…'

'But we can soon start spending weekends together again at Boisgeloup…'

'Which still leaves me stuck on my own. I never know where you are, what you're doing, or who you're doing it with, I can't stand it. And you never touch me any more, do you..?'

'But you were pregnant, for heaven's sake! And you've been breast-feeding and all.'

She broke free from his embrace, backed away from him again, the blue eyes flashing.

'You just don't want me any more. At least you used to want me,

38

and now you think you can palm me off with Maya so that I won't say I'm lonely any more or 'do something silly'. Well I'm lonelier than ever, Pic, and I don't care who knows I was under-age all those years ago, I'm not going to be hidden away at Boisgeloup or anywhere else any longer, for if I am I'll go mad and do something *really* 'silly' this time…'

'Stop it, Marie-Thérèse!' he shouted, taking her in his arms again. 'I won't put up with that talk!'

As he stood there, containing her movements as she struggled in his embrace until the sobbing and trembling subsided and she was just quietly weeping in his arms, he found himself staring at his own early drawing – so early it amounted to evidence – of a happy schoolgirlish Marie-Thérèse sitting smiling beneath a floppy hat in a rowing boat on the Marne.

It looked as though all this was going to take some time…

Sabartés was looking forward to a quiet and productive day.

He had already sorted out the correspondence, replied where it was possible to do so without consulting Pablo and established a priority list of items that required to be followed up. And now he was just getting into his stride on the typewriter, when the doorbell rang.

On the pavement stood a tall handsome man of around forty, while in the middle of the street in her fur coat and hat was Olga, shouting and waving an umbrella.

'You'd better come in' said Sabartés hastily, quickly closing the door behind them.

'I thought she was going to hit me with her umbrella! Who is that woman?'

'Who knows?!' Sabartés found himself saying. 'You get all sorts in Paris these days. The name, you said, is…?'

'Paul Eluard.'

'Eluard? Oh yes,well, yes, do come in, Monsieur Eluard' said Sabartés, very flustered. 'I've read some of your poetry, of course.'

'Nice of you to say so. And you are…?'

'Sabartés, Jaume Sabartés. You'd better come through, Monsieur Eluard.'

'Oh, *Paul,* please' said Eluard with a smile, as Sabartés took his overcoat, led him into the room in which he had been working and showed him to a chair.

'Pablo is in, I take it?'

'He's not, I'm afraid.'

'Will he be back shortly?'

'Not today, I'm afraid.'

'That's unfortunate. But he will be here tomorrow?'

'Well, actually…' said Sabartés in some embarrassment, 'he's away.'

'Ah. So he's away?'

'Yes, he's away dealing with some personal business' said Sabartés reluctantly.

'I see. But he will have left instructions?'

'Instructions…?'

'Oh I'm sorry' said Eluard graciously, 'I was assuming…'

'Yes well I do act as his secretary, but I'm also a longstanding friend of his.'

'Then do please forgive the misunderstanding. The point is that we do need to finalise the choice of exhibits.'

'Exhibits?'

'Yes, the pictures for the exhibition of new Spanish painting in Barcelona and Madrid in January. You're informed about all that presumably?'

'Ah yes, he did mention it.'

But did he mention it? Not that Sabartés could remember, he didn't! You could bring some order to correspondence, but not quite bring order to Picasso.

'Then he'll have told you that I'm involved in setting up this exhibition and that I'll be giving a lecture on Picasso in Barcelona. Miró and Salvador Dali will be turning up in person and of course I was hoping to persuade Pablo to come.'

'Oh yes?' said Sabartés, a little uncomfortable at the mention of Dali, since it was well known that Eluard's first wife Gala had left him for Dali.

'And frankly' Eluard went on with a modest smile, 'I was also hoping to persuade him to illustrate a new poetry collection of mine.'

'Well, I'm afraid – er, Paul – that he hasn't left any clear information and that I can't easily contact him at the moment.'

'Really?' said Eluard, looking increasingly bemused. 'But is he away for long?'

Sabartés hesitated, but he could hardly tell him that Picasso had taken Marie-Thérèse off to Boisgeloup to 'stabilise the situation', since Eluard wasn't supposed to know about either Boisgeloup or Marie-Thérèse or God only knew what else.

'I'm afraid I could only speculate' he said, 'It's a little difficult to explain.'

'I see…'

He could see Eluard eyeing him with discreet curiosity. You'd almost think he'd killed Pablo and done away with the body, for God's sake!

'Well, I'm afraid that leaves me at a loss' said Eluard. 'But at least, since I'm here, I'd been thinking that we should be quite up-to-date and showcase some of his current paintings. You have them here, do you?'

'Well, actually' said Sabartés, 'he hasn't been painting for some time now.'

'Really? So he's sculpting?'

'Well no…'

'No…?'

'Actually' said Sabartés reluctantly, 'he has given up painting.'

'What?!' said Eluard with a sudden laugh. 'But Picasso can't stop painting! He's the greatest painter we have – how can he give up painting?!'

'Well, that's what he says.'

'But that's dreadful. I'd no idea he'd been so badly affected' said Eluard. 'So you, er…Jaume, are here on an extended visit to help him through this, are you?'

'Well not quite, I'm here on a permanent basis.'

'I see…'

'Well he really did need someone.'

'Yes, perhaps he did' said Eluard. 'Well, look, Jaume, all I can say is that, if you do manage to get in touch with him, I'd be most grateful if you would tell him about my visit.'

'I certainly shall' said Sabartés, handing him his overcoat and seeing him, with a doleful little smile, into the street.

And as he walked back down towards the Champs-Elysées, Eluard hardly knew what to think. Was his Spanish trip on or off? Was Picasso even going to offer exhibits? Would he have to forget about the illustrations for his new collection that he was banking on to keep himself solvent? And where had this strange, bespectacled, almost clerical Sabartés come from? Had Picasso really given up painting? And, if so, why would he need a secretary…?

All because of the break-up with that Russian wife of his?! It was ridiculous! He could soon tell Pablo – if he could lay his hands on him! – that there was life after a break-up with a Russian wife. Hadn't he been there himself with Gala?! What Picasso needed was another woman. Not the Philistine that Olga apparently was, but a woman who could understand his creative work as a painter. And not one who was middle-aged like her, but a woman who was young and spirited and glamorous – one who could get the creative juices flowing again. Somebody like Dora Maar for heaven's sake!

Dora watched her father fuss over his breakfast croissants and watched her mother also watching him fuss over the breakfast croissants with her longsuffering, ironical little smile. Parents… And everybody had them…

Although she lived in the same spacious apartment in the Latin Quarter in the Rue de Savoie, she did not so much live with her parents as live alongside them in an independent fashion. Indeed she was only having a late breakfast with them because she didn't go to the studio on Saturday, and because she felt a little guilty at not spending more time in the apartment. Especially on account of her mother, who no longer had her hat shop to keep her busy and who was not a happy woman. But that might not be entirely her fault and, happy or not, she was there, she existed, everybody had a mother, you only had one and you should always make the effort.

'I do like that woollen dress you're wearing – nice shade of blue' she said to her mother to break the silence. 'Where did you get it?'

'The Trois Quartiers.'

'You know, I've got a necklace I think might go very well with that – amber, with different shaped stones, so you get a fine play of light. It should set off that blue very nicely. I'll look it out for you.'

Monsieur Markovitch looked up as though briefly taking the measure of this conversation from another world, and went back to spreading quince jam with some precision on his second croissant.

As she sometimes said jokingly, Dora was of mixed background in more ways than one. To begin with, her father Joseph was a Croatian architect from Zagreb, while her mother was a French Catholic from Tours, whom he met and married when, after finishing his studies in Vienna, he came to live in Paris. Again, although she was born in Paris, she had been transplanted at the age of three to Buenos Aires, where her father had been commissioned to construct various buildings, including the Austrian-Hungarian Embassy, for which he was honoured by the Emperor Franz Josef. She had therefore spent her teenage years in Argentina – speaking fluent Spanish as well as French – before returning to Paris at the age of nineteen.

And she was conscious of other oddities about her upbringing. There was of course the early discovery that she was the 'wrong way round' in that she was left-handed when everybody should be right-handed and was forced to switch, so that it was only gradually that she was able to change back for drawing with the left. Then there was the fact that she was an only child, which made her tend to be shy but, paradoxically, forced her to dare to be bold.

Above all, there was the fact that her room in the Buenos Aires apartment had a glass door with a curtain on the outside, often only half drawn, so that not only could she observe the ballet of her parents bickering over her flighty father's infidelities, but she was open to inspection by them at any time. If her father, who treated her as his good buddy, happened to see her undressed, he just smiled or winked and, while she trusted him completely, she had once or twice looked at her developing breasts and thighs in the mirror afterwards to try to imagine how he saw her. All this left her with an early sense of herself as something or somebody *watched,* and she sometimes joked that this was why she had taken up photography so early, so that she could watch others and get her own back.

Except, of course, that the joke also turned back on you, since you not only photographed others but were inevitably drawn to photograph yourself – to become the watcher of yourself. Contradictions, no end of contradictions. But then you had to live with the contradictions. They could be tragic or funny, but they at least forced you to be aware, made you think, made you read books, made you attempt to be yourself – whoever that was or could become –rather than just be the off-the-peg model of the young middle-class French woman from the standard family background.

'So what are you up to today?' asked her mother, as though expecting the unconventional.

'I think I'll trawl some of the boutiques on the Boulevard St-Germain and then do the market stalls – see what I can dig up.'

'Props for your work?' asked her father, welcoming the change in the conversation.

'Yes, but I might also find something for myself. And then I'm lunching with friends.'

'And which dashing avant-garde figures are you favouring with your presence at lunch today?' said her father teasingly.

'Paul Eluard and his wife.'

'Isn't that Eluard a Communist?' asked her mother.

'No *Maman,* He's a Surrealist.'

'Is there any difference?!'

'There is and there isn't' said her father, restored to his sardonic jollity by the croissants with quince jam. 'They're both pseudo-religions, but they're wrong for quite different reasons!'

'You're just an old sceptic' said Dora, laughing. 'You don't believe in anything.'

'You can say that again!' said her mother with feeling.

'It's the beginning of wisdom' said her father with a smile.

Of course she could see that the incompatibility between her parents was not simply due to the fact that he was a seasoned sceptic while she was a Catholic. People didn't always actually believe what they thought they believed, and such a conflict of values could probably be overcome if people cared deeply enough for each other. But that hardly seemed to be the case, whether because the marriage had simply been a mistake, or because any trust between them had long since been eroded by those infidelities of her father that she had seen and heard argued over as a child from behind the glass door. And what was left was habit, the fact of sharing a dwelling and sharing a daughter, a weary acceptance that things were unlikely ever to change.

Yet if Dora felt guilty, it was because she recognised that her mother was more a prisoner of this situation than her father. After all he had his professional contacts, while his very scepticism led him to take a critical interest in what was going on in the world, just as he had been able to take an informed interest in her career as a photographer. And if she got on more easily with him than with her mother, it was basically because he was the freer of the two. Indeed, though she could not quite remember exactly how it had started years before – had her mother really always been content to opt out and pursue her church-related activities? – she often lunched on a Sunday with her father alone. Always at the same table in the same restaurant at Sèvres-Babylone, when in between tormenting the

45

waiter with his legendary fussiness – which he practised as an ironical art form – they could talk, as he put it in his grimly humorous way, 'man to man'. Dora had several times tried to persuade her mother to join them, but whether she really didn't want to, whether she felt she wasn't wanted, or whether it was a perverse way of demonstrating that she felt she wasn't wanted, she always refused. Which, as usual, left things the way they were.

'I must go, *Maman*' Dora told her mother, 'but I'll look out that necklace to go with your dress. It will just add something.'

She kissed both of them goodbye and was soon out enjoying the enlivening crisp morning air as she walked up to the Boulevard Saint-Germain to begin her trawl. It was nice to feel free. One way or the other, you had to be free…

Sitting in the Metro carriage, opposite a flustered young mother with two small staring children, Dora was reviewing her purchases – a small ebony bust and thick beads from the African stall that could also come in handy.

'*Bonjour*' she said to the children, showing them the little ebony figure.

However, since that merely made them stare all the harder, she contented herself with a sympathetic smile to the young mother.

She was looking forward to seeing Paul Eluard again and reflecting that he was in fact her closest male friend and the only man with whom she might have thought of forming a long-term relationship – if he had not already been married to Nusch. It wasn't because he was tall and handsome, or because he was a sociable *bon vivant*, but because with all that he was warm, honest and reliable. And what was particularly attractive about him was not only his sympathy and admiration for women, but a quite unusual generosity of spirit. There was an unusual simplicity about him and about his poetry, a simplicity which he had achieved the hard way. And not just through his horrendous experiences in that awful World War.

Returning as a pacifist after the war, having married his Russian sweetheart Gala, he had to share her for a while – painful though he found it – in a *ménage à trois* with the German painter Max Ernst, who ironically had been shelling his trenches in 1917. He was devastated when Gala left him for the painter Salvador Dali, who was not only flamboyant but extremely wealthy – a joking anagram of his name being '*avida dollars*' – and when he suddenly disappeared his friends feared that he might commit suicide. When he returned six or seven months later, after an apparently life-changing journey – to Tahiti and Indonesia perhaps, though he refused to talk about it – he was the calm, even-tempered Paul of today. Having decided that jealousy was a moral weakness to be overcome, that you must respect and love people whether they respond in kind or not, he remained on friendly terms with Gala and went on his way alone. At least until Nusch entered his life…

As the train clattered to a stop at Vavin, Dora got out and went up the steps to arrive outside the big Dôme brasserie. But it wasn't there that they were lunching, or at the Coupole or even the neighbouring café where the American expats hung out, but at some cheap place called Chez Jules in the neighbouring Rue Delambre. For Paul, who lived mostly by buying and selling pictures, combined being frequently hard up with a flair for finding the kind of matey cheap restaurants where you talked to the diners at the adjoining tables almost as much as to your friends. Of course these restaurants tended to be crowded and it was a moment or two, when she entered Chez Jules and peered through the smoke, before she discovered Paul and Nusch crushed around a table in the far corner. '*Bonjour, Mademoiselle*' said several of the diners admiringly or even suggestively as she fought her way through the tables to where Paul was already on his feet, arms aloft, waiting to greet her.

'A-dora-ble Dora! You see how you set the place alight?!'

'You flatter me, Paul – but keep going! *Bonjour* Nusch.'

She embraced and kissed both of them, opened her coat, threw it over the back of her chair, told Nusch she looked lovely as always and brought out her purchases, which Nusch – and Paul, doing his best to take an informed interest – duly admired.

'So where's Jules?' she asked finally, gazing around her. 'Is there a Jules?'

'Nobody knows' said Paul. 'There may once have been a Jules, or he may be an entirely mythical figure, or perhaps some owner named Sébastien thought his name was too upmarket for a joint like this, or perhaps he named it after his father to compensate for having being an ungrateful son– who knows…?!'

'You clearly don't!' laughed Dora.

'What I do know is that the place – like all good things and even the cosmos itself – is actually run by a woman. Called Ginette.'

'And a right old battleaxe Ginette is!' said Nusch, laughing her trilling laugh.

'But with a heart of gold?'

'They all do' said Paul. 'Can I pour you some of this rather young and brash but engaging house white? We've been drinking quite a lot of it already.'

'I can see that!' Dora laughed.

'I love your laugh, Dora. It's so musical. And you laugh a lot, doesn't she, Nusch?'

'She does, I'm glad to say!'

'Well I suppose' said Dora, laughing, 'that there's an awful lot in the world to laugh about!'

'Or cry about!'

'And they're often the same things!' said Dora, laughing again. 'So can you eat here as well as drink?'

'You eat what's on that slate on the wall' grinned Nusch. 'Or else Ginette will come and get you!'

Dora loved the Alsatian accent. Nusch was of course a nickname that Paul had given her – her real name was Maria. He had got talking to her several years before somewhere near the Opéra one fine May evening when he and Breton were strolling aimlessly around the boulevards. She was out of work at the time, having done

48

various jobs as a minor actress, a hypnotist's assistant and a travelling acrobat – she could still do an impressive number of somersaults in a row. And even discounting the Surrealist idea that apparently chance encounters were pre-ordained by fate, Paul found himself suddenly smitten by this young woman – slim, with fine features, dark curly hair, smiling easily, totally unaffected: a child of nature.

If everybody liked Paul, as Dora knew, everybody absolutely loved Nusch. However drawn you were to Paul, you couldn't be jealous of Nusch if you tried. And even less could you be jealous since Paul, though he obviously worshipped and could not stop writing poems about Nusch, carried his determination to transcend sexual jealousy to the point that he was prepared to share her with certain close friends in wife-swapping situations. And if Dora saw a slightly sad and comic paradox in all this, she knew enough about their intimate relationship to understand how it could suit them both.

'So what have you been up to, Nusch?' she asked.

With her pretty face, slim high-breasted figure and natural air, she had modelled for Picasso and Magritte as well as for Dora herself. And indeed she had become a minor artist in her way.

'I've been pottering about with some collages recently' she said, then added with a laugh. 'At least it helps a bit with the insomnia!'

For that was the only mystery about this child of nature, that someone apparently so totally carefree should suffer from insomnia.

'I know, I know' said Paul, stroking her arm tenderly. 'I don't understand it.'

'But of course it only happens at night' said Nusch with a grin. 'Anyway let's eat something. Here's Bernard.'

Bernard the waiter was short, bald and bustling.

'So the starter is mixed hors d'oeuvres?' asked Paul. 'Anything other than that?'

'Mixed hors d'oeuvres.'

'Then I think we'll all have mixed hors d'oeuvres, shall we?'

'Three mixed hors d'oeuves – three!' roared Bernard over his shoulder towards the kitchen, before bustling off again.

'All that nonsense of actually *choosing* what you want to eat...!' joked Paul.

'Shocking!'said Dora with a grin. 'It's bourgeois individualism!'

'Not the sort of thing you could tolerate in leftwing politics,is it?!'

But as the mixed hors d'oeuvres arrived – and proved to be both copious and tasty – Paul began to talk about the recent split between the Communists and the Surrealists at the International Writers' Congress in Paris. After André Breton, who was due to read a paper, ran into the Soviet delegate Ilya Ehrenbourg in the street and slapped him across the face – twice.

'Was he challenging him to a duel or what?' asked Nusch.

'No, though it almost sounds like it!' smiled Paul. 'He was furious because Ehrenburg said the Surrealists weren't serious revolutionaries, but just a crowd of poofs and nancy boys interested only in dreams and psychoanalysis and the Marquis de Sade – and you know how André hates homosexuality.'

'Why exactly is he so opposed to that?' asked Dora.

'Well he thinks some of it is just experimental and fashionable, but it's mainly because he thinks it goes against the natural 'dialectic of desire' between man and woman – and so do I, for that matter. Which is why both André and I have each got a beautiful, mysterious Muse' he said, removing a sliver of celery from his mouth before kissing Nusch tenderly on the lips.'Have I not, Nusch?'

'So you tell me, Paul' she said, rolling her eyes with a comical smile towards Dora.

Dora smiled in return. No, you just couldn't be jealous of Nusch...

'Anyway' Paul was saying, 'it became quite farcical after that – almost surreal in fact!'

'But the split was bound to happen sooner or later, wasn't it?' said Dora. 'The Communists wanting to change society and the Surrealists wanting to change themselves – it's not quite the same thing in practice, Paul, is it?'

'Well, certainly not with the way the Soviets are going, with the cult of Stalin, the expulsion of Trotsky, and all the rest of it. But then the Surrealists did need to attach themselves to a significant political movement.'

'Except that they were never more than the tail trying to wag the dog.'

'What's this?' cried a throaty voice. 'No dog meat here, I can tell you!'

It was the 'battleaxe' Ginette, come to salute 'Monsieur Paul' and to ask loudly how he managed to go around with *two* such beautiful young women at his time of life.

'But I'm only forty, Ginette. It's my youthful maturity that attracts them.'

'You randy old bugger' she said affectionately. 'So what would you all like for your main course?'

'What's the choice?' asked Nusch with a grin.

'You can either have *boeuf bourguignon* or – if you're good – *boeuf bourguignon.*'

'I think I'll have the former' said Nusch..

'You know, I think I'd prefer the latter' said Dora.

'And after due reflection' said Paul, 'I'll go for the *boeuf bourguignon.*'

'A wise choice, Monsieur Paul. And you'll need a bottle of *gros rouge* with that.'

'I'm entirely in your hands, Ginette.'

'That'll be the day, Monsieur Paul!'

The *gros rouge* and the *boeuf bourguignon* arrived, courtesy of the short, bald, bustling Bernard and in turn they pronounced it to be good, very good and excellent. But they were by now exchanging bantering chat with the people at neighbouring tables, some of whom clearly had a head start with the *gros rouge,* and it was some time before the conversation turned to being serious again.

'Anyway' Paul was saying, 'the ridiculous thing is that the Surrealists can still say they're internationalist, anti-patriotic and anticolonialist, while the Communists are becoming more conservative, more nationalistic and more tied to Moscow by the day.'

'But that simply means, doesn't it, that the Surrealists are politically marginal, that they have nowhere to go?'

'Except that there are other non-communist revolutionary groups they could combine with. And Breton is busy combining with one in particular to form Contre-Attaque.'

'You mean with Bataille's lot?'

Paul didn't wish to embarrass her, but everybody seemed to know that she had had that brief relationship with Georges Bataille. Including Nusch, clearly, since she was smiling mischievously.

'So what's he like, Dora?' she was asking. 'Is he as wild as they say?'

'Not really. He's quite a gentle sort of guy, who just happens to go in for a kind of upside-down anti-Christian mysticism.'

'Oh God!' said Nusch, rolling her eyes in bafflement.

'Well, not quite' said Dora with a slight laugh, 'God is present, but only as an absence.But I don't think, Paul, that the Surrealists would gain by adding that lot to their political platform. They would only make themselves more irrelevant.'

'You could be right, Dora.'

'In fact I think it may be too late for Surrealism. With Hitler threshing around and the League of Nations falling apart, wouldn't the only sensible thing be to come in from the margins for the fight against Fascism?'

'It's beginning to look like that, Dora.'

Fortunately, a little light relief turned up in the bulky person of Ginette, who – perhaps as a gesture to Paul – came over in person to accept compliments on the *boeuf bourguignon*, collect the empty plates and deliver the dessert, which was *Tarte tatin* and no nonsense.

'Tell me, Madame, we've been wondering' asked Dora. '*Is* there a Jules?'

'That *would* be telling, dear.'

'I mean, if there is, where is he?'

'Where I want him to be!' said Ginette with grim satisfaction.

She turned away, leaving them eyeing one another over their *Tarte tatin.*

'You'd nearly think she'd killed him' said Nusch,

'He could be under the floorboards' said Paul.

'Poor Jules' said Dora. 'But I'm not sure that would be the best place to hide a body. Not in a restaurant.'

'You mean people would notice?' asked Nusch.

'I mean there's a better way of making sure people don't notice.'

'You're not saying ...?' asked Paul.

'I'm afraid I am saying...'

'What do you mean 'you're saying'?' asked Nusch.

'Well it's all too obvious, isn't it?'

'What's obvious?'

'He was in the *boeuf bourguignon.*'

'Oh no!' shrieked Nusch, before starting her trilling laugh again. 'How am I going to eat my *Tarte tatin?*'

'Don't worry, there mightn't have been enough of him left to go into the *Tarte tatin.*'

'Thanks a lot!'

'But you might care to think twice before you drink any more of that rough, strangely gravelly red wine.'

'I think' said Paul, after he stopped laughing, 'that I can feel a bad poem coming on.'

'And have you a bad title for it?'

'"High Mass Chez Jules on a December afternoon'. It will complete my new collection.'

'It will be a change from poems about me' smiled Nusch.

'I'm hoping to get Picasso to illustrate them, but he's away at the moment and I can't get much out of that friend he's got living there now. His marriage has broken down, of course.'

'So it's some new woman friend?' asked Dora.

'No, it's a man, a rather odd Spanish guy. Anyway, I'm hoping to persuade him to come with Nusch and me in the New Year to

Barcelona for the exhibition of new Spanish painting I've been involved in setting up – his mother is there apart from anything else.'

'I'm looking forward to it' said Nusch. 'I've never been to Barcelona.'

'Oh, you'll like it' said Dora. 'It's a very lively and interesting place.'

'You've worked there, of course' said Paul. 'haven't you?'

'Yes, I did some documentary work there.'

'And of course you speak Spanish! So why don't you come along with us, Dora? Make a party of it?'

'Yes do!' said Nusch. 'It would be lovely.'

'Oh I don't know' said Dora with a smile. 'I've got a couple of commissions lined up for January.'

'Well, do think about it, Dora.'

But she was already thinking about it. And thinking with amusement that her old friend Paul had better not be taking this 'sharing' business to the point of lining her up for some sort of four-handed Spanish orgy with – of all people – Picasso.

On the other hand, of course, if it was a civilised trip to the exhibition in Barcelona, she couldn't immediately think of anything more exciting than getting to know Picasso…

3

There was an occasional snowflake drifting down from a leaden sky as Eluard turned right from the Champs-Elysées just before two o'clock and walked up the Rue La Boétie towards Number 23. He needed to finalise the entries for the exhibition, to try to persuade Picasso to attend the opening in Barcelona and – more immediately given the state of his finances – to get him to agree to illustrate his new collection of poetry.

At least the angry lady was not on hand today with her umbrella. He suspected, despite what Sabartés had said, that she must be the abandoned wife Olga – a suspicion reinforced when no sooner had he rung the bell than a flustered Sabartés suddenly appeared, checked him out through thick glasses, glanced up and down the street and quickly drew him inside.

'I hope this isn't a bad time' said Paul.

'No no no, absolutely not. Pablo is back, everything is in order, back to normal, we've been sorting out the paintings for the exhibition, they've been put in a crate and already sent off, so it has all been done, you see…'

'He did it all himself?' said Eluard, disconcerted.

'Yes, he said he wanted it over and done with. I don't know if he wants to be available today.' He looked embarrassed, hesitated. 'But perhaps I'll just go and see, shall I?'

He went off and it was what seemed like a long time before Picasso appeared – alone.

'So, Pablo…' said Eluard.

'So, Paul…'

It was the same thick Spanish accent and the same sardonic voice as before, the voice of the games player. They shook hands, sat down and looked at each other.

'Well' Paul began cautiously, 'you've been away, it seems…'

'Yes' said Picasso with his distinctive, almost whinnying laugh. 'And now I'm back.'

'I was just a little surprised when I came last week and your friend Sabartés opened the door…'

'Yes, Jaume always comes as a surprise. It's the beret that does it. More the sort of thing you see in the markets at Les Halles than in the respectable Rue La Boétie. But if anybody asks – not that they would dare, since they're so fucking polite – I'll tell them he's a Spanish Surrealist.'

'Yes, that should drain the blood from their over-refined faces! But what really surprised and indeed shocked me, Pablo, was that he said you've stopped painting.' He laughed. 'And at the most unfortunate moment, as it happens.'

'And why's that?' said Picasso. Getting up and starting to move around a little, digging in his jacket pocket for something or other.

'Well for one thing I was about to ask if you would illustrate my new volume of poetry.'

'Oh I'm sure, Paul, that it will sell without any squiggles from me.'

Eluard watched him produce a packet of Gauloises and go on digging in his pocket.

'Are you looking for a light by any chance?'

'No no, no light' he said distractedly, producing a matchbox, but leaving it and the Gauloises side by side on the table beside him.

'However, the main thing I wanted to do was to try to persuade you to attend the exhibition in the New Year in Barcelona. As you know, I'm supposed to give this lecture about your work, but I can hardly tell them you've packed up painting just when you're being honoured in this exhibition.'

'But it would make it all the more interesting, Paul – 'the last works of Pablo Picasso'.'

'You know that Miró and Dali will be there?'

'Dali? Big deal!' he said, fishing out of his pocket a small piece of green pottery, looking at it, then laying it on the table beside the Gauloises and the matchbox.

'It's still an honour, though. From your motherland, after all.'

'But I've been out of my 'motherland' for thirty years, Paul!'

'And your own mother is still alive and living in Barcelona, isn't she?'

'Except that the last time I went there I swanned around with Olga in the Hispano-Suiza and stayed like a princely prat at the Ritz. I'm not sure either my mother or my motherland is dying to see me again.'

'Well, it could be politically useful, you know' said Eluard, changing tack. 'Now that the left-of-centre parties in Spain are getting together to try to form a Popular Front against the threat of Fascism.'

'But I'm not political, Paul. I don't do propaganda.'

'That's the point – that it wouldn't be propaganda.'

Eluard watched him extract a small pebble from his right trouser pocket – a bluish pebble with limestone streaks – and examine it briefly before laying it down beside the green pottery fragment. It was clear that Pablo – perversely perhaps – was enjoying saying no in this little verbal joust that was developing.

'They don't really know anything about your recent work down there, do they? Though of course they'll remember the earlier stuff: the Blue period obviously...'

'Sentimental shit – of course they'll remember it!'

'Come off it, Pablo!' said Paul, smiling as he watched him grope down into his left trouser pocket for some other *objet trouvé* as it seemed, 'I wonder what you would say of your Pink period!'

'*Pink* sentimental shit. It's a good thing I didn't have a Green period or an Orange period or a Magenta period – they'd have liked them even more.'

'Do you think' asked Paul teasingly, beginning to enjoy this playacting almost as much as Pablo obviously was, 'that they'd prefer those gigantic great women of your neo-classical period?'

'Probably, since it was naked neo-classical kitsch. But then', he said, extracting a golf ball from the left trouser pocket, 'I blame all that on my aunts.'

'You blame it on your aunts? And what on earth are you doing with a golf ball?'

'It's a beautiful object, all those little dimples. Yes, I had these neo-classical aunts – two of them no less.'

'You mean the ones with arms and legs like tree trunks who used to gambol romantically along the beach?'

'No, that was artistic licence – they were almost too heavy to get up from their chairs, let alone gambol along the beach. They were terrifying with their fat legs and thighs when you were under the table.'

'And what the fuck – with or without a golf ball – were you doing under the table?!' asked Paul, laughing.

'Hiding from these two aunts – I was very small of course. But I was scared I would get so gigantic myself that I'd blot out the whole sky. Or else get so tiny I'd disappear into nothing at all and nobody would know I'd ever existed – not even me.'

'I can see why you sent them trundling along the beach! Not that I'm suggesting your lumbering maidens were in any way ugly.'

'Why not? The uglier they are the more people are prepared to pay for them. I can produce rubbish and it makes no difference to those idiots. If I wiped my arse and signed the bog-paper there'd be some delicate English aristocrat or American millionairess who'd pay big bucks for it – to stick it in a bank vault most likely! It has become an investment business, Paul, a racket. Painting lost its place to photography donkey's years ago and there's an end to it.'

Eluard watched him take a child's top from one pocket, a small rusty ring from another pocket, and lay them with a sort of finality beside the other objects on the table.

'Photography or not, you can't tell me you produce rubbish, Pablo, that's just masochistic nonsense.'

'I'm fifty-four all of a sudden, Paul. It's time to stop pretending.'

Paul got up, picked up the bluish pebble from the table, looked at it and began to walk around slowly.

'Look, I just do not think you can give up painting. You're clearly the sort of guy who thinks with his fingers – you can't stop fiddling with things, transforming things, trying for some reason to turn them into something else. I mean, look at all this stuff. Have you ever in your life thrown anything away?'

'Not up to now. It would be like throwing a bit of myself away, I suppose. That's me there on the table, Paul. All that's left of the painter Picasso. Not much, is it?'

He stood looking at the little pile of objects with a sardonic grin, then suddenly swept them off the table and across the room.

'But isn't it time I offered you a drink?' he said.

'I thought you'd never ask' said Paul.

He watched him go to a cupboard, take out a bottle of Armagnac, splash some into a glass and hand it across.

'You're not joining me?'

'Yes I am' said Pablo, producing a bottle of Vittel water and filling a glass for himself. 'It's just that I've given up alcohol – an old ulcer. But here's to... whatever.'

'Yes, whatever!' said Paul.

He picked up the packet of Gauloises and the matches from the floor, offered a cigarette to Pablo, took one himself and lit them in turn. What could he say that would get through the self-protective armour of this man? For beneath the playacting and the touch of self-pity, there seemed to be a real loss of belief and self-confidence.

'Tell me, Pablo' he began cautiously, as they were sitting down again, smoking their Gauloises, 'this decision to give up painting.

Are you sure it's not just a temporary reaction to the break-up with your wife – Olga, isn't she? Believe me, there's life after separation from a Russian wife – I know, I've been there.'

'Oh yes, Gala – before she left you for Salvador Dali? Or was it for Salvador Dali's dollars?'

It was clear that Pablo, who doubtless also knew about the *ménage-à-trois* with Max Ernst, wasn't going out of his way to make it easy for him.

'Well it was certainly all very painful, I don't mind admitting that! So painful I had to go halfway round the world to get over it. But I did get over it, Pablo. I learnt to share. I learnt to let go.'

'And Gala clearly learnt to let go, since she went off with that wanker Dali! Fortunately, I've no trouble letting Olga go. Anyway, they all go, Paul. Even if they don't die or kill themselves, they all float away from you in the end.' He paused, drew on his cigarette, then frowned down at it. 'The one I really shared with, the one I could never paint for some reason, I can tell you what we shared – as I watched her spluttering and dying of tuberculosis in that freezing bloody winter in wartime while the rest of you were happily slaughtering each other heroically in the trenches. Eva she was called – where's she these days, she's not sharing any more, is she? They all go thataway, Paul. The world is a ridiculous, murderous place.'

'I know, but isn't that precisely why we have to go on sharing, to try to prevent those horrors from happening again – sharing our humanity, sharing our idealism, sharing our love?'

'So you say in your poetry at least.'

'But I'm also living it, Pablo. I'm with Nusch now, and she's wonderful, we share everything, we share ourselves. And of course she'll be coming with me to the exhibition. So why don't you come along with us, to Barcelona?'

'But I know Barcelona, Paul. I've lived in Barcelona. I left Barcelona.'

'You could visit your mother, couldn't you? And see people – Miró...'

'And Dali!'

'Come on, Pablo, come with us, share Barcelona with Nusch and me, share the exhibition with us, share *us* with us. And she'd be a great model for you, would Nusch. Get you going again, get you painting again, for God's sake!'

'I don't think so, Paul. The way I feel, there's nothing to paint, nothing to paint with, and nobody to paint for.'

'And I could try to get Dora Maar to come – you know, the young Surrealist photographer? She's young, she's lovely, she's intelligent, she could help you stoke the old fires again. What you need, Pablo, is another woman…!'

He stopped as he saw Picasso shaking his head and smiling sardonically as he stood up to indicate that the visit was at an end.

'If you understood anything about my present situation, Paul, you would realise that the last thing I want is another woman!'

Which saw Paul ushered out a few minutes later, with at least the compensation of an invitation to Boisgeloup to show for his pains. To walk back through thicker snowflakes towards the Champs-Elysées, wondering increasingly about this strange new relationship with Sabartés, who with his dark clothes and beret looked more like some officious country priest than the companion to a Picasso.

Meanwhile, Sabartés had come in to find Picasso sitting brooding over his glass of Vittel – untouched as usual, since he only ever ordered it for the sake of appearances and rarely drank from it.

'So are you going to Barcelona?' he asked finally.

'No, I don't want to go to Barcelona or anywhere else.'

'Eluard will be disappointed.'

'Yes. But since he has obviously been putting himself to a lot of trouble over this exhibition – and since I don't want to illustrate these new poems of his – I've invited him and his wife Nusch to Boisgeloup for a few days. It will at least get me away from Olga.'

'So when will you leave?'

'Tomorrow.'

'And what about Marie-Thérèse…?'

'She can go on staying at her mother's. That's all right for now since it's winter time and the baby is still very small. I'll go out the odd time to see her at Maisons-Alfort and perhaps you can come too. The situation is manageable for the moment, but it will have to be watched – and of course kept absolutely under wraps.'

'I see' said Sabartés, looking thoughtfully at Picasso, who still seemed to brooding about something. 'He's a good fellow, Paul Eluard, isn't he?'

'Yes, I like Paul. And he's about the only one among that lot who actually seems to know about painting.' He paused. 'Except, somehow or other…'

'Except…?'

'Well he has been through the mill, of course. Even so, these Frenchmen…!'

'You mean they're not quite Spanish?'

'They're nowhere near Spanish. Can you imagine sharing a woman – your Mercedes say – in a *ménage-à-trois?*'

'Well, it would only be half the trouble, I suppose' said Sabartés, realising guiltily that he could imagine such a scenario without too much difficulty. 'Anyway, he's a Surrealist, isn't he?'

'He seemed to be offering to 'share' his wife.'

'The Eskimos do that as well, I believe. It's a form of politeness – unless it's due to the cold.'

'The trouble, Jaume, is that I wasn't sure if he wanted me to share her or if he wanted to share me. It's just that he's a little too delicate in a way, too civilized or something. No machismo.'

'Not Spanish?'

'Definitely not Spanish! And then he tells me I need another woman.'

'Which might be one too many just at the moment!'

'I tell him that painting has been killed off by photography, so what does he do?!'

'So what *does* he do?'

'He tries to fix me up with some flaming Surrealist photographer…!'

Dora was in her studio in the Rue d'Astorg in late afternoon staring at this strange, blind, unformed little creature, with its threateningly sharp claws held up to its pointed snout as though in supplication, that she had removed from its news paper wrapping and placed in front of her.

She occasionally dropped into the animal shop on the right bank of the river close to the Pont Neuf, just to look around or possibly find a subject, but she had not quite bargained for this: an armadillo foetus that the shopkeeper had shown her as a curiosity and been about to throw out.

'It's a salmon pink fairy armadillo' he had told her. 'They come from South America.'

'I know' she said. 'I've lived in Argentina. They eat armadillo down there. It tastes like pork. Can I have it?'

'To eat?!'

'No no, to photograph! I'll drop in a print next time I'm passing.'

The shopkeeper looked as though he could get along quite happily without such a print, but that in itself was telling. Lit from below against a stark black background, with a hint of an alien terrain at bottom left, this complex little creature could become a mysteriously frightening yet frightened monster from another world. It could have a formidable effect at an exhibition.

Yes, but that would still only be to neutralize it, control it at the level of photographic composition. In the silent reality of this studio, what could not be neutralized was the disturbing fact that this pathetic little lump of organic matter that had never made it into the living world would gradually disintegrate and disappear. That was what was mysterious, and rather frightening. Enough to make her decide to visit Jacqueline a little earlier than planned – and not to mention it in view of the forthcoming baby.

The Metro was rather more crowded than usual for this time of day, with women shopping for Christmas and the New Year. It wasn't clear whether Jacqueline's baby was late, but it was beginning to look as though Dora might miss the birth. The trouble was that she was due to leave the following week for the Alps, to do a photo-reportage on the mediaeval silver mines of the Grandes-Rousses and to join a group including her screenwriter friend Louis Chavance, the actor Jean-Louis Barrault and the poet and screenwriter Jacques Prévert. But they said first babies tended to be late in any case, didn't they? Late or early, all this just seemed to have happened so quickly. One minute you were a pair of students living it up together and all of a sudden one of you was married and having a baby...

She got out at Place de Clichy, walked down the Rue Fontaine to Number 42 and rang the bell. To produce almost immediately the impressive figure of André with his swept back hair and his trademark black velvet jacket, black shirt and swirl patterned tie.

'Dora! The most colourful butterfly in the kingdom. How are you? Do come through, but we'd better go quietly. Jacqueline is resting.'

'How is she then, André?'

'She's fine, I think. All's well. Let me take your glorious coat and your so surreal scarf.'

As he disappeared briefly, Dora looked around the room, with the familiar large stand on which André was again displaying everything from engravings or manuscripts to exotic objects from Africa or the South Seas. Since, like Eluard, he lived by his pen and by buying and selling pictures, he had no consistent source of income and was sometimes hard up. And, again like Eluard, he had been forced some years earlier to sell his collection to make ends meet.

'You're building your display up nicely again' she said when he returned.

'Yes, it's coming along. I've just got hold of some Indian artefacts from the western coast of Canada, Salt Spring Island in fact. And that little propitiatory group from Nepal.'

He took down and handed her a small, rough-hewn wooden

bowl, containing three tiny carved wooden figures standing upright within it – a little family: man, woman and child.

'They look so desperately vulnerable' said Dora.

'Not so long as they're inside the bowl' he said with a smile. 'It exorcizes the evil spirits that bring about death and disaster. Let me get you a drink.'

'Thanks, André. When is the baby due then?'

'They can't really say with a first one, we're told. It might be sometime between Christmas and the New Year. Here you are – a quiet white wine, from Vouvray.'

'Oh thanks. Aren't you joining me?'

'Well I won't, if you'll forgive me. Actually, Dora, if it's not too much of an imposition, I was wondering how long you intended to stay...'

'You mean you'll throw me out noisily after my quiet drink?'

'Trust you, Dora!' he said, laughing. 'No, but I clearly can't leave Jacqueline alone and – if it wasn't a dreadful inconvenience for you, obviously – I could usefully go out for an hour or so...'

'Yes, of course I'll stay' said Dora. 'Do go out and get some fresh air.'

'That's wonderful, Dora. It's a meeting to set up an organization we're calling Contre-Attaque, with Georges and one or two others.'

'Georges Bataille?'

'Yes. You'll be all right here, will you? If Jacqueline doesn't emerge shortly, you could perhaps peep in and see if she's still sleeping?'

'Yes of course. You go along to your meeting. With Georges...'

Which left Dora quietly drinking her quiet white wine while wondering just why André, who had for years seen Bataille as anathema and indeed as a serious rival for the leadership of the Surrealist movement, was now collaborating so closely with him in this business of Contre-Attaque.

'Dora!'

It was Jacqueline, padding in from the bedroom, dressed in a short frilly nightdress which possibly made her look even bigger than she was. She made a comic helpless grimace as she advanced ponderously to exchange kisses.

'I didn't realise you were here. Where's André?'

'He went out for a short while to organize a meeting.'

'Oh God yes, meetings! When he isn't writing he's going to meetings. And with being stuck so much indoors for the past ten days or so because of me, he has been like a caged lion.'

'Then it's good to let the lion out for a runaround' said Dora, smiling. 'But how *are* you, for heaven's sake?!'

'How am I?!' said Jacqueline with another helpless grimace. 'I don't know how I am. I'm big, I'm anxious, I'm getting impatient to get it over with, I've got fluid retention but I keep going to the lavatory, I'm waiting for these contractions they've told me about – and I'm wondering how on earth I'm going to manage when and if this child is ever born. It's just so exhausting.'

'But of course you'll manage, Jacqueline. And André is supportive, isn't he?'

'Yes, he's lovely in his way. But there isn't any money to spare and he's not a man for household chores. And the laundry and the washing up don't do themselves.'

'You'll have to train him.'

'But I'm not so good at it either. And can you imagine anybody training André Breton?!'

'Well, not easily, no' said Dora. 'But he obviously loves you.'

'Oh yes, he loves me to death – except that I'd still like to live a little. It's so long since I held a pencil or a paintbrush in my hand that I can hardly remember it. But then, as you may remember telling me, I'm his 'Muse'.'

'Well, I think you're just naturally a little apprehensive before the birth, Jacqueline. I'm sure it will all go splendidly and you'll be delighted with this baby. Are you hoping for a boy or a girl, by the way?'

'Oh, it will be a girl.'

'How do you know?'

'André said so.'

'But how does André know?'

'The way André knows everything else' smiled Jacqueline. 'André just knows.'

To cheer Jacqueline up, Dora went into the kitchen to tackle what was indeed a large pile of dirty dishes and pots, and soon they were joking and giggling like schoolgirls.

'Here's a strange and ridiculous story for you' said Dora.

'Good! I like strange and ridiculous things.'

'My old friend Paul Eluard was suggesting a trip to Barcelona with Nusch and himself and Picasso.'

'Great! Go for it! Picasso, no less!'

'Except that Paul told me this morning it has fallen through.'

'Why?'

'Partly because Picasso, Paul seems to think, has switched his interest from women to some new live-in man friend he's got.'

'Then maybe it's good that it fell through!' said Jacqueline with a laugh. 'Still, that really does surprise me. He never looked that way to me.'

But Dora could see that she was beginning to tire again, and became a little concerned that André was taking so long to return.

It was more than two hours before he came back, full of apologies and enveloping Jacqueline in tenderness and concern.

'*Mon grand amour,* don't you think you need to go and lie down again,?'

'Yes, perhaps I should, André.'

It was a very pretty scene, no doubt about that. But as Dora left them together and made her way back to the Metro to go home, she was thinking that it was possibly less than heavenly to be a 'Muse'.

The big Hispano-Suiza was cutting a fine dash through the festive night-time traffic as it sailed across the vast expanse of the Place de la Concorde and on to the Quai des Tuileries, with the Louvre showing up on the left and the gloomy Conciergerie looming beyond the Pont Neuf on the right. Driving through Paris on New Year's Eve, with the Eiffel Tower lit up, drivers hooting and honking in celebratory fashion and the odd firework already shooting up over the river, was a joyful experience.

Not that joy was uniformly felt by all the occupants of the Hispano-Suiza. Marcel, absent-mindedly humming Maurice Chevalier's *Ma Pomme*, would rather have been at his brother's family party and was hoping for some compensation in the form of a fat tip. Picasso, beside him in the front seat as usual, was more single-minded than joyful. In the back seat, Sabartés and his very dark, plump wife Mercedes were pleased at being included in the outing, but uncertain about what to expect.

But the Hispano-Suiza was certainly equipped for a New Year's Eve party. On the seat beside Picasso was a large hamper filled with fine hams, cheeses, *pâté de foie gras,* Bordeaux wines and champagne. And on the back seat beside Mercedes there were parcels containing pretty little embroidered pink dresses and caps, a large doll and heart-melting baby bootees. All of this supplied by Mercedes, the appendage to Sabartés that Picasso had not welcomed but who was after all a competent housekeeper who had her uses. And Mercedes, even without knowing about other purchases that Picasso himself had made, was privately astonished at how much he had allowed her to spend.

'Charenton' announced Marcel, abandoning his preoccupation with Maurice Chevalier's apple in response to a premonitory clearing of the throat by Picasso. 'It won't be long now.'

And indeed they were soon clambering out of the car in front of the house in Maisons-Alfort, with Marcel and Sabartés carrying the hamper and Mercedes carrying the parcels, while Picasso, holding a bunch of roses, rang the bell. Which quickly produced Marie-Thérèse's mother, with a red paper crown on her head.

'Pic!' she said – quite warmly on this occasion.

'I see you've started without us' he said with a laugh.

'Not at all' she protested, 'but we knew the traffic might be slow this evening'

'*Bonne Année!*' he said kissing her on both cheeks and handing her the flowers.

'*Bonne Année à vous tous*' she said and led them through the hall into the normally dreary living room, now enlivened for the occasion with background music, bunting and a candlelit table with flowers – and with a radiant Marie-Thèrèse standing waiting with a hesitantly smiling Maya in her arms.

As Picasso went to her at once and kissed her and the baby, the others were more or less left to introduce themselves, with a little help from Marie-Thérèse's mother. There was the older sister Geneviève, who had her man Jean-Charles in tow, and the younger sister whose name Picasso could never quite remember, who was also with a young man. Which was all to the good since, once the introductions had been scrambled through, this young man helped Marcel to open up the hamper and lay out the contents, while Jean-Charles took charge of the drinks, dealt expertly with the champagne and, after toasting Marie-Thèrèse, Pic and their baby Maya, left them to talk together in a corner while he got the others talking about how long it had taken them to get here, what a rough year 1935 had been, how well Sabartés and Mercedes spoke French, how nice Pic's drawing on the wall of the teenage Marie-Thérèse in the rowing boat on the nearby Marne was, how she hadn't really changed all that much – whatever.

And then as they started eating and drinking, moving around and settling in various parts of the room, the party began to go quite well. Geneviève and Mercedes talked about the cost of living, while Sabartés talked to Jean-Charles about living in South America and Marcel talked to the others about Hitler and the horsepower of the Hispano-Suiza. Meanwhile Picasso went on talking to Marie-Thèrèse and her mother, until Genevieve and Mercedes came over to admire little Maya again – and he deemed that it was time for the ceremony of the presents.

So they all gathered around with due solemnity for the presentation of the little embroidered dresses and caps for Maya, which brought the traditional murmurs of appreciation, then the sweet little bootees, which brought a few cries of 'bravo', and finally the large doll, which produced real applause and laughter at Maya's vaguely flapping attempt to clutch it. Then Picasso produced his gift for Marie-Thérèse's mother, a blue cameo bearing the profile of Aphrodite, which he handed to her and, to further applause, gallantly kissed her hand. Finally, as expectation gathered, he produced a diamond necklace for Marie-Thérèse, which he arranged around her neck. before producing a matching diamond ring which he slid on to her finger as she stood, her eyes shining with tears of pleasure and gratitude, while he kissed her and Maya as the applause began and Jean-Charles proposed another toast to the happy family.

It was as the party got going again, with another round of food and drinks, that Marie-Thérèse's mother drew Picasso aside for a quiet word.

'Thank you so much, Pic. You can see how happy she is.'

'Well, I'm glad.'

'She was terribly worried, you know, eating herself up. All these delays with the divorce.'

'I know, but it's the legal arguments over the settlement, you see.'

'I mean, I'm glad to have her here for the moment, but I can see she's pining to get away.'

'But the difficulty is that we can't use La Boétie because of Olga and I'm likely to be forced to give her Boisgeloup – which would be too cold for her and Maya at this time of year in any case.'

'So what… are you thinking of, Pic?'

'Well, if she could stay here till the winter is over, I could take her down to the Côte d'Azur, get away from all these complications, get a bit of warmth and sunshine. It could be fine, you know.'

'A real honeymoon!' she said with a smile.

Meanwhile the party was getting noisier, with more drink being poured, jokes being told and the laughter getting louder. When Marie-Thérèse took the baby into the bedroom to feed her and put her to bed, Picasso followed and assured her that he would stay over.

'But what about Marcel and that funny little man Sabartés and Mercedes?'

'It's New Year's Eve, *mon amour*, we can't throw them out before midnight!'

'Oh God, I don't think I can wait. It's been so long, Pic!'

'Well you'll just have to wait!' he said, laughing, kissing her on the forehead.

And wait is what they did, as the talk and the laughter went on, with Jean-Charles telling convoluted funny stories about the Auvergne, Marcel giving interminable imitations of Maurice Chevalier, Mercedes hitching up her skirt and performing a plump Spanish bolero and gradually involving everybody in inexpert and increasingly drunken dancing – until at last it was midnight and they could toast the New Year, embrace and wish everybody good luck for this new unknowable year of 1936.

But it was another half hour before Marcel and the others were packed off in the Hispano-Suiza and Picasso and Marie-Thérèse were alone in the bedroom, where she started crying and almost ripping off her blouse.

'*Maman* says you were talking to her about a honeymoon, Pic?' she said, dropping her bra to reveal her swollen breasts.

'Well, I was saying we could go down to Juan-les-Pins in the spring.'

'Oh but that's wonderful, Pic!' she cried, throwing her arms around his neck. 'I've been dying for you here. I thought that after the birth I mightn't want you so much, but I want you more and more. I was coming all by myself out there tonight, I was getting embarrassed. I want it, Pic, please, Pic, I want it, I want it, I want it…!'

'So you had a good time then?' asked Madame Markovitch.

Dora, having just returned from the Alps, had dropped in to wish her parents belated best wishes for the New Year.

'Yes, we had a splendid time – a bit of ski-ing, a lot of eating and drinking and, believe it or not, I even got some work done.'

'What was that then?' asked her father.

'I got some good coverage of the old mediaeval silver mine at the Lac Blanc, above the village of Huez where we were staying.'

'So who were you with then?' asked Madame Markovitch.

'Oh, there was a whole group of us' said Dora, who was in the habit of giving her mother correct information, but not too much. 'The actor Jean-Louis Barrault was there, by the way. He tells me he rehearses round the corner in an attic in the Rue des Grands-Augustins.'

'So that explains those raffish looking characters I've noticed in the *quartier*!' smiled her father.

'Have you any news yet about Jacqueline's baby?' asked her mother.

'No, but I'm going to Rue Fontaine to find out.'

'So what age would she be now, Jacqueline?'

'Twenty-five' said Dora, adding drily 'that's right, *Maman*, three years younger than me. But tell me, *Maman*, what have you two been doing?'

'Not much beyond eating and drinking. Nothing new except that I saw a poor old man run over on my way to Mass and your father has suddenly taken to listening to German radio!'

'Have you, *Papa*?'

'Oh it's just a holiday distraction, I suppose. But I've been getting some rather disturbing news from my old student friend Furst in Vienna and, since I couldn't find Viennese newspapers on sale on the boulevard, I've been listening on and off to Berlin.'

'So this friend of yours…?'

'Is also an architect and he's thinking he'll have to leave the country if he is to get any commissions. He's Jewish.'

'But there's no official anti-Semitism in Austria, is there?'

'No, but it always was a highly anti-Semitic place and there was that attempt by the local Nazis to seize power last year. You begin to wonder if this clownish character Hitler couldn't begin to upset the whole European applecart.'

'Certainly there's growing anti-Jewish feeling here in France.'

'We-ell...' said Madame Markovitch, in an apparently significant manner.

'What do you mean, *Maman*?' asked Dora, smiling.

'Your father is Jewish' said her mother tranquilly.

'What?!' said Dora, laughing in surprise.

'It's true.'

'That's nonsense, Julie!' said her father.

'Well, it says so on our marriage licence.'

'That's only because they wouldn't put me down as agnostic – it had to be a recognized religion, you all said. So they put that.'

'But were your parents Jewish then, back in Zagreb?' asked Dora.

'Yes, but it didn't show particularly – certainly not with my father.'

'But, *Papa*, doesn't that mean that you're technically Jewish?'

'Whatever I may or may not be 'technically'' said her father with a laugh, 'I'm an agnostic – so much so that I can't even be bothered to call myself an atheist.'

Dora looked from one to the other in a kind of dazed surprise.

'Why did neither of you ever talk about this before?'

But no sooner had she said it than she realised it had never been relevant. Except that it might conceivably just have become relevant...

'This doesn't make me Jewish, does it?'

'I don't think so. It comes down on the mother's side. At least as far as the Jews themselves are concerned. As for how the Nazis define it, I wouldn't know...'

But when she left them to go and see Jacqueline, and sat studying the different faces in the Metro, Dora's sense of relief at – probably – not being Jewish was becoming tinged with a touch of unease at having felt such relief. As if it wasn't enough to have her mother fishing and going on about Jacqueline's baby! What freedom would she have to work and play with interesting people in the Alps if she was lumbered with a baby...?!

'She's lovely' said Dora, her eyes filling with tears. 'Those perfect little fingers, it's astonishing, she's so beautiful…! I can't get over her…!'

'Neither can I!' said Jacqueline, laughing down at the baby sucking at her left breast. 'I'm so amazed, I almost wonder where she came from.'

'And she's a girl – a little Jacqueline…! So André was right!'

'André is always right' said Jacqueline, smiling. 'He'll tell you so himself.'

'And she's called Aube? A new dawn – how wonderful…! But how are *you*, Jacqueline?'

'I'm splendid, I think. I mostly sit here in a kind of pleased daze and make milk – in between little trips to the lavatory.'

'I brought you a present' said Dora, taking out a framed photograph of Jacqueline looking out of the broken window of a ruined building almost overgrown with greenery.

'That's very nice of you, Dora. I look a little anxious there, don't I, as though I'd no idea what was going to hit me – and so slender, my God!'

'You'll be slender again, don't worry. Can I do anything to help?'

'Well, actually' said Jacqueline, wincing slightly as she removed Aube from her breast, 'you could hold her for me while I make another little trip.'

'Of course' said Dora, carefully taking the baby from her, 'though I've no experience of babies.'

'Neither have I!' said Jacqueline with a grin.

It was true, thought Dora as she was left alone with Aube, that she didn't seem to have any siblings or cousins or even close friends who had had babies. So to be holding this strange, beautiful little creature who was searching with her tiny quivering mouth to find again the nipple she had been sucking at was startlingly strange and new. And worrying, as the baby's anxiety communicated itself – so much so that she was almost tempted to pull up her woollen ski jumper and put Aube to her own breast. But she just sat there, wondering what it felt like to feed a baby from yourself while rocking Aube gently to keep her from crying, until Jacqueline came back.

'I think she's still hungry' she said, handing Aube back to her.

'Yes, she generally is!' said Jacqueline, starting to feed her again. 'André is out, by the way. He did an hour or two of domestic chores earlier, so as a reward he's now meeting Bataille to talk about this new group called Contre-Attaque. You know about that?'

'Unfortunately yes' said Dora with a smile. 'However, I expect you've been having lots of visitors, have you?'

'Yes, they've been coming and going. I just sit here – when I'm not dozing – and let it all revolve around me, so I'm not sure if I can even remember everybody who's been here. But of course Paul Eluard came with Nusch, before they left for Spain. They'd been staying with Picasso for a few days before Christmas, they said.'

'Had they?'

'Yes, at some château he has somewhere, called Boisgeloup or some such. Paul seems to be getting quite chummy with Picasso. And, between you and me and little Aube here – who can be trusted to keep a secret, can't you, my sweet, of course you can – Paul isn't the only one.'

'No?'

'Alice Paalen has been making eyes at him, it seems. And Alice, as I don't have to tell you, has those devastating big blue eyes.'

That was certainly true. Alice, the wife of an Austrian artist and a Surrealist painter in her own right, was a spectacularly attractive, bright brunette of dazzling vitality, whose charm was somehow rendered the more winning by the misfortune of having a limp.

'But Paul seemed to be saying – you remember? – that Picasso, now that he has separated from his wife, has swung towards a man friend these days.'

'Well, unless he's swinging both ways, Paul seems to have got it wrong.'

'So is Alice's own marriage in trouble then?

'Oh I don't imagine so. It's the big name, isn't it? It's Picasso. All the young women artists want to knock off a Picasso. They want to be – guess what!'

'A Muse.'

'Right first time, a Muse.'

'Even so' said Dora slowly, 'the man must be in his mid-fifties, Jacqueline. Is he up to it?'

'From what I hear' grinned Jacqueline, 'he's more than up to it! Anyway, that's not the point, is it?'

'I know, I know!' said Dora 'They just want to be a 'Muse'.'

But as she left shortly afterwards, hit the Metro in the rush hour and was forced to stand just as she was beginning to feel tired, she was not amused. It was bad enough to arrive back from a splendid holiday in the Alps to be told you might be Jewish, without having Paul Eluard spreading confusion all over the place – and all this demeaning nonsense of women artists wanting to be somebody's 'Muse'!

Dora was sitting at a table in the corner eating a *croque-monsieur* and sipping at intervals from a glass of *rosé d'anjou*.

The Deux Magots on a mid-February evening had a more intimate atmosphere, if also a smokier one, than in the summer, when the terraces were in use. She quite often dropped in here of an evening on her way home, for while the Surrealists also met in the Café Cyrano or in Breton's apartment, their more or less accredited watering hole on the Left Bank was the Deux Magots on the corner of the Place St-Germain-des-Prés. And the ambiguity of the name itself set off surreal resonances since, although the word *magots* originally referred to figurines from China, it was also suggestive both of hoards of money and of Barbary apes.

In fact she had not been doing much socializing over the five or six weeks since the New Year – she had been working too hard on commissions. Also Paul and Nusch had been in Barcelona for the exhibition of Spanish painting and had only returned a few days ago. Paul was disappointed that Picasso had not accompanied them and also seemed unlikely to agree to illustrate his new collection of poetry. Not that it had anything to do with Paul's nonsense about Picasso's change of orientation, since only the other evening she had glimpsed Alice Paalen turning down into the Rue La Boétie as she herself was leaving the studio. But that was a piece of gossip she saw no need to pass on to Paul and Nusch, when they turned up to go along with her to this meeting of Contre-Attaque.

And she was not exactly looking forward to this launch meeting of Contre-Attaque. While it described itself as an anti-Fascist group which aimed to 're-establish the revolutionary principles betrayed by the Communist and Socialist parties' – since of course these had joined with the moderate Radical-Socialist party in the electoral pact of the Popular Front – she was inclined to think that this might be a tall order. Also, she wasn't entirely looking forward to seeing Georges Bataille again – especially, since he was now operating in tandem with his old enemy and Jacqueline's husband, André Breton.

'Dora! I hope I haven't kept you waiting?'

It was Paul, in a heavy overcoat and scarf, kissing her on both cheeks.

'Not really. But I think we'd better get going. It will take us a good fifteen minutes to get to this meeting. Is Nusch not coming?'

'No' he said with a grin, 'she finds the dialectics and the decibels don't help her insomnia.'

As they left the café and started to thread their way through the early evening crowds on the boulevard, she explained that she was getting pretty uneasy about Contre-Attaque. A concern not lessened when they got to the large bare attic room in the Rue des Grands Augustins and found less than forty people there, all of them – including Bataille and Breton, who were sitting together – rather obviously middle-class. With the Communists and Socialists excluded, was this just a few self-indulgent bourgeois playing at being against the bourgeoisie?

77

Indeed there was something comically middle-class about the procedure adopted to ensure neutrality in the election of a chairman, which eventually established that only those third from the left in each row would be eligible. Of these, one declined to stand to muted murmurs of disapproval, one withdrew in favour of another who he declared would be more effective, and in the run-off vote between the remaining two – in which each voted honourably for the other – the ultimate winner to emerge was a rather startled-looking bespectacled young man, who now clambered his way to the front to routine and, to some slight extent perhaps, ironical applause.

'Democracy isn't quick' murmured Eluard, 'but I suppose that's what's good about it.'

'So long as you're not facing an urgent threat!'

However, a motion attacking the values of 'fatherland and family and the domination of the country by the 200 richest families' was now being proposed by a greying young man who gave a confident analysis in Marxist terms of the damage caused in bourgeois society by such tribalist values as family and fatherland. It was supported by others in much the same vein, until Breton and then an intense young woman in mauve moved on to attacking the Communist Party, not only for itself falling back on such patriotic and paternalist values but for 'joining with bourgeois parties like the Socialists and the Radical Socialists in a so-called Popular Front'. And it was as they were moving towards a vote that Dora raised her hand to speak.

'The chair recognises…er…?'

'Dora Maar' said André helpfully.

'Thank you, André' she said. 'But I'm afraid I find much of this fanciful. You may have good reasons for disliking the Communists and you may think the Socialists are bourgeois, but it is they who have the troops in the working class and the unions. And what's the point of attacking the Popular Front when it is in practice the only force capable of standing out against Fascism and the attacks on Jews that are gaining ground every day right across Europe? What exactly is Contre-Attaque attacking? And what, if it isolates itself from the existing centre-left forces, is it attacking *with*?'

'I think you've started something!' murmured Paul, as she sat down, a little flustered and embarrassed at having clashed with André.

And indeed she had, for the discussion started afresh, with several speakers now moving towards her viewpoint, arguing the need to relate their counter-attack to the workers and to existing political structures – until Georges Bataille, saying the starkest things in his usual mild and courteous fashion, mounted his own counter-attack. Weren't they in danger, he said – without aiming his remarks directly at Dora – of falling back into the old habits of bourgeois capitalist society that they were trying to escape from? Of compromising with the dead old political parties of a corrupt parliamentary system? Of putting up with the useless drivel of pseudo-democratic politicians and their diplomats at the footling League of Nations? Shouldn't they be beating the Fascists at their own game? Shouldn't they be using the Fascists' own weapons *against* the Fascists? For you didn't energize the working masses with bureaucratic trade unions, you did it by inspiring them! By binding them emotionally and spiritually to a collective cause of great mythical power, by giving them large-scale ceremonies in which they could celebrate their oneness with the great common cause…!

'And by giving them a common enemy?' interrupted Dora sarcastically. 'Such as the Jews?'

Bataille stopped, as though suddenly unsure of himself, and stared at her.

'It's madness' she went on, hearing her voice quivering with anger. 'It's glorifying emotionalism and fanaticism. It's treating ordinary people like cattle. It's trying to fight Fascism with Fascism – and at least the other lot know what they're doing! It's politically suicidal!'

This created a silence, after which the discussion swayed this way and that until the bespectacled young chairman put the motion, which was by now half-forgotten, to the vote. It succeeded but, since there were around a dozen abstentions, by a less than convincing majority. Not that this relieved Dora's feeling of embarrassment at the hostile tone in which she had attacked Georges Bataille in the course of the meeting.

Nor was her embarrassment lessened by the brief exchange on the way out in which Georges said it was nice to see her again, and André said he would think hard about the points she had made in the discussion.

'Come on, Dora' said Paul with a grin. 'You can buy me a rum grog.'

With the temperature outside falling below zero, the Deux Magots was not only steamed-up but sufficiently draughty for Dora to be wearing her black gloves with the little red appliquéd flowers as she sat at the same corner table sipping a cognac next evening. She was trying to concentrate on the editorial in *Ce Soir*, but finding her attention lapse at intervals as her mind kept drifting back to various unsettling happenings that left her feeling vaguely irritated..

For no sooner had she come back in fine form from a happy and fruitful holiday in the Alps than there was that curious conversation with her father about Jewishness – an issue perhaps still unresolved. And though Jacqueline's baby was wonderful, of course, there was that irritating business of young women artists throwing themselves at middle-aged painters and settling for being a magical 'Muse'. Then there was that stressful meeting of Contre-Attaque, with the embarrassment of criticizing André Breton – ridiculous though the feeling was, but he was after all Jacqueline's husband – and the mixed emotions involved in clashing so openly and so heavily with Georges Bataille, when many in the room would have known she had had a relationship with him.

Might they have suspected that her motives were personal? Might they even, to some extent, have been right? Oh God, the political situation was complicated enough without having to worry about your own and everybody else's feelings being hurt. It left you feeling irritated without quite knowing exactly what it was you were irritated about. Which meant you were even irritated at feeling irritated…!

Going back impatiently to the editorial, she groped absently in her large black-and-white handbag for her Gauloises and then for her ivory cigarette holder, which chanced to come out along with the small decorated penknife she used for odd jobs in the studio and even on occasion as a dry point, for scraping special effects on photographic plates. This had seen some action during the holiday in the Alps as it happened, since her poet friend Jacques Prévert had borrowed it to demonstrate a Surrealist game of which he was a leading exponent and which consisted of driving a blade at increasing speed between the fingers of his outstretched hand on the table.

It was a game for which it was better to be sober, as Louis Chavance had amply and bloodily illustrated, or else to have the natural actor's timing of Jean-Louis Barrault. She had not seriously tried to compete with them, but now that she had the knife in her hand and was idly opening the blade, now that she was feeling irritated without knowing quite what she was irritated about, now that she was laughing at the absurdity of being irritated at being irritated, she began to tap the knife in sequence from left to right between the fingers of her right hand, slowly at first, then slightly faster, then faster still, then as fast as she could until she felt a sharp cut in one finger but went on regardless driving the blade harder and harder between the fingers until she heard a voice saying in Spanish that she was too beautiful to be an intellectual and looked up to find three heavily muffled up figures standing staring at her: Paul Eluard, a man in thick-lensed glasses wearing a beret, and a short stocky man with striking dark eyes whom she recognised as Picasso.

'Thank you for the compliment, kind sir' she said ironically in Spanish. 'But why do you believe intellectuals should be ugly?'

'I'm sorry' he said, with a rather high-pitched laugh. 'I didn't realise you spoke Spanish. I'm Picasso.'

'Yes, I recognise you. I saw you on the set of *Le Crime de Monsieur Lange*.'

'Ah yes, the Jean Renoir film?' he said in his thick Spanish accent. 'How could I have failed to notice you?'

'Perhaps because I was working!'she said coolly. 'I was the set photographer.'

'Let me introduce my good friend Dora Maar' said Eluard. 'And this is Jaume Sabartés, an old friend of Pablo's.'

'*Bonsoir*' said Dora, noting that Sabartés was looking at her askance through his thick-lensed glasses.

'I was admiring your skill and your courage with the penknife' said Picasso.

'Oh, I'm just a beginner.'

'A Surrealist form of self-expression, is it?'

'It's a café game I was introduced to by Jacques Prévert over the New Year holiday.'

'And a game I remember soldiers playing in the army' said Eluard.

'But a violent game. Your hand is bleeding slightly, I think.'

'So it is.'

'May I?'

He looked down with a gleam in the big dark eyes, took her gloved hand in his and kissed it formally, then gently removed the glove and kissed her hand, lingering softly over the drop of blood on the middle finger.

'I kiss it better.'

'You're very galant, Monsieur!' she said with a dry smile.

'I'm very Spanish, Mademoiselle! May I?'

He drew up the only chair available and sat down opposite her, leaving the others standing as he offered her a cigarette from her own packet, watched her insert it into her ivory holder, then lit it for her.

'So you're called Dora? May I call you Dora?'

'Why not? It's my name! And I'll call you Picasso.'

'That will do' he said, smiling. 'And you're a photographer?'

'Yes.'

'With a studio in the Rue d'Astorg, Paul here tells me. Which is just round the corner from where I am, in the Rue La Boétie.'

'So it is' said Dora, aware that a slightly embarrassed Eluard and a visibly unhappy Sabartés were left standing looking at each other and wondering what to do.

'So, Dora, what kind of photographic work do you do?'

'I do the whole range, Picasso – from publicity to artwork.'

'Dora exhibits quite a bit in Surrealist exhibitions' said Paul, intervening in an attempt to relax the slight tension in the situation.

'Really? And have you such projects in hand?'

'Yes, I do. But I'm afraid' she said, gesturing slightly towards the others, that Paul and your Spanish friend may be getting a little impatient...'

'What a pity' he said. 'Do you have a business card?'

'Of course' she said and produced one from a small card holder in her bag.

'29 Rue d'Astorg' he read aloud from the card and then, with the gleam returning into the big dark eyes, he asked if she would grant him a great favour.

'That might depend' she said, with a glinting smile.

'Would you allow me to keep this glove as a memento? I would be honoured.'

'Well, in that case!'

He took the glove, stood up and kissed her hand again.

'Au revoir, Dora.'

'Au revoir, Picasso.'

She watched him walk out with his rolling gait between the similarly short Sabartés and the much taller Paul Eluard. Then sat smiling to herself. So that was Picasso...!

Who had a Spanish accent you could cut with a hatchet, who had taken her card and pointed out that her studio was just round the corner from his place,… Who had looked at her with those gleaming dark eyes, kissed her bleeding hand and asked for her glove as a memento… And who was doubtless just like that with all the pretty young things who dreamt of becoming the 'Muse' and the plaything of a famous male painter…

At least she had probably done enough to send him back to Alice Paalen…!

4

Walking up to the Place Saint-Augustin in warm Spring sunshine – so welcome after the freezing March weather – Dora was on her way to see Jacqueline after work. Wondering as she went down into the Metro, where the time seemed to have gone to.

Some of it, of course. had gone into looking after her parents, who had succumbed one after the other to the flu that had been raging in Paris – her mother, in particular, had suffered quite severe complications that affected her breathing. This had required Dora to work longer hours than usual in the studio, particularly with the two commissions from *Madame Figaro* for the autumn collections – which incidentally seemed a little eerily, in the faintly military cut of jackets and the new line in peaked hats, to be anticipating a tenser Europe in this year of 1936.

As well they might, she thought, for political tension was increasingly in the air. There was concern about the news from Spain, where a Popular Front coalition including the Communists had won a narrow victory in the February elections, which raised the fear that the army might be planning a military coup. And Hitler had just marched his troops boldly into the Rhineland – 'wiping his arse on the Treaty of Versailles' as her father had colourfully put it.

But there was tension also at the Rue Fontaine, for no sooner had she reached Number 42 than André himself suddenly emerged, looking grim and in a hurry.

'You will forgive me, Dora, I'm in a rush.'

'Yes of course, André.'

And he was gone. Leaving her to ring the bell and wait for several minutes before Jacqueline appeared, looking flushed.

'You ran into André?' she asked as they moved indoors.

'It was more that he ran into me!' said Dora, attempting to lighten the tone.

'Yes, he's in a huff.'

'It happens!'

'It's happening rather too often, I'm afraid.'

Dora removed her hat and coat, followed her into the living room and admired little Aube, lying sleeping peacefully in her cot in front of the display stand with its Indian artefacts and the small Nepalese bowl enclosing its tiny wooden figures – keeping the little family safe from harm.

'He doesn't want me to go with him to Tenerife next week' said Jacqueline as they sat down.

'Oh, I didn't know you were going there. He has been invited for some Surrealist do, has he?'

'Yes. He doesn't actually say he doesn't want me to go. He says it might be difficult for me with Aube, that she might be too young to travel, that it might make it difficult to move around when we get there – that sort of thing. If I thought it was a question of money, I wouldn't mind, but it appears they're giving him enough to cover us both.'

'You're sure' asked Dora tentatively, 'that he's not genuinely concerned about travelling with a baby three months old?'

'But that's precisely what makes it easy, Dora. If she was crawling or walking it might be different. It's part of a pattern, that's the trouble.'

'Oh dear. You think so?'

'He's good, he's kind, he's honourable, he loves me to bits, but it's funny, you know, I hardly know how to put it, it sounds ridiculous…'

'Well…?'

'It's that he loves me so much he doesn't even see me. Ever since we've been together I've been attending the Surrealist meetings and participating actively in all the events. I speak, I say things, I paint, I draw – baby or no baby, I'm a painter, for God's sake, and they tell me I'm not a bad one. But he never comments on that, never acknowledges it and somehow – I don't think it's deliberate or even conscious – he never even seems to notice!'

'I see.'

'So I'm wonderful, I'm a mythic creature, I'm destiny, I contain in my boobs and my belly the deepest secrets of Nature itself, I'm a *femme fatale* like no other, which is fine up to a point. But if his dinner isn't on the table when he comes home in the evening he is surprised, he doesn't understand, he wonders what I could have been doing, he feels hurt, he feels I'm letting him down – he even feels I'm letting *myself* down! So we have rows.'

'Lots of them?'

'No, it's more that we have the same row over and over again. But since he's brusque and nervy and I'm proud and stubborn – as you know! – it's a pretty big row.'

'But you do eventually get to eat in the evening?' asked Dora, laughing despite herself.

'Yes, but the *femme fatale* mightn't get around to slaving incompetently over a hot stove before eleven o'clock in the evening' said Jacqueline, laughing in her turn. 'Oh God, I never gave you a drink, did I?'

'You never did. Have you any more of that 'quiet Vouvray' André gave me last time?'

'Well I've never heard it make a noise, if that's what you mean.'

She poured Dora a glass of the Vouvray and they sat smiling a little helplessly at each other.

'Well at least' said Dora, giggling a little, 'if you must be a Muse to somebody you've picked one who is well-known and honourable and quite goodlooking.'

'Yes, it could be worse. I could be like poor Alice Paalen.'

'What's poor about Alice Paalen?'

'Did I not tell you? She's been chasing after Picasso.'

'And she appears to have caught him. Since I'm pretty sure I saw her in the distance going down his street one day.'

'Well, whoever caught whom, it seems she didn't enjoy it.'

'Did he?'

'Yes, but he wouldn't let her enjoy it, so she says. Rough sex maybe, I don't know. He's Spanish of course.'

'Yes well, I've been hearing a little too much recently about Picasso's sexual inclinations. I don't think we need any more details.'

'Men…!' said Jacqueline with a wry grin.

And 'Muses', thought Dora. You could either have a hard time with Picasso or be not noticed by Breton – tough choice!

'Men…!' she echoed with a smile. But look, Jacqueline, would you like me to help you to cook something before André comes home? Give him a nice surprise?'

'That would be lovely. I never realised you were a good cook, Dora.'

'I'm not, but we could invent something between us. You do have the raw materials, do you?'

'Yes, more or less. I've lots of carrots and things.'

So Dora soon found herself preparing vegetables, while Jacqueline sorted out saucepans and attended to the baby.

'This trip to Tenerife then' said Dora at one point. 'Will you be going or not?'

'You're damn right I'll be going!' said Jacqueline. 'Did you think I wouldn't?!'

Dora had dealt with some correspondence and was prioritizing the day's tasks when the phone rang just after ten o'clock a couple of days later.

'Dora?'

'Hello Paul.'

'Are you busy?'

'I'm not quite sure yet, I'm not long in.'

'I'm round the corner, at Picasso's place.'

'Oh yes?'

'The thing is that Roland Penrose, the English Surrealist fellow, you know, wants to buy a picture from Picasso, a *Nude on the Beach* he's been raving about, and it happens to be out at this château of Picasso's at Boisgeloup…'

'So…?'

'So Picasso is suggesting that we make a trip of it and all drive out there together. And he wondered if you might like to come along.'

'Was this your idea, Paul?' she asked suspiciously.

'No no, Dora, not at all. It was his idea. And Nusch will be coming.'

'Well, I just don't see where I come in. He only met me for five minutes in the Deux Magots.'

'But I think he meant you to bring your camera and take photographs. He expects to be losing this place soon in a separation settlement and would like some record of it.'

'Well, if I was going as photographer…' she said hesitantly, 'I suppose that might be a little different…'

'Yes, do come. The car will be arriving in half an hour, if you'd like to come round – it's Number 23. Or perhaps we could pick you up?'

'No no, I'll come round.'

Which saw Dora, still in two minds, arriving at Number 23 to be received rather coldly by Sabartés, before being warmly greeted by Picasso, Paul and Nusch, and then being introduced to the tall, lean-faced aristocratic Englishman Roland Penrose – who told her in quite reasonable French that he been impressed by some exhibition pieces of hers that he had seen. Which, together with a glass of punch and a Normandy biscuit or two to sustain them for the journey, left her feeling reasonably relaxed.

However, she became rather less relaxed when Picasso, who had been showing Penrose a series of etchings on a side table, drew her over smilingly to look at them. And she became somewhat suspicious when he said it was a Minotaur series he had done for the magazine *Minotaure* and mentioned that Georges Bataille had been involved in giving it that name.

'You know Bataille, do you?' he asked lightly.

'Yes, I know him and a number of the others involved' she said equally lightly, beginning to wonder if he was testing her. 'They're in sequence, the etchings, are they?'

Penrose put them back in order and stood aside smilingly as she looked at the first one, of a rather middle-aged Minotaur, with his bull's head looking oddly innocent, carousing with an opulent nude on a bed.

'Beautifully drawn' she said, as she saw Picasso eyeing her expectantly. 'I like the innocence and the bushy tail.'

But the next etching, as she came to it, showed a raging, hairy-backed Minotaur – far more bull than man this time – ferociously pinning to the ground and assaulting a naked girl.

'Not so innocent on this one, is he?' she said with a smile. 'Ravishing her right back to her ribcage. It's a very powerful rape scene.'

'Why do you call it a rape scene?' asked Picasso.

'What would you call it?'

'Isn't it just the battle of love?'

'Except that he's the only one fighting it. Why do these innocent, helpless young girls enrage our bull-headed men so?'

Fortunately, perhaps, Sabartés arrived at that moment to say that Marcel had arrived with the car and they all moved out to install themselves in the Hispano-Suiza, Penrose with Picasso alongside Marcel in the front seat and Dora and Nusch on either side of Paul in the back. And off they went, up the Champs-Elysées, towards the Porte de Saint-Cloud and on into Normandy, with mostly separate conversations going on in the front and the back for the next hour and more until they arrived at Boisgeloup.

Dora was in working mode from the moment they arrived at this quite elegant but strange château, where they were confronted by the enormous skull of a hippopotamus in the hall as soon as they entered. It soon became clear that Picasso had been less interested in the château itself than in the outbuildings. For most of the rooms were totally devoid of furniture except for the odd large Picasso on the wall, giving a ghostly impression of painting addressing itself to the long-dead people who once walked and talked in these seventeenth century halls. The outbuildings, on the other hand, had seen the real life of Picasso's tenure, for the ivy-covered chapel and the various barns still contained a number of statues and other signs of the work he had carried out here. And since there were also freestanding statues in the grounds, mostly of the same young female model – perhaps the same one as the girl in the Minotaur etchings – the whole place felt like an abandoned, secret Picasso museum, hidden away in deepest Normandy. If it was true that he might be losing this place, it was as though he was abandoning a part of himself here.

Meanwhile, as she went around with her camera – while exploring the empty rooms with Nusch, observing Roland Penrose's sustained delight in front of the striking, stylised *Nude on the Beach* that he lusted after, or listening to Paul's views on various paintings – Dora had the increasingly disturbing, yet exciting feeling that those big dark luminous eyes of Picasso were constantly upon her. It was not so obvious as to be impolite, you couldn't really catch him at it, but you knew that it was insistent, that he was watching you, stalking you. It was not at all like some man glancing down your blouse, it was far more invasive, for those big dark practised painter's eyes seemed to be seeing right through to your nakedness, to your full breasts, your slightly heavy thighs, so that you were becoming uncomfortable, flustered, almost awkward in your movements, conscious of your clothes, your underclothes, disturbingly aware of a throbbing dampness at your crotch and afraid and resentful that you were flushing and reddening and giving yourself away.

And it was to turn the tables on him that she began to scrutinize and at intervals photograph him, either without comment or, on occasion, controlling his movements for the purpose.

'Could you stop there for a moment, with that statue to the right of you? That's fine, thanks. No need to pose.'

She had taken a number of shots of him in this fashion, noting that he seemed not only pleased but challenged by this exercise, when he smilingly turned the tables back on her by asking her if he might borrow her camera.

'Of course.'

He took over the camera, asked her about its controls, practised lining it up and pronounced it a fine instrument. He then proceeded to follow her around, apparently casually but scrutinizing her and lining her up at moments in the same fashion – leaving her feeling even more uncomfortably self-aware and challenged than before.

'I'd like to try a few interior shots' he said eventually.

'You'll have to compensate for the light. It's rather dark inside' she told him.

'Let's see if I can manage it.'

She did her best to appear to be unconcerned as he photographed her in profile and apparently absorbed in a newspaper. He then took a more deliberately composed three-quarter profile shot of her sitting and looking thoughtful, asked her to keep the pose but kept her waiting and waiting and waiting, with the result that when he took a direct face-on shot her eyes looked a little sad or even pleading.

'I can see you've done this before' she said tersely, all too aware that the others had been standing around observing them.

'I'm not as skilled as you, Dora' he said smilingly, handing back the camera, 'but at least I had the benefit of a beautiful subject.'

'You're too kind!'

As they were preparing to leave shortly afterwards, she could see Nusch and Paul looking at her in a slightly glinting, amused fashion.

'Did you notice?' whispered Nusch. 'He couldn't take his eyes off you.'

'I noticed!' she said grimly.

'Yes' chimed in Paul, 'you were really striking sparks off each other.'

When they got back to the car, Penrose had a word with Picasso and then announced that he would like to celebrate his acquisition of the *Nude on the Beach* by inviting them all to a late lunch in Gisors, the nearby mediaeval town of which he happened to be fond – an announcement which was received with murmurs of warm approval.

As they started out, he half turned in his seat to speak enthusiastically about the eleventh century castle of Gisors, the church with its fusion of Gothic and Renaissance features, and the association of the town with the religious order of the Knights Templar.

'But the most relevant thing about Gisors at this precise moment is the restaurant La Table des Templiers, and I can promise you we'll eat better than the Templars ever did.'

And that certainly looked like being the case, as soon as they were warmly ensconced with a glass of champagne in hand to lighten the burden of reading through the lengthy menu, with starters ranging from Terrine of Goose Liver with spiced fig and Marsala jelly or Dressed Crab Roll with avocado and Charentais melon to Smoked Salmon with sweet lemon and oyster or Mosaic of Quail with compressed apple, dates and walnuts.

'A little more variety than Chez Jules', murmured Nusch.

'Yes, though there it wasn't so difficult to choose!' said Dora, now feeling more relaxed.

For the difficulty continued with the even longer list of main courses, ranging from the Normandy Pork with cream and apples or the Lobster with grapefruit and apple – Normandy being of course apple country – to the Venison Pie with truffles and mushrooms or the Perigord fillet steak with creamed mushrooms. All of which caused some serious heart-searching until it finally emerged that Penrose and Picasso would have the Normandy Pork and that both Dora and Nusch would have the Venison Pie, while

Paul concluded, since he was unable to choose between the Lobster and the Normandy Pork, that he could only resolve the dilemma by having the Périgord fillet. After which strenuous exercise they were delighted in advance with whatever wines Penrose might propose – although Picasso would stick to his glass of Vittel.

Certainly the wine produced a warm feeling and spurred on the conversation as the meal progressed. Picasso was smiling and relaxed, but Dora sensed that he was still keeping an eye on her and felt he was waiting for the chance to test her out further. However, they went on to talk about Gisors and Boisgeloup and about the sculptures which had only been revealed by the successful Picasso exhibition of four years earlier. And then there was a lengthy discussion of Picasso's painting – mostly between Paul and Penrose, since Picasso said that you could either paint or talk about painting, but you couldn't do both – after which the Englishman tried to explain just what it was about the *Nude on the Beach* that fascinated him. So it wasn't until they came to the cheese that Picasso saw an opportunity – after Paul had introduced the subject of politics.

'I'm afraid that Dora and I both feel that Contre-Attaque has gone off the rails' he was saying, 'with this ridiculous tract saying it 'prefers Hitler's anti-democratic brutality to the drooling banter of democratic diplomats and politicians' – if you'd believe it!'

'Yes, it's near-Fascist nonsense' said Dora. 'We've both refused to sign it.'

'Ah yes now, Contre-Attaque' said Picasso, as though trying to remember. 'Is that not the group led by your Surrealist friends Bataille and Breton?'

'Yes, but I disagree with them on this. And I'm frankly disappointed by André.'

'But not by Georges Bataille?' he asked smilingly – a little too smilingly.

'Oh I'm fond of Georges and he's had a difficult background, but I think he's becoming a little confused.'

'Why would that be then?'

'Well, for one thing, he got rather over-excited at seeing some famous torero being gored to death by the bull. In Spain, of course' she added, with a sweet smile towards Picasso. 'And this got him talking almost as though he envied the torero, going on about 'exquisite suffering' and so on – like that martyred saint being grilled on hot coals who invited the executioner to turn him over and toast him nicely to match on the other side. A kind of inside-out Catholicism really, martyrdom with no heaven to go to, all a bit back-to-front. And for another thing, of course, he has fallen like some other Surrealists for that ridiculous macho myth of the Marquis de Sade.'

'So you don't care for the Marquis de Sade?'

'Not really' said Dora, beginning to enjoy herself. 'I don't think a homosexual nobleman who whips prostitutes and practises sexual abuse on children has much appeal – to women at least. Anyway, he's another one who's confused and gets it all back-to-front.'

'This is a most interesting viewpoint, Dora' said Penrose. 'How do you mean?'

'Well he didn't believe in God, but he ran around blaspheming against this God he didn't believe in and giving him hell for not existing – he wasn't very bright. And I would only add' she said with a smiling nod to Penrose, 'that this camembert is absolutely wonderful!'

'But surely' said Picasso, who had been staring intently at her, 'you can't deny that Sade broke taboos?'

'Well, some taboos may be worth breaking – like no meat on Friday or sex outside marriage – but most are there for obvious human reasons. He only seemed to feel free when he was brutalizing women and denying their femininity by sodomizing them – which seems to allow some men to release any latent homosexuality, by the back door as it were. And as for expressing your freedom by eating excrement, I really don't think – since Contre-Attaque is supposed to be a revolutionary movement – that turds on toast with a nice glass of chilled urine is a plausible political programme for the proletariat. I'm sorry' she said, bursting out laughing, 'there were probably too many 'p's in that proposition.'

They were all laughing now, Picasso along with them in his odd high-pitched whinnying laugh, but she could see from his expression that she had hit home in some way. Was he also a breaker of taboos? She was aware that her brief affair with Bataille might have given her a certain reputation – rather undeserved since Bataille was all talk and little action – so it did no harm to make it clear that she wasn't the kind of woman who could be kicked around as Alice and some others seemed to have been.

They went on to other things, the trip back to Paris was alternately quiet and jolly, Marcel had progressed to Jean Sablon's current creamy number *Vous qui passez sans me voir* and, as she was dropped outside her studio, Picasso told Dora that he would be interested to receive the photographs – and of course the invoice.

'Yes of course. I'll send them or drop them round.'

'Or perhaps I could call round here, now that I've seen where your studio is?'

'Well, I can't say when they'll be ready' she said firmly. 'It will be simpler to send them or drop them round.'

Dora was less than enchanted to be interrupted by an unexpected visitor to 29 Rue d'Astorg around two thirty in the afternoon a few days later. She was working with an inexperienced young model called Zette, who had decided to go by the more glamorous name of Catalina, which was fine except that she hadn't learnt the difference between artistic nude and normal naked and, being nervous and rather fidgety, was not good at retaining the pose. In short she was a little trying to work with and Dora, as she went to the door in her white working coat to deal with this interruption, was not at her most welcoming.

'*Bonjour!*'

96

It was Picasso. Still wearing the worn *canadienne* open over the old jacket with bulging pockets which seemed to be his habitual attire. And smiling.

'Oh *bonjour*...' she replied.

'I happened to be passing Am I interrupting?'

'Well, actually' she said, 'I do happen to be busy with a model – Catalina there.'

Picasso glanced at Catalina, who had come out of curiosity to stand in the inner doorway and was switching self-consciously from naked to nude and back again as she felt his eyes upon her.

'I'm sorry, Dora. I can see you're busy. I should obviously have phoned.'

'Well, I'm afraid I'm tied up for the moment. I assume it was for the Boisgeloup photographs?'

'Yes. I was curious.'

'Well, I could drop them round to you around four o'clock, say?'

'Four o'clock will do very well. But why don't I save you the trouble and come here?'

'Well, there's no need, you know...'

'But it will be a pleasure. Sorry again to have interrupted.'

He smiled at Catalina, smiled again at Dora, and was off. Leaving an outmanoeuvred Dora to get back to work, just so long as she could keep Catalina still and preferably silent.

'He looks familiar, that man' said Catalina. 'I think I've seen his picture.'

'Yes, he's a painter.'

'He's pretty old, but he has got marvellous big dark eyes, hasn't he? Would give you goose bumps.'

'Well, try to keep your bumps under control while I'm doing the close-ups, Catalina.'

For it really was cheeky of him to turn up out of the blue like that, entirely without warning – and then not take no for an answer. Especially since he might normally have found her working with

Assia or another of the best known models and instead he had found her struggling with a beginner like Catalina, so that he had no idea of the real work that went on in this place.

'What's his name?' asked Catalina.

'Who?'

'That painter.'

'Picasso.'

'So that's Picasso?'

Yes, that was Picasso. Turning up unannounced in his old *canadienne*, wanting to see his Boisgeloup photographs Well, when – or if – he bothered to come back at four o'clock, she would show him photography...!

And when the bell rang at three minutes past four, she went to the door with her camera in hand, let him in and, as he stood looking around curiously, took an angled shot and watched him smile in slight surprise.

'So your model has gone, has she?'

'Yes, she's young and really only good for youth fashions, but she's trying to break into the beauty market and she hasn't quite grasped what's required.'

'So what is required?'

'A bit of distance and dignity. As you probably noticed, she can't tell nude from naked. Do take your *canadienne* off if you would find it more comfortable.'

He began to take his *canadienne* off and she shot him in the process. He smiled a faintly quizzical smile this time.

'Yes, I know what you mean about nude and naked. But perhaps that's the difference between photographers and painters – we want to start with our models naked. After all... well, I won't quote Renoir at you...'

'You mean 'I paint with my prick'? And here was me thinking that had to do with the high price of paint brushes at that time!'

As he laughed, relaxed and then leant casually against the wall, she stepped back and took him again.

'But that does tend to leave women painters at a distinct disadvantage, doesn't it?'

'Yes, I'm afraid it does, Dora.'

The casualness with which he said it surprised her. Did he really believe that...?

'Do smoke if you feel like it, won't you?' she said, camera still poised.

'Thanks, Dora, I think I will.' He smiled. 'And then you'll be able to have a shot of me smoking.'

'And then, as you say' she said with an answering smile, 'I'll be able to have a shot of Picasso smoking. And perhaps go on to complete the series with Picasso sitting full on, Picasso sitting in profile, sitting on the floor or standing on his head.'

'Poor bloody Picasso – his soul is being possessed,. But, you know, Ingres said that the best way to possess a woman was to paint her. I'm not sure it works with photography.'

'But Ingres also said, so they told us in art school, that a photograph was better than a drawing, though you weren't to tell anybody. Anyway, I doubt if Ingres's model ever felt 'possessed' by him – she was probably thinking about her lunch. You can reveal things about a subject, but I don't believe you can 'possess' anybody.'

'So you have never been possessed, Dora?'

The banter was getting bolder and it occurred to her that, though she was the one with the camera, the big dark eyes were scrutinizing her just as closely and that she would be more comfortable if she hadn't shed her white coat.

'Not that I noticed' she said.

'Never?'

It felt once again as though the long practised gaze of those painter's eyes could penetrate right through her dress and see her not just nude but naked...

'I don't think you can ever really possess somebody else's freedom' she said slowly. 'But perhaps you feel that you yourself have been possessed?' she added lightly 'Hundreds of times perhaps?'

'No' he said with his high-pitched laugh. 'But then I rather think it's supposed to work the other way around.'

'Though if you actually look at what happens' she said with a smile, 'you might conclude that you're being fooled and that it's women who possess men. Still, you think old Renoir was right, do you? Men paint and possess with their prick, which obviously leaves women out in the cold, doesn't it?'

'I'm afraid it does.'

'Seriously though, do you really believe that women can't paint?'

'I'm not sure that anybody can paint.'

'I rather thought you could paint. What are you saying?'

He looked as though he thought he had said too much, as he sat down on the far side of the small table, seemingly reluctant to continue. She sat down on the near side of the table, put the camera down between them and looked across at him curiously.

'I think painting is dead' he said finally.

'So who killed it?'

'You did, Dora' he said with a slight laugh. 'You and people like you. All you need to do now is to start using the new colour film and we can hold a nice funeral.'

'So it's all due to photography?'

'Yes, until photography came along painting had a clear central function – it provided the record of people, places and events. And then you lot came along and took all that away – tore the heart out of it'

'So…?'

'So we don't have a proper tradition since then, no artistic order. The Impressionists just started painting what they *felt* about things because you lot were coming along and making copying look silly. And on top of that some crazy little guy called Einstein said you could forget about perspective since space was just time or some such bollocks – and that was the tradition buggered up good and proper!'

'But you surprise me! Surely you of all people can't regret the tradition.'

'Of course I regret it. What do you think Braque and I were trying to do with Cubism? Trying to invent a *new* tradition, a style so objective that nobody could tell whether a picture had been painted by Braque or myself.'

'And it worked, didn't it?'

'No, it failed. Because everything was against it and we also wanted to do our own poky little individual things in the end, And now there's nothing left but so-called 'abstract art', and that way lies madness, masturbation or wallpaper design – or all three at once. It's over, Dora.'

'But it can't be over' she said hesitantly, 'if you're still painting.'

'I'm not.'

'You're not?!'

'Didn't I tell you?' he said with a sardonic smile. 'I was the last painter.'

She sat staring at him, quite taken aback by this serious, confessional turn that the conversation had taken. He was a bit of an old actor, of course, and the sardonic smile was self-protective, but that very fact suggested that there might be real feelings to protect. Was this whole spiel real, or was it simply designed to cover up the fact that he was in his mid-fifties by the look of him and possibly running out of steam or self-belief? From a man with his reputation, it was disconcerting…

'Well I can't quite believe that's the case' she said. 'And I really hope it isn't.'

'Anyway, to hell with all that!' he exclaimed suddenly, jumping to his feet with the high-pitched laugh. 'What about those photographs we took at Boisgeloup?'

'Oh yes, we were forgetting about those, weren't we?' she said, relieved at this sudden change of subject.

So she went over with him the whole range of photographs she had taken at the château, including the group shots, the ones she had taken of him wandering around the grounds, and a striking one of him looking oddly lonely in those large empty rooms with his paintings on the walls on either side of him.

'And then there are these three that you took of me' she said a little wryly.

He looked at the profile print showing her pretending to be absorbed in the newspaper, then at the three-quarter portrait of her sitting looking thoughtful.

'That's nice' he said.

'No, I'm afraid it came out a little dull, that one. The light inside just wasn't up to it. So I had to work hard in development to bring up the lighting in this one' she said, handing him the direct face-on portrait that he had kept her posed and waiting so long for.

'And you've done a lovely job on it, I must say.'

'I rather wish I hadn't. I've brought up the light in the eyes so much that I look quite tearful.'

'So you do, Dora' he said with a smile. 'I'm afraid that, though I always think of you as laughing, I've turned you into a weeping woman.'

'*Cher Monsieur*' typed Sabartés clatteringly on the heavy machine, 'while Monsieur Picasso is of course deeply appreciative of your kind invitation...'

Which is as far as he got before exploding into a racking, spluttering cough and reaching again for the rum-and-lemon grog with which he had been fortifying himself for the past few days. April in Paris, he had been told, tended to be rather a cold month and this April, after a false Spring, was ending up colder than most. At all events, it had given him a severe bout of flu, with fever, headaches and heavy catarrh.

Of course, with Picasso not being around, he could have gone to bed for a day or two, but since he refused to give in to such things he was now sitting in blue dressing gown and beret dealing with Pablo's correspondence, which consisted mostly of begging letters, inquiries from dealers or invitations to implausible events in Bordeaux, Besançon or even Venezuela. Pablo might have told him not to bother, but Sabartés was not the man not to bother. Except, unfortunately, that he had been obliged to fall back so heavily and so frequently on the rum-and-lemon grog that he was now not only even more feverish than before, but lightheaded and bordering dangerously on feeling frivolous.

'Where was I?' he went on. 'Yes, 'while Monsieur Picasso is of course deeply appreciative of your kind invitation…' – which he would doubtless describe as a right royal pain in the arse – 'he nevertheless finds himself unable to accept due to pressure of ongoing work…'- except that there's no work either ongoing, outgoing or even likely to be upcoming . 'Needless to say…' – which is of course why I say it – 'Monsieur Picasso extends his best wishes for the successful completion of your admirable project, which if he ever had the misfortune to hear of it he would consider a meaningless, mercenary load of crap…' Oh God, I've typed that, I don't feel right, I'd better go and lie down or something, I need some more of that grog – is that the doorbell? No…? Yes…?'

He listened again. It was indeed the doorbell. He didn't need to answer. Yes he did.

He went and opened the front door. To find Eluard staring at him strangely.

'I'm sorry, Jaume.' said Paul, 'I hope I'm not interrupting anything?'

'What do you mean?'

'Well you're in your dressing gown and, if I may say so, you look flushed and flustered.'

'I'm a bit woozy. I've had the flu.'

'Then I won't linger. I did phone, but you said…?'

'Yes, I'm under strict instructions not to give information…' he said, breaking into his spluttering cough, '…over the phone.'

'Well, can you tell me in person where Pablo is? As I told you, we had an arrangement to meet last week and he never turned up.'

'That's unfortunate.'

'It certainly is unfortunate. So can you tell me where he is, so that I can contact him?'

'I'm afraid I can't, Paul. He's travelling incognito.'

'Incognito? But he's travelling?'

'He will have stopped travelling by now.'

'So do you know where he was travelling incognito to?'

'Up to a point.'

'So can I contact him?

'He said no direct contacts – since, as I said, he's been travelling…'

'Incognito, I got that. So can *you* contact him on my behalf?'

'Well, Paul…' He coughed again, a painful racking cough, then drank some more of the rum-and-lemon grog. 'I suppose, since it's you, I could try.'

'Then would you remind him about my deadline? For the illustrations? *Please?*'

And he was off. Leaving Sabartés reaching groggily for the rum-and-lemon grog and wondering if he wasn't feeling a bit incognito or rum-and lemon himself.

'May the Second and *Le Figaro* and *Le Temps* are not happy' said Eluard with a smile.

'And they're quite restrained as compared with the harder right-wing papers, who seem to be thirsting for blood' said Dora. 'Have we turned the world upside down?'

They were sitting with Nusch on the terrace of the Deux Magots, now open to the boulevard on this fine spring evening, discussing the victory of the Popular Front coalition in the first round of the elections a week earlier.

'The world is certainly upside down' grinned Eluard who was still wearing the lily of the valley he had been sporting at the big May Day parade of the previous day, 'when you get the Communists sounding so conservative and telling people to 'vote for stability'.'

'And the unions marching united for once in the parade' said Nusch.

'Yes, it's extraordinary' said Eluard. 'And it all takes my attention away for a little while from thinking about Picasso and my deadline.'

'Are you sure he's still away?' asked Dora.

'Yes, I tried Sabartés again last week, but he makes the mystery the more impenetrable every time you talk to him. And Pablo must have been away for five or six weeks now.'

'You're concerned about him, are you?' asked Dora.

'Well. I was concerned mostly because I simply do need those illustrations. If I get them I sell far more copies for a higher price and I'm frankly in dire need of the money. But I'm also getting a bit concerned. Why should he just go off 'incognito' like that? I mean, he's unlikely to have gone to Spain – I couldn't persuade him to go to Barcelona for that exhibition, even though his own mother's there. He seemed a bit lost after the breakup of his marriage and even talked about giving up painting.'

'He said the same thing to me' said Dora. 'Even described himself as 'the last painter'.'

'When was that?' asked Nusch, with a glance at Paul.

'A week after that Boisgeloup trip. He came for the photographs we'd taken.'

'Then you must have been about the last one to see him' said Paul.

'But you make it sound like a murder inquiry!' laughed Dora. 'You don't think there's something sinister about this, do you?'

'No, but where the hell is he? He can't just have buggered off for no reason. It's almost as though he's running away from something.'

'Perhaps he's running away with *someone*' said Dora, reflecting that she hadn't seen Alice Paalen around recently.

'Or running away *from* someone?' said Nusch with a grin. 'Perhaps you, Dora, since you seemed to be having such a go at him at that restaurant in Gisors.'

'What nonsense, Nusch! That would hardly have frightened away Picasso!'

'But that's what *attracted* him' said Nusch. 'If he's running away from anyone, it might just be you.'

'I somehow don't think that's likely!' said Dora with a laugh. 'But from what I saw of him, I would think – if he *is* running away – that he's running away from himself.'

5

Picasso was lying on his right side staring into the darkness, aware of the arm lying loosely across his stomach and the breasts pressing softly upon his back from behind. Why had he done it…?

Why had he brought her to this exact same place, Juan-les-Pins, that he had brought Olga to in 1920? Why had he done the exact same things with her? Taken her to bathe on the Garoupe beach? Visited the old fishing village of Golfe Juan? Wandered through the botanic gardens of the Villa Thouret? And got Marcel, still crooning *Vous qui passez sans me voir*, to drive them for day trips to Nice and Cannes? Why had he done it? Was he trying to prove something? Was he trying to bury Olga…?

Juan-les-Pins. This was where the contradiction had become crystal clear to him. This was where he could see that, because of Olga, friends like Braque and Matisse were moving away from him. This was where he sensed the falsity of the life stretching ahead of him. This was where he had killed off the myth of Olga the ballerina by depicting her with fat swollen legs. But this was also where he discovered that Olga was pregnant, where he was so thrilled at the idea of being a father that he even drew the baby before the baby arrived. But had he been more interested in the baby than in the mother, and less interested in the baby once it grew into Paolo? At all events, now that Paolo had been taken over by Olga, whose

Russian pride made her so deeply vengeful, that son would be lost to him. Olga was not to be buried so easily. And, on top of that, what kind of predicament had he landed himself in now…?

'Are you asleep, Pic?'

'Almost. I'm about ready to drop off.'

Yes, drop off… But drop off into what? He had tried to get back into working mode, since the light down here on the Côte d'Azur was so tempting, but it was not easy. He had done a bit more on the Minotaur and, as so often, she had laughed in bafflement at it. And of course he had obviously had to paint her and the baby. For that little Maya was wonderful, a redemptive reincarnation of the long dead little sister, a miracle – he loved that baby. But babies do not come unattended, the same contradiction still seemed to be there and he had allowed himself to get irritated in the late afternoon when, having done some mother-and-baby drawings over previous days, he was now trying to get them on to canvas. And it had started with something as silly as a chocolate…

'Are you all right, Pic?'

'Yes, of course. Goodnight.'

Yes, chocolate. He had just been raising the brush to begin when she took a chocolate from the box, playfully offered it to Maya, then popped it into her own mouth, laughing delightedly.

'Ready, Marie-Thérèse?'

'Yes, we've got to be good, Maya, since *Papa*'s going to paint our picture *specially*. But is this blouse all right, Pic?'

'Yes, why not?'

'You said you liked the blue one, but you've done me before in this pink one.'

'The pink one is fine,'

'Not that you could really tell it was pink' she said, laughing, 'since I was hanging out of the front of it and you only got a suggestion of pink on the sleeve it looked like, you know the way you mix everything up. But if you'd prefer the blue one…'

'The pink one will do, Marie-Thérèse – really' he said firmly, raising the brush again to make a start.

'Just one little thing, Pic…'

'What?!'

'I'd love it if it was one I could show my mother this time. I mean, if you could do one that sort of looks like me, you know?'

'One that looks like you?' he said, rolling his eyes in exasperation. 'Where have I heard that before?!'

He paused, waited for her to settle, then raised the brush again to make a start.

'Oh and Pic' she interrupted, 'if you're doing Maya you will do her nicely, won't you?'

'Nicely? You want me to do her 'nicely'?'

'Well, just so her eyes aren't going in all directions like she had a squint or something.'

'Oh this is madness – fucking madness!' he had said, flinging down the brush.

So there had been tears and whatnot, with her saying she was sorry, him saying it didn't matter, he shouldn't have got angry and all that. No real row, but silences and a sense of strain. And now he was lying looking into the darkness with her body lying close behind him…

'Pic? Are you asleep?'

'No.'

'I'm sorry about…'

'It's all right, Marie-Thérèse. It doesn't matter. Goodnight!'

'Goodnight.'

Silence again. The darkness didn't seem so dark when you stared into it. You could distinguish volumes, shapes. And, of course, sense time moving on. With you or without you…

'Pic?'

'Yes?'

'Are you very tired?'

'Well it's been a long day…'

'Of course, if you don't want to…'

'It's not that I don't want to, Marie-Thérèse.'

'I mean, if you liked, we could, you know, do it your other way.'

'Marie-Thérèse, I don't want to do it any fucking way, I'm tired and I want to go to sleep! Goodnight!'

He stared again into the darkness. The hand lying loosely across his body was slowly withdrawn. There seemed gradually to be a very faint tremor in the body behind him. Was she crying…?

He went on staring into the darkness. There were times when you just went on staring into the darkness.

Dora. in black-and-white summer two-piece and dashing matching hat was crossing the large square in front of the Saint-Sulpice church in glorious June sunlight on her way to Sèvres-Babylone. She was meeting her father for Sunday lunch – for the first time in weeks, as it happened, for she had been caught up for the past month in the whirl of events following the victory of the Popular Front in the national elections.

Of course the new government was never going to find life easy. For a start, the prime minister Léon Blum was Jewish, which inflamed the anti-Semitic right-wing press. And then the coalition itself was shaky, largely because the Communists, who had gained many seats, offered only passive support and refused to join the cabinet. And above all the workers had begun to celebrate the victory of the Popular Front by going on strike and occupying their factories. Which had led Dora to drop her commissioned work for several days and – with Paul and Nusch for part of the time – to tramp with her camera around this astonishing carnival of a Paris where the Metro was often not working, where there were workers' meetings or entertainments going on not only behind the closed gates of Renault and other factories, but in major stores like the Galeries Lafayette and even, here and there, in the street. It was like a revolution, bordering at moments on a Surrealist revolution.

Not, she thought with amusement, that any kind of revolution would be welcomed by the habitués of the Lutétia, the grand Art Nouveau hotel on the corner of the Boulevard Raspail where she was meeting her father for lunch. What would they think of the bold programme Blum had announced? For he was not simply introducing a maximum forty-hour working week and a two-week annual paid holiday – which would enable many people for the first time in their lives to see the sea. He was even, miracle of miracles, appointing three women to the cabinet – and this even though women were not allowed to vote. It was as though he was opening wide a door that people hadn't known existed.

As she entered the elegant restaurant, she was received by the *maître d'hôtel* with a smiling greeting and a knowing nod to where her handsome, white-haired father sat at his regular table, submitting the menu to his usual stringent examination. Monsieur Markovitch's exacting little ways were known here.

But he seemed almost serene as he got up to greet her with a kiss and tell her she looked ravishing, before sitting down again with a smile.

'You seem very pleased about something, *Papa*.'

'Yes' he smiled. 'I think I've been touched by grace.'

'And how could that conceivably have come about?'

'I've just been to church. At Saint-Sulpice.'

'You do surprise me!'

'Not at all. I'm an architect after all and it's an interesting building – a bit of a jumble of course, but that's why it's interesting. However I was actually there for the Sunday organ recital by Marcel Dupré. He's good, but the organ is better, a really complex and subtle instrument. You know, those Christians, they're a bit like you and your Surrealist friends, aren't they?'

'I hadn't noticed.'

'Well, you're both looking for the supra-real, aren't you? For something beyond material reality.'

'Except they think they've found it.'

111

'And you're still looking? What if it doesn't exist? And you don't even have the music?'

'You mean you think the music you heard in Saint-Sulpice has spiritual significance?'

'No, I think it's entirely material. But it has a pleasant effect on the neural networks of the brain. Are you hungry?'

And he was in such a serene mood that he barely quibbled with the service or the dishes as the meal progressed. True, he complained to the long-suffering waiter Gaston that the wine had not been properly chilled, then complained when it was brought back that he had said chilled and not frozen. But he pronounced his starter of Creamy Scrambled Eggs with roasted wild mushrooms from Corrèze to be distinctly less than disastrous. And if he complained that his Sole with Lobster and vermouth sauce was insufficiently crisp at the edges and that the sauce was all vermouth and no lobster, he did not demand to see the cook or the *maître d'hôtel* and the matter was comfortably handled by Gaston, who knew this game backwards.

Dora, as usual, was amused by this comic ritual. But she was a little puzzled at her father's mood and it wasn't until she was watching with some fascination his strategic approach to his Bergamot Tea Custard Cream Cup in orange blossom flavour that she began to wonder if he was quite as serene as he had seemed.

She was enthusiastically describing her reportage on the occupied factories when he asked teasingly if she had chosen her red nail laquer that morning to celebrate the triumph of the revolution.

'You don't approve of the Popular Front government, *Papa?*'

'Well at one level I do, but I'm beginning to wonder' he said with a slightly sardonic laugh, 'if we might not have been wiser to stay in Argentina.'

'What are you suggesting? Why on earth would you think that?'

'I think ironically that we may have had a clearer view from outside of the depth of the upheaval caused by that World War – the people in Europe were a bit too close to it. And with Hitler walking blithely into the Rhineland, the upheaval may be only beginning.'

'But the Popular Front is a response to that, is it not?'

'Yes, but it will provoke a reaction here and probably also in Spain and in Germany, don't you think?'

'Well, there's always the danger of that, I suppose.'

'Between you and me and this misbegotten Bergamot Tea Custard Cream Cup in so-called orange blossom flavour, Dora, it will sharpen the division in Europe.'

She was leafing through the magazine *Vendredi* while awaiting the arrival of Picasso. He had phoned a week before – giving due notice this time – saying that he would be interested to see the range of her photographic work and that he might have a favour to ask of her. And while she was prepared to show him her work, she did not care to speculate on what he had in mind as a favour.

She had known for some time that he was back in Paris. In fact it was weeks since she had caught another glimpse of Alice Paalen – so easily distinguished unfortunately by her limp – hurrying up the Rue La Boétie towards the Metro station late one afternoon. And since she had a short red-haired woman shouting and gesticulating behind her, it was a reasonable supposition, firstly that Alice was coming back from Picasso's and, secondly, that the pursuer might well be his apparently unreconciled wife – if poor Alice really was Picasso's lover, it did not look like a comfortable option. But since then Nusch had told her that she had disappeared mysteriously from Paris, and that it was rumoured that she might have been ill or been taken off somewhere by her husband. So whether it was because of Picasso, Alice herself, the husband or the gesticulating red-haired ex-wife – or some combination of these – it did seem that any affair there might have been between Picasso and Alice Paalen was over.

Meanwhile, Paul had told her gleefully that Picasso was back and working again, and had done the illustrations for his poems. Indeed he had since sent her a copy of the volume with a dedication both by himself, saying that 'she joined the dawning day with eternal loving happiness' – a bit flowery, but then he was a poet and, being Paul, probably meant it – and by Picasso, with the pleasant little conceit 'Adora, Picasso', which meant what it meant.

Whatever all this meant, it was a new Picasso that she opened the door to when he arrived. Gone were the worn anorak and the tired jacket with bulging pockets, replaced by an elegant light summer suit, blue shirt and white tie. And he looked different, even younger.

'So you've been in England, did I hear?' he said.

'Yes, I went to London the week before last for the Surrealist exhibition, as well as doing a bit of reportage. And you're back in Paris and working away, Paul tells me?'

'Yes' he smiled, 'I must be responding to the change of season.'

'And you said you'd like to see what I do here?'

'Yes' he said with a grin, 'I need to keep tabs on the competition, don't I?'

So she first showed him a few examples of her routine fashion and beauty magazine work, before going on to the documentary reportage. They went through the Barcelona series, where of course he recognised many of the locations, then on to the London series – on which he commented that she had a sharp eye for irony and loneliness.

'Well there's not much loneliness in these' she said, bringing out the recently developed work on the workers' occupation of the factories.

'No, it's like one big happy party all over Paris' he said as he leafed slowly through them.

'But I'm really most interested in the photo-montages and experimental stuff I do in my own time.'

And she showed him several examples of these, with their often disturbing juxtapositions of figures, periods and places, noting that his interest was essentially in the techniques involved. He asked how she controlled the lighting on the figures lying prostrate on the ceiling of a curved vault, and was particularly curious about the stages involved in building the montage depicting a hand with lacquered nails emerging from a shell to finger sensuously the sand on an alien beach.

'I think you could teach me things – though I can at least see where the lacquered nails come from' he said with a smile.

'A fair guess!' she said with a smile. 'But here's one that I'm exhibiting in London at the moment.'

She brought out the recent one with the armadillo foetus and watched him study it in silence for a moment or two.

'A very powerful image' he said finally with a little nod of approval. 'I can't imagine what that strange little monster is, or where it comes from.'

'And I'm not telling!'

'Quite right too. And have you any other monsters up your sleeve?'

'Well, actually' she said with a smile, 'there's another series I've been toying with. You remember those shots I took of you the last time you were here?'

'I do. You were climbing all over me.'

'In the nicest possible way, I hope! Anyway, here they are.'

And she showed him a series of flexible negatives – shots of him sitting in profile, leaning against the wall, or smoking – in which black and white and light and dark were inverted and the large dark eyes, most disconcertingly of all, had become strange white hollows.

'My God' he said, 'I look as though I'm just not there, I'm a ghost, or no more than a memory, not really alive – it's a kind of death. It's black magic, Dora.'

'Then I hardly dare show you this one' she said lightly.

He stared at the full-on shot on which she had scratched with her little penknife a wide area all round the face, cutting off the ears and part of the eye on one side, leaving a narrowed, grim visage staring outwards with blank dead eyes.

'You see what you've done this time, Dora? You've monstered me with a vengeance! But while your own little monster had a little

115

bit of pathos, even a little charm, you've turned me into some sort of frightening angel of death.' He looked at her curiously and smiled. 'Are you punishing me for something?'

'Oh, I just thought you were a good subject' she said lightly. 'Though it does serve you right for trying to turn me into a weeping woman that time.'

'No wonder I was suspicious of photography' he said with a wry grin. 'I hardly dare after that to ask you for the favour I had in mind.'

'Well of course if you don't dare…!' she said with a twinkle.

'I'll risk it! You know that the Popular Front government is planning on have a big spectacular Bastille Day? And that they are putting on this big play about the Revolution, *14 Juillet*?'

'Yes, and it will have hundreds of actors for the crowd scenes and massed choirs and music by the big French composers.'

'So they tell me. But the point is they've asked me to do the stage curtain.'

'Well, that's a great honour! It should be a historic occasion.'

'So I was wondering, Dora, if you would like to act as photographer – not just for the curtain, but for the different stages in the process of creating the painting, which I think might be a more interesting exercise and is very rarely done. Would you?'

'Yes indeed. I'd be pleased to, Picasso.'

'Dora' he said with a smile, 'why do you call me Picasso?'

'Because you're a painter again.'

In the rather rainy run-up to this highly symbolical Bastille Day, meant both to celebrate the victory of the Popular Front and to act as a riposte to the growing Fascist tendencies in France and elsewhere, Dora had the heady feeling that history had suddenly begun to matter to everybody. It mattered to the Jewish refugees who were now straggling in from Hitler's Germany. It mattered to those middle class people who were reading dire press warnings that France was in the grip of a Communist revolution. It mattered to those wealthy individuals who were already squirreling their money out of the country. It mattered to ordinary workers who, after years of recession, found it hard to believe that they now had some protection in the workplace, that the working week was limited to forty hours, and that they had before them the dream of a paid summer holiday of two whole weeks. And it mattered the more because of the uneasy sense, following what amounted to the collapse of the League of Nations, that the hardening underlying conflict was not simply French but European. Whether you wanted it resolved in this way or the opposite way, it mattered.

And the degree to which it mattered was evident in the way she and her friends – not only Paul and Nusch, but Picasso and even Sabartés on occasion – were tending to congregate at the end of the day in the Deux Magots to discuss politics. That the heated political atmosphere was also tending to increase personal tensions was evident in the fact that Paul had broken off relations with André Breton, complaining about what he described as André's overbearing manner. Meanwhile, there was some surprise about what appeared to be Picasso's move to the left.

'You realise, Pablo, that not so long ago the Communists were writing you off as reactionary and decadent – and now they're quite keen on you?'

'That's their problem, Paul. They may have changed, but I haven't changed.'

And that remark lingered in Dora's mind as the time approached for the painting of the curtain for *14 Juillet* at the Alhambra theatre. For it turned out rather disconcertingly that this was to be based on an earlier small drawing entitled *The Remains of the Minotaur in Harlequin Costume*. It showed a giant human figure with the head of an eagle holding a dead Minotaur in Harlequin costume and confronting a ragged human figure holding out a begging bowl, but doubled up under the weight of a dead horse apparently ridden by a young boy. And Picasso was certainly right to say that he hadn't changed, since he was obviously still playing with the same elements of what appeared to be a personal mythology. But did this seem appropriate for the occasion?

Of course there was part of a ruined building suggestive of the Bastille, while you could see the man with the bowl as representing the starving people and the figure with the eagle's head as representing the fabulous phoenix. But that was about as much as even a sophisticated audience could read into it as an allegory of 1789. And while it was interesting that, having seemed in his earlier work to identify with the Harlequin and latterly with the Minotaur, he seemed here to be killing them both off, these were still elements of a purely personal iconography.

'How do you see the painting as relating to the Revolution?' she asked him directly, as he stood surveying the enormous canvas spread out on the floor.

'That's for them to decide, Dora. They want a Picasso, they get a Picasso!'

Was he simply painting Picasso? Or was he engaging in history at least at a symbolical level? But as she observed the intensity with which he worked on the curtain for days on end, she realised that for Picasso himself the question was largely meaningless. He simply painted, painted passionately – and only seemed to know what he might have done when he had done it. The 'meaning' was something that came afterwards, something for other people and over which he had no control. He wasn't an intellectual – he was an artist.

And if that made him sometimes hard to fathom, it made him all the more interesting to her as they spent time together over these days working on the canvas. They talked during the work, they talked in the nearby bar at lunchtime, they joked and laughed a great deal and they gradually became very much at ease in each other's company. So much so that she felt a keen disappointment when he said the day before Bastille Day that he wouldn't be accompanying Paul, Nusch and herself on the great parade.

'The stage curtain is one thing' he said, 'but I'm just not political.'

'Well we'll miss you' she said. 'However I understand.'

'But I'll be happy to see you all after the show at the Alhambra. Have a good parade!'

And they did. Especially since they decided not to join in from the start at the Hôtel de Ville, but to go ahead to a point on the Rue Saint-Antoine and see the whole procession as it passed. When they got there they had to wait for around twenty minutes, but it was spent happily with the spectators already lining the route – most wearing rosettes, children eating waffles, a whole family sitting on the pavement eating frankfurters, a group of older men standing with full glasses outside a bistro giving a ragged rendering of the *Marseillaise*, children and adults enjoying the merry-go-round and the swings of a mobile fairground installed at a corner along the street, and of course small traders loudly offering their wares from barrows on either side of the street.

'It's a pity there's no sunshine' said Nusch.

'The sun is right-wing, everybody knows that' grinned Paul. 'Still, the rain hasn't started – not yet!'

But the parade was already on its way, preceded by two young stewards in blue shirt and red tie, each standing on the roof of a taxi with a loudspeaker and singing the *Internationale*. And then the procession arrived, the marchers twenty abreast and often linked arm-in-arm, interspersed with brass bands, flute bands or pipe bands, for hours and hours: the political leaders, the president of the League of Human Rights, the bemedalled war wounded in wheel chairs or on crutches bringing sobs and applause from the crowd, the scouts, the sports organizations, a folklore dance group, the trade unions, the Front Populaire deputies wearing their parliamentary sashes, women's organizations with banners demanding equal rights, and then the cultural groups: writers, journalists, artists, actors, film directors and members of political groups.

'Right!' said Eluard, 'this is us.'

And they stepped into the parade – among the journalists as it happened, not that it mattered.

119

'They say the whole thing takes three hours' said Nusch. 'And these are new flat shoes.'

'But at least we're not at the end' said Dora. 'We're ahead of the Renault workers, the miners, the construction workers and all.'

Eventually, after frequent stops enlivened by bits of impromptu dancing and singing, they arrived at the thronged Place de la Bastille, where they managed to find two free chairs on the terrace of a café, which enabled Dora to sit and Nusch to sit on Paul's knee while they listened to the singing and the speeches by the various political leaders, ending with Léon Blum. Finally they fought their way through the crowds and through sudden heavy rain to get to the Alhambra theatre, for the performance of *14 Juillet*.

And as the music swelled and hundreds of voices sang, as the Bastille Day of 1936 merged with the Bastille Day of 1789, Dora felt that for her, as for many of those around her, history had become intoxicatingly alive.

The exhilarating feeling of surfing on the wave of history only became the more intense for Dora with the bad news that began to emerge a few evenings later at a soirée in the home of her friend Lise Deharme.

Lise, some ten years older than herself, was not only a writer and the editor of a Surrealist review, but something of a society hostess who ran a salon for the cultural avant-garde. She also had an enhanced status among Surrealists as 'the Lady of the Glove', a glove kept and treasured by André Breton, who had once suffered an unrequited passion for this slightly long-faced brunette. And of course her interior was a byword for its studiously Surrealist style, with greenery growing inside the house, pictures and objects covering the walls, every flat surface and even the floor – leaving Lise's Persian cat Charmante to pick her way fastidiously through the artistically organised disorder.

The conversation among the usual collection of writers and artists had been going on for several hours and nothing particularly notable had happened. Except, perhaps, that Dora had been invited by Lise to join her at her summer place at Saint Tropez, where she would be in residence by the start of August. And then, of course, there had been that rather unfortunate episode with Jacqueline, after Dora found her laughing tipsily in a large circle of people. For when she innocently asked her if André was around somewhere, Jacqueline replied merrily that he was at 42 Rue Fontaine – with Aube.

'That's very noble of him' Dora said jokingly. 'You've got him trained?'

'He can train himself. I just walked out and told him to damn well get on with it.'

Since this was said loudly and with a defiant laugh in the hearing of quite a few people, and since gossip about the Bretons would quickly do the rounds, it did not bode well for her impulsive friend's marriage.

However, it was around midnight when Lise's husband came into the room with the news from the radio that some army generals had started a rebellion against the Popular Front government in Spain. It had begun with the army in Spanish Morocco and was apparently beginning to spread to the mainland. Which led to heavy speculation as to whether this could end up in a full-scale civil war. And if so, could France be dragged into it in support of a sister Republican government? Or indeed Germany be dragged in on the other side, since the rebellion seemed to be directed by Fascist elements in the army? These questions were tossed around into the small hours, but it was clear only that the political scene had darkened.

And from the following day onwards, Dora found herself meeting up most evenings at the Deux Magots with Paul, Nusch, Picasso and occasionally Sabartés, trying to follow what seemed to be a confused situation. While the Nationalist rebels seemed to have gained control over a third of the country, the situation remained both fluid and bloody, with assassinations taking place on both sides.

And a prime consideration, since Picasso's mother and sister were there, was the situation in Barcelona, where heavy street fighting had broken out – though the rebel troops were being successfully confronted by a combination of loyal army units and workers' militias.

'So your mother should be quite safe' Dora told Picasso.

'I hope so, but it sounds as though the Ramblas will be running with blood.'

'Still, we're holding on to Madrid as well as Barcelona' said Eluard, 'so the chances are the rebels can be defeated.'

But once the army Junta set up an opposing Nationalist government in Burgos, it became ominously clear that Spain was in for a civil war – and even more ominously clear that a civil war in Spain threatened to turn into a general war in Europe. For if the French started sending a few obsolete aeroplanes to the Republicans, the German and Italian air forces were soon actively engaged on the side of the rebels.

'It's up to Léon Blum and the British to stand firm' Dora was saying. 'If we don't support the elected government in Spain, what signal does that send to Nazi Germany and Fascist Italy?!'

Blum did declare his support, but not only was he being fiercely attacked in the right-wing press by those who saw Fascism as part of the defence of European civilization against the 'red peril' of Communism, but he got no encouragement from the British. So he was forced into the humiliating about-turn of joining with Britain in a non-intervention pact which – though it was broken immediately by Italian aircraft operating in Spain – preserved at least a pretence of peace in Europe and postponed what many were beginning to see as the inevitable. Especially as all this coincided with the spectacular Olympic Games in Berlin, where a triumphalist Adolf Hitler was taking the salute from the athletes of the nations of the world.

Dora found herself so caught up in the rhythm of these events that she decided not to accompany Paul and Nusch on their way down to Lise Deharme's place at Saint-Tropez, but to stay a little longer in Paris. Since she was collecting signatures for a declaration by French intellectuals of support for the Spanish Republicans, she was often in the Deux Magots, where she was tending to run into Picasso, either on his own or with Sabartés. They were increasingly speaking Spanish, which in itself created a certain intimacy, and gradually they found themselves talking freely about all sorts of things. But she was not finding it easy to persuade him to sign her declaration.

'Look, Picasso...' she was saying.

'Why the devil, Dora' he said with a laugh, 'do you keep calling me Picasso?'

'But it's your name, isn't it?'

'Well it is and it isn't, as it happens.'

'What does that mean?'

'It means it's the name I paint under.'

'So where did it come from?'

'Well, actually...' he said, a little reluctantly as it seemed, 'it was my mother's name.'

Dora was slightly surprised. Although there was good reason for concern about his mother's situation in Barcelona, he tended not to mention her.

'Well, Pablo might be a reasonable name for a teddy bear, but Picasso is what you're known as, and it's as Picasso the painter that I'm trying to get you to sign this declaration, so that I can get on a train and go down to Saint-Tropez and swim in the Mediterranean.'

'Then you'd better tell me what difference my signature would have on the course of the civil war – in which there have been atrocities on both sides.'

'Yes, but one side is still better than the other. And it's an important moral gesture.'

'But I'm not into moral gestures, Dora. And, as I keep saying, I'm not political.'

'We're all caught up in this political situation whether we like it or not, Picasso – your mother in Barcelona more than most.'

He looked at her almost resentfully, as though she had dealt him a low blow.

'All right' he said finally. 'But if anybody ever asks me to paint propaganda, I'll kill you and me both, Dora Maar.'

'That seems entirely reasonable, Picasso' she said with a smile.

'So when are you leaving to swim in the Mediterranean then?'

'As soon as I can get a train – it's the August holiday rush, of course.'

'And where are you staying, did you say?'

'At Lise Deharme's place at Saint-Tropez. With Paul and Nusch – and various others, I believe.'

'Sounds like a jolly party. I'll be going down shortly as well, to Mougins further along the coast. I might manage to drive over there one day – and catch up with you all.'

'Yes, we'd all be glad to see you.'

'Have you got the address?'

'No, that's back in the studio, I'm afraid.' She hesitated. 'But I think I have the phone number here. I'll write it down for you…'

'What are you smiling at?'

It was Nusch, grinning down at her as she lay in her red swimming costume on the striped beach towel.

'Was I smiling?'

'Yes, you've been smiling ever since you arrived.'

'Well I'm nicely relaxed after swimming. And Paris and all that bustle just seem so far away, don't they? It's as though the world is in suspension down here.'

The Deharme's villa at Les Salins on the edge of Saint-Tropez was roomy and pleasant, with direct access to this wonderfully unspoiled sandy beach, which had the added advantage of being sheltered from the mistral. And of course the guests were very familiar. In addition to Paul and Nusch, there was Cécile, Paul's daughter from his marriage to Gala, who was a charmingly natural girl of eighteen. And then there were Christian and Yvonne Zervos.

Christian – or Kristos, since he was Greek in origin – was a handsome man in his late forties who had founded the influential art magazine *Les Cahiers d'Art* and was engaged in the complicated task of cataloguing Picasso's works from the beginning. His wife Yvonne, a pleasant brunette of around thirty, had been running a gallery before they got married and they had since operated in the art world very much in tandem.

They had all passed the days pleasantly in various ways. They had strolled around Saint-Tropez, admiring the unspoilt character of the village and the old port – although Lise told them that, since the fashion designers Coco Chanel and Elsa Schiaparelli had spent time there, Saint-Tropez risked becoming 'a little too fashionable'. Beyond that, they visited some of the villages fortified against the Saracens, picnicked on the beach, danced a little, amused themselves by working out horoscopes at Lise's instigation – and almost succeeded in keeping the big wide world at bay.

But not quite, for the world kept breaking in with news from Spain, where the poet and dramatist Garcia Lorca had been murdered by Fascists in the most shocking fashion.

'Forced to dig his own grave before being murdered, can you imagine it?!' said Paul,

'I'm afraid I can' said Christian. 'Writers are dangerous.'

'I just wish the Anarchists in Barcelona weren't looting and burning all those churches' said Cécile diffidently.

'I'm afraid civil wars are the worst' said Christian. 'They can tend to make one side as bad as the other.'

Depressing as all this was, it did not stop the sun from shining, or the blue sea from being tempting, or the group from playing a primitive form of beachball in the cool of the evening on the fine damp sand. Since Dora had discovered that Cécile was as fond of swimming as she was, they had been swimming together out to some of the moored yachts and back. And it was when she was again lying on her striped beach towel that she found Nusch standing over her with that same mischievous grin.

'You're still smiling that smile, aren't you?'

'It's the only smile I've got, Nusch.'

'No it isn't, it's a special smile – there's something mysterious going on.'

'There always is, Nusch. And if I had the answer to the mystery I would tell you.'

'I believe you!'

'Of course you do!'

But the world kept breaking in again, this time provoking an argument between Paul and Christian, which took place rather comically with each of them straddling one of the old cannons on the Citadel. For the news had been coming in about the trials going on in Moscow, in which Zinoviev, Kamenev and other prominent members of the Communist Party were being tried for treason.

'But it's laughable' Christian was saying. These are old Bolsheviks, for heaven's sake! It's grotesque that the prosecutor should be calling them mad dogs and just not credible that they would confess to treason like a row of zombies.'

'Yes, it's disturbing' said Eluard. 'But what worries me is the effect this might have on the unity of the left.'

'It just splits it in half. It means you can't rely on Stalin's Soviet Union.'

'Except that whatever you think of Stalin's Soviet Union, it's the only power to have come out cleanly in favour of the Spanish Republic. If you exclude that, what are you left with to fight against Fascism – the weak democracies in France and Britain?!'

'Which just practise appeasement' said Dora. 'It's all quite ominous.'

But, ominous or not, the heady feeling of living in exciting times did not leave her as Paul and Christian dismounted more or less elegantly from their cannons and they all strolled to the bar of the Citadel where they lounged around on the terrace. Discussing the relative merits of various apéritifs, telling funny stories, commenting on the yachts dotting the wide blue sea, watching the sun move imperceptibly on its great westward arc and generally feeling how good it was to be alive.

'You're smiling that little smile again' murmured Nusch, who was sitting beside her.

'And you're grinning that mischievous little grin again, aren't you?'

'You're smiling at some secret, aren't you?'

'I'm smiling because it's not so much a secret as an unlikely hunch.'

'And what is that supposed to tell me, Dora?'

'Nothing, I hope!'

At dinner, when they eventually got to it, they talked among other things about art and Christian, who was something of an expert on prehistoric art, spoke of the difficulty of interpreting the cave paintings.

'It's funny, you know' he was saying, 'about the only contemporary painter who gives me that same sense of mystery, and even then only in some of his recent work, is Picasso. Incidentally, is he on the Côte d'Azur this summer?'

'Yes, he did say he would be coming down, I think' said Paul. 'Perhaps you know, Dora?'

'He said he intended to, though I don't know when he was leaving. But he did say he might drive over to say hullo to us all.'

She had tried to speak very casually, but she could see at once that Nusch – though she remained discreet about it – had somehow sensed that what she had called an unlikely hunch had to do with this visit from Picasso.

However it was two more evenings before Picasso turned up halfway through the dinner, greeted them all, said he really wasn't able to stay, but that he wanted a word with Dora.

'Perhaps we could talk on the beach?' he said.

'All right' she said.

It was dark on the beach, but a three-quarter moon was reflected on the sea and on the wet sand near the water, the air was balmy and there was the strange, savage sound of crickets somewhere as they began to walk slowly away from the villa. He had taken her hand, was playing tentatively with her fingers.

'I want you to come back with me to Mougins. I'm afraid this may be very unexpected, Dora.'

'Not entirely, Picasso.'

'I'm fifty-four years old and you are…?'

'Twenty-eight.'

'So I'm almost twice your age. I have a wife called Olga I'm trying to get a separation settlement from…'

'I did know that.'

'And I have had a long-term relationship with a young model called Marie-Thérèse who has a small child by me, a daughter, just under one year old.'

'That I didn't know.'

She moved automatically to withdraw her hand, but he grasped it firmly.

'I don't want to live with her, but she needs support and I'll probably have to spend some weekends with her – though I need to find a new place for her.'

'I see…'

They walked on in silence beside this vast moonlit sea. She could hear the sucking sound of their feet on the damp shiny sand. A bird cried briefly somewhere – in pain, was it…?

'That's about it, Dora. Will you come?'

There was still this sucking sound of their feet on the shining sand. And that strange savage sound of the unseen crickets…

'Yes.'

'Good. Marcel is waiting to pick us up a little further along this beach.'

'And my things?'

'Marcel will come back and pick them up in the morning.'

Dora laughed briefly and he laughed in response. That he was so sure of himself seemed to go with the sense of inevitability she had been living with right up to the moment of this slow walk in moonlight along this shining beach. And there was little said, or needing to be said, as they reached the car and got into the back seat.

It was with a grave expectancy, a kind of solemnity that they sat hand in hand and almost silent in the back seat as Marcel drove them, for Dora had no idea how long, through the warm moonlit Mediterranean night. And it was with the same solemnity, later that night, that he lay beside her and, slowly feeling every inch of her skin as though sculpting her body with his fingertips, led her through rhythmic stages towards an ecstasy that went beyond awareness of skin, or body, or even self.

6

What on earth had she done to Picasso, Dora asked herself with amusement, to turn him into an oversized small boy dressed only in shorts and playing at making cardboard masks?

Wrapped in a bath towel, with her red swimsuit drying on a chair beside her, she was sitting on a lounger on the terrace of Vaste Horizon – a quite modest hotel which lived up to its ambitious name with a sweeping view over the bay of Cannes and the Valmasque forest.

As for Mougins itself, a charming mediaeval hilltop village with narrow cobbled steets and houses clothed in purple bougainvilleas, they had barely noticed it. For the past three days – apart from the previous evening when they had dined at L'Amandier – had been spent eating, sleeping and making love at all sorts of strange hours. The lovemaking, if sometimes vigorous, had been pretty conventional – if only because Picasso, though he would allow her to make love to him up to a point, seemed to want to have the last word.

This morning was the first time they had managed to go down to the beach for a swim, although she had failed to persuade him to swim along with her, since he was much too busy wading up to the waist and looking down into the water for pebbles to collect. It was such an enthusiastic performance that it took her some time to realise that it was designed to conceal the fact that he couldn't swim. And now he was sitting in his shorts finishing off a painted mask of a black bull's head to go with the white horse's head mask already completed.

'What do you think, Dora?' he said, placing the bull's mask on his head.

'I think your Minotaur obsession' she said, laughing, 'has visibly gone to your head.'

'This is the way we played as youngsters, you know. One of us would wear a wickerwork mask with horns and a little kid would be the picador, sitting on a bigger boy's shoulders and using a broomstick to goad the bull. We even had a toy trumpet and a little drum – for when I came charging into the arena.'

'For you were the bull, of course!'

'Well any fool could be the picador, but with the mask on you could almost *be* the bull – feel its fear, its courage... Here, try it.'

She laughed protestingly, but let him place the mask over her head.

'This is ridiculous' she said, laughing, as she was forced to hold the mask in place with her hand so that she could see straight.

'So what do you feel, Dora?'

'Hot.'

'Good, because you're furious and frustrated, aren't you?'

'No, but I could get that way!'

'Because you've rushed out of the dark into the blinding sunlight, haven't you? And been goaded into charging – go on, charge...charge! – three times! And you're maddened by the six banderillas you've had stuck in your neck, yes maddened!. And now you're desperately pawing the sand – go on, paw, paw..!'

'Paw...?!' she gasped laughingly, beginning mockingly to paw the ground.

'And now it's the *faena*, the moment of truth.'

'For the bull?'

'And for the matador! For I now have only this small *muleta*.' he said, picking up her red swimsuit from the chair. 'But first I must ask the President's permission...'

As he bowed to the imaginary President and held up an imaginary sword in crusader fashion, she found herself drawn further into this fantasy.

'And now I must offer the kill to some beautiful woman in the crowd…'

He doffed an imaginary hat, tossed it away, then turned in a threateningly stylised way towards her.

'And now there's only you and me, and you're charging me – go on, charge! – and I'm turning you with the *muleta* – like that, yes!- and again… and again… and over again! And once you stumble – that's right, stumble! – it's the moment of truth for both of us, when I pick my spot and run you through with my sword – *voilà*! Until you stagger… and look at me blindly… and fall dead.'

Dora, sufficiently absorbed in this playacting to have ended up on her knees, removed the mask, got up and shook her hair loose. Picasso's big dark eyes were gleaming.

'Well?' he said with a grin.

'Well, it's obviously fun to spin me like a top and mock me before impaling me on your imaginary sword. But isn't this rather a roundabout way to kill cattle?'

'That's ridiculous, Dora! It's not 'mocking' the bull, it's bringing out the bravery, the nobility of the bull.'

'Bulls aren't brave or noble, Picasso. The bull is just being a bull.'

'You're impossible, Dora' he said with a laugh. 'But then you've probably never seen a proper bullfight, have you?'

'I did once, in Ronda – and I wouldn't have called it 'proper'.'

'Because you never got into it, the deeper meaning of it. It's a symbolical battle against a powerful force of nature, that's what it is. Why do you think the crowd sits there so thrilled by it?'

'Because they're killing by proxy and in comfort?'

'Because they admire the courage of a great matador – the artistry, the style, the chivalry. That's why you see them throwing in cigars, jewels, gold watches, sombreros by the dozen…'

'Well, that should keep him in cigars and sombreros, but I wonder if a Popular Front government would want to hang on to this old Spanish custom. It's primitive.'

'Of course it's primitive – life is primitive. But look how the primitive element is controlled by style and ritual. It's the central ceremony of Spain, I'd have you know. It's the real life-and-death tragedy that leaves your Greek tragedy looking like poncey posturing and the rest of your so-called artists looking like phoneys and wankers. The bullfight *is* Spain, Dora!'

'More of a Fascist fantasy of Spain, I'd say, with people prancing around in those silly feudal costumes. It's like a cross between the circus and a crucifixion – except that it's an animal that's being tormented and crucified.'

'All right, so it's like a kind of savage Mass, if you like. But try at least to get inside it, Dora. Stop intellectualising and start *feeling*, for Christ's sake. Here, try this, this is more like it, this makes more sense for you...'

'You think so?'

She was laughing, but she let him take the horse's mask and place it over her head, and then watched him place the bull mask back over his own head and start to circle threateningly around her again.

'Can't you feel the *rhythm* of the mare as she's being ridden around the arena, the oneness of the mare with her rider, the dignity of the mare, the beauty of the mare...?' he was chanting, circling closer. 'Can't you feel the trembling of the mare..., the fright of the mare as these big horns come closer..., the panic of the mare as you feel them coming closer and closer to plunge deep into your belly...? Don't you feel the tremor, the sexual excitement at the sight of those big horns he's got, at the sight of those big balls he's got...?'

He was suddenly behind her, pulling the bath towel from her body, seizing her breasts...

'Don't you feel the hot breath and the thrill and the agony as he comes violently on to you, to thrust himself into you, to penetrate you...?'

'I do, I do!' said Dora, laughing, 'and if a bit of Fascist foreplay is what it takes to get the old Minotaur going...'

He seized her harshly by the hair and was bending her over as though to mount her when there was a cry of *'Bonjour'* from somewhere behind them and they turned round – Picasso in shorts wearing the black bull's mask, Dora naked except for the white mare's mask – to find Paul, Nusch, Cécile, Christian and Yvonne staring at them.

It was Eluard who finally broke the silence.

'Perhaps this isn't a very good time...?'

For Dora it almost felt like the Surrealists by the seaside, especially when Roland and Valentine Penrose turned up. They were staying nearby, as were Christian and Yvonne, and since Paul, Nusch and Cécile were staying for part of the time at the Vaste Horizon and part of the time in the villa of a relative of her fellow photographer Man Ray, it was the old avant-garde network in action.

And it was like one long party. They met up on most days in varying combinations, to bathe in the sea, lie in the sun, eat a picnic lunch or perhaps try a local restaurant, after which the order of the day would be the siesta. In the late afternoon, they would play cards, at which Christian and Paul were adept, and on and off they would discuss poetry or painting or politics, especially the situation in Spain. At intervals they drove around the area, discovering among other things the pottery-making tradition of the old town of Vallauris, which particularly enchanted Picasso, who tried his hand at a few simple statuettes. Dora took photographs, of course, while Roland took some heroic shots of herself and Picasso emerging godlike from the sea, with Picasso looking as though he had swum fearlessly through many oceans It all felt like serious fun, especially since there was time for heart-to-heart conversations, one of which – the more disconcertingly since she had not previously seen much of Valentine – took place between Dora and Valentine Penrose.

Valentine, with an attractive, rather grave face and long dark hair, was from the Bordeaux area and had rebelled against her military family to become a Surrealist poet. She was much admired by Paul, and her poetry was said to resemble Paul's own. The difference, of course, was that Valentine was into alchemy, Hindu philosophy and the occult in general and was a follower of an unusual guru in the form of some Spanish count.

'Of course' she said as they walked together along the beach close to the rippling water, 'Roland and I are about to split up.'

'I'm sorry to hear that.'

'Oh it's all very amicable. The marriage hasn't worked for some time now.'

'I see.'

'It's not Roland's fault – he's a very honourable Englishman and I'm fond of him. But I'm not sure that man-woman relationships are very nourishing in any case. It's like chalk and cheese, you know? You can't find a common perspective on reality, a common search. I know I'm something of a witch' she said with a comic grimace, 'but I do think increasingly that truth and reality are feminine. So it's convenient that Roland doesn't want to come to India with me.'

'Oh yes, you've been there before, I believe?'

'Yes and I'll be going back to the same ashram for the same communal, meditative life. You can no longer pursue a spiritual journey in Europe, after all. Even André Breton is betraying Surrealism now by ranting on and on about politics. If the Surrealist quest isn't about transcending everyday reality at the personal level, Dora, it is about nothing. Don't you agree?'

Dora was rather taken aback by the question. Her interest in Surrealism seemed to have faded into the past recently.

'I'm afraid I think that Surrealism has been overtaken by events, Valentine. When we're all so bogged down in a threatening everyday reality, it surely has to be about enlarging that reality for everyone. But I wish you luck in India. When are you leaving?'

'In about a month's time.' She grinned. 'As soon as we get ourselves organised!'

'So, you're not going alone then?'

'Oh no' she said with a laugh, 'I'm going with a soul sister, another refugee from the man-woman prison, another pilgrim in pursuit of the 'eternal feminine''

'And you won't tell me who this paragon is?' asked Dora, laughing in turn.

'Well, I shouldn't really. Dora. It's someone who's just coming out of an attempted suicide following a disastrous affair. Though of course' she smiled, 'you'll know who it is anyway, won't you?'

Dora felt a sudden chill run through her.

'You don't mean…?'

'Yes, I assumed you knew, Dora..'

'It's Alice…?'

'That's right, Alice Paalen.'

Jolly as the party atmosphere was, there were so many comings and goings that it was not so easy for Picasso, though his enthusiasm had revived, to get much painting done. However, he worked while the others were enjoying their siesta and, as the days passed, Dora could see herself gradually becoming part of his imaginative world.

While walking on the beach, or while pretending that he was too busy to swim, he had been collecting pebbles and bits of bone or driftwood on which he inscribed her face, transforming her into an ancient Greek damsel, a female Minotaur, a bird, or whatever his fancy dictated.

However, she entered his world much more directly in an arresting drawing done with Indian ink and coloured pencils, in which as Dora – since she was treated quite naturalistically and was entirely recognizable as herself, down to her lacquered fingernails – she was being ravished by the much larger, darker horned Minotaur with a glaring, rather humanised face. In this classical rural landscape, the Minotaur was almost the colour of the angry red sky behind him, whereas the very white body of Dora chimed with the mellow sunset behind her, so that the rape scene had the effect of a clash of two irreconcilable worlds. This was some way from Valentine's pursuit of the 'eternal feminine'…

'It's very powerful' she told him, then added jokingly, 'though some might think that, as couples go, they're not entirely compatible.'

'Well, it's mythological, isn't it?'

Yet it seemed at best semi-mythological, since the depiction of herself was so literal as to suggest that the Minotaur was a flattering fantasy image of himself.

'Your Minotaur looks oddly guilty, doesn't he?' she said. 'Is he driven to this violation despite himself – by his bull-like nature or his destiny, say?'

'He's driven to it, I think.'

'So he's a sort of tragic figure. But he's not just attacking women, is he? He's really attacking pretty well everything – the way the world is?'

'Oh I can't answer such questions, Dora. You'd better keep it and then you can tell me one day what it signifies. That's if you would like to have it?'

'Yes, I would. Thank you.'

'So how should we title it?'

'Well it looks very much' she said with a laugh, 'like *Dora and the Minotaur*.'

Since he clearly didn't like analysing paintings in such terms, she didn't persist. And yet the question lingered. Did femininity somehow represent the seductive appearance of a hostile world? Perhaps not so very far from Valentine Penrose after all. Or from Alice Paalen…

However, a more intriguing indication of her absorption into Picasso's imaginative world was the very large oil painting he was embarking upon, to be called *Reclining Nude with Stars*. For this was her again, not depicted realistically but translated into his new language of emblems or signs. Yet it was entirely her, for he was obviously starting to define her in terms of the varying colours of her nail lacquer – purple or light green mostly, but also blue and black. She was beginning to colour his world, entering into his system of signs, becoming part of his mythology.

It was flattering, but it was also faintly frightening. For it implied being possessed more profoundly than by the non-existent Minotaur. She could be endlessly transformed within this man's system of signs, be swallowed up by it. It was wonderful to be part of this great painter's mythology – but would she ever, if it came to it, be able to get out of it? She suddenly remembered that walk on the beach, the savage sound of the crickets, the sucking sound of her feet on the wet sand…

'I love you, Picasso' she said.

'And I love you too, Dora Maar.'

'I could teach you to swim, you know.'

They had gone down to the beach in the evening, after the others had left. It was dusk and the reddening sky in the west was like the sky behind the Minotaur.

'And what would be the point of that?'

'It would stop you having to go to such lengths to conceal your embarrassment – for a start.'

'It's dangerous to swim. There are fishermen around the Mediterranean who refuse to learn to swim.'

'But they could fall overboard from their boat and drown in the harbour. That's absurd.'

'No no, it's wise. They don't want to tempt fate.'

But it was Picasso himself who tempted fate the very next day by ignoring Marcel's view that, if a car crash ever did happen – by another driver's fault, naturally – it was safer to be sitting in the much larger and heavier Hispano-Suiza. For when Roland Penrose proposed a trip to Grasse to view the Rubens and Fragonard paintings in the cathedral, suggesting that rather than wait for Marcel they should go in his Ford, he allowed himself to be persuaded by Roland's view that the Ford might also be better adapted to the narrow winding hilly roads than the big six-cylinder Hispano-Suiza, especially since only the three of them – Picasso, Dora and himself – would be travelling.

It was a pleasant outing, with visits to the cathedral, to the Fragonard museum and to a perfume factory, where Picasso chose one that he favoured for Dora. And it was on the way back and, ironically, only a mile or so from Mougins that a battered tradesman's van suddenly loomed up at a bend in the road and, as Roland tried to swing right to avoid it, smashed loudly into the Ford from the left. Picasso, in the rear, was flung forward and sideways against the car door and Dora was flung against him, while Roland, to his extreme embarrassment, emerged miraculously unharmed.

And it took time to sort out. There was an argument between Roland and the other driver as to who was responsible. A passing motorist informed the local police at Mougins, so they became involved. Which meant inevitably, as Picasso realised since he had dropped his incognito for this visit to the Côte d'Azur, that the news was likely to leak out to the press. Meanwhile, Roland was apologising profusely to Picasso, who, though he was clearly shocked and in pain, was telling Roland that it was only a few minor bruises, a story backed up reassuringly by Dora as regards her own bruises. But it was a relief when the car was finally towed back to Mougins and they could rest at the Vaste Horizon.

Fortunately for Picasso, since it meant he could stop pretending about his bruises, Roland was off the scene a day or two later. There were reports of clashes in Barcelona, which was largely under workers' control and where there were conflicts between Anarchists, Communists and Socialists. A priest had apparently been imprisoned and later executed, which had led the Pope to condemn the Spanish Republican government for its 'satanic hatred against God'. Roland, with his English Quaker's conscience, decided along with Christian Zervos to go at once to Barcelona to find out the truth of the situation.

'We could look up your mother for you, Pablo' said Roland.

'No no, no need.'

'Are you sure?' Roland went on, anxious to make up for the car crash.

'She's an old lady of eighty, she has been widowed for years. It would only disturb and upset her.'

'But surely you'd like to know how she's managing in Barcelona?' said Dora.

Which led him reluctantly to agree, although he seemed all the more relieved to see Roland disappear. Anyway, he now began to groan with pain if he made any significant movement even in his sleep. Certainly, he had bruises on his right shoulder and down his right side. So indeed did Dora, but hers seemed less serious. When he still seemed slightly shocked and in pain two days later, she suggested that he should go to Cannes and see a specialist.

'What could he do?'

'He could examine you and give you an X-ray.'

'I don't believe in X-rays. It was bad enough you turning me into a ghost with your fancy negative photography, I don't want a machine seeing right through me.'

'But you might have broken ribs or a broken collar bone. It's common sense.'

'Yeah, common sense…!'

But she eventually managed to persuade him. And next day, with Marcel driving at an almost funereal pace to underline the superiority of the professional chauffeur, while almost brazenly crooning Tino Rossi's latest hit about the gypsy woman with the big black eyes, *La Bohémienne aux grands yeux noirs*, they drove solemnly into Cannes.

The specialist Dr Emile de Mourgues was smooth bordering on smarmy and already aware from *Nice-Matin* of the 'unfortunate accident that had befallen Monsieur Picasso'. It was especially unfortunate, if he might say so, in the case of a distinguished artist – a word, as Dora knew, that the painter Picasso detested. So the X-rays were taken and she sat beside a tense, glowering Picasso until the doctor re-emerged beaming almost ecstatically.

'Congratulations, *cher collègue* if I may so call you, since I am myself something of an artist in a very modest way. You have been remarkably fortunate. You have no breaks at all, not so much as a crack. No more than a few bruises that should heal nicely in a day or two. Would you like me to send the invoice to your address here or to Paris?'

'Don't look so disappointed!' said Dora, laughing, as they moved back to the car.

'You think that wasn't a total waste of time and money?!' growled Picasso.

'Of course not!'

'Well, what did he find, your 'artist'? Nothing!'

'Because there was nothing to find, for heaven's sake! Do you *want* to have broken bones?!'

Seeing her laughing, Marcel started off with some brio, but a glance at Picasso's face and a threatening clearing of the throat led him both to reduce his speed and to abandon his crooning liaison with the gypsy woman with the big black eyes. Meanwhile, Dora sat marvelling that this man who had a superstitious fear of the sea, of illness, of a car crash or of X-rays should behave with such lordly freedom in his painting. Was it because he was ill at ease in the world that he tried to transform it?

She stroked his arm gently and slipped her hand into his. She was beginning to understand the vulnerability of this Minotaur – and to feel the more for him.

'No, not so, sir' Sabartés was insisting in his brave effort at English, 'Monsieur Picasso was not hurted. I tell you, sir, no violence was done to him. He carries himself very well. And Sir Penrose did not suffer any wounds in addition. Thank you. Goodbye, sir.'

He replaced the receiver with an irritated grunt. If it was bad enough when Picasso travelled incognito, it was even worse when he didn't. For there was a mention in several papers that he had been in a car crash along with the young photographer Mademoiselle Dora Maar, his *amie*, implying his mistress, and that he had been obliged to have X-rays taken at the clinic in Cannes. And since there had also been a mention of Roland Penrose – one version hinting darkly that an English Surrealist might not be adept at driving on the right on French roads – one or two British newspapers had been inquiring as well.

And it wasn't only car crashes and mentions in newspapers. There was this sudden affair with Dora Maar. Alice Paalen was bad enough, but going on holiday for weeks on end with this damned woman Dora Maar – and not even incognito – was worse. Just when it looked as though, with his marriage ending, he could have settled into some sort of family life with Marie-Thérèse and the baby Maya – and provided a stable environment for Mercedes and himself – he had thrown everything up into the air again. Was he trying to live three or four different lives at once?! It didn't even dispose you to want to answer the door bell – it could be some other newspaper snoop or possibly Olga delivering some fresh threat or other. Let them wait outside there in the stifling Paris heat…

But since the bell-ringing persisted, he eventually went to open the door. To find Marie-Thérèse, flushed and distressed, with little Maya in her arms.

'I was just going away again. I thought you wouldn't open for me.'

'No no, of course not. Come in, Marie -Thérèse, come in…!'

'I had to carry Maya the whole way, I couldn't get the pram into the Metro. And it's so hot…!'

Sabartes brought her in, gave her a glass of Vittel, asked if she needed anything for the baby.

'No, she's all right for the moment. But you realise he missed her first birthday?! It was on the fifth.'

'Yes, I'm sure he's very sorry about that. But he should be back in Paris shortly.'

'He's not a bit sorry. He's down there with that woman. He writes

142

me these letters saying he loves me and the baby, and loves me more and more – and all the time he's screwing some fancy photographer.'

'Oh well, I'm not sure we can say that, Marie-Thérèse. She's one of a whole group of people – artists, writers and so on.'

'Well I know Pic, and if he isn't doing it with me – and he hasn't really been, if you must know – he must be doing it with somebody else. He can't just treat me like a tart, you know, Monsieur Sabartés...'

'Oh, but I'm quite sure...'

'It's all right for him, isn't it? But what am I supposed to do? I can't even imagine being with anybody else – anyway he's so jealous he wouldn't let me. But if he doesn't want me any more and treats me like this, then there's no point, is there? No point at all.'

'Oh, but you mustn't talk like that. I'm quite sure Pablo is fond of you.'

'But he's not fond enough to get a divorce, is he?! Or to take me on holiday with his fancy friends, is he?! So he asks me to write to him, but you can tell him that I'm not going to write to him! For he needn't think he can keep me in a closet even more now that I've got this poor, lovely little Maya so that it's even harder for me to think of...' she broke off, crying, '...ending it all... one way or the other way...'

'Oh, Marie-Thérèse, please, you really mustn't' he said, watching helplessly as she went on sobbing and weeping.

'For there isn't even anybody on my side, is there?' she went on sobbing. 'There's never anybody on my side...'

Sabartés sat for a moment looking at this pretty young weeping woman and at the little Maya, who had become agitated and was joining in her distress.

'Don't worry, Marie-Thérèse' he said. 'I'll be on your side.'

On returning to a rainy Paris, Dora had *Dora and the Minotaur* framed and given pride of place above her mantelpiece. In other respects, however, it was not a comfortable homecoming.

For a start, if she managed to convince her mother that she had no ill effects from the car crash, she clearly failed to convince her about Picasso. And while her mother, as she knew, worried about her much more than she normally cared to reveal, she was now sufficiently concerned to be more open. Asking pointedly whether Picasso was still married – and what age he was…

'I'm afraid, Dora' she told her after an awkward conversation, 'that your father's influence has not been good for you.'

And then there was that disturbing phone call from Nusch, to the effect that Jacqueline had left André Breton – possibly a spur-of-the-moment thing, she thought. She and Paul had visited André and found him having to cope alone with little Aube, while Jacqueline was off – apparently with some man – in either Algeria or Corsica, Nusch wasn't quite sure which. It was so painful and embarrassing, she said, that they hardly knew what to say to him.

Dora called that evening at 42 Rue Fontaine and found André alone with Aube. While he obviously felt humiliated – to the point of saying he would never love anyone else – he was also very dignified. He said he had not realised that she needed so much space for her painting and that there had also not been quite enough money for a child minder, but that he had now made a temporary arrangement and that, since Jacqueline had written to say she was coming home, he hoped that they could put this episode behind them. That being so, Dora did not seek to know the details of what seemed to be a passing fling and assured him she would help in any way she could.

Beyond that, the autumn weather was not good, nor was the news. At home the government was having difficulty with the economy and with unemployment. In Spain, General Franco's rebel forces had captured Toledo and Germany was sending in its élite Condor legion of ten thousand men. Meanwhile, at the broader European level, Hitler and Mussolini were forming the Axis alliance.

Picasso had been appointed honorary director of the Prado museum by the Spanish Republic, but had resisted suggestions that he might make at least a token visit to Barcelona, if not Madrid, to mark the event. He was preoccupied at this time with the final negotiations over his legal separation from Olga, who was demanding possession of Boisgeloup – which meant that he would need to have his paintings and sculptures removed in good time. It was clear to Dora, although it was never mentioned, that he had been seeing his Marie-Thérèse there at weekends, but it seemed that he was now being lent an alternative place by his old dealer Ambroise Vollard at Le Tremblay-sur-Mauldre, at a similar safe distance from Paris.

There had been no suggestion that Dora should move in with Picasso, nor would she have been entirely happy to live in that apartment in Rue La Boétie, especially since she never found Sabartés welcoming and saw little of his wife Mercedes. As the visible mistress of Picasso, as opposed to the concealed Marie-Thérèse, she shared his social and artistic life, while retaining her independence. He phoned her every day, they visited galleries together, they frequented the Deux Magots and the Café de Flore, and often dined together or with friends at the Brasserie Lipp. They also on one occasion drove down to the Saint-Benoît-sur-Loire in the centre of France to pay a surprise visit to the poet and painter Max Jacob, a very close old Jewish friend from Picasso's early years in Paris who had converted to Catholicism. But the greatest satisfaction, as a damp dull autumn gave way to a harsh wintry cold that lasted well beyond Christmas, was that for much of the time they were not only socializing and sleeping together, but working together and learning from each other.

For Picasso was especially interested in Dora's experiments with photoengraving, which had already gone far in moving photography into the domain of art. And he followed intently her procedures as she created pieces for an exhibition of her work at the Galerie de Beaune in the New Year. He particularly followed the sequence of steps involved in building up the disquieting image of a headless doll in an off-the-shoulder dress in a sinister curving cloister with a disproportionately small figure in the distance – a piece which André Breton, who had seen it when he dropped in one day, had described as a self-portrait of the unconscious. In these experiments, as Picasso recognised, she was getting close to the drive behind his own work.

However, Picasso was not interested merely in blending photography with engraving. While he mirrored Dora's techniques for creating increasingly complex effects – by modifying the length and degree of exposure, or controlling the image by graduated screening of the negative – he was going beyond this by painting the glass plate itself and creating further effects on that. In fact, he was performing what amounted to a determined takeover of photography, reducing it to the rank of artist's materials like paints or brushes – subordinating it to painting.

'Are you trying to kill off photography altogether and do me out of a job?' she asked him jokingly.

But he was clearly trying to do more than that. For he was not so much 'killing off photography' as killing off the principle of resemblance which it embodied. In his Cubist paintings, where the subject might be seen as through a prism, it had still been possible for the viewer to reconstitute it as normally perceived, but in rendering faces he was now moving even beyond the stylised distortions of cartoon or caricature. In the *Reclining Nude With Stars*, which he had begun at Mougins and had now completed, the only objective reference to Dora was the colours of her nail lacquer. The nude body was a physical impossibility while the face, with its oddly placed eyes and mouth reminded her of some of the portraits of Olga which she had noticed at Rue La Boétie, where the face was reduced to a malignant scream. Picasso was moving beyond resemblance towards an algebra of ideograms, a painting of signs and symbols.

And the consequence, Dora reflected, was both exciting and rather frightening. For by abandoning any reference to external reality, he was left to paint directly out of his own unconscious – Picasso painting a largely unknown Picasso. Which meant that, except at the level of technique, he did not understand what he was doing. He was walking a tightrope – and so, she sensed, was she.

Dora was enjoying the crunch of her winter boots on the fresh snow as she walked down the Rue La Boétie towards Number 23. It was late February and this white, silent, almost funereal Paris seemed eerily in tune with what already promised to be a strange 1937. Franco's troops were mounting an offensive against Madrid, there were further treason trials in Moscow and, at home, the Popular Front government had been forced by economic problems to call a halt to the reforms.

Yet her mood was buoyant. As the consort of Picasso she could not help noticing that she now enjoyed a quite special status. Also, he was proclaiming that he didn't know a woman could be so intelligent and he was regularly doing portraits of her – the latest being a 'Spanish' one of her wearing a mantilla. Morever, he had been commissioned by the Spanish Republican government to paint a large mural for the Spanish pavilion at the Paris World Fair due to open in May and, although he had expressed some doubts about the project, she was looking forward to being closely involved with it. Meanwhile, he had been asked to contribute some artwork for a fundraising event for wounded Republican soldiers and their families, and she had offered to do the photography involved. They were now meeting to discuss what might be appropriate before going out to dinner.

But having crunched her way to Number 23, she had to ring the bell three times before Sabartés appeared, in blue dressing gown and beret.

'Mademoiselle?' he said coldly, without moving aside.

'May I come in?' asked Dora with a slight smile. 'It's rather cold out here.'

'I'll take you in.'

He led her with some formality, as though she was not a regular visitor, into the reception room where he had his desk.

'Will you tell Picasso I've arrived?' she said, removing her scarf and beginning to loosen the buttons of her coat.

'I'm afraid I can't do that, He's not here.'

She stopped loosening the buttons and looked at him.

'Where is he?'

'He's off dealing with a family matter.'

'A family matter?'

'Yes, the sort of thing that crops up in families from time to time. His little daughter is ill – and of course he's quite besotted with her. They both are.'

'You're saying he has left for Le Tremblay?'

'Yes, that's their new country place. They like their weekends in the country and of course he gets some sketching done then.' He gestured towards several folders lying on a side table. 'I expect you've seen all the recent stuff, have you?'

Dora hesitated, sensing a false casualness about his manner.

'I'm not sure that I have' she said.

'Oh well then, since you're so used to these things after all, I expect he wouldn't mind terribly…'

He pulled out the second folder, entitled *Boisgeloup/Le Tremblay 36-37* and opened it for her. Leafing over it briefly, she saw that it contained some nice studies of the child and a number of Marie-Thérèse, including some very frank nude treatments. It also contained, startlingly, a portrait of her in exactly the same posture as in her own 'Spanish' portrait, wearing the exact same mantilla.

She closed the folder and looked levelly for some moments at Sabartés.

'You resent me, Jaume, don't you?'

'Not at all, Mademoiselle. I recognise you have a professional interest in Pablo.'

'Professional?'

'But perhaps you might recognise that his close relationship with Marie-Thérèse is a very longstanding one. And that he does have family responsibilities.'

'I think we should perhaps respect his own view of those responsibilities. Did he leave a message? Or any artwork? I offered to make slides of any engravings he might wish to contribute to this fund for wounded Republican soldiers.'

'Yes, he did leave this. He said it was the only readymade series of engravings that might be suitable – that wasn't too personal for the purpose.'

As he handed her the top folder, she opened it and flicked briefly through the set of engravings of the Minotaur.

'I've seen one or two of these, but I'll have a look at the rest and see if they're 'not too personal for the purpose', as he put it.'

She turned to go and Sabartés saw her with almost comic formality into the street.

But as she started to walk down towards the Champs-Elysées, the crunch of her winter boots on the snow sounded much louder – and angrier – than before.

'I'm sorry about yesterday' Picasso was saying on the telephone. 'I had to leave at very short notice. It was an emergency.'

'So I gathered. I hope the child is better?'

'She is, but I don't quite know what Sabartés told you…?'

'Well he told me rather more than I needed to know in fact. About your family responsibilities and the sketching you get done out there at weekends, and whatnot.'

'So what *did* he tell you?'

'Oh he didn't just tell me' she said with a laugh. 'He showed me the sketches.'

'Did he…?!'

'Yes, in the *Boisgeloup/Le Tremblay 36-37* folder. I did like some of the studies of the child, though some of the nude treatments of your model – Marie-Thérèse isn't she called? – I found excessively gynaecological.'

'You did, did you?'

'Well, you do seem to be fascinated by the female crotch' she said laughingly. 'It's almost as though you'd like one like that of your very own.'

'Well I've heard of penis envy, but not vagina envy. Perhaps we could swap sometime.'

'Somehow I don't think you'd find that comfortable, Picasso.'

'Meanwhile, I'd be interested to know what you thought of that Minotaur series. Are you free tomorrow at five?'

'No, but I might be free the day after.'

'So I'll see you here at five on Thursday?'

'No, I'd prefer to meet here in the studio.'

'All right' said Picasso tersely. 'If that's what the lady would prefer.'

But he might well have been having even terser words with Sabartés by the time he turned up on Thursday at five, for he apologised for having placed her in a difficult situation and for Sabartés's action in showing her the folder of the drawings of Marie-Thérèse.

'Oh that's all right' said Dora airily. 'We're hardly going to descend to the vulgarity of being jealous – not even in a bourgeois *quartier* crawling with money and privilege like this one. I've just made some tea. Would you like some?'

'Yes, why not?'

'You know, Picasso' she said as she poured the tea into two striped cups, 'I sometimes wonder how you can bear to live in this area.'

'By not noticing.'

'Quite. I just wonder how long you can go on not noticing' she said, handing him his cup and saucer. 'Is that all right for you?'

'Yes it is.'

'I find it a little sad, actually.'

'Sad?'

'Well, look at you, going on living in that shell of a bourgeois apartment inside the ruins of a bourgeois marriage – and nursemaided by an old nanny like Sabartés. And proposing, I imagine, to project your weekend erotic fantasies on to the wall of the Spanish pavilion at the Paris World Fair? You did say you were thinking of the *Painter and his Model* as a suitable subject, didn't you?'

'Yes I did.'

'Well, I examined the Minotaur etchings you'd left for me. I thought we might look over them together – when you've finished your tea.'

'I have finished my tea, thank you' he said with an ironical glint in the dark eyes. 'It was delicious.'

'Good' she said as she took the cup and saucer from him, opened the folder and laid it on the table between them, 'There's a clear sequence to them, isn't there?'

'Yes, I would say so.'

'This I'd seen before, of course' she said, holding up the one showing the Minotaur with the bushy tail carousing with a reclining nude. 'He looks contented in his middle age, doesn't he? And then this other one I saw that day we went to Boisgeloup, if you remember.'

'I remember.'

'Ah yes' she said picking up the second etching, 'this is the very different Minotaur, dark and hairy, ferociously assaulting this poor young thing. A powerful composition, I must say.'

'Thank you, Dora' he said ironically.

'She doesn't seem too responsive, poor girl!' said Dora with a laugh. 'But then it isn't really about her, or even about sex as such, is it?'

'Isn't it?'

'No, it's more about his rage and resentment at the desire she innocently causes. That's what's so infuriating about these plump juicy bimbos, isn't it? You may not think much of them, but they still have this power to make you want to fuck them.'

'At least they do have the power – perhaps more than some others.'

'I'll ignore that remark!' said Dora with a smile. 'Of course we can forget about Theseus killing the Minotaur and finding his way out of the labyrinth and all that old classical stuff. This is all about the poor old Minotaur himself, isn't it?'

'If you say so.'

'Especially' she went on, picking up the study of a blind Minotaur being led away from an adult Marie-Thérèse figure by a small girl carrying a dove, 'when he's blind, and searching, and lost in what looks like his own personal labyrinth. With the sea suggesting eternity, I suppose?'

'You could be right.'

'And the boatman waiting to collect him for the last journey to death? Except that he's being saved and led away by the child with the dove. Who of course has the same face as your grown-up Marie-Thèrése, hasn't she? Is this an actual memory of her as a small child?'

'No, of course not!' he said, his face reddening suddenly.

'So you've made her even more of a child then. And now she's absolutely central to this night-time version of the same scene' she said, picking up the next etching. 'All those big stars your blind Minotaur can't see. His only hope is this innocent little child. It's beautiful, Picasso – and it's awful…'

'Why is it awful?' he asked, disconcerted.

'Because you can sense how the whole sinister business is going to come to its inevitable end in this one' she said, picking up another night-time scene in which the Minotaur with his horns has ripped open the mare's belly to reveal the naked female body inside it.

'But what's sinister about it?'

'What's sinister is putting a naked woman inside a horse's belly. And what's even more sinister is killing off your grown-up Marie-Thérèse along with the mare, so that she's only left as the child. Shining her little light on the terrible murderous thing he has done – with him trying to shield his eyes from it. It's shocking, Picasso!' she said, her eyes filled with tears suddenly, 'truly shocking…!'

'But why are you so upset?' he asked uncertainly.

'Because there may never be a way out of that labyrinth. It's the same old paralysis, isn't it, the old fear of women…?'

'What do you mean?'

'Can't you see?! His desire for the woman is bound up with rape and rage and murder. He can only accept her in the pre-sexual form of the small child. That's what's so sinister, so tragic…'

She closed the folder with an air of finality, pushed it towards him along the table, got to her feet and stood briefly looking out of the window at people passing in the Rue d'Astorg.

'So I take it that you didn't do any slides?' he said, getting to his feet also.

'No' she said, turning towards him, 'I really couldn't present this stuff at a fundraising do for wounded Republican soldiers and their families.'

'Why not, for God's sake?!'

'Well it's supposed to be an anti-Fascist event, Picasso.'

'Are you saying I'm some sort of Fascist?!'

'Oh, I'm not saying you're *consciously* a Fascist or an old bourgeois sugar-daddy exploiting that poor child-woman of a model of yours…'

'What the fuck do you mean? You've never even met her!'

'Well if you keep her locked away for purely personal use like a slave girl in a gilded cage…!'

'Well now' he said mockingly, mimicking her voice, 'you wouldn't just be 'descending to the vulgarity of being jealous', would you?'

She slapped his face suddenly, he slapped hers in response, and they were standing staring at each other when the telephone rang. And went on ringing for what seemed like a very long time before it stopped.

'I'm sorry, Dora' he said.

'Yes well, so am I' she said with a slight comic grimace. 'I don't normally slap people.'

'Well, you're the first woman who has ever managed to slap me. It's a shock.' He grinned suddenly. 'Quite a sexy shock!'

'That wasn't the message! Look, Picasso' she said with a faintly weary smile, 'your Minotaur was just a high priest of King Minos in Crete who kept order by scaring the life out of a poor ignorant populace with a bull mask on his head – presumably a more convincing one than your little boy's cardboard version.'

'He was a fraud, you mean – like me?'

'He was even more of a fraud because he was probably just as scared as the people he was scaring. So stop hiding in this decadent bourgeois *quartier*, Picasso. Get a studio over on the Left Bank or somewhere, stop living this aristocratic existence shielded from the world by old Sabartés.'

'Get a job as a house painter, you mean – or as a car mechanic with Renault?'

'I mean take an interest in what's going on all around you – not in some mythical old labyrinth, but here and now, in 1937. There's rape and rage and murder going on for real out there.'

'On both sides, as I observe.'

'Yes, but you can't sit on the fence any more. It's not just a Spanish civil war we're looking at now, but a *European* civil war. And you know what that means…'

'No' he said with a grin, 'but I've a funny feeling you're going to tell me'

'It means there's no fence left to sit on. It means the choice is between Fascism and anti-fascism. It means you've got to be either the hammer or the anvil.'

'But it sounds, Dora' he said with a laugh, 'as though you're the hammer and I'm the anvil!'

'Oh, this is hopeless!' she said, turning away impatiently. 'We'd better stop even *trying* to communicate!'

'Oh well, I don't think it's quite as bad as that…'

'Yes it is, it's pointless. Anyway, it's not fair of me to try to influence you.'

'What does that mean?'

'Well, you're not a young man after all' she said deliberately. 'You have your own settled way of life. I have no right to be disappointed…'

'You'll have me dead and buried in a minute! What's so disappointing?'

'Oh, just that it's such an honour to be asked to do that mural when your country is fighting for its life against Fascism – and you don't even seem to recognise it.'

'Of course I recognise it.'

'An enormous mural in between the Soviet Russian pavilion and the Nazi German pavilion, it's a historic opportunity.'

'A historic opportunity to display the same blown-up bollocks that they'll be displaying!' he scoffed. 'I may have doubts about painting, but I'm buggered if I'm going to paint propaganda.'

'Nobody's asking you to paint propaganda. But could you not at least make some gesture towards the big wide world outside your own tormented little fantasy land?'

'But where else do you think the painting comes from, Dora?! I can only get at your big wide world through me – and even then I don't know what me is. That's why I was painting so much at night. Because painting is like working out a dream, or even a nightmare, and I never really know what it means' – he laughed sardonically – 'until some feminist intellectual with brightly coloured nail lacquer explains it to me And if you think that's an 'aristocratic existence', it can be very very scary.'

'And is that the real reason you stopped painting?' she asked after a moment. 'It got too scary?'

'I don't know, but it was certainly eerie painting all alone in the middle of the night, feeling somehow guilty about chasing after this dangerous dream. I could hear my own breathing, I even felt like the matador facing up to his hidden terror of the bull, or' – he gave a sudden nervous laugh – 'like some lonely new God re-creating this whole fucked-up world and everything in it.'

'Including your Marie Thérèse? And the likes of me…?'

'Of course! Don't you know that real painters are cannibals?'

And he was laughing as he seized her by the hair and drew her towards him. And still laughing after she slapped his face.

'But it's your own fault, Dora.'

'How could it be my fault?!'

'Because you've got me working again – you've awakened the sleeping cannibal' he said, stroking her face. 'And I doubt if I could

155

even attempt that mural if you weren't there to slap me around the place.'

'You devil, Picasso!.'

For he was still holding her by the hair, fingering her lips, running his hand up under her skirt and into her knickers to find her crotch, grinning as she twisted and struggled, and kissing her violently on the lips until she was responding, reluctantly, then willingly and then passionately as he was pulling her skirt up above her waist and unbuttoning his flies and asking her grinningly if she didn't want to fuck...

'You old devil...!'

7

Sabartés was reading *Le Populaire,* or at least he was going through the motions of reading *Le Populaire,* for he was preoccupied about the atmosphere in the apartment over the previous week or two.

He left down the newspaper and looked out of the window. The days were longer now that it was halfway through the month, but the Rue La Boétie did not look any more engaging in the cold March daylight. Even granting that Picasso had a superstitious fear of any change to his domestic routine, Sabartés knew him well enough to sense by his recent uneasy, slightly offhand manner that something was troubling him that might uncomfortably affect himself. Could he be planning to bring that Dora Maar into the apartment on a permanent basis…?

These reflections were interrupted by the noisy arrival of Picasso himself, wearing his usual battered *canadienne*.

'Ah, you're there' he said.

'I believe so. And you're there.'

'Yeah, we're both here.'

'Though that's probably neither here nor there.'

'No.'

Sabartés watched him hesitate, then take off the *canadienne*, then hesitate again as he ran his finger speculatively along the grain of the side table.

'How is Dora?' he asked finally.

'Fine, fine' he said in his offhand way, then paused. 'Actually, Jaume...'

'Yes?'

'Well, she has been looking around for a more suitable studio for me. One big enough to take this bloody mural for the Spanish pavilion.'

'So you've finally found a subject for it then?'

'Well I have and I haven't, but it's the sheer size of the thing, you see. And Dora thinks she has found this studio over on the Left Bank. Just round the corner from her place, as it happens.'

'That's convenient' said Sabartés. 'Where is it?'

'The Rue des Grands-Augustins. It's a big attic where actors used to rehearse and where that leftist outfit Contre-Attaque held its meetings.'

But Sabartés sensed that this surplus of detail, and the pause that followed it, was a way of not saying something else.

'Pablo, you're not thinking, are you, of selling this apartment and moving in with her permanently?'

'No, I'm not proposing to do that.'

'That's a relief.'

'But of course, now that I'll be working over there, I'll be spending less time here.'

'That would certainly seem to follow!' said Sabartés with a laugh. 'So I'll be holding the fort here on my own?'

'Except that there would no longer be any real work for you to do, would there? And any routine correspondence could be handled by me – or by Dora herself, I imagine.'

'You 'imagine'?'

'I mean I'm sure she would be willing if I asked her.'

'Are you saying, Pablo' asked Sabartés slowly, 'that Dora wants me to leave?'

'There you are, you see, blaming Dora!' Picasso burst out, slapping the table suddenly. 'How do you expect her to come here when you're sticking those sketches of Marie-Thérèse under her nose and interfering in my private life, eh?!' He calmed down suddenly, looked embarrassed. 'I'm sorry, Jaume, but I think it would be better.'

'I see…'

'Well, she's the only woman I've ever been able to talk to about painting – or anything else for that matter.'

'And she just happens to be young and attractive into the bargain?'

'I need her, Jaume.'

'For a man who has a problem with women, Pablo, you always seem to need to have a problem with two of them at once. I'll be gone by this evening.'

'So where are you off to today?' asked Madame Markovitch over the Sunday morning *café au lait*, in a tone which implied that Dora might be rushing off to any place this side of China.

'Well, I'm going to see Jacqueline, which means I'll first have to find some suitable present for her little girl Aube. Who must be sixteen months old by now.'

'Ah, Jacqueline?' said her father, who had met and liked – and probably fancied – Jacqueline. 'How is she?'

'I think she's fine. They had some marital problems, but I expect they've blown over.'

'Marital problems?' said her mother ironically, as though she had never heard of such things.

'Fortunately' said Monsieur Markovitch in his smoothly sardonic way, 'your mother has been spared any such problems. And are you busy in the studio?'

'Yes, and you'll be interested to know, *Maman*, that I've been doing commercial ads for hats this past week, which means I'm getting more free hats, Schiaparelli this time. I must bring them along for you to try on.'

'Oh, fashions have changed so much since I was selling hats, I don't think I'd dare go out in one of those new-fangled creations.'

'No, it mightn't go down too well at Mass' said Monsieur Markovitch slyly.

Madame Markovitch ignored the remark, apart from looking at Dora to ensure that she appreciated what her mother had to endure.

'So how is your friend Picasso?' she asked warily.

'He's well, I think. He's trying to work up a subject for a mural for the Spanish pavilion at the World Fair.'

'So will it be Surrealist or something?'

'Well it shouldn't be *too* incomprehensible' said Dora with a smile. 'It actually sounds very conventional – the *Painter and his Model*.'

'That's if anybody ever gets to see it!' said her father. 'What's your Popular Front government going to do about this Paris World Fair, Dora? It's a shambles, isn't it?'

It was true that the whole project was terribly far behind schedule, so much so that even some at the Spanish embassy were complaining. Of course there had been the flooding of the Seine early in the Spring, but the main problem was that the workers wanted the strict application of the new forty-hour week and were asking for increased wages into the bargain.

'It's blackmail by the unions, *Le Figaro* is saying' said her mother.

'But the workers aren't being entirely unreasonable, *Maman* – they're worried that once the Fair is over they'll be out of a job again.

'One way or the other they're sabotaging their own government' said her father. We're well into April and they're clearly not going to be able to open on May the First.'

'Yes, but let's hope it won't open too late. And, you know, there are going to be fifty countries participating and thousands of exhibitors. Let's remember the aim is to promote peace and co-operation between the nations.'

'Except that nobody seems to have told the Germans! Or the Soviets for that matter! I passed that way the other day and I found those two pavilions squaring up to each other on the same bank of the Seine, each as pompous and aggressive as the other. And I think they're telling us something, Dora – that in this ideological war between them they're not going to stop at bad architecture. I'm afraid that in the present European climate this Paris World Fair may be doing more harm than good.'

Dora was strolling over the Pont St-Michel in the mid-April sunshine on her way to see Picasso at the new attic studio in the Rue des Grands-Augustins. He had phoned to ask her to call in on her way home from work, to discuss some problem concerning the mural for the Spanish pavilion. And since there had been a certain underlying strain in the relationship over the previous few weeks, she was not exactly rushing to meet him.

To begin with, he had been delighted with the new studio to the point of saying, as though unaware of the dust floating around in the old attic, that he could breathe freely there at last. But then, as though the absence of Sabartés was beginning to weigh upon him, he started to complain about the inconvenience the move was causing and to suggest indirectly that it was all the fault of Dora. That was until he suddenly switched to calling Sabartés a treacherous swine for having gratuitously, as he put it, given evidence to the magistrate adjudicating on his legal separation from Olga.

But Sabartés, as Dora had learnt over lunch one day from Nusch, had done rather more than that. For he had seemingly been avenging himself by telling all and sundry that Picasso was mean with money, that he left his mother and sister in Barcelona in poverty and would not allow them to sell any of his pictures and finally – a point of more direct interest to Dora – that he was violent with women. And if she had heard this from Nusch, it was almost certain that Picasso would have heard it as well, from one of his Spanish acquaintances at least.

'So you've got a problem, Picasso?' she said as she arrived.

'You can say that again!'

'So what is it?' she asked, amused by his expression, which

seemed both sullen and uneasy. 'You haven't changed your mind about the *Painter and his Model*?'

'Of course not. That's not the point.'

'So what *is* the point?'

'The point is I've received the measurements for the mural: 7.82 metres by 3.51 metres. That's bloody enormous.'

'Well then, you'll just have to do a bloody enormous Painter and a bloody enormous Model' she said laughingly. 'What's the problem?'

'The attic isn't high enough, that's the problem' he said, pointing to a measuring tape lying on the floor. 'It's a good ten centimetres too low.'

'Ah!'

'Exactly!'

'But the canvas will be on a frame, won't it?'

'Obviously.'

'Well, can't you just lean it a little against that long beam there?'

'I don't know. I suppose so. It's all such a mess. And then there's that bastard Sabartés…'

She sat on a stool and watched him move uneasily around the studio.

'Sabartés?' she said.

'Yes' he said and paused. 'I don't know if you heard anything…?'

'I did hear that he had been saying critical things about you.'

'You see?! He even said I was an exhibitionist, for God's sake!'

'He also seems to have said that you beat women.'

'What nonsense! I might have lost my temper once or twice with Olga, but I have no need to beat women.' He grinned. 'Even when they slap me around as you did.'

'Just so long as it stays like that, Picasso' said Dora sweetly, getting to her feet. 'And now I've a few things to go and do before dinner.'

'I'll come down with you.'

'So Sabartés said you were an exhibitionist, did he?' she said with a mock-innocent smile as they went downstairs.

'Yes. Would you believe it?!'

There was music in the background at the Deux Magots, Yvonne Printemps singing *C'est la saison d'amour,* but nobody on the terrace was listening. And nobody would have agreed this evening – not with the grim black-and-white photograph on *Ce Soir* being passed around – that it was the season for love.

'It's shattering' said Dora, staring at the headline saying 'Holy City of the Basques in Flames.'

'Guernica reduced to ashes... fleeing civilians bombed and machine-gunned...' read Nusch in an almost wondering voice from the newspaper. 'It's barely believable.'

'It's all too believable' said Eluard grimly.

The event had taken place early in the week, there had been conflicting reports about it and it was only now, on this Friday evening, that the newspaper was presenting an apparently reliable account, complete with photographs, of what had been done to this ancestral capital of the Basque people, Guernica. It seemed that the German Condor Legion, using Junkers and Messerschmitts supported by elements of the Italian airforce, had carried out successive bombing raids in broad daylight, flying frighteningly low over the undefended town and strafing civilians trying to escape. Within a few hours Guernica was largely in ruins, while it was claimed that there were up to 1,800 casualties among the population of around 5,000.

'But it wasn't near the front, it wasn't a military target' Dora was saying. 'It was pointless.'

'That *was* the point' said Eluard.

'Because it had such enormous symbolical importance for the Basques?'

'Yes, and precisely because it was a defenceless, non-military target.'

'Old people' said Nusch, crying as she looked at the photographs, 'children, babies, pregnant women… It's terrifying.'

'It's meant to be terrifying, Nusch. It's terror bombing, Blitzkrieg, total war.'

'With no such thing as civilians any more, that's the message' said Dora.

'And it's merely a rehearsal for what Hitler will be doing to us in a year or two, if we don't all wake up' said Eluard. 'Another war, my God, another world war…!'

'And these same Nazi murderers are all set to display their wares at our Paris World Fair…!' Dora was saying as the short stocky figure of Picasso could be seen rolling towards them along the crowded boulevard.

He greeted them in turn, pulled up a chair, asked the waiter for a Vittel, gazed at them in turn and said with a dry smile that he had seen them look happier.

'That was before this happened' said Dora, pushing the newspaper photo towards him.

'Ah yes, Guernica.'

'Isn't it shocking, Pablo?' asked Paul.

'Yes it is. Though it doesn't seem altogether clear yet…'

'What do you mean: "it's not clear"?' asked Dora sharply.

'Well some papers are saying it was the Republican forces themselves that did it…'

'What?!' exclaimed Dora, pointing to the photograph. 'Are you telling me the Basques would do that to themselves?!'

'*Le Figaro* is suggesting that the Republican forces could have done it to cover their retreat.'

'But that's grotesque! *Le Figaro* is only saying that because it supports Franco!'

'And because it's banking on Hitler attacking the Russian Communists rather than us' said Eluard.

'All I'm saying is that it's not yet totally clear, Paul. And strange things do happen in civil war…'

'What strange things?!' interrupted Dora.

'Well, don't you at this very moment have Anarchists fighting Communists – a civil war amongst the Republicans themselves…?'

'Oh, that's just a cop-out, Picasso!' said Dora.

'Things are perhaps more complicated than you think, Dora!'

'Well' said Paul, to calm things down, 'we'll soon find out if it really was German bombers – though I confess nothing else would seem to make much sense.'

'Or any sense!' Dora muttered.

'*Garçon*' roared Picasso suddenly, '*ma Vittel, nom de Dieu!*'

'*Mais voici, Monsieur*' said the waiter, who was in fact at his elbow. 'But *Monsieur*' he added disarmingly, 'never drinks his Vittel.'

'That's neither here nor there. If I order a Vittel, I expect a Vittel!'

'*Parfaitement, Monsieur.*'

And the waiter went off muttering audibly that he didn't drink Vittel either, leaving Picasso looking slightly ridiculous.

'Anyway, Pablo' said Paul, 'I gather you've got yourself a larger studio. Does that mean you have decided on a theme for your mural?'

'Yes, more or less. Though I haven't gone beyond a few preliminary sketches.'

'Miró has already finished his own mural, I gather – it's on the theme of the Reaper. So what have you chosen?'

'Well, it's a traditional subject…'

'A *very* traditional subject' said Dora ironically.

'It's only a painting, Dora – it's not going to change the world. Anyway, Paul, it's about painting.'

'A painting about painting' said Dora cuttingly.

'I'm calling it the *Painter and his Model*.'

'And why not?!' said Dora, 'Everything is falling about our ears and Picasso is going to cover the wall beside the Nazi pavilion with the Painter and his suitably Aryan-looking blonde model!'

'Do you want me to cover it with dark-haired anti-Fascist

feminists and revolutionary slogans?!' asked Picasso angrily. 'Or just copy this photograph here?!'

'Oh I'm sure none of us would want any kind of innocent socialist realism' said Paul laughingly in an attempt to avert the row that was brewing. 'It's just that this news about Guernica is so devastating. I can tell you this coming Monday is going to be something.'

'Yes. the May Day parade' said Nusch, trying to sound sprightly. 'The biggest for twenty years, they say.'

'And perhaps the last chance to demonstrate against Franco and Fascism everywhere' said Eluard grimly.

Picasso, still visibly angry, was sitting turning his full glass of Vittel round and round on the table, spilling it slightly in the process. Dora, face flushed and trying to control herself, was staring into the middle distance. Yvonne Printemps had come around again in the background, assuring them that it was the season for love...

'Pablo' asked Nusch innocently, to break the silence, 'will you be joining us on the march?'

There was a pause in which Picasso and Dora glanced at each other.

'Well actually, Nusch' he said eventually, 'I'm going to be otherwise engaged this weekend.'

'Oh well, if you're going to be otherwise engaged...' said Paul.

'You must understand, Paul' said Dora bitterly, 'that Picasso is going to be otherwise engaged this weekend. Guernica or no Guernica, Fascism or no Fascism, Picasso is going to be otherwise engaged this weekend!'

'Yes' said Picasso harshly, 'I'm going to be otherwise engaged this weekend!'

'Just look at this photograph!' said Dora, jabbing down at it with purple fingernails. 'Wholesale slaughter of women and children in his own country, but Picasso can't join the May Day protests because Picasso is going to be otherwise engaged this weekend. And that' she said, holding up the newspaper in front of him, 'is because Picasso is scared to face up to the reality in black-and-white there in front of his face!'

He snatched the paper from her, got to his feet angrily, then stood for a moment staring at the photograph.

'Yes, black-and-white!' he said with a sardonic glint in the dark eyes. 'Black-and-white is what it is!'

And he was soon lost in the crowd on the boulevard. Leaving the others staring at one another to the sound of Yvonne Printemps singing *C'est la saison d'amour*.

Dora was just finishing a shoot on the following Wednesday with Assia, perhaps her favourite model, when the phone rang.

'*Bonjour* Dora' said the sardonic voice. 'I was wondering if you could suggest the name of a good photographer.'

It was Picasso, who hadn't been in touch since the argument on the previous Friday at the Deux Magots.

'Well I might just be able to advise you there' she said coolly, 'but I'll have to phone you back. I'm tied up with Assia.'

'That sounds sexy. Would you like me to come and join in?''

'I think that might strain your resources.'

She wrapped up the shoot, said goodbye to Assia and called him back. His voice, when it came, was teasing and jocular, but perhaps a little self-protective.

'So how did the May Day Parade go?'

'Very well indeed: lots of people, bands and speeches. How did your weekend go?'

'Hard to tell. I was working all through it.'

'On the famous *Painter and his Model*?'

'Oh no, I've dropped that!'

'Have you?!'

'Yes, and since this mural is such a big thing it will doubtless have to go through a number of stages. So I thought it would be good if I could find a photographer to record the whole sequence.'

'I think I might be able to suggest one. I'll call in on the way home.'

He had certainly been working very hard, to judge by the clutter she found in the attic when she got there. There was a scattering of drawings on the floor, mostly in pencil, others in pencil and gouache, and some torn up or tossed away unfinished. They were studies in his usual cartoon-like style of particular details, such as a screaming face or the agonized head of a wounded mare – which also featured on a stark oil on canvas study propped up against the wall.

'You've been busy, haven't you?' she said.

'I'm going to be even busier. I've ordered the canvas, but he can't deliver it for another week. He has to concoct a folding frame, so that we can get it up and down the stairs.'

'So that will leave you only two or three weeks to paint it?'

'Yes, I'll have to use ordinary household paint, I fancy, gallons and gallons of Ripolin.'

'And those are thematic studies for the whole mural, are they?' asked Dora, looking across at two larger treatments, in pencil and oil on plywood, propped up against the far wall.

'More or less.'

He lit a cigarette and sat on a chair watching her as she went over and examined the plywood sheets, which presented two versions of the same scene.

The first portrayed, in Picasso's very schematic manner, a bull with a human face running guiltily away after apparently having killed the mare, which had collapsed on top of a dead warrior carrying a spear. Meanwhile a woman was leaning from a top window on the right, holding out a lamp as though to bear witness to this act of wickedness. In the second version, the bull was just a bull and was staring away from the killing as though indifferent, while the mare was rearing up in agony and the fallen warrior looked more like a woman – whose profile, like that of the woman with the lamp, was reminiscent of that of Marie-Thérèse.

168

'So?' said Picasso eventually.

'Well, it's not the *Painter and his Model*!'

'Not unless the bull and the mare are becoming my real models – as you hinted some time ago.'

'Well, you're obviously using the same elements as before. It will depend what you do with them, I suppose.'

'You don't sound wildly enthusiastic, do you?'

'But it's too early to say anything useful, isn't it? Especially since you'd presumably need to develop the scene further to fill up the space?'

'I've no idea how it will develop. That's why I thought it might be a good idea to record the different stages – and that it might be nice to discuss our mural over dinner at Le Catalan.'

'*Our* mural?'

'Of course. Wasn't it you who made me change my mind about the subject?'

'When?'

'Last Friday evening at the Deux Magots.'

'How?'

'By holding up that photograph in front of my face and insisting that the truth was there in black-and-white, black-and-white. So it will be our black-and-white painting.'

'And will it have a title, our black-and-white painting?'

'*Guernica* – what else?!'

One afternoon a week later, Dora was on her way to photograph the first day's work on the actual mural. She had got Manuel to bring the necessary equipment from the Rue d'Astorg in the Hispano-Suiza, had bought an extra lamp so that the canvas could be lit evenly from both sides, and had already done the set-up in the attic. She was now looking forward to seeing how far Picasso had brought together the various studies he had been working on into a coherent whole that might live up to its title *Guernica*.

At least there were no other visitors at this time of the afternoon. Whereas there had been no casual callers to the apartment in Rue La Boétie, Picasso's move to the Latin Quarter was encouraging acquaintances to drop in. Moreover, his favourite restaurant Le Catalan was nearby and some of the Spanish regulars tended to come along before lunch. And as Picasso was seen as controversial and a celebrity even before the word had spread that he was painting a mural called *Guernica*, a regular group of interested parties was tending to form around midday. The problem then was how to get rid of them, since Picasso always worked alone, the only exception for the mural being Dora – and just possibly Eluard, who might look in briefly and unobtrusively.

'So the courtiers have all gone?' asked Dora brightly as she entered the attic.

He was sitting on the floor in a striped sailor's jersey, cleaning his hands with a rag.

'Yes, thank God. I don't know why they come here.'

'You know perfectly well why they come here' she scoffed. 'My God, but it's big, this thing!'

She moved back to get a better view of the whole length of the canvas, which stretched right across the wall of the attic. The scene was basically as before except that to give added width there was now a screaming woman on each side, one holding a dead child, while the house from which the woman with the lamp was leaning was now on fire. Also, the defeated warrior was now holding a broken sword rather than a spear and raising a defiant fist.

'So…?' came the ironical voice of Picasso.

'Well…'

'You think it's the same old Fascist fantasies, do you? The same old Picasso bric-a-brac of over-personal bits and pieces – the brutal bull, the wounded mare, the lamp and all that?'

'Not quite' said Dora lightly. 'We've now got a bull with a faintly human face instead of a man with a bull's face. Also the child holding the lamp has grown into the woman holding the lamp. And then there are these other women, one with her dead baby, screaming up at the sky…'

'So you think I'm improving, do you?'

'I think' she said smilingly, 'that you're perhaps beginning to put your Spanish obsessions – with sex, violence, suppressed Catholic guilt and all that – into a public context.'

'Sounds as though I'll soon be exposing myself to those classy females on the Boulevard St-Germain.'

'I wouldn't risk it, Picasso, if I were you.'

'You mean they'd have me arrested?'

'I mean that with all those fancy boutiques around they'd never even notice. Which might be seriously deflating to your oversized Spanish… ego.'

'Ouf!' he said with a grin.

'All I was saying, to be serious, is that your symbolical sexual struggle between the bull and the mare could now have a political dimension. Indeed, it will obviously have to, won't it?'

'What do you mean?'

'Well, if you're going to call this thing *Guernica*, it's bound to be seen as a symbolical treatment of the destruction of Guernica, isn't it? With the bullfight representing Spain, I suppose?'

'Oh I don't like this 'symbolical' talk – it's a *painting*' said Picasso, getting up from the floor. 'But you could be right, Dora Maar, damn you!'

'Sorry!' she said with a smile. 'And I won't say another thing.'

'Which only means you've more to say, doesn't it?'

'No no. I'll set up the camera.'

'So say it, Dora.'

'It's really not important.'

'Say it!'

'Oh well, it's just that your fallen warrior has a broken sword rather than a modern rifle, doesn't he? So it's a sort of *neo-classical* symbolical painting, is it?'

'Oh God, I don't know, I suppose so.'

'But then that defiant raised fist there' she said, pointing to the fallen warrior, 'that's the Republican salute, isn't it?'

'I probably put that in to please you, Dora.'

'Mmmh…'

'You think it's out of place?'

'Do *you* think it's out of place?'

'But it's the only direct reference to the civil war there is.'

'Then could that be why you possibly think it's out of place – that you're not quite following your own symbolical approach?'

'Intellectual women, my God! With sexy painted fingernails into the bargain! If I took out the raised fist, wouldn't the whole middle of the painting fall flat?'

'Ah, so you think that might be the real problem, do you?'

'Are you sure you wouldn't rather paint the damned thing yourself?! You keep telling me it doesn't hang together…'

'But I haven't said a word, Picasso' she said, laughing. 'Not a word!'

'Yes you have, Dora, that's the trouble! Too many words. I don't trust words. Let's stop using words.'

'So what do we do?' she laughed. 'Stand in silence?'

'We could go to bed. No need to use words in bed.'

'And what about photographing the mural?'

'You could do that later. Anyway, it's maybe not worth photographing at all – not unless you can tell me what to do with this unholy great thing.'

'How would I know?! Though…'

'Though what…? More words? More fucking words?'

'Well, I just wonder if it mightn't be the same central problem as before – the relationship between the bull and the mare.'

'Back to that, are we? Sounds sexy, Dora!' he said, imitating the bull and moving threateningly towards her.

'Only if you like your sex with suffering, Picasso.'

'Sounds even sexier, Dora!' he grinned, pulling her close to him.

'You monster' she said, laughing and wriggling, 'you monstrous old Minotaur…!'

'Look at me' growled Picasso. 'I've been slogging away at this bloody thing for a week, I'm covered in black paint, I reek of turpentine, I'm either squatting on the floor or up and down this stepladder like a monkey on heat, I don't know whether I'm coming or going, but that doesn't matter – and why? Because every Tom, Dick and Harry of a would-be art critic that comes in off the street for a free apéritif or three before lunch, as if this was some sort of charity bar open to all comers, knows far better than I do what's wrong and could obviously – if he just happened to have a free moment in his busy schedule – paint the fucking thing far better than I ever could!'

'It doesn't sound as though you've had a great day!' said Dora with a laugh.

It was true that he had smears of black paint on his forehead as well as on his striped sailor's jersey and that he reeked of turpentine. And it was true that the painting was physically demanding, whether he was having to bend down to the bottom of the canvas or stand on the stepladder stretching sideways with the brush tied to the end of a broom handle. But his real anger was obviously due to some critical reaction from his morning visitors.

'Well, if you will hold a late morning court even though you don't like talking about your painting, you can't guarantee the courtiers and hangers-on will say the right thing.'

'So what do you want me to do when Roland Penrose turns up with some English sculptor called Henry Moore or some such – throw them out?!'

'Not hold court in the first place. So it was Penrose?'

'And then André Breton. Just what I needed!'

'So what did they say?'

'Nothing. They said nothing. Henry Moore even said it in English.'

'But they can't just have remained silent!'

'Oh, Penrose talked about that Hindenberg Zeppelin disaster and Breton talked about Breton. In a word, nothing!'

'But they know it's still a work in progress. They were being discreet. So why worry when you don't even know what they think?'

'I know exactly what they think, Dora! They think what you think!'

She could see that he was indeed worried and that he was not so much angry at his visitors as at himself. She could also see that he was looking to project that anger on to someone else – which happened to be her. So she declined to take the bait and was quietly completing a final take of the mural when there was a '*Bonjour!*' from the doorway and Eluard came in, with a bright smile.

'Am I intruding?'

'Not in the least, Paul, you're just in time!' said Picasso with a wicked grin. 'Dora was about to tell me what is wrong with my mural.'

'Dora was not!' she said.

'She thinks it's formalist and defeatist.'

'That's what Picasso himself seems to think, Paul.'

'Oh but I think it's coming along well, Pablo' said Eluard. 'I like the contrast of the black and the white – very strong.'

'Ah, but is it *too* strong, Paul?' said Picasso, making a great show of pondering the question. 'I wonder if I shouldn't throw in a touch of blood-red here and there – or stick on a bit of patterned fabric for the dress of the fleeing woman on the right. What do you think?'

'Mmmh…' said Eluard, obviously unconvinced.

'Something like that very pretty pattern there' he said, pointing to Dora's dress. 'May I…?'

With Dora staring at him, he coolly lifted the hem of her patterned dress up over her thigh and held it out towards the painting for some moments as though to gauge the effect.

'I wonder…' he said. 'What do you think, Paul?'

'I think it looks better on Dora than it would on the painting.'

'And what do you think, Dora?'

'I think you're being offensive. I also think you're being rather confused. You seem to be trying to use the black-and-white of photography to demonstrate the superiority of painting over photography, so you'd be sabotaging your own critique if you introduced colour or collage before you've even got the overall composition right.'

'You see, Paul?' said Picasso, 'I haven't even got the overall composition right!'

'Oh I don't think, Pablo, that we should have a civil war over *Guernica*' said Eluard with a soothing smile. 'Dora is surely right about not adding colour – it would detract from the starkness. Especially now that you've given such a strong diagonal line to that fleeing woman on the right – which of course helps to create the pyramid effect that's beginning to hold the composition together.'

'That's *'beginning'* to hold the composition together, Paul?'

'Oh well, I'm assuming that you're still at an early stage of the work, Pablo. It's a very ambitious project.'

'So you *both* see the same central weakness then? Which of course Dora thinks is due to my failure to resolve some contradiction in my own miserable Spanish symbolism.'

'Well, Pablo, it does have to be seen as a symbolical work, I imagine. But I wasn't criticizing...'

'It's all to do with the relationship between the bull and the mare, Dora tells me. Because Dora sees the mare as her own private symbol, so Dora naturally thinks it should be the centrepiece of the mural. Is that not so, Dora?'

'Stop it, Picasso!' said Dora with controlled anger. 'It's *your* symbolism and *your* mural and you're the one who wants to call it *Guernica*, except that there isn't any Guernica. There are no aeroplanes, no bombs, no sides in battle, no *enemy* for that matter – only something like a nightmare in a bullring. And since the only symbolical conflict in your symbolical bloody painting is between the bull and the mare, and since it's the mare that's being crucified, she's perhaps entitled to a proper place in your symbolical bloody picture. That's if you had the imagination to understand her suffering in the first place!'

And she swished out of the studio.

'She's so proud, that woman!' said Picasso eventually, with a reluctant smile.

'I know' said Eluard. 'Isn't she wonderful?!'

'I must say' said Picasso, standing back to survey the whole mural, 'that the greys really do hold the whole thing together.'

'Yes' said Dora, who was on her knees, painting little vertical lines to indicate the hairs on the mare's leg. 'Black-and-white photography itself is mostly about different shades of grey.'

It was already early June and the light outside the attic window was wonderfully inviting, but Picasso had been working straight through the past two weekends in order to bring this vast canvas to a conclusion. There had been further sporadic arguments between them, since Picasso, in his mischievous fashion, enjoyed testing her – and in this situation actually needed to test her, for he was often uncertain. But the painting itself had brought them together, to the point that for the past week she had been acting not just as photographer but as collaborator, dealing diplomatically with visitors, seeing to the supply of paints and brushes and even, as now, painting minor sections of the mural. And it was in an atmosphere of tired serenity that they were now approaching the end of their efforts.

'Yes, the composition is so much clearer now' mused Picasso. 'Though perhaps I've overdone it a bit with that electric light bulb in the middle of the sun.'

'You mean' said Dora, getting to her feet to have a better view, 'it's too close to the lamp the woman is holding?'

'Yes, but I'll leave it. They've got to realise it's neither night nor day, nor indoors nor outdoors – not any particular place or time or perspective.'

'Like one of those nightmares of yours? With everything terribly clear, but still ambiguous…?'

'Yeah well, this was one big punishing nightmare – I'm glad it's over.'

'Well almost. I've still got some more strokes to do on the mare.'

'And I still have to tidy up that top left-hand corner a little. But let's have a breather.'

He took a packet of Gauloises from his shirt pocket and offered one to Dora, who fetched the cigarette holder from her bag on the chair by the window.

'Anyway' he said, as he lit her cigarette, 'you've now got your martyred mare enthroned in the centre of the nightmare – even though I had to bend my bull in half to make room for her.'

'Sorry about that!' she said with a smile.

'Well she's you all over, isn't she?' he said with a laugh. 'All deep feeling and defiance.'

'And your bull's you all over, Picasso. Looking both ways and saying it's not his fault!'

'All right, but don't just think I'm the bad bull and you're the good mare, Dora. I'm the bull *and* the mare *and* the dead warrior and this whole great screaming Spanish omelette.'

'You mean you *are* a kind of Spanish civil war?'

'I don't know. Anyway, to hell with all that! The bloody thing is over and done with.'

'Not in Spain it isn't. Men and their wars… At least women tend to be above that kind of violence.'

'You think so?'

'Well look, you just show them as suffering and screaming.'

'But that's what women seem to be about, isn't it – suffering and screaming? In fact I wonder…' he said broodingly, but stopped short.

'Yes?' said Dora, looking at him curiously.

'Oh' he said reluctantly, 'I just wondered once or twice…'

'Mmmmh…?'

177

'But it's nothing, nothing at all! You never really know where these screaming nightmares come up from, for God's sake, and it's safer not to inquire!' he said with a dismissive laugh, stamping out his cigarette on the floor.

'You may be right.'

'So let's put an end to this thing and and get it to hell out of here' he said, starting up the stepladder, but then turning with a theatrical wave of the hand. 'After we've both signed it, of course!'

'You do me too much honour' said Dora with a laugh. 'But I must say, Picasso, now that you've finished it, I do think it's tremendous.'

'Don't tell anybody, Dora, but so do I!'

'I thought you might!'

She finished the strokes on the mare, cleaned her hands and slung the camera around her neck to take some final shots of Picasso at work on the canvas.

'We've certainly put a lot into this' he was saying, perched high on the stepladder and stretching awkwardly across to his left.

'Well, *you* certainly have' she said as she shot him at an angle from below.

'So what about a nice summer holiday at Mougins? Survey the world from the Vaste Horizon?'

'Sounds delightful.'

'We could lie in the sun…'

'Stroll along the beach…'

'Sleep in the deep Mediterranean shade…'

'Swim in the deep Mediterranean sea…'

'Guzzle on those big lobsters from the port at Golfe-Juan…'

'Make pictures all day long…'

'Make love all night long…'

'Oh yes…?!' cried an angry voice from behind them.

Dora turned to find a young, red-faced blonde woman glaring at them from the doorway, with a child in a pushchair behind her – Marie-Thérèse it had to be…

'So this is why you've been too busy to see me' she said to Picasso, still perched high on the stepladder. 'You've been busy doing it with her!'

'She's been helping me!' said Picasso, smiling down.

'I can see how she's been helping you – 'making love all night long' you said!'

'She's been taking photographs.'

'I can imagine!'

'Photographs of the *painting*!' he said with a laugh.

'You call those cartoon horses and things a painting?! Wouldn't you be better painting something about the war in your own country?!'

As both Dora and Picasso gave an involuntary laugh at this, she became incensed and turned on Dora.

'You uppity bitch! You think this is funny, do you?'

'No I don't, but…'

'Do you know how long I've been with this man?'

'A long time, but that's not my affair.'

'He's the father of my child sitting in that pushchair out there – is that your affair?!'

'Well hardly…'

'You don't give a damn, do you?!'

'I'm simply saying it's his choice.'

'Well, don't think he'll choose you! Will you, Pablo? Go on, tell her! Is it going to be her or me?'

Picasso looked down on them from the stepladder, seemed to hesitate, then said nothing.

'Say it, Pablo, say it! Is it her or me?!'

'It looks' he said eventually, with a sardonic glint in the dark eyes, 'as though you'd better sort it out between yourselves.'

'So you can get out of here now' said Marie-Thérèse, snatching at the camera slung from Dora's neck, 'and take that thing with you!'

'Leave it alone!' said Dora. 'You'll break it!'

She was jabbing at Marie-Thérèse to try to wrest the strap of the camera from her grasp, but was pushed in return and dragged forward as Marie-Thérèse pulled on the camera, until Dora jerked it back suddenly and Marie-Thérèse stumbled, but recovered sufficiently to slap Dora on the face, prompting a slap on her own face in return, leading to a tussle which ended up with the pair of them hair-pulling and wrestling each other in an undignified fashion until there was a cry from the child, alarmed by the disturbance, and the two women were left sitting shamed and staring at each other on the floor – until Marie-Thérèse got up, looked despairingly at Picasso and rushed out sobbing bitterly, to the diminishing sound of the pushchair bumping noisily down the stone stairs.

Dora got up, hot-faced and humiliated, brushed down her dress and stared up at Picasso who, on his lofty perch, had been affecting an air of sardonic detachment.

'Well, I had to protect the camera, didn't I?!'

'Yeah sure. Especially since "women tend to be above that kind of violence."'

'My God, you're just like that great bull of yours, aren't you? Turning away from the awful suffering females. You *are* Guernica, aren't you?!'

She picked up her bag and left him high on his perch.

For the next three days Dora refused to take calls from Picasso, putting down the receiver on him even when he attempted to apologise profusely for the incident in the attic. So she was startled when he practically stormed into her studio in mid-afternoon and accused her of being perverse.

'Perverse?! Me?!' she laughed. You're saying I'm the one that's perverse?!'

'Yes I am. You've been quite unreasonable, with no understanding of my position.'

'Your position was that you visibly enjoyed humiliating not just one woman but two women from up there on that stepladder of yours!'

'But look at the position I was in! What could I have done?! She *knows* I'm with you, she could *see* I'm with you – do you want me to tell her *in front of you* that I'm with you?! I was in an impossible position!'

'And what do you think my position was?! Or hers?'

'It's her I have to worry about, Dora. She's the one who went off crying, isn't she? She's vulnerable, she might do something silly, so I have to keep her stable. I had to go out and see her, spend a day with her – and I can tell you it wasn't easy.'

'Oh God, Picasso…' she said, slumping into a chair and smiling helplessly at his indignant reversal of the situation.

'So I'm very sorry it happened and I'd be pleased, since you put so much work into 'our mural', if you would come to the attic tomorrow at five for the viewing by the architect of the Spanish pavilion, Sert. Paul will be there.'

'I'll think about it' she said finally.

She did think about it, decided she had to live with the fact of Marie-Thérèse's existence, and turned up next day for the viewing, to find Paul attempting to reassure Picasso, who was less than happy at the idea of having his work 'inspected'. And his mood did not improve when Josep Luis Sert, who turned out to be a distinguished man in his mid-fifties, shook hands pleasantly and declared himself impressed by the overwhelming size of the mural, but could not quite conceal the fact that he was taken aback.

'I imagine, Don Pablo' he said diplomatically after some minutes, 'that you are likely to be asked to explain the painting.'

'You can't explain paintings' said Picasso. 'If you could you wouldn't paint them.'

'I do think, though, that the ordinary visitor might well find the mural a little difficult to interpret without some accompanying explanation. I can well see, for example, someone demanding to know what the bull represents.'

'The bull represents a bull.'

'Yes, but the title does suggest some sort of allegorical reference to the events at Guernica' said Sert with a smile, 'and I wonder whether, in your own interest…'

'In my own interest?'

'Well, I'm embarrassed to mention it, but you are probably aware that there is an unfortunate – if no doubt unfounded – rumour circulating in some circles that you are not actually a supporter of our Spanish Republic.'

'You mean that I support the Fascists?' said Picasso. 'What nonsense!'

'Even so, Pablo' said Eluard, 'I think in the circumstances that some statement might indeed be helpful.'

'Then I'm sure you and Dora here could knock one up' said Picasso sarcastically.

Which is what Paul and Dora proceeded to do that evening, with a statement signed by Picasso declaring that in *Guernica* he was expressing his 'abhorrence of the military caste that has sunk Spain into an ocean of pain and death'. However, this did not quite settle the issue. For over the next few weeks the Spanish authorities were rumoured to consider the mural not merely formalist but anti-social and ridiculous. Indeed there was some suggestion that it would not be displayed at all, were it not for the political embarrassment that this might entail.

These rumours further annoyed Picasso, who was expected to appear at the formal opening of the Spanish pavilion, but who was anxious to get down to Mougins and frustrated by the continuing delay in completing the pavilion.

'This would-be World Fair' he was grumbling in the Deux Magots, 'was supposed to begin on May the first and now they're talking about only opening the Spanish pavilion in mid-July, ten or eleven weeks late. Will there be any visitors left to bother to visit it?'

'Of course there will' said Dora.

However, her own early visit to the Fair had been disappointing. At one level, of course, it was indeed a success. With so many national pavilions and some ten thousand exhibitors, it had taken over much of the centre of Paris, stretching along the river and incorporating the Trocadéro Gardens and the Champ de Mars. It had also provided a brand new Palais de Chaillot and a Museum of Modern Art. But the intended emphasis on peaceful progress in industry and in public services had been overshadowed not only by the failure to open on time, but by the larger political tensions symbolized by the stark confrontation of the German and Soviet pavilions on the bank of the Seine. And for Dora and Eluard there was something more disconcerting still.

With Nusch visiting her mother in Alsace – and Picasso affecting disinterest in the whole business – they had gone along together for a second look. And now, sitting on a stone seat in the Soviet pavilion, they were staring at a large fresco of Stalin and the Soviet leaders. For *Paris-Soir* had printed a large photograph of the original fresco under the mocking title 'Stalin in the Kingdom of Ghosts', in order to emphasize that leading figures in the group, notably Radek and Zinoviev, had since been denounced as mad dogs and executed as traitors. And this had caused some ribald speculation as to how the Soviet pavilion might deal with this embarrassment. Would it leave the 'ghosts' in place, or paint them out, or perhaps replace them with newcomers? In the event it had settled for an even more desperate solution.

'I don't believe it' said Eluard.'It's grotesque!'

'That's not Radek disguised by a black beard, is it, Paul?'

'It is. And that's Zinoviev buried under that ridiculous wig.'

'So they're not only dead, they never existed!'

'My God, it's like a grisly pantomime! Those trials in Moscow were hard enough to swallow without this.'

'It's Stalinism just turning into the mirror image of Fascism.'

'All we need now is for the Spanish pavilion to fail to open or for something to go wrong over *Guernica*.'

In the event, the pavilion did open on July the twelfth and the overall impression was favourable. The building was a fine example of modern architecture in the transparent Le Corbusier manner, there were numerous paintings and sculptures by Miró and other prominent Spanish artists, there were displays recording the struggles in the civil war, – and of course there was *Guernica*.

The mural was visibly disconcerting to most visitors and Picasso, on being interviewed, refused to offer any explanation. However, on being reminded of his role as honorary director of the Prado, he did say that the true protectors of the Prado were the soldiers and airmen who were fighting to defend Madrid. So the event passed off rather better than Dora and Eluard might have feared.

But it was all far too late. The visitors were scarce and the press was absent except for the Communist daily *L'Humanité*. So the contribution of the mural to the Republican cause could at best be marginal.

'It really does look' said Dora sadly, 'as though history has passed us by.'

8

'Oh, Dora's far too dignified to get involved' said Picasso jokingly.

She was sitting in her swimsuit on the terrace of the Vaste Horizon in Mougins watching him clown around self-consciously with his visitors. Always theatrical and provocative, he enjoyed having an audience and, since Dora was now regarded as the official *maîtresse en titre* and therefore the one closest to him and the least likely to take offence in public, she was logically the one to be provoked. And his expectation was that she would play the game, throw the ball back and stand up to him.

'Not at all, Picasso!' she replied smilingly. 'I used to love pillow fights, I really did, I enjoyed every moment of pillow-fighting.'

'So what happened then?' he asked

'Well, it was all rather sad. I left kindergarten and had to grow up' she replied to general laughter.

She was not as relaxed as she tried to appear. For one thing, now that they were on holiday and spending every night together, she noticed that Picasso – as though the mural had not relieved him of his devils – was having nightmares. And since he sensed that she knew, his unspoken embarrassment had much to do with the forced jollity he was displaying. For another, given the number of friends who were staying locally and dropping in and out, she tended to find herself cast in the testing role of hostess in a seaside comedy bordering on erotic farce.

On this particular late afternoon there were three other couples in addition to Paul and Nusch. There was Man Ray, the American photographer with his darkly cynical eyes and an interest in the Marquis de Sade and bullfighting, who was accompanied by Ady, a dazzling dusky young dancer from Martinique a good thirty years his junior. There was the tall slim Roland Penrose, no longer with Valentine who was of course now the lover of Alice Paalen, who had recovered from her attempted suicide after her affair with Picasso, so Penrose was now with the beautiful blonde American model Lee Miller, who had previously been a lover of Man Ray. Then there was the English painter Eileen Agar, who like Dora had spent part of her childhood in Argentina and who was with the expatriate Hungarian writer Joseph Bard. And as though to complete the circle of connections, Paul and Nusch had recently returned from a wife-swapping holiday with Eileen and Joseph in England. So though you could not quite say that absolutely every character had slept with everybody else, it did look like a promising cast.

Of course they were not merely amusing themselves. Picasso worked every day, as indeed did Dora, who had decided to devote herself seriously to painting, while Man Ray was busy working up illustrations for a poetry collection by Eluard, who gave a reading of a new poem every evening. Nor were they unaware of the great world outside. On the previous evening they had discussed the news reports of the exhibition of so-called 'Degenerate Art' in Munich, in which several of Picasso's paintings had featured alongside works by Cézanne, Renoir, Van Gogh and Matisse.

'I see that Goering has removed sixteen thousand modernist works from German museums and art galleries' said Penrose.

'And Hitler has made some speech saying all this is Jewish art' said Eluard. 'That it's all due to a 'serious sexual perversion' and that such unfortunates – the likes of you, Pablo! – should be sterilised.'

'It's almost too silly to be believable' said Lee.

'But I think we'd better start believing it' said Dora.

'Because if we were to end up surrounded on all sides by Fascism in Spain as well as in Germany and Italy' said Eluard grimly, 'how long would it be before France went Fascist itself? And where would that leave people like us?'

'We're the first ones they would come for, aren't we?' said Man Ray.

'And some of us happen to be Jewish' said Joseph Bard pointedly.

A slight unease flickered around the group. It was known that Bard was Jewish and believed that Man Ray was as well, although he would never admit to it.

'It's chilling' said Dora. 'Very chilling.'

But that was yesterday and on this afternoon, with Nusch, Lee and Ady already bare-breasted in the sunshine, the mood was tending towards a little sexual frivolity. There had already been a certain amount of flirtation, casual kissing and light lesbianism, with Dora – who stuck to her swimsuit and her camera – duly photographing the nude trio of Lee, Nusch and Ady posing as the Three Graces, or the naked Ady and Nusch rolling together on a rug for the particular delectation of the men. But now the mood was for fun and games and, if Dora became quietly watchful, it was because Picasso seemed bent on orchestrating them.

'I know' he said. 'Let's see if we can swap names and identities.'

So Dora found herself becoming Dora Agar, while Man Ray became Roland Ray, Joseph Bard become Paul Bard, and so on – until there was only one exception.

'Who are you swapping with, Pablo?' asked Lee.

'Oh, I'll be Don José Picasso.'

'But who's Don José?'

'He's my father' said Picasso, a little reluctantly.

'But you can't swap with your father!'' said Nusch, laughing.

'He's not really swapping with his father;' said Dora with a grin. 'He's swapping with himself!'

So, amid much risqué discussion, rules were drawn up whereby your new identity could be tested in various ways and, if you forgot it or failed to answer basic questions concerning it, you could be made to pay a forfeit, like balancing a jug of water on your head or singing the *Marseillaise* in the nude. But if you survived the tests, you got the prize of sleeping with a partner of your choice.

'Oh, this is all getting too complicated for me' said Dora, laughing. 'I think I'll opt out and act as official photographer for the coming chaos.'

Privately, apart from the fact that she did not fancy the other men present – with the possible exception of Paul Eluard, who was too old a friend – Dora found the whole exercise a little vulgar. And she suspected that it might be an artificial situation set up by Picasso – who would have been madly jealous if she had slept with someone else, but who was guessing that she wouldn't – to accept Eluard's standing invitation to 'share' the sweet, innocent Nusch. But she could see that Picasso was dazzled in particular by the beautiful blonde Lee Miller and by the dusky young Ady, and she could not have tolerated him sleeping with either, so she hinted casually when they were alone that night that he mightn't want to offend Penrose, who had just come together with Lee, or run into trouble with legal minors in the form of the seventeen-year-old Ady. And she took Eileen Agar out of the equation by persuading her to go to the beach for a swim next afternoon before dinner, which was the recognised time for sex romps.

That left Nusch, who was used to 'sharing', who had her own reasons for not minding it and who was not a direct threat. And though Dora certainly did not want it to happen, she suspected as she swam with Eileen that it might well be happening, but was determined that, if it did happen, it would never happen again.

'By the way, I did it with Nusch this afternoon' said Picasso in a would-be conversational tone that night as they were preparing for bed.

'Yes, I thought you would' she said in the same tone. 'You've been planning to do it with Nusch for some time, haven't you? Where did I put that new jar of cream, I wonder…?'

'I don't even find her attractive. Nice though she is, she's a bit thin for my taste. But I can hardly insult Paul, when he seems to be offering her, by suggesting that his wife is undesirable, can I?'

'Yes, I know, you did it for Paul. That kind of thing is actually fairly common among men, I believe. Here it is – I put it in the wrong drawer…'

'What kind of thing?'

'Well, Paul and you are good friends, aren't you?'

'So…?' he said, standing naked and idly rubbing the grey hair on his chest.

'So by possessing the good friend's lover you possess the good friend – and it works both ways. But I shouldn't worry about it? It's unconscious.'

'What's unconscious?'

'The homosexual element. It's latent. I'd only get concerned about it if it were to become habitual – or if you started offering me.'

He looked at her uncertainly for a moment, then frowned heavily.

'That bloody man Paul…!' he said.

'Oh no, that's rather unfair. It's doubtless quite unconscious with him as well.'

'Unconscious?!' he snorted. 'It's all too damned conscious the way he does it with Nusch.'

'I'm surprised she told you.'

'I asked her.'

'That was surely indiscreet of you' said Dora, creaming her face.

'He does it sitting down, if you'd believe it!'

'Yes, so I gather. But you've got to remember that you had it easy during the World War, since you were exempt as a foreigner and would probably have been too old in any case.'

'So?'

189

'So you should recognise that Paul has weak lungs because he had tuberculosis and was then severely gassed, which is why I get concerned about him smoking so much. I don't know what Nusch told you, but they do have their problems, those two, quite apart from her insomnia. Anyway, you've no ill effects, do you?'

'Ill effects? What kind of ill effects?' he said, stopping rubbing his feet and staring at her.

'Oh, I shouldn't worry, it would be too early for them to show up in any case. Right, that's me ready for bed.'

'What ill effects?'

'Well I do happen to know that they have great difficulty making love regularly, I imagine because Paul had been 'sharing' a little too lavishly around the place and caught whatever it is.'

'What *is* it?'

'It's herpes, it seems, though there can be different kinds. It produces some sort of bad rash and blisters around the genital area – quite painful, I believe, though I haven't seen it myself. But I wouldn't worry about it now.'

'Why not?' asked Picasso.

'Well, it probably only shows up after a few days. I mean, I wouldn't start rushing off to see a doctor – especially knowing your superstitious dislike of doctors and illness. You can wait and see if anything develops.'

She smiled nicely as she watched him take a small mirror and twist this way and that in the attempt to examine his genital area.

'Is there nothing I can do in the meantime?'

'Well, I suppose you could use iodine to disinfect as a precautionary measure. They might have some in the hotel if you ask them in the morning. You'd need to put it on all around the danger area. I must say I'm quite ready to sleep.'

'Wouldn't iodine sting a lot?'

'Yes, a fair bit.'

'And wouldn't it colour the whole damned area purple?'

'No, it's more of a yellowish brown, if I remember. Not an

attractive colour, but you're hardly going to be waving your bits and pieces around the hotel, are you? Did you enjoy it at least?'

'What has that to do with anything?!'

'Well, nothing I suppose.'

'Fuck' he said as he laid himself with exaggerated gentleness down on the bed. 'Fuck,fuck,fuck, fuck, fuck!'

'Yes, I know' said Dora with grim satisfaction. 'That's the problem!'

'The summer is moving on, isn't it?' said Dora as they sat staring at two yachts that appeared to be racing each other along the white-topped waves on quite a choppy blue sea.

'Yes, there's already a little chill in the air in the evenings, as I've noticed' said Jacqueline.

As the summer moved on, so did the visitors. However, Jacqueline and André Breton had arrived the previous week, without Aube who was staying with André's family. And there was another newcomer, but not one that Dora cared to think about.

'You know, I really think André only came down to make sure I didn't get involved in lecherous threesomes' said Jacqueline.

'Well I've recorded some nude antics in the bedrooms' said Dora, 'but I haven't come across any threesomes.'

'So I haven't missed anything! And you, Dora? Are you being as faithful as I'm apparently being forced to be?'

'I'm trying to be faithful to myself, Jacqueline, which is quite hard enough! But how is it all going these days?'

'By 'all' you must mean André!' said Jacqueline with a grin. 'Oh, we rub along in a kind of a way, you know? We're not really compatible, I suppose, but then I'm not sure I'm all that compatible with any of the men I've come across. They don't seem designed to take women too seriously. Which is maybe' she said with a laugh, 'why they don't seem to know a lot about women – or women's bodies.'

'I think I know what you mean!' said Dora, laughing in response.

'I am fond of him, you know, and he's very brave and honourable and all that, but he's so damned portentous and puritanical – I call him Moses for fun sometimes. The trouble, of course' she said with a comic grimace, 'is…'

'That he loves you?' said Dora, laughing.

'Yes, that's it exactly. Isn't it terrible?!'

'I don't know. I think you may be the lucky one.'

'But you've got the great Picasso!' said Jacqueline, then hesitated. 'Don't you think he loves you?'

'Oh yes, he does in his way'said Dora, 'but he's not easy to get really close to.'

'And why's that, do you think?'

'Oh well' said Dora reluctantly, 'he has his own nightmares and he's self-protective about it. The closer you get, the more he puts you through it. But we'd better go back, I suppose.'

'There's a very proper threesome over there' said Jacqueline as they came back to where Breton was involved in earnest conversation with Eluard and Penrose in an arbour.

'Quite oblivious to that disgusting Dali, squatting up there above them.'

'Yes, I wouldn't fancy him in a threesome!'

For the other newcomer that Dora preferred not to think about was Dali – not, in the event, the extravagantly theatrical Salvador Dali, but a wildly mischievous capuchin monkey that Picasso had insisted on buying in Nice one day, when they happened to be passing a shop grandly called Le Royaume des Animaux. While the group had volunteered alternative names – such as Monseigneur or Mussolini – Picasso decided to call him Dali, on the grounds that he had the same imperial gaze and the same view of his own importance. In fact, this other Dali was a creature whose sanitary and social training left a lot to be desired. In particular, apart from tending to snatch the food or the paintbrush from your hand, he had apparently been conditioned to lift up women's skirts, reach down the front of their dresses and, indeed, with a faraway look in his eyes, strong rhythmic movements and eerily soft staccato squeaks, to attempt to conduct sexual intercourse against their legs. Picasso was delighted with Dali and used him to tease the ladies, especially Dora, who had been incensed at finding the monkey in their bedroom.

'You're beginning to laugh like the monkey' she told him tartly on one occasion, when Dali was sniffing around the thighs of Jacqueline and herself. 'Though why you should want such a close relationship with a male monkey is rather beyond me.'

However the monkey was not the only form of pressure to be resisted. For Picasso had been working intently ever since *Guernica* on variations of the theme of the 'weeping woman'. None of the three distressed women in the mural could actually be said to resemble Dora – quite apart from being in Picasso's standard cartoon form, they had more obviously the classical Greek profile of Marie-Thérèse. But in developing this emblematic figure of female suffering over the past couple of months – even though he had also produced a beautiful portrait of a radiant Dora as herself – he was increasingly lending to what was becoming the *Weeping Woman* her own characteristically bright colours of purple, red, blue and green. And as he always displayed the new version in the evening, the expressions of Jacqueline and Nusch in particular as they glanced at Dora betrayed a questioning unease.

'Don't worry' laughed Dora. 'Picasso isn't painting me, Picasso only paints Picasso. He works through polar opposites – light and dark, blonde and brunette. And since his blonde model stands for childlike happiness, the brunette has to stand for grown-up awareness and grief. And he's still trying to work out some personal buried nightmare underlying that *Guernica* mural – am I right, Picasso?'

'You always are, Dora' he said with an ironical smile.

'I just wonder what you'd do if one day I actually did start to cry all over the place. I must try it and see.'

And in a certain fashion she was trying it. For in between taking photographs of the comings and goings and the odd naked goings-on in the bedrooms, she had been working at her painting almost as hard as Picasso. Having heard that artists tend to develop by copying a style and then progressing beyond it, she had started to paint in the style of Picasso and, indeed, had painted quite successful portraits of Picasso himself in that style. Moreover, she had been studying his technique in the portraits of the *Weeping Woman* and had been producing her own series, copying and modifying the image even to the point of parody. So that, on another evening, when he displayed his latest version, she was able to produce a caricatural version of the similarly dislocated face of a grief-stricken woman – now smoking and wearing a perky little yellow hat. Picasso look startled, but then laughed louder than all of them.

'Dora' he announced, 'is going to be a great painter.'

'As great as you, Pablo?' asked Penrose with a smile.

'Eventually, Roland! Eventually!'

The incident passed, but it came up in conversation when they were at dinner that evening.

'He really admires you, you know?' said Paul quietly.

'And I admire him, Paul, but he can be a little testing.'

'Well, you do fire each other up. But he's always quoting you – Dora says this, Dora says that…'

'Which doesn't seem to make him any less testing' she said with a smile.

And, as it happened, Paul soon got a glimpse of how testing his friend could be, when Picasso started doing costumed caricatures of some of them – flattering ones of the lovely Lee Miller, who thanked him with a kiss on the lips for not turning her into a 'weeping woman', but also a curious one of Paul as a woman suckling a cat. Paul made no comment, but Dora was embarrassed for him, knowing as she did that Picasso's Spanish *machismo* did not lead him to admire Paul for sharing his wife.

However Paul soon got his revenge when Dali, tiring of

Picasso's attentions, turned on him suddenly and bit his finger. Which occasioned a solemn discussion about whether it was poisonous, whether it required medical attention and whether in the meantime Picasso – who of course took any threat to his health with doom-laden seriousness – should go and lie down.

'We'd better drive into Nice tomorrow and show it to a doctor' said Dora.

'Yes, you should, Pablo' said Paul with a sly glance at Dora. 'I seem to remember that the king of Greece was bitten by a monkey. Or was it the king of Bulgaria?'

'And what happened to him?'

'Yes, on reflection, it probably was the king of Greece.'

'So what happened to him?'

'Are you sure it wasn't the king of Romania?' asked Dora.

'Well it was the king of somewhere or other. Anyway they called in their best medical experts – as you would obviously expect.'

'What happened to him, for Christ's sake?!'

'Oh, didn't I say? He died, poor devil.'

'So you'd better ask for an injection' said Dora.

'But can anything be done in the meantime?'

'I'll put some iodine on it. That's if you haven't used it all up on your... whatsit.'

'That bloody monkey!' said Picasso.

'Perhaps you just got a little too close to him. Wouldn't you say, Paul?'

'Yes, monkeys don't always return your affections – so it was said, if I remember, in the case of the king of Greece – or wherever.'

'I knew I shouldn't have called him Dali!'

'Don't worry, we can take him back with us to Nice in the morning. Unless you think you would like to keep him?'

'Why the hell would I want to keep him?!'

'You're quite sure you wouldn't miss him?' asked Paul.

'Why the fuck would I miss him?'

'Quite right, Picasso' said Dora sweetly. 'You can do it without the monkey.'

L'Amour est passé près de vous Marcel was singing on the drive back from Nice, though it was not quite clear from his rendering of this latest Maurice Chevalier ditty who exactly had missed out on love. At all events, Marcel too seemed to be sad that they were coming to the end of their summer in the Riviera sun.

'*C'est triste, Marcel*' said Dora, emerging briefly from a reverie about the significance of this last visit to Nice..

'*Ah ça oui, Mademoiselle Dora, on peut bien dire que c'est triste.*'

'Sentimental slush!' snorted Picasso, who also seemed to have been brooding about the visit. The usual visitors had gone, although the Bretons had passed through again briefly before returning to Paris. But there had been one unexpected latecomer, apparently staying somewhere in Mougins, who had made surprise appearances at different venues – sitting twenty yards away from them on the beach, or sitting at a nearby table in the restaurant when they were dining with the Bretons, on each occasion making distinctly uncomplimentary remarks about Picasso. Having once before seen this red-haired person chasing Alice Paalen up the Rue La Boétie, Dora recognised her as the unhappy, unreconciled Olga.

'Can you do something?' she asked Picasso in the restaurant.

'Like what?' he said, apparently unembarrassed.

'Speak to her, or something!' said Dora, very aware of André's unspoken disapproval.

'That only tends to make it worse' he said, smiling.

'You mean it has happened before?'

'Oh yes, it happens at intervals' he said with a shrug.

'You didn't tell her you were going to be in Mougins, did you?'

'I suppose I might have mentioned it in a card to Paolo.'

Fortunately, she soon gave up and left the restaurant. But on the very next day, they were suddenly confronted in the village by the same angry Olga, her red hair merging almost comically with the flaming red flowers of the bougainvilleas. To avoid any further embarrassment Dora insisted on returning at once to the hotel.

'This is ridiculous!' she said in exasperation. 'Are we going to see any more old flames jumping out of the bougainvilleas?'

'You never know' he said with a grin.

However, once Olga had disappeared as mysteriously as she had arrived and the Bretons had also gone on their way, it was time for Picasso, before leaving, to call on 'Mademoiselle Matisse', as he referred to his old sparring partner Henri Matisse. And it was from that visit that they were now returning.

Dora had been delighted to meet this other iconic figure of modernist painting, and had found the bearded and bespectacled older man both gracious and charming. For Picasso, however, this visit over a *five-o'clock goûter* of tea and cakes, in which he felt constrained by the presence of Matisse's rather proper wife Amélie, tended only to confirm his prejudices. Beyond congratulating each other ironically on featuring in the Munich exhibition of Degenerate Art, there had been little enough time to talk about painting – although when shaking hands on leaving, they had agreed to keep in touch since, as Matisse said pleasantly, they 'needed each other'.

'What a way of life!' said Picasso broodingly. 'Forty years of bourgeois marriage – a day's work in the studio, followed by tea and cakes, a spot of violin-playing and then bed at ten o'clock sharp.'

'Not quite your style!' said Dora with a smile.

For these old rivals were clearly polar opposites, and not simply because of the dignified lifestyle of the more polished Matisse, who saw himself as the balanced French northerner as opposed to Picasso's volatile Spanish southerner. Indeed he had initially seen this newcomer as some sort of barbarian bursting on to the pre-war French art scene.

'No it's not my style' said Picasso with a grin. 'It's more like the world of the respectable bourgeois young lady – harmony, serenity, beauty and all that bollocks.'

'So he's 'Mademoiselle Matisse' then, just as I've heard you refer to Braque as 'Madame Braque'? Are we back to the artist 'painting with his prick?' You think of genius in terms of conquering sexual energy, so that the Braques, the Matisses and the Eluards, who have a softer view of the world, are all effeminate? Are you really saying you don't even take Matisse seriously?'

'On the contrary, he's the only one I take remotely seriously – which is why we've been competing with each other for the past thirty years. The point being that we started out together on the same journey, but somehow ended up at a different destination.'

'And you find that mystifying, do you?'

'I suppose I do. I mean, we both realised that the tradition was being killed off by your damned photography and we were each trying to renew it by transforming it. He attacked the standard illusionist approach by using bold, illogical colours, while I went further and attacked representational art altogether by turning it into a system of signs.'

'Yes, but there's also the temperamental difference, isn't there? Matisse is still reflecting the classical harmony and elegance of the French tradition – and of the calm, ordered life he tries to live.'

'But ironically, even though he was the one who introduced me to those African masks, he didn't grasp what they were about. Painting isn't some nice polite aesthetic activity you indulge in before a civilised *goûter* with tea and cakes. It's about trying to exorcise the horrors of this strange, hostile fucking world we're living in.'

Which left him trying to dig down into the nightmare, thought Dora. Trying to pursue its hidden origin until he had at least stabilized the nightmare symbolically as in *Guernica,* or trying to go on and on dislocating the face of the *Weeping Woman* until he had achieved at least some formal finality – not so much painting the world as painting his own onslaught on the world.

'I recognise your mystery…' Marcel was crooning sadly.

The sun was already casting shadows across the road from a line of pine trees to the left and on the dry undulating hills up ahead of them. The air had changed subtly. The summer was ending.

The mystery, Dora reflected, was not simply that Matisse was painting the world he loved and that Picasso was painting Picasso, or that their very differences made them curiously dependent on each other. The mystery was where the inspiration came from in the first place. Certainly, nobody but Picasso could have dredged up from somewhere deep within himself such a private emotional equivalent of the horror of Guernica.

But where did the horror come from…?

'You'd never guess who I ran into the other day' said Picasso teasingly, 'standing in front of the Sainte Chapelle.'

'Who was standing in front of the Sainte Chapelle, you or… whoever it was?'

'He was. Though by the end we both were.'

Dora was in high spirits. Picasso had painted a wonderfully happy portrait of her and immediately presented it to her, after which he had made love to her with unusual tenderness. And now, after hurrying through the dark wet autumn evening, they were dining at the Brasserie Lipp – dining *à deux*, though as usual many other clients tended to greet them or else eye them discreetly.

'So who was this mysterious person in front of the Sainte Chapelle then?' she asked, with her knife and fork poised over her sautéed chicken breast.

'Guess.'

'Well, if it was the Sainte Chapelle, it must be a person of spiritual significance – was it the Pope?'

'No' said Picasso laughing, 'he just looks like the Pope blessed with thick spectacles.. It was Jaume.'

'Sabartés? Is he still around?'

'Yes, he's back in Paris, managing all right, so he says. But I think perhaps I didn't treat him all that well.'

'But you thought he didn't treat you at all well, spreading all those rumours. Anyway, I know you don't like talking about this, Picasso, but what are we going to do about *Guernica*?'

'I've done all I can do, Dora. I painted the damned thing!'

'Yes, but it was all too late and now it's just going to waste with nobody seeing it!'

'They didn't much like it when they did see it! Some Communist thought it was effete, somebody said I was in an ivory tower, and somebody else said it was a 'personal brainstorm that was entirely self-referential' – whatever that means!'

'Yes, but Christian Zervos countered that the best way to address problems of reality is to surmount them.'

'Which suggests I leapfrogged over political reality and never even noticed it!' He laughed his sardonic laugh. 'It doesn't sound all that different!'

'You're not taking this seriously, are you? The point is that they didn't know how to look at that mural.'

'They looked with their eyes.'

'Yes, but they hadn't seen your earlier work, they couldn't read the emblems, they didn't know how you had worked up to *Guernica*.'

'Yes, but paintings aren't just for art critics, Dora.'

'Picasso!' she said with an exasperated laugh. 'You seem to be bent on demonstrating that you painted a bad mural! What *do* you think after all that's been said about it?'

'Well actually' he said with a grin, 'I think that a painting that has been rubbished by the Nazis, by the Vatican and by the Communists – not to mention the Spanish Republicans who commissioned it in the first place – can't be all bad!'

'Well then, why don't we make sure that more people see it? Why shouldn't it go on tour – England, America, perhaps Scandinavia? And the obvious place to start is England, since Penrose is there. I'll write to him tomorrow morning – all right?'

'Well, if you have the time' replied Picasso with an airy wave of the hand.

Dora did find time for it next day, although she was having a busy transition year. She had long been moving increasingly towards art photography and had exhibited at the Galerie Gradiva, named after the Surrealist Muse Gradiva, the mythical classical figure who walked through walls – though for want of financial management she very soon hit the wall. She had also recently published photographic etchings done in collaboration with Picasso. Nevertheless, she was drawn more and more towards painting, which she felt to be the purer form of self-expression, and she was intent on breaking out from under Picasso's shadow to develop her own style. So she was trying to limit her photography to recording his own production.

And it was with that purpose in mind that she arrived in the attic the day after his fifty-sixth birthday to find Penrose and Eluard looking almost greedily at a brilliantly coloured version of the *Weeping Woman,* a canvas on which the paint was still wet.

'You've just finished this?' asked Dora.

'Yes, and I imagine it's the last of the series' said Picasso with a smile.

'Well then, the series is ending in glory' said Eluard. 'Isn't it, Dora?'

'Yes indeed.'

'I don't suppose, Pablo' asked Penrose diffidently, 'that you would sell me that?'

'What do you think, Dora?' he said with a meaningful grin. 'Should I sell?'

'That's entirely a matter for you, Picasso.'

'I'll offer you two hundred and fifty pounds for it' said Penrose.

Eluard and Dora looked at each other in surprise. At two hundred and fifty pounds the picture would be going for a song.

'Oh well, since I'm sure Dora doesn't *really* like it' he said, 'why not?!'

And with a dismissive wave of the hand, the deal was done. To the discreet dismay of Eluard, who probably felt that, at that price, he could have raised the money himself and made a killing on it. And to the discomfort of Dora, who felt that Picasso was playing games with her, and who was not entirely reassured when he told her the next day that he could hardly haggle over a price with the man who – thanks largely to her – was willing to promote a tour of *Guernica* in England.

Nor was she entirely reassured by his explanation on another matter, when they were returning from a formal homage to Apollinaire before the poet's tomb in the Père Lachaise cemetery. The whole avant-garde had turned out for the occasion, including the leading Italian Fascist writer Marinetti, who at one point came to shake hands with Picasso, only to be rejected with the brusque reminder that Italy was attacking Picasso's homeland Spain.

'I'm impressed.' said Dora with a smile on the way back. 'You're almost becoming political!'

'I've doubtless got you to thank for that, Dora. But, speaking of Spain, there's something I wanted to say to you.'

'What's that?'

'I've decided to bring back Sabartés.'

'But why?'

'There are things to do with dealers and exhibitions, not to mention other bits of business, that have got to be covered.'

'Couldn't I cover much of that?'

'Yes, but it would be totally unfair to ask you, now that you are becoming a serious painter. You must be free to get on with that and have your work exhibited.'

'Oh well, I suppose… So when would he be back?'

'Tomorrow.'

It was ridiculous, thought Dora as she sat in the Metro after work on her way to photograph whatever drawings or paintings Picasso might have accumulated over the previous two weeks. For there seemed to be no escape from people directly or indirectly reminding you that you were thirty – and therefore no escape from the expectations of others that went with being thirty.

It was all the more surprising because she had not normally been aware of being thirty – she had been much too busy to be thirty. Nor had she been aware of looking thirty. And yet, perhaps there was no escape from being thirty. For the faces around her in the carriage did seem to fall broadly into the standard decades, from the bright twenties of the laughing girls sitting opposite her to the muted seventies of the grey-haired man coughing intermittently in the corner. They bore their age on their faces as a fatality.

It had started almost accidentally at the annual birthday lunch with Jacqueline, who phoned to say she was unable to find a babysitter and would Dora mind if she brought Aube along? Of course, she had told her, do bring her along, it would be lovely to see her again. And indeed Aube was a lovable, lively two-year-old, who got on well with her 'Auntie Dora' and who charmed other clients in the restaurant with her antics. So, with Jacqueline being in an equally lively mood, they had all spent an enjoyable few hours together. Yet it had somehow not been quite the same…

And then, of course, there was her mother. Increasingly strained as she got older and unable to conceal her concern at her daughter's unconventional lifestyle and associations. While she was generally discreet and even a little nervous about it, she had been rather more direct on the previous Saturday morning, when Dora had dropped in to see them over the coffee, the croissants and her father's quince jam.

'I just can't believe you're thirty, Dora' she began casually.

'Neither can I, *Maman!*'

'You realise I was your age when I had you?'

'I suppose that's so. I hadn't really thought about it.'

'Do you think perhaps' said her mother cautiously, 'that you ought to start thinking about it?'

'You mean it's time for me to get married?'

'Yes, so that you can be happy ever after' said her father with a mischievous smile.

'I mean, if you don't have children when you're the right age, you might regret it later on' her mother persisted. 'And not all marriages are the same, you know.'

'Aren't they?' said her father with a comic show of astonishment.

'No, she might find a husband who's kind and reliable, believe it or not!' said Madame Markovitch with feeling.

'Not if she goes on looking where she's looking!' said her father, whose view of Picasso seemed less than favourable.

'Then I suppose I'd better start hunting around for a husband' said Dora lightly. 'Though I'm not sure that this is a good time to be bringing children into the world.'

'You can say that again' her father had agreed.

That remark by her father had helped to put an end to the conversation, but the episode had left her feeling mildly irritated. And as she emerged from the Metro into the brightly lit Place Saint-Michel to make her way to the Rue des Grands-Augustins, she was already anticipating what she would find there. For Picasso had lately been spending every weekend at Le Tremblay and it had been obvious for some time from the work he produced there that his interest had shifted from Marie-Thérèse to little Maya, from the mother to the child. Indeed it was almost as though the mother came with the child, rather than the child with the mother. As though there was redemption in this child. It seemed to be all about this child.

'*Bonjour*, Dora' said Sabartés politely. 'It's chilly out there, isn't it? Shall I take your overcoat?'

Sabartés, now quite changed, apart from the beret, was clearly on his best behaviour – under instruction perhaps?

'Thank you, Jaume.'

'Pablo is in the attic.'

And so he was, sitting on a stool wearing a thick sweater with a scarf around his neck, making tiny figures out of white clay.

'Ah, the recording angel' he said.

'Let's hope the works are as angelic' she smiled.

And indeed when, after a glass of wine, she began to leaf through a collection of drawings, obviously from Le Tremblay, angelic is what many of them turned out to be. For they were delicate, affectionate treatments of the little girl Maya, who would be just a few months older than Aube and who seemed to be every bit as lovable.

'They're lovely' she said, 'really lovely.'

'Yes, she's wonderful, that little Maya. I do love small children, don't you?'

'Yes, there's an innocence about them.'

She went on looking through the drawings and, as the silence gathered, she somehow knew what he was going to say. He had once hinted jokingly that she was too intelligent to be a normal woman and she had heard him say that every young woman needed a child to make her happy…

'Would you not like to have a child, Dora?' he asked eventually.

'I might well' she replied with a smile, 'but to be fair to the child I would want it to be within a relationship that's stable and emotionally secure. So can I take it that you are proposing marriage, Picasso?'

'Ah well now, Dora' he said with an awkward laugh, 'That's a big question.'

'It's a pretty clear question.'

'Well I'd love to, of course, you know that perfectly well, but I just couldn't, could I?'

'No?'

'I mean with Marie-Thérèse. God knows what she would do. She could do something silly, she might even kill herself, perhaps even hurt little Maya. And I have to think of the child. You do recognise that, don't you?'

'That you have to think of the child…?' said Dora, staring down at a tender study of this sweet sleeping two-year-old that he had fathered.

'That's right. Above all, I have to think of the child.'

'We've hardly exchanged a word all evening!' said Marie-Laure some time after one o'clock in the morning at Lise Deharme's soirée.

'I know' said Dora with a laugh. 'The place is like the Gare Saint-Lazare at rush hour!'

The two friends nodded appreciatively at each other's evening dress, Marie-Laure's in aubergine and Dora's a cerulean blue.

'I haven't seen Pablo in the crush.'

'No, he's away from Paris this weekend.'

Marie-Laure, the Vicomtesse de Noailles and known to be a distant descendant of the Marquis de Sade, was a friend of Dora's and, like their mutual friend Lise, a wealthy patron of the artistic avant-garde. Dora had accompanied Picasso to Marie-Laure's even more prestigious mansion in the sixteenth *arondissement*, but when on her own tended to prefer the slightly more familiar company she found amid the greenery, the outlandish creations and the *objets trouvés* of Lise Deharme's Surrealist interior.

'So you're on your own?' asked Marie-Laure.

'Well, trying to be actually. Don't disappear, will you?'

'You're being pursued? How wonderful! Is it a man and a heterosexual one at least?'

'Yes it is' smiled Dora, aware that Marie-Laure's husband had turned out to be otherwise inclined.

'Well then, I shall glide away and let him have his prey.'

'No no, please don't!' said Dora, laughing.

'I wonder who it might be' said Marie-Laure mischievously, looking around. 'Now I saw you talking, let's see, to André Breton, who seems unlikely, and then to that oddly theatrical, dandified young psychoanalyst called I know not what...'

'He's called Jacques Lacan – and it's not him. It's the one lurking three paces to your left, our painter friend Yves Tanguy who seems to imagine I dropped him unkindly when I met Picasso. Would you give me cover as far as the door, so that I can collect my stole and slip silently into the night?'

'Sounds a rather operatic exit, Dora, but I'll be happy to.'

And within a few minutes, after a brief goodbye to her hostess Lise, she was getting into a taxi beneath a wonderfully bright moonlit and starry sky.

'*Bonsoir, Madame*' said the middle-aged driver.

'*Bonsoir*, it's a beautiful night, isn't it?'

'It is indeed, and so mild! Where to, Madame?'

'Rue de Savoie. Well no, actually it's such a nice night I'd like to drive around a bit. If you don't mind?'

'Not in the least Madame. Which direction do you fancy?'

'West I think. We could go out by the Porte de Saint-Cloud.'

'And why not, Madame? Did you have a nice evening?'

'Oh yes.'

She had too, she reflected, although it was not so easy to explain Picasso's absence on weekend occasions. Did Marie-Laure really believe that he was 'away for the weekend'? Nobody ever queried this explanation, but that might mean either that they accepted it – or that they didn't. Did anybody among his friends know about Marie-Thérèse…?

'Tell me' she said as they approached the Pont de Saint-Cloud. 'isn't Le Tremblay-sur-Mauldre out in this direction?'

'Yes, it's in Seine-et-Oise, not far from Versailles. But it's a fair bit.'

'Still, it's such a nice night. Would you mind if we drove there? There's a house I'd like to check on.'

And after exchanging a few routine remarks with the driver, she sat gazing out at the moonlit landscape, sinking into a lengthy reverie until eventually she realised with a start that they were parked in an empty square in the middle of the night in front of the small town hall of an eerily moonlit hamlet which must be Le Tremblay. And that the driver was turning to look at her with real curiosity.

'Do you know which house it is, Madame?'

'No, it's actually a farm, with a wall round it – I just saw a photograph of it.'

'Does it have a name, do you think?'

'Well, it was lent to the person concerned by a man called Vollard, though of course there's nobody to ask at this time of night, is there?'

'No, Madame.'

'But it seemed to have a kind of double arch at the entrance, with perhaps a date in the centre. Do you think we could just drive around for a little and see if we can find it?'

'Yes, if you wish.'

So they drove around the hamlet for about ten minutes, setting dogs barking in several directions until they came upon a walled farm that looked as though it might be be the one. She got out of the car, followed by the driver, hitched up her evening dress and, since the locked gates themselves were too tall, struggled in her high heels through long grass to see if she could look over the wall. Finding that she was too short, she looked a little helplessly at the driver.

'Do you want me to look, Madame?'

'Yes, would you?'

He pulled himself up, looked over the wall, said there was just a farmhouse, with no lights showing – and looked at her hesitantly.

'Would you like me to…?'

'Yes, would you mind?'

He braced his back against the wall, lifted her up and she gazed for some moments at the farmhouse with its outbuildings looking almost dreamlike in the milky moonlight. Little Maya would be asleep there. Picasso would be asleep there, with Marie-Thérèse beside him, perhaps with his arm across her. All tucked up together for the night in the middle of this strange landscape. Almost like the tiny family kept safe in the little Nepalese wooden bowl on André Breton's display stand…

'All right, Madame?'

She realised with a start that she had the taxi-driver's head on her breast and his arms locked around her thighs in the depths of Seine-et-Oise in the middle of a moonlit night.

'Yes, thanks.'

She grimaced apologetically as her dress rode up when he was lowering her to the ground, and then walked back with him to the taxi.

It was about ten minutes after they had been driving in silence back towards Paris that a great raw sob rose up from within her and she began to shake and weep so convulsively that the driver was soon turning and pleading with her – and eventually stopping the car.

'Please, Madame' he was saying, stretching a hand back towards her 'I know it's hard. It's still hard for me too, my wife died earlier this year, you see, she was only forty-six and...'

'I'm sorry, I'm sorry...'

But this had only made her cry the harder, which set him crying, so that they were both sitting holding each other's hand across the back of the front seat and crying in this stationary taxi on an empty moonlit roadway – until Dora controlled herself, apologised for upsetting him and, as they drove on again, started asking about him and his family. He told her that he was really a trained fitter who had lost that job in the recession, that his wife had died of tuberculosis and that their daughter had been very good with her, especially helpful since their son was always away in the navy. And by the time they were reaching the lights of Paris again, the current of sympathy between them was such that Dora was apologising again for reminding him of his loss and inviting him to join her for a night-time supper at Les Halles.

While it was not entirely unusual to see late-night revellers ending up with chance partners for onion soup in the central markets, with meat porters and fruit porters pirouetting around them, it was still a little surprising to see a taxi-driver and a lady in evening dress having a heart-to-heart conversation over *bifteck frites* at three o'clock in the morning.

'But I don't quite understand' he was saying hesitantly in his gravelly Parisian accent. 'So it wasn't your husband out there, but your lover?'

'Yes, that's right.'

'So is that his wife he was with?'

'No no, he's separated from his wife.'

'Well then, forgive me, but was that a new mistress?'

'No, that's a woman he sort of has to spend weekends with.'

'Oh?' he said, with his knife suspended over his steak.

'It's not quite the way it sounds' she said with a laugh. 'It's simply that he has known her for many years and, and since she's vulnerable and she has a child by him – a little girl – he feels obliged to see them both at weekends. It's the child, you see."

'Yes? And you don't feel…?'

'No no, because I'm his real mistress, the one he goes out with and goes on vacation with. And we work together on artistic projects, you see.'

'Yes, well, if it suits both of you…' he said, gazing thoughtfully at her as she stopped to chew her steak and sip her red wine.

'He's a man you have to stand up to, of course' she went on, 'but then he's a great artist, world famous in fact, you'd be bound to know his name.'

'Oh well, artists's names and me…!' he said with a smile.

'Well he's Picasso, as it happens.'

As he gave an apologetic shrug, she looked disbelieving, then laughed.

'Well you can take it from me that he's a great artist. And it's exciting working along with him.'

'So you're happy then?'

'Yes… And luckier than most, I imagine.'

'I mean' he said hesitantly, 'I just wondered when you got upset out there tonight…'

'Well yes, but that's the price of freedom, isn't it?'

'But you believe that he loves you?'

'Yes, and I love him. And just between you and me' she said with a laugh, 'I will never, ever let him go.'

He laughed in his turn and sat gazing at her for several moments.

'I think, Madame' he said eventually, 'that you are very brave and very proud, but I hope…'

'Yes?'

'Well, I just hope that you're not too proud for your own good.'

9

Dora, drying herself vigorously after getting out of a late-night shower, stopped and surveyed herself in the mirror. She had found herself doing this increasingly – lifting the quite full breasts, judging the width of the hips, running her hand over the belly. It was like discovering yourself to be a kind of question mark, she thought with a smile. Should she or shouldn't she? Would she or wouldn't she…?

Not that these early months of 1938 provided an encouraging backdrop. The Popular Front government was threatened with collapse, there had been further implausible treason trials in Moscow, and Hitler had marched into Austria. Of course an unusually warm and flowering Paris spring went on regardless, Dora had made good progress with her painting, and had photographed a whole series of works by Picasso – including tender portraits of both Marie-Thérèse and herself. But the harsh newspaper headlines tended to make everyday reality seem a little hollow and even Picasso, who had the knack of ignoring bad news, could not escape the report that the Italian air force had bombed his home city of Barcelona.

There had been one further occasion on which the question of her having a child had arisen, in relation to what Picasso saw as Olga's attempt to discredit him in the eyes of their son Paolo.

'Marriage is a prison' he was saying, 'a legal nightmare. It just poisons relationships.'

'Oh I don't know' said Dora. 'The Eluards and the Bretons seem to do rather well on it.'

'And what difference would it make to them if they weren't married?. It's just a piece of paper, for God's sake!'

'But you just said it was a prison!' she said with a laugh. 'It's a commitment.'

'Well, you know the difficulties of my situation, Dora. And you should also know that, if you want to go ahead and have a child, you have all the commitment from me that you need.'

And that was where they had left it. But the question mark was still hanging in the air as she set out one fine April afternoon to visit the Bretons before they left for Mexico. It had become a more pressing question now that she sensed that Picasso himself was keen for her to have his child. But she was not convinced by his argument that every woman needed a child to make her happy – had it made Marie-Thérèse happy, or had it locked her away in a different kind of prison? And while to have a child by a man might be a standard way of trying to hold him, that was not a game that she could see herself playing. The decision whether to have a child was too serious for that.

Yet motherhood didn't seem to be weighing too heavily on Jacqueline, as she discovered when she arrived at Number 42, to be met at the door by André and little laughing Aube, holding up to be kissed a surreal doll with a yellow face, blue arms and red legs.

Dora duly kissed the doll, then Aube and finally André, before following him into the living room with its familiar display of engravings and exotic objects – now enhanced by two new portraits of André and several childlike drawings on the wall.

'As you see' said André, pointing, 'we have now added the early work of the future painter Aube Breton, haven't we, Aube?'

'Clever girl!' said Dora to the giggling Aube, who was clutching her hand. 'And fresh portraits of *Papa*?'

'Yes, but they're by Jacqueline' said André.

'That's because I'm turning him unto my Muse' said Jacqueline, coming into the room. 'Nice of you to come and wave us off, Dora.'

'But it's an honour. A government commission for a cultural visit to Mexico indeed – I'm quite envious!'

'Except that we'll never get there if I don't go and pack' said André. 'If you'll forgive me, Dora.'

He reached her a drink and went off, while Aube climbed on to her knee demanding to be read to from her picture book, leaving Jacqueline to sit smiling at them.

'You'll let Auntie Dora drink her wine, won't you, Aube?'

'Oh she's fine. Aren't you, my sweet?'

'Quite a Mother and Child scene, Dora' said Jacqueline with a grin. 'You're not thinking…?'

'Oh no, not you as well, Jacqueline! I'm getting hints from all over the place.'

'Sorry!'

'Tell me about Mexico instead. How long will you be away?'

'A good few months, I expect. André will be lecturing, but he wants to stay on to meet lots of people, including Leon Trotsky.'

'Sounds wonderful. And what about our little friend here?'

'Oh, she'll be staying behind.'

'Will she?' said Dora with surprise.

'Yes, Rose and André Masson have agreed to take her. 'She'll be fine.'

'I'm sure she will…'

But she never quite got over her surprise. And as she lay in bed that night, thinking over the events of the day, she decided that, if she had a child as young as Aube, she could not contemplate leaving her in that fashion. Ironically, as it seemed, she now seemed to be moving beyond the expectations of others in relation to having children towards her own. But after all, she reflected as she stroked her belly lightly, to bring a child into the world to live in time beyond yourself was a grave and beautiful thing to do. It should only be done responsibly, for the right reasons and in the right circumstances. Yet it was an idea, as she stared up into the darkness, that did not seem to be going away.

'Does he think he's bloody Superman?!' asked Eluard rhetorically, as though calling upon every drinker in the Deux Magots to bear witness to this enormity.

For André Breton might have gone to Mexico, but he had left behind him a bomb in the form of a written instruction to members of the Surrealist group to cease all contact with Eluard because he had not publicly condemned the treason trials in Moscow.

'I wouldn't call him Superman' said Dora, laughing. 'More like the Pope. André is really a very moral person, and respectful of women. Poor old Nietzsche's Superman was not.'

'Why do you call him, 'poor old Nietzsche'?' asked Picasso.

'Well, because of his views on women. Give them a child to shut them up, don't forget to use the whip, and all that pathetic nonsense.'

'You might think it's wrong, but what's 'pathetic' about it?' asked Picasso.

'Just that he never really knew any women. He went to a brothel once when he was young, got syphilis and that was as far as he got. If he'd ever met a real woman, he would have run a mile.'

'Are you saying' asked Eluard, 'that the hostility to women is based on fear?'

'What else?! But I'm also saying, Paul, that though André's exclusion order against you is simply silly, he's right to say it's ridiculous to condemn all those Soviet leaders as agents of Hitler. It's no more likely than that Stalin himself is a Hitler agent, paid to wreck the Soviet government.'

'Yes, well...' said Paul, 'I'm not saying it's not a troubling business.'

Clearly, external events were eating into personal relationships, just as they were eating into Picasso's painting. And, as the year moved on, Dora realised that the nature of her relationship with Picasso was changing.

On the surface, apart from the return of Sabartés, there was little difference. While they did not live together, they spoke on the

215

telephone every day, they dined together at Le Catalan or the Brasserie Lipp whether à *deux* or with the usual artistic or literary friends, they made love fairly regularly and, in short, they were recognised publicly as a leading couple on the art scene. But she found that she was coming to know him in a much more profound and sometimes disconcerting way through the recording of his paintings. Indeed it occurred to her that it might be possible to know someone too well. For while in their everyday dealings they could preserve a civilized distance, maintained by a competitive form of humour and talk about everyday events, this continuous engagement with the mind behind the art – though, paradoxically, it helped her to move away from him in her own painting – could seem disturbingly close.

It was becoming clear that the mood engendered by bad news from Spain or from Germany – even if he did not consistently look at newspapers – was increasingly reflected in a marked disturbance in Picasso's painting. Of course there were sunny intervals, as expressed in tender drawings of Maya or in happy portraits of both herself and Marie-Thérèse but, as the summer wore on, the mood darkened to a degree that Dora found disquieting.

They had come down as before in the big Hispano-Suiza, to spend the summer at the Vaste Horizon in Mougins, with Marcel treating them to Maurice Chevalier's latest ditty *On est ce qu'on est* – saying bleakly that you are what you are and you had better get used to it. And the Côte d'Azur being as attractive as before, they had sunbathed, splashed in the sea and made the usual trips to Cannes and Vallauris. But there were fewer friends than before, with only Paul and Nusch apart from the odd passing visit and an unwelcome appearance by Olga, who shadowed them naggingly for several days in a row. Also there was no monkey on this occasion, no flirtatious games in the bedrooms, no swapping of partners and no demand for iodine. And as the news worsened day by day in the lead-up to the Munich Agreement, opening the way for Hitler's expansionist ambitions in Europe, so Picasso's vision darkened.

While he had done a number of variations on the theme of the

Crucifixion over the years, there had been nothing like the *Crucifixion* he produced towards the end of that sweltering month of August. For this was quite shocking in its violence and its mockery. In a scene lit by a strange square sun, it portrayed an ecstatic Christ on the cross having his penis sucked by a hysterical Mary Magdalene, while the Virgin Mary was joyously drinking the blood spurting from her son's side from a wound caused by the lance of an indifferent Roman centurion on horseback.

'How do you react to that?' Dora asked Paul when they had a quiet moment together.

'Well it's Spain again, I suppose. The crucifixion is a traditional subject for a Catholic country and the centurion looks just like the picador entering the bullring.'

'And the Vatican has recognised Franco, now that he is all too likely to win, so there might be some point to the blasphemy. But it's so ferocious!'

Even more ferocious, however, were the female faces he was producing, following on from the Weeping Woman theme, but testing it to destruction. For he was dislocating these faces – of Nusch, Dora, Marie-Thérèse, or whoever –with extraordinary violence. He was even grossly dehumanizing them by giving a face a muzzle like that of a dog or a trunk like that of an elephant. Even Nusch, who normally did not take any of this too seriously, was taken aback.

'What's got into him?' she asked Dora

'That's just what I'm wondering, Nusch.'

'I've heard him joke about the trouble he has had with women!'

'He should be joking about the trouble women have had with him!' said Dora with a laugh.

But it was not really a laughing matter. Picasso might be depressed by events and might be attacking Franco's Fascist version of Catholic Spain, but why the emphasis on bloodsucking, lubricious women? Why not mangle the landscape, or the faces of men – like his own or Eluard's for that matter – rather than degrade and mangle the images of women? This was surely more than the old swaggering Spanish machismo, the idea that you master a woman and break her in like a mare. Did he at some deep, unconscious level hate women, fear women? The thought was an unnerving one – especially since it cast such a black shadow over the idea of having his child.

And that thought lingered on until the end of September when, just as Hitler was meeting the innocently smiling British Prime Minister Chamberlain at Bad Godesberg, they were driving back to Paris in the big Hispano-Suiza. With Marcel combining with Maurice Chevalier to remind them at intervals that you are what you are, and there may not be too much you can do about it.

'What exactly went wrong between you and *Maman*?'

They were having Sunday lunch again in the splendid Art Nouveau restaurant of the Lutétia at Sèvres-Babylone. The atmosphere was discreetly convivial, the *maître d'hôtel* was masterfully charming, the waiter Gaston had negotiated a civilized truce with her father in the obligatory negotiations over the successive dishes, Monsieur Markovitch was now about to engage with his Old Rum Baba with Chantilly Cream and Malaga ice cream – and it was this moment, of all moments, that his daughter chose to ask him what had gone wrong with his marriage…!

'Dora, I was about to eat my dessert!'

'Yes, *Papa*' she said with a smile, 'but I'm not sure that a man of your years and complexion should be gorging on Old Rum Babas swimming in Chantilly cream and Malaga ice cream.'

'You think I should be eating your Tangerine Tartlet, do you? The answer is that a lot of things went wrong, but the basic reason is that we had incompatible backgrounds and she was conventionally religious, whereas I was not. If things had worked at the sexual level, none of that might have mattered, but they didn't. A lot of it was my fault of course, but I'm not persuaded that marriage works too well anyway.'

'So what made you stay together?'

'Habit, I suppose, and probably guilt on my part. *Now* can I eat my Rum Baba?!'

'I'm sorry. I've just been wondering what makes relationships work. But can I just have a tiny spoonful of your Rum Baba?'

'Oh God, Dora! However, now you have decided that we should talk so frankly, what are you doing with that playactor Picasso?'

'But he's the greatest painter we have. And *Guernica* is touring Britain and the United States to raise money for the Spanish Relief fund. It's an enormous privilege for me to be part of all that.'

'And you love him?'

'Of course I do.'

Mr Markovitch proceeded silently for several minutes to deal respectfully with his Old Rum Baba, leaving Dora to tinker with her Tangerine Tartlet – and wonder what else he seemed to be about to say.

'You see' he said eventually, 'I'm a bit concerned. He's a foreign national for one thing, he's now politically exposed because of that *Guernica* mural and, with the Spanish Republic quite obviously going down the drain, his status is not secure – any more than yours is, Dora.'

'What on earth do you mean, *Papa*?'

'Look around you, Dora. Your Popular Front is dead and those Nazis in Germany are serious. They only waited five weeks after the Munich Agreement before they produced that night of smashed glass they've just treated us to.'

'Yes, the Kristallnacht, I know' she said impatiently.

'A thousand synagogues burnt down, a hundred people killed, thirty thousand arrested and who knows how many sent to concentration camps? We can't say we haven't been warned, can we?'

'No, but I don't see..."

'There is shortly going to be a major war in Europe, Dora. And I don't intend to hang around to see it.'

'You mean you would leave France? To go where...?'

'Back to Buenos Aires, why not?'

Gaston came over at that moment to inquire if Monsieur Markovitch was enjoying the Old Rum Baba with Chantilly cream and Malaga ice cream.

'Yes, it's not too bad, Gaston, not botched at all. But you could tell the chef to alter the balance slightly in favour of the Chantilly cream.'

'I'm quite sure he'll be delighted to have that advice, Monsieur Markovitch. And Mademoiselle's Tangerine Tartlet?'

'It's fine' said Dora impatiently.

'Of course' said Mr Markovitch as Gaston backed away elegantly, 'there would be no need for your mother to come along if I do have to go off. Good French and Spanish Catholics, as you can see, are quite at home with Fascism.'

'I think you're scaremongering a bit, *Papa*. We don't have Fascism – not yet anyway.'

'But if there's war and Hitler wins over these soft democracies, you will have. Even if there's no war and you're surrounded by Fascism in Germany, Spain and Italy, you're all too likely to have something similar here. Look at the anti-Semitic forces you already have in this country.'

'Yes, I know, *Papa*, but...'

'Believe me, Dora, it's not a good time to be a Jew.'

'But I'm not a Jew!'

'Neither am I. But Adolf Hitler and his friends, I have to tell you, would insist that we are.'

'He's in agony' said Sabartés in a hushed voice as he opened the door on a freezing day in December. 'Agony!'

'What's wrong with him?'

'It's from his thigh right down to his right foot' he said in the same hushed, doom-laden voice. 'And he can't feel it, you see.'

'Can't feel what, Jaume? I mean, if he's in agony...?'

'Can't feel his backside or the back of his right leg.'

'So there's numbness. Has he seen a doctor?'

'No, you know what he thinks about doctors.'

'Yes I do. I'd better go up and see him.'

She took off her heavy winter coat, went upstairs and found Picasso lying on the bed, half-dressed and propped up on pillows.

'So you've come to visit the poor old bugger, have you?' he said with a sour grin.

'Yes' she said, kissing him lightly. 'I thought I'd better see if the old Minotaur is on his last legs. So how is it?'

'It's agony if I change position. And agony if I don't!'

'It's terribly cold weather, of course. Could you have caught a chill out there in the wilds at Le Tremblay?' she asked, feeling his forehead. 'What are you grinning at?'

'Oh, it's just that Marie-Thérèse was in earlier and her theory was that I must have caught a chill here at Grands-Augustins, so I should stay at Le Tremblay. Isn't that funny?'

'Not really. Anyway, it can't be too bad if you don't want to see a doctor.'

'You're always trying to drag me to see a doctor – like that clown in Nice, who couldn't find anything wrong with me.'

'Because there wasn't anything wrong with you! Can you get up?'

'Just about, but it's hellishly painful.'

'Then you really ought to see a doctor.'

But it took another two days to persuade him. And even then he would only agree to see a doctor he knew. Which meant Jacques Lacan, who moved in avant-garde circles.

'But Lacan is basically a psychoanalyst, Picasso! Do you think you're just imagining the pain you're feeling?!'

'At least, if he knows me, he's less likely to try to trick me.'

Dora turned up as arranged for the visit of Lacan the next day, and was talking to Sabartés when she found to her embarrassment that Marie-Thérèse was also just arriving with Maya.

'I'm sorry' she said. 'he didn't tell me…'

'No' said Marie-Thérèse, equally embarrassed, 'he didn't tell me either.'

'He seems to be well enough to play games!' said Dora grimly.

Lacan arrived and was met by Sabartés, who received his feathered hat, elegant beige overcoat and multicoloured silk scarf. He then greeted Dora, who introduced Marie-Thérèse and, to his mild surprise and amusement, the two women accompanied him up to the bedroom, leaving a hesitant Sabartés behind.

Lacan greeted Picasso, asked a number of questions, announced that it looked like a straightforward case of sciatica, prescribed painkillers and bed rest, and said that with any luck there should be no need to call for Klotz.

'Call for Klotz?!'

'Yes, if it comes to cauterizing the sciatic nerve.'

This idea alarmed Picasso sufficiently to keep him motionless on the bed while Lacan escorted the two women downstairs, telling them they should leave him to rest.

'I sense' he told them confidentially, 'that your charge is quite a nervous patient who will need quite a lot of mothering. But to keep him fairly quiet' he added with a slightly roguish smile, 'I recommend that you take it in turns.'

And he was off, leaving them looking awkwardly at each other.

'Well, it's harder for you than for me' said Dora after a moment, 'since you have farther to come and you've got Maya to think of – you won't want her staying up late in this cold weather.'

'That's right, I wouldn't' said Marie-Thérèse uncertainly.

'So if I knew when you were coming, I could make sure I didn't get in your way. You could let me know through Sabartés or maybe directly by telephone – I'll give you my number. I mean, we'll have to be sure he's being looked after. And if you want to stay on now, I'll go off. All right?'

Marie-Thérèse, though still feeling overtaken by events, was sufficiently reassured to agree to this arrangement. And over the next week or so, up to the Christmas holiday, they did speak several times on the telephone, rather awkwardly at first but then more easily until they were taking each other, if not for granted, at least as a fact of life. However, it became clear that Picasso's condition was not improving and they agreed that they must both urge him to undergo the special treatment by this mysterious Dr Klotz.

This two-pronged attack having finally succeeded, they both turned up at the appointed time to support a deeply distrustful Picasso. Who, wincing as he strained to see what was happening, looked on askance as Dr Klotz, an impressively earnest and methodical man with a strictly ordered black beard, set up his elaborate apparatus for the operation.

After persuading Picasso to turn over and lie on his stomach, he explained carefully, as he identified the appropriate spot, that the process was one of conduction using a metal probe heated by an electric current.

'You're going to electrocute me?!'

'Not in the strict sense of the term, no. Keep quite still, can you?'

'I can't do anything else!'

'Now!' said Klotz.

As he applied the probe, there was a faint plosive sound and a small flash.

'Was that it?' asked Picasso.

'No, I'm most terribly sorry, but a fuse has blown. It may be your wiring, or it may be my equipment. It could possibly be the transformer.'

'Can I turn over at least?'

'Yes, of course. So sorry.'

All of which meant that the operation was postponed until the following day, that Picasso predicted at length that this would-be miracle of electrocution would never work, that it was folly for Dora and Marie-Thérèse ever to think that it could, and that the best it could achieve was to blow all the fuses and leave them in darkness while the whole house went up in flames. It also meant that Dora and Marie-Thérèse, since he was also complaining of the pain of having turned over, decided to leave him to rest, went out together laughing a little hysterically and ended up, at a suggestion from Dora, in a cafe at Saint-Michel, where they ordered coffees and a croissant with jam for little Maya.

'He *is* a bit of a big baby, isn't he?' said Marie-Thérèse, with a slightly nervous laugh.

'Yes, needing 'mothering', as Lacan said.'

'That portrait of you I saw in the attic, with that Spanish thing over your head...'

'The one with the mantilla, you mean?'

'He's done the exact same one of me.'

'Yes, I know' said Dora. 'With the same mantilla!'

'Yes, and a dusty old thing it is too. Did he tell you where it came from?'

'No, he didn't.'

'It was his mother's – I asked him' said Marie-Thérèse, then paused. 'She's not well, is she?'

'No, she's not. I think she may even be dying.'

As though they might have said too much, they sat silently for some moments, looking out at the bustling life in the square outside – until the background music switched to Rina Ketty's popular new number *J'Attendrai*.

'I hate that song!' Marie-Thérése burst out suddenly. 'Waiting, that's all I ever do. It's all right for you, you know. You go with him to all those fancy shows and restaurants and places and all I do is sit and wait.'

'But I don't live with him either' said Dora, seeing her red-faced and angry. 'I only go out with him when he asks me. The one who sees most of him isn't me – or you. It's Sabartés.'

'Yes, but you're all classy and educated and can talk about art and stuff. And all he thinks I'm good for is to wait for him to come and fuck me front or back as he fancies and then do a bit of sketching. And in between he's sending me lovey-dovey letters to make sure I don't do something silly – like doing away with myself...!'

As she collapsed into weeping, little Maya started to whimper and Dora was reaching out instinctively towards the child when Marie-Thérèse pushed her hand away angrily, stood up and yelled down at her furiously.

'That child is mine! How dare you touch that child!'

And with that she was gone, dragging Maya by the hand behind her. Leaving Dora to meet the stares of the customers at the other tables in a silence filled only by Rina Ketty promising to go on waiting day and night in *J'Attendrai*.

'I've stopped wishing people a Happy New Year' said Eluard. 'It's quite clear that 1939 is going to be a bloody awful year.'

'I'm afraid that's what it's looking like' said Dora.

It was Saturday and she was having a snack lunch with Paul and Nusch at the Deux Magots.

'Did you see that Hitler has been saying that the coming war – the 'coming war', if you please, he's just taking it for granted!- will see the destruction of the Jewish race in Europe!'

'He sounds like a lunatic' said Nusch.

'Except that he's in charge of the asylum' said Dora.

'Yes, war just seems inevitable now, after that sell-out at Munich' said Paul.

'Meanwhile, nothing can stop Franco winning in Spain.'

'And Pablo's mother is very ill, isn't she?' said Nusch. 'Will he get to see her?'

'Well, Barcelona is still free, but I'd be a little surprised if he went' said Dora. 'I'll find out on Monday.'

'But he is all right again?' asked Paul.

'Yes, Klotz's second attempt with a new transformer worked a treat, though Picasso was so convinced it wouldn't that he was almost disappointed' said Dora with a smile.

But she wasn't smiling at Picasso's opening gambit when she went along on Monday afternoon to photograph some of the December work. And found him sitting in the old wooden armchair in the attic studio, doing a charcoal sketch of a large ox skull he had picked up on the beach in the summer.

'So you've got to know Marie-Thérèse as a result of all this sciatica nonsense?' he asked, with a mischievous little smile.

'Yes, I've got to know her to an extent, I suppose.'

'And what do you think of her?'

'Do you really want to know?'

'Of course. Why wouldn't I?'

'I think she's unhappy, I think she feels badly treated, and I think she feels trapped.'

'What the hell are you saying?!'

'I thought it was clear.'

'What do you want me to do? Marry her?!'

'That's for you to decide.'

'What's got into you today?!'

'I also think, while I'm about it, that you should go and see your mother in Barcelona before it's too late.'

'That's also for me to decide, Dora.'

'Except that you never do decide. You wouldn't go to Spain even though they made you honorary director of the Prado and I just do not understand your attitude to your mother. You adopt your mother's maiden name and call yourself Picasso. You paint both Marie-Thérèse and me – and others before us, for all I know – wearing your mother's old mantilla. But you won't bother to go and see your mother, even though you know she's sick and dying.'

Picasso got up angrily and walked towards the attic window.

'It would only put pressure on her and the family.'

'Put pressure on *you*, do you mean?'

'Why are you so harsh and critical about everything today?'

'Perhaps because we live in harsh times, Picasso. I think we're sleepwalking towards a terrifying war.'

He turned from the window, glanced at her irritably, looked down at the eyeless, weather-beaten ox skull he had been sketching, then turned it over with his foot.

'I'll think about it' he said.

But Picasso, as Dora guessed, had already thought about it.

He did not go to see his mother in Barcelona, did not attend her funeral when she died eleven days later, and did not speak about it then or after Barcelona fell to Franco's forces at the end of January.

Dora did not speak about it either, although she knew that he was very aware that she was avoiding doing so. While he was heavily armoured against the world through his celebrity, his wealth and his sardonic distance, she was very conscious of the cracks in that armour: the superstition, the dread of illness, the reluctance to face intimate emotional situations. And she felt that there was more to his silence than casual indifference.

But she was not prepared for what happened one night early in March when they returned from a jolly evening at the Brasserie Lipp with the Eluards, Man Ray and Ady and a whole boisterous bunch of people. Since it was understood that Dora was staying the night, they went up laughing and joking to the bedroom. But when she returned after a few minutes in the bathroom, she was astonished to find Picasso sitting slumped fully dressed on the bed – crying.

'What is it?' she asked, stroking his face. 'What on earth is it?'

'Oh, it's nothing – and it's everything' he said, looking at her helplessly as tears rolled down his cheeks. 'It's war and death and disease and fucking and screaming and having to try to paint your way out of it – this world is a shithole…'

'But you *can* paint your way out of it' she said, kissing his cheek. 'You're a great painter…'

'But you shouldn't *need* to have to paint your way out of it – and you can never get out of it anyway. It's a living graveyard this world, it's a nightmare…'

'Did anybody say anything this evening to disturb you?' she asked cautiously.

'No no, nobody said anything, nobody ever says anything. What does it matter what anybody says…?'

Worried and still surprised, she kissed him repeatedly, helped him off with his jacket and eventually persuaded him to lie down beside her, half-undressed, under the top blanket on the bed. Stroking and kissing him until the crying subsided and they were just murmuring softly.

'That electric light bulb beside the lamp. And the women screaming…'

'The women screaming…?'

'It took a lot out of me that screaming. Like hearing my mother screaming in there somewhere…'

'Your mother…? But didn't you tell me once she was very cool and dignified…?'

'Yes, but there was this thing that happened when I was very small – only about three, maybe, and just when Lola was being born…'

'Your little sister…?'

'We were in this terrible earthquake in Malaga…'

'An earthquake? You never mentioned an earthquake.'

'No, but it was an enormous earthquake and that fucking mural sort of brought it back, because it was the same screaming and wreckage and confusion – and flames, you see, flames as well as this awful shuddering…'

'How dreadful…!'

'Yes, because my mother was screaming all big-bellied and naked and my father was yelling at her to get dressed for Jesus's sake, and then he was carrying me in this cape with these blood-stained crying women screaming at us and my mother screaming and crying along with them, so that no matter how dignified she was afterwards I could always remember her screaming naked through that earthquake and Lola being born and this basin with blood in it, red blood in it I could always see her screaming. And that's maybe part of why I didn't want to go back – because I felt so guilty, you see…'

'Guilty…?'

'I know, it's strange…'

'Because you'd seen her naked and screaming?'

'No, it was more than that. I was very small, of course, but it was as though it was me that had caused the earthquake, the screaming of the women, my mother's screaming during Lola's birth, that basinful of red blood and everything else. I must have thought deep down it was all my fault…'

'How terrible for you…! Poor little boy…!'

She was kissing his face softly, stroking him, saying she loved him, reassuring him, saying that little children blamed themselves for all sorts of impossible things, that it was all so unfair, that he could try to forget it all now and stop worrying…

And gradually, with the light still on, they stopped murmuring, became drowsy and fell asleep in each other's arms for perhaps an hour, or possibly two or three hours – Dora, happy and relaxed, neither knew nor cared how long. Until she woke up to the realisation that his hands were moving over her body and down to her crotch, and she was smiling drowsily as she turned towards him to find his trousers undone, and blinking in surprise at the bright light as she found herself being violently turned over and almost flung face downwards until he was on top of her, forcing her legs open with his knees and holding down her struggles as he tried, and failed, and tried again and half-succeeded in penetrating her anally, grunting and grunting in anger and frustration until he finally stopped and she lay there, half-roused and shocked and angered, slowly becoming aware of liquid sliding down between her thighs…

It was some minutes before she got up, went to the bathroom, washed herself and came back to find him sitting half-dressed on the bed as before.

Nothing was said as she found her clothes, dressed slowly, glanced at him briefly, went down the stairs and out into a dark and totally deserted Rue la Boétie.

She was doing a still-life of a jug, staring from the canvas to the jug, and back again.

It was a large grey earthenware jug, a handmade countrified jug with an amateurish floral pattern around it. A straightforward still-life by ordinary standards, but how could you convey the reality of such a jug? You could represent its appearance, just as you could confirm its function by placing a few glasses alongside it. But how could you convey the simple weight of it, or what it meant to the potter who made it? Or convey why that or anything else should exist in the first place? Or even say why she herself had chosen to paint it when for three days, in a dazed, circular fashion, she had been thinking about nothing but Picasso?

She had felt betrayed at first by what had happened and then a cold anger. It was not really the act in itself that mattered, messy and unsatisfactory though it was. Nor indeed was it exactly a revelation, given what Marie-Thérèse had implied and his own mentions of Sade. But he had never attempted it with her, perhaps out of respect, and it had been such a shocking change from the tenderness that preceded it. What really mattered was the intention behind the act. And the intention had clearly been to punish her.

But to punish her for what? Of course she had criticized the way he treated Marie-Thérèse, as well as his failure to go and see his mother before her death. But there was clearly much more to it than that. Wasn't he punishing her for having seen him crying and, above all, for having penetrated the armour which he had developed over the years and seen deep into the vulnerability that lay beneath? Punishing her for having found the timidity dictating the need to play the showman or the superman? Punishing her for having glimpsed the origin of the Minotaur, with his guilty sense of being driven by some monster within him and his obscure feeling that the sexual act in itself was somehow evil?

But it was not only her that he was punishing. Wasn't he also punishing himself? For openly revealing his inner self, his own private Guernica and for the advantage which he apparently felt that he had allowed her. Perhaps even for the brutal clumsiness of his attempt to retrieve the advantage, as suggested by the grunts of his apparent frustration and his slumped appearance when she found him sitting half-dressed on the bed as before. It had all been a little pathetic, an unedifying event that neither of them might find it easy to recover from.

Which was why she had not answered the telephone for the past three days. Why she had not responded to a wryly amusing cartoon slipped yesterday through her letter-box, showing a dominant, upright Dora turning away from a bowed, remorseful Picasso. And why she had still not decided how to respond to a simpler message, slipped through the letter-box that morning, saying that he would call at seven o'clock to see whether she would care to go out to dinner. At least, she thought as she gazed at the grey earthenware jug, he seemed to have understood her feelings about the incident and be trying to apologize in his own pictorial fashion.

In any event, was she perhaps making too much of what had happened? Was she, in fact, punishing him in her turn? Was she, indeed, missing the essential? Hadn't she seen through to the frightened, lost little child overwhelmed by that awful earthquake in Malaga, assuming guilt for a disaster far beyond his comprehension let alone his control? Wasn't she the more moved by his vulnerability in that she had found him still within the grown man? Wasn't that why he was bold in his painting but superstitious, fearful of change and unable to throw anything away? Wasn't that why he was kind and generous with others, but penny-pinching with his family and often cruel to those close to him – as though needing to keep testing his own power? Wasn't that why this man so attractive to women could not quite open himself up to them, and why this superlative showman was a little shy? And wasn't it in fact those contradictions, that weakness within strength, that she loved in Picasso…?

And if loving meant understanding, was it not her role, and her privilege, to help him to release that little boy from his anguish, to help make Picasso whole? In love you had to go beyond pettiness, beyond calculation, you had to be prepared to go the whole distance. Indeed, if he really had been trying to 'punish' her, was it not also because she had not demonstrated enough trust in him to show herself willing to carry his child…?

Not only could there be no question of letting go of Picasso but, strangely or not, the unexpected event of three nights earlier had led her to the realization that she wanted to have a child by this man.

She took a last long look at the earthernware jug, put away her palette and her brushes, and went off to sort out something rather special to wear for dinner.

With events beginning to dictate everything in 1939, it seemed to Dora that, in seeking to become pregnant, she was swimming against the tide of history.

For every month seemed to bring a new turn of the screw. At the end of January, after the fall of Barcelona, France opened an internment camp for 'undesirable foreigners'. In February, Britain promised to support France if attacked, which in effect announced the line-up for the coming war. In March, Hitler tore up the Munich agreement and marched into Czechoslovakia, just as the Spanish Civil War was ending with Franco's capture of Madrid. And then April capped all this with the enormous, triumphalist parade in Berlin for Hitler's fiftieth birthday, which seemed to set the stage for what was to come.

With these events going hand in hand with Dora's equally momentous design to bring new life rather than death into the world, the year wore on until they went south early in July – this time to Antibes, where Man Ray had lent them a modern apartment. They both worked there for two weeks until the next disaster, one that was closer to home, for Picasso's dealer Ambroise Vollard was travelling in his car when a bronze sculpture propped up on the back seat fell forward suddenly and broke his neck. Picasso saw a sinister omen in this occurrence since Vollard's chauffeur was called Marcel, just like his own. Which drove him to take the train when he went up to Paris on his own for the funeral.

Dora was less than pleased when he returned with Sabartés, and even less so when he took advantage of Jacqueline Breton's arrival to go off with him on a five-day jaunt to attend a bullfight.

'It's just a boy thing' said Jacqueline with a smile. 'Getting away from the women and all that.'

'Yes, but it happens to be inconvenient. Between you and me, I'm trying to get pregnant.'

'I must say, Dora, I admire your spirit. I spend my time trying *not* to get pregnant!'

They talked a great deal over the following weeks about Jacqueline and André's trip to Mexico, about their meeting with Trotsky and about Jacqueline's lesbian adventure with the Mexican painter Frida Kahlo. They painted portraits of each other, agreed that they were both moving beyond Surrealism and, on Picasso's return, featured as two carefree young women licking ice creams while observing fishermen savagely spearing fish in his canvas *Night Fishing at Antibes*. But all this was dwarfed by the bombshell of the Hitler-Stalin pact, which suggested strongly that war was imminent and sent them hurrying back by train to a confused Paris, where Dora visited her mother while Picasso tried to find a way of removing to a bank vault the many paintings piled up at Grands-Augustins.

Forced to give up after four frantic days, he left with Dora for Royan, the seaside resort just north of Bordeaux where he had placed a complaining Marie-Thérèse for the summer – and where they arrived the day before war began with Hitler's invasion of Poland at the start of September. He booked into the very tame Hotel du Tigre, a fair distance from the villa where Marie-Thérèse and Maya were staying, and also booked a so-called studio in that villa so that the locals would not be too scandalized as he moved freely between the two women.

This was a difficult situation for Dora, and it was not relieved by the arrival of Jacqueline with Aube, in search of a refuge now that André was on attachment to the air force, for Picasso insisted on introducing her to Marie-Thérèse, on the grounds that this would enable the two little girls to play together. The arrangement worked all too well, thereby leaving Dora feeling isolated, especially as Picasso chose to spend much of his spare time wandering around with Sabartés. But perhaps the most painful thing was his otherwise charming habit, although he normally declared that only effeminate men went in for dancing, of leaving her alone in the afternoon to fetch little Maya and, with her little feet on his, go dancing to jazz in a nearby bar. It seemed to be all about children all over again – and not even Jacqueline appeared to understand the depth of her isolation.

Feeling imprisoned by the war in a false situation, she tried to cope by painting. But she also went quietly to consult a local doctor, a florid middle-aged man by the name of Legat, who appeared to feel that her concerns about pregnancy were a little frivolous on the day it was announced that the Russians had joined in the invasion of Poland. Irregular periods, or discomfort during what he insisted on calling coitus? All very common. And if she and her, er, partner, had only, as he understood it, been, er, aiming at this result for some months, well it was much too early to come to any very firm conclusion – it often took a year or more. The secret was relaxation, difficult though that might be at this dreadful time. It was useful that she recognised the time of the month when she ovulated, and it would be helpful to cut down on alcohol and on smoking, but the real secret was relaxation – never forgetting, of course, regular and satisfying coitus. And were she and her, er, companion planning to stay long in Royan…?

Not totally convinced by this, Dora took advantage of the opportunity to accompany Picasso when he had to return to Paris to obtain an official residence permit. She managed to make an appointment with a consultant gynaecologist named Desforges on the Boulevard Malesherbes, but first she comforted her mother, who was concerned that her husband was intent on abandoning her for good by leaving for Argentina. She also talked privately with her father, who argued that her mother would be well provided for, that what he was doing was simply prudent, and that Dora should consider leaving as well.

'But why on earth should I? I can't possibly leave.'

'Well in that case, Dora, you might just be glad one day that your Jewish father did leave.'

Still troubled by all this, she went to her appointment with the gynaecologist Dr Desforges, a highly precise, grey-haired man who asked her a whole series of questions about sexual frequency, about her periods and about any related pelvic or lower back pain. Following that, he undertook a quite lengthy internal examination – apologising for the pain it was causing as he went along. At the end he said that, while she could of course seek a second opinion, his own view was that a combination of symptoms – especially the heavy periods, the occasional pelvic pain and, indeed, her often acute discomfort during his examination – would lead him to conclude that it was a case of endometriosis.

'Oh? And how is that treated?'

'Well, it's possible to remove adhesions or cysts by surgery, but I'm afraid the conventional view is that the condition –while not in any way fatal, of course – is not curable.'

'And your own view?'

'I can only agree with the conventional view, I'm afraid.'

'So what exactly does this mean, Docteur?"

'It means, Madame – and I'm deeply sorry to have to tell you this – that you are almost certainly infertile.'

She thanked him with great dignity, went out, crossed the boulevard, went into a small public garden, sat down on a bench, stared up into the branches of a chestnut tree, remained still for several minutes – and then burst into sobs that shook her whole body. It was perhaps half an hour before she got up, mindful of her arrangement to meet Picasso for the return journey to Royan. Mindful also of his superstitious dread of any illness or weakness, which determined her to keep this matter secret – and not be seen to cry.

The whole way back to Royan, she talked about this and that – and didn't cry.

It was the lack of freedom that was so shocking, the fact that she had never had the choice to get pregnant in the first place…

10

'Thank the stars for that!' said Picasso. 'The last thing I needed was Maurice Chevalier crying!'

'Yes, but do you think this is any better?' said Dora with a smile, as the café music switched from Chevalier's *Je pleurais* to Edith Piaf singing *Je n'en connais pas la fin*. 'If she doesn't know how it's going to end, neither do we.'

'All I know is that this bloody man Hitler is making my life hell!'

'Yes, he obviously miscalculated.'

'Miscalculated what?'

'The degree of inconvenience to which Picasso might be subjected by world war, of course.'

'Yeah, very droll, this *drôle de guerre*!'

This *drôle de guerre*, or 'phoney war', was both irritating and mystifying. Since France and Britain did not go to the aid of Poland, it hardly seemed that they were in the war at all. It was the more inconvenient for Picasso since, unlike those leaving for America, he could not even imagine doing so. He could not contemplate abandoning his pictures, which filled two rooms in a bank vault. In addition, he had Marie-Thérèse and Maya, he had Dora, he had Paolo and even some lingering financial obligation to Olga. Above all, he had his superstitious suspicion of change. In any event, while his application for naturalization was refused, he expected a degree of protection from Dubois, the senior detective in the Sûreté who had intervened to get him the residence permit. And since there was no indication that France would lose, the obvious thing to do was to stay put and not tempt fate.

As though to emphasize the unreality of these eight months of the *drôle de guerre,* Picasso found himself being advantageously photographed for the magazine *Life* in such typical Parisian haunts as the Brasserie Lipp and the Café de Flore, all this as publicity for the retrospective of his work at the Museum of Modern Art in peaceful New York. But the frequent comings and goings between Royan and Paris were dictated more by the need to check on the studio, to buy canvases or simply to try to find out what was going on. Dora, who accompanied him on many of these often lengthy trips, was delighted to escape from Royan and from the stifling atmosphere of the Picasso stable that had formed there – which Picasso himself had tried to escape by taking a studio on the top floor of a seafront villa, which he kept strictly to himself.

The familiarity of Paris enabled her to relax, to visit her mother and to see friends – including Eluard, on leave from his posting as a lieutenant in the supply corps. But above all, perhaps, Dora was relieved to escape from the troubling atmosphere of Picasso's painting at this time. For it was clear that this eerie waiting for the fighting to begin was wearing him down and, since he tended to express his revulsion against the world by distorting and dislocating the female form, she sometimes felt – as she told him tartly on one occasion – that he was trying to do to her what Hitler was doing to Poland.

However, none of this deterred him from complaining about the disruption and the sheer wear-and-tear of this ominous interlude of the *drôle de guerre.*

'What the hell is this clown Hitler playing at?!' he burst out one day in May 1940 over lunch in Le Catalan. 'This is getting unbearable!'

'You were cross at him for declaring war' said Dora, laughing. 'And now you can't wait for him to attack! Don't worry, he will!'

And he did. He attacked through Belgium two days later and the effect was stunning. For the French and British armies already seemed to be collapsing when they left for Royan six days later, just ahead of the streams of refugees blocking all roads leading south. By mid-June, they heard that Paris had fallen, a week later they heard that an armistice had been signed, and by the end of the month they could see with their own eyes the red flag with its inset swastika flapping triumphantly in the sea breeze from the flagpole of the town hall in Royan. It was bewildering.

And that was only half of the disaster. For France had not only been divided into two, with direct German occupation in the north and a so-called free zone in the south. It now acquired an authoritarian right-wing government in Vichy under Marshal Pétain, who assumed full powers, suspended elections and trade unions – and took little time to meet Hitler and promise collaboration with the Germans. All this was worse than Dora and Picasso could have imagined, and it was something of a nightmare when they returned at the end of August to a dazed Paris – to find German soldiers strolling the streets, German officers dining in the Brasserie Lipp, and the Gestapo installed both in the Avenue Foch and in the Rue de la Pompe.

But if Paris itself had become a mysterious threat, they still had to find a way of living in it. There was the curfew, there were food and fuel shortages, and a rapidly developing black market – though not for artists' materials, which sometimes saw Picasso reduced to painting on newspapers. However, for Dora, more politically aware than Picasso, there was the overarching tragedy of the alliance of Nazi Germany and the Soviet Union. Also, her father had gone, leaving her mother desolate, Man Ray and so many others among their Jewish acquaintances had left, while Jacqueline and André Breton were also planning an escape to America.

Paradoxically, while Dora and Picasso were drawn closer by their situation at this time, the very closeness led to rough badinage and even mischief-making by Picasso, who liked to try to knock Dora off what he saw as her pedestal. Since Le Tremblay had been largely wrecked by the Germans, he had installed Marie-Thérèse in an apartment on the Boulevard Henri IV on the Right Bank. But if he did so on the grounds that she should be kept at an appropriate distance from Dora, he was still tempted on occasion to liven things up by setting them one against the other.

Having arranged for a dress which had been made for Dora to be wrongly delivered to a furious Marie-Thérèse, he engineered a repetition of the confrontation that had taken place during the painting of *Guernica*. When Marie-Thérèse demanded that he finally choose between them and marry her, Dora allowed herself to be drawn into saying that it was her that he loved. Which enabled him to exploit the opportunity in the grand theatrical manner.

'Dora Maar' he declared solemnly, 'it is Marie-Thérèse Walter that I love.'

This led a triumphant Marie-Thérèse to start a scuffle by which she eventually forced Dora to leave. It also led, as Dora anticipated, to a subsequent phone call from Picasso saying that the encounter had been unfortunate.

'I'm glad you realise that' she replied coldly.

'Well, I hope you understand why I said what I said.'

'I understand perfectly why you said what you said. Do you?'

'What do you mean? You don't think I intend to marry Marie-Thérèse?'

'Of course I don't think that. But does *she,* poor woman?'

For she knew that Picasso would never wish to be seen with Marie-Thérèse in the sophisticated artistic circles in which he and Dora moved. Nor, indeed, could he allow her to grow up beyond his own image of her.

'You do sound very annoyed, Dora.'

'Oh, not really. It's just that schoolboy tricks are better left to schoolboys – they do it better.'

You had to play Picasso's game, hit the ball back, stand up to him. But the game was getting harder. For it was no longer just a matter of standing up to Picasso, but of standing up to this all-enveloping war.

'What is this war doing to people?' asked Dora rhetorically over lunch in Le Catalan one wet November day.

'Making them thinner' said Picasso.

'If only that was all it was doing to them. It certainly doesn't seem to be making them better people.'

For the war was not just something far away in the Atlantic or North Africa, it was here in France, an everyday presence, a cancer in the nation.

'At least I'm glad I'm not Jewish' said Dora.

'I wouldn't say that too loudly' said Picasso, glancing around the restaurant.

'Why not?'

'Because somebody might wonder why you're saying it.'

Certainly, the Jews were being systematically targeted. Within months of the defeat they had been excluded by Pétain's new government from public office and the media, by May 1941 they were required to wear the yellow star, and by June they were excluded from jobs in banking, universities and the liberal professions. More threateningly, the government had already, of its own volition, set up an elaborate commissariat for Jewish affairs, charged with creating a national database of all Jews in France. This was accompanied by a large exhibition in September designed to demonstrate the Jewish threat to France, then by the great round up of Jews for the concentration camps in the summer of 1942. And this was not the Germans against the French. This was the French against the French.

And not just against the Jews. For resistance to the occupier had been growing, particularly after the Germans attacked the Soviet Union, which brought the Communists back into the anti-Fascist camp. With the killing of some German soldiers, the savage reprisals that ensued, and the sense that there might be spying eyes upon you in the Metro or in the restaurant – even Le Catalan – the city had become an uneasy place.

'You're not suggesting' said Dora, resuming in a low murmur. 'that I myself am Jewish?'

It occurred to her that Picasso knew that her full family name was Markovitch. Could he also believe that she might be Jewish?

'I'm suggesting' replied Picasso in a non-committal low tone, 'that there are other things to talk about.'

And there were indeed other things, but they were not necessarily safer things. For the increasingly bitter division in the country was glaringly obvious from the controlled newspapers and the official radio, not to mention the choice of films in the cinemas or topics in the magazines. And of course all this had been sanctified, in a sense, by the Church declaring its allegiance to Marshal Pétain, a move which did not improve relations between Dora and her mother.

'But it's a Fascist régime, *Maman*' she had said.

'It's defending Christianity against Bolshevism, Dora.'

'But it's destroying all our republican freedoms, it's deporting innocent people…'

'Well maybe that's the price you have to pay to get away from all that atheism and Communism that was corrupting the country and making us lose the war. The Marshal is trying to redeem us.'

'I'm not sure the people he's punishing are feeling redeemed!'

'Well, perhaps they were too involved in all that Surrealism and stuff. I'm afraid your father and you have a lot to answer for, Dora.'

'But *Papa* has never been a Communist or a Surrealist – quite the opposite.'

'Well, whatever he was, he's not here, is he? He has left me alone in the middle of a war with only the Church to help me.'

'But *I'm* here, *Maman*. I'll help you.'

'Except that you're still living in sin with that foreigner Picasso, aren't you?'

242

'Oh, not again *Maman*, please…!'

For there was no escape from it. It was as though the real war was in the mind. It was everywhere, in politics, religion, even the popular song, with Maurice Chevalier now hated for singing to German audiences. But most directly worrying for Picasso and Dora was the sinister war that was being waged over painting.

For in October 1941 a number of painters, including Vlaminck and Derain, had accepted an invitation to go on a cultural tour of Germany. This was lavishly promoted in the collaborationist press and was followed up in the summer of 1942 by a fierce attack on Picasso by Vlaminck, of a violence matching his own stormy landscapes. For Picasso, he argued in a resounding article, had all but killed off French painting, by leading it 'beyond the dead end of Cubism to negation, helplessness and death'. And all this was bolstered by savagely personal comments about him as a 'sort of monster', with 'the eyes of an inquisitor' and as 'impotence in human form'.

'This isn't art criticism' raged Picasso. 'It's an attempt to get me deported or assassinated.'

'And you can't afford to do a thing about it' said Dora.

The controversy was the more damaging in that it fed into the Fascist idea that it was Jewish influence that was responsible for the 'decadence' of modern art. And since Picasso was seen as the prime example of this decadence, a non-naturalised immigrant and the painter of that monstrous mural for the defeated Spanish Republic, he could be suspected of being halfway to Jewishness and at least of associating with Jews. Which was a thought that was particularly alarming for Dora.

She believed she was not a Jew, she had never felt herself to be a Jew, nor did she want to be a Jew, but she had noted her father's warning that she might have Jewishness thrust upon her. And she was now uneasily grateful to him for having left the country, since he would doubtless have been on the national database and it would then have been easier to get to her. But her connection with

Picasso – who might or might not believe that she was Jewish – now seemed to be even more alarming. She knew that the address in the Rue des Grands-Augustins was regularly watched, so they would certainly have seen her coming and going and investigated her. So, in this worsening atmosphere, could she be safe?

It was lucky at least that she was not present when there was a raid on Picasso's studio by the German police, and lucky also that Dubois, his protector at the Sûreté, was there to mediate. Of course they had long since made an inventory of Picasso's works in the bank vault, but this was the first hostile visit. They looked around, called Dubois a degenerate for his trouble, mocked works which they found mystifying, kicked a canvas or two and went off. But they threatened ominously to come back and both Picasso and Dubois were sufficiently alarmed to call on Jean Cocteau. Picasso had never liked Cocteau, quite apart from the fact that he was well in with the German cultural authorities and had just written a piece welcoming an exhibition by Arno Breker, the German sculptor whose monumental male nudes were hailed by Hitler as the highest expression of Aryan manhood.

Cocteau having reported back that he had phoned the German Ambassador Otto Abetz, who if required might contact Arno Breker, Dora was left wondering if the world she was living in was some sort of lunatic asylum. As a non-Jew who might yet be defined and killed for being a Jew, she could be dependent on Picasso, who was dependent on the dubious Cocteau, who was dependent on Otto Abetz, who might have to depend on Arno Breker, who might or might not be able to depend on his possible access to Himmler or Hitler. And that was if any of them got the message, or had the time, or could be bothered. It all seemed so frighteningly flimsy and implausible.

Dora cried that evening at the shame, the humiliation and the sheer impossibility of her position. Just as she had no freedom of choice about whether to have a child, so she had no choice about being seen as Jewish or non-Jewish. She was the plaything of forces she could not even identify, let alone control.

But she did not let Picasso see her crying. Nor did she mention the other frightening possibility, that since she might already be listed on the Jewish database, they could get at Picasso through her – that instead of her being dependent on him, he might be dependent on her.

What, in this corrupted France of suspicion, rumour and revenge, was going to happen to them – either singly or together?

'Well, Dora my darling, I hope I have done you justice' said Cocteau, wiping his hands delicately.

In the five or six months since he had come to be seen as potentially useful, the gay flamboyant Cocteau had begun to drop in fairly frequently and today, at Picasso's invitation, he was painting Dora's portrait in her own studio.

'I've a horrible feeling that you have!' said Dora, with a wry laugh.

'Well, perhaps it's just a teeny bit severe, but we're all suffering from this silly war.'

But Jean Cocteau, thought Dora, wasn't suffering in the least from this war. A life-and-death struggle might be going on at Stalingrad, the Allies might be landing in North Africa, the Americans and Japanese might be fighting epic naval battles in the Pacific, but Cocteau clearly thought that to take sides in a world war was slightly vulgar. His loyalties were to art, to drugs obtained with the complicity of the Germans, and to the pleasure of the moment.

'You did say Pablo was coming over, did you, Dora?'

'Yes, he should be here by now.'

'Well, I do have a rendezvous' he smiled. 'But I can leave them panting for me a little longer. Which will give me time to admire your pictures.'

And for the next few minutes he looked at the pictures on her walls, but kept coming back to the *Dora and the Minotaur* over the mantelpiece.

'It must be wonderful to have been desired like that' he said broodingly.

Given the possible inference, intended or not, that she was no longer desired like that, Dora was relieved to see Picasso come in. To go straight to the easel and examine the portrait intently from every angle, leaving them watching in silence as he appeared to meditate at length before turning gravely towards Cocteau.

'It's brilliant, Jean' he said. 'Brilliant.'

While this sent Cocteau happily on his way, it left Dora eyeing Picasso quizzically.

'You overdid it a little, didn't you?'

'You can't overdo it with Cocteau' he grinned. 'That man's capacity for absorbing flattery is bottomless.'

'So what *do* you think of the portrait?'

'It's superficial. It's outside-in instead of inside-out. However, it's correctable.'

'Correctable?'

'Yes, I'll make a few changes – that background for a start.'

And over the next week and more, he worked at intervals and without using Dora as model, to correct Cocteau's portrait. Until she was seen as oddly off-centre against a dark gloomy background and her image had become transformed. For he imagined her in a green-and-red striped dress, with a pathetic lace collar and trimmings, of a sort that might have been worn by a housemaid, the effect being strengthened by the tightness with which the vertical red and green stripes contained the body. But the really telling effect came from the eyes. He had simplified the face, enlarged the eyes and given them great black pupils so that the strained face, staring straight ahead, suggested desperation. This, as Dora recognised with something approaching horror, was the real inside-out portrait. It was not what she looked like, but what Picasso thought – perhaps even rightly – that she had become.

And it was just when she was skirting around the subject of the portrait with Picasso in his studio one evening that she received yet another call from her mother, complaining that she had not been to visit her.

'But I dropped over yesterday, *Maman*, and you weren't in. And I've been quite busy. I have things to do as well, you know...'

Since her mother was obviously angry, the argument went on for several more minutes, with Picasso looking across irritably at moments – until her mother stopped speaking.

'Hullo?' said Dora. 'Hullo? Hullo? Hullo...?'

'She has put the phone down' said Picasso curtly.

'No, she hasn't, I can still hear it. There's something wrong.'

'She's playing games.'

'No, she's not. I'd better go round there.'

'You can't. It's after curfew. You'd be picked up. You can go in the morning.'

Dora stared at him. The risk was indeed real. But the awfulness of not doing anything, the shame of it...

'You can't do it! It's too dangerous – for both of us' he said with a look that warned her not to weaken and cry.

'Yes – for both of us...' she said coldly.

Dora was stunned by what she found next morning. Her mother lying dead with her face distorted and the telephone receiver still clutched in her hand. Her cat moving around questioningly, mewing for attention and probably food. The indignity of it. Not a glorious, patriotic death on some world war battlefield, just an ordinary, modest civilian death of the kind that went almost unnoticed every day. But it was her mother, her not very happy mother. And now she would have to be put in a box and buried in the ground.

But there must be things to do: the death to be registered, a funeral to be arranged, the neighbours and any remaining relatives of her mother to be informed, her father to be contacted somehow – not that he could ever attend. Where to start?

She phoned Lise Deharme and Marie-Laure de Noailles for advice, got helpful information from a widowed neighbour, contacted her mother's doctor, visited the local funeral director's office, had the body removed, registered the death – and was left with the embarrassing task of approaching the Church.

Rather than operate through the funeral director, she went directly to her mother's place of worship, which she knew to be Saint-Sulpice. A little daunted as she entered, she sat down for a moment at the back, getting used to the filtered light of the interior. So this was where her mother worshipped. Where her father had come that day to have his 'neural networks' stimulated by the playing of the famous organ, now silent. This was where, as she had learnt over the phone, Marie-Laure's ancestor the Marquis de Sade had got baptized, where Victor Hugo had got married. This was a place that was steeped in history.

And that was how it worked, she reflected. They hit you with two thousand years of history. The enormous height of the nave dwarfed you to miniature size, the stained glass windows annexed the daylight in the service of the Bible story, the Latin reduced your involvement to uncomprehending mumbles of assent to propositions in the language of a bygone Roman empire. And this was where her poor mother had regularly come to seek solace…

Seeing a duty priest moving around near the altar, she approached him diffidently, unable to bring herself to address him as 'Father'. But he turned questioningly towards her, a relatively young priest, with a respectful but easy smile.

'I have to arrange a funeral' she said. 'It's for my mother, who has been a regular worshipper at Saint-Sulpice. You may not have known her. The name was Markovitch.'

'Madame Markovitch? Madame *Julie* Markovitch?'

'Well yes…'

'Oh, I'm so sorry. You have my sympathy, er… Madame…?'

'Mademoiselle.'

'Yes, we knew her well here. She helped with the flowers and the magazine display. What a pity.' He smiled. 'So you're the famous daughter?'

'Am I?!'

'Oh yes, she was very proud of you, always talking about your career.'

This conversation brought Dora to tears when she got back out to the church square, so disconcerted that she walked around aimlessly for some time before coming upon a café in the Rue de Vaugirard and ordering a cognac.

In the event, the funeral went quite well. While Picasso did not attend, it was partly because he would not have wished to and partly because his presence might have attracted undue interest – the presence of Marie-Laure, being a Vicomtesse, created interest enough. Eluard, now in the underground Communist Party, was away in the Resistance, but Nusch came along with Lise, while her mother's cousin and a nephew were there, along with neighbours and friends, so that the presence of a group by the graveside made the burial tolerable.

But for weeks afterwards, as she cleared up her mother's affairs, Dora brooded on her life and death. Had she been fair to her mother? Had she been partly responsible for her obvious unhappiness and lack of freedom? Had she identified unconsciously with her errant father in an attempt to escape her mother's fate? And, most troubling thought of all, was she herself any more likely, with this war poisoning everything, to achieve freedom and fulfilment…?

'I must say your restaurant is getting livelier by the minute, Pablo' said Charles.

'You could be right' said Picasso, looking around the crowded Le Catalan. 'It must be the black market beef.'

It was a fine May evening in 1943 and Marie-Laure de Noailles and her handsome husband the Vicomte, both formidable collectors of modern art, had come over to the Latin Quarter to see what Picasso, who of course was unable to exhibit, had been up to. And while they had responded warmly to his new sculpture the *Man with a Sheep*, they were visibly taken aback by the harshness of much of his recent work.

'It's always interesting how different artists react to their models' Charles had said in his exquisitely courteous fashion, attempting to disguise his surprise at some of the treatments of what he took to be a dislocated Dora.

'Don't worry, Charles' said Dora, 'He's not waging World War Two against me, he's waging World War Two against himself, isn't that so, Picasso?'

'Psychology and nonsense!' he retorted. 'But it *is* mysterious' he added with a wicked grin. 'You might even think that Dora didn't attract me any more!'

'I know!' said Dora, trying to match the grin, 'And you might even think that this little sixtyish grey codger didn't attract me any more!'

Even a highly sophisticated couple like Charles and Marie-Laure – he was basically gay, while she compensated with a succession of lovers – were a little disconcerted by the banter between Picasso and Dora. But then, as Dora had murmured to Marie-Laure as they were strolling across to the restaurant, the war didn't just draw you together, it flung you together – and it could hurt.

Meanwhile Le Catalan had gradually filled up while they were eating the black market beef – courtesy of some crooked arrangement, which might even be tolerated for their own reasons by the authorities – and had indeed become livelier.

'Perhaps it's because people have just got used to the war?' said Marie-Laure.

'Or been cheered up by the German defeat at Stalingrad' said Charles. What do you think, Dora?'

'Oh Dora probably thinks it's just 'psychological', don't you. Dora?'

'No, I think the war is reaching a tipping point…'

'A 'tipping point'?' interrupted Picasso. 'What does that mean?'

'Oh, it just means that the Allies look like winning – though with Hitler unlikely to surrender, things could well get worse before they get better.'

'And I'm supposed to be the pessimistic one!' said Picasso mockingly.

'Meanwhile' said Dora with a smile, 'I'm ashamed to say I did enjoy that black market beef.'

'Pity they don't run to real black market coffee' said Marie-Laure. 'Still, you do get a colourful crowd in here. That's Alain Cuny there, isn't it? Did you see *Les Visiteurs du soir?*'

It was indeed Alain Cuny, the tall gaunt actor who had played a minstrel in the recent Marcel Carné film, sitting at a neighbouring table with two young women of around twenty, possibly drama students to judge by the striking green turban worn by one and the elaborate makeup worn by the other. Dora had already noticed them – and noticed that Picasso had noticed them.

'Oh, Dora didn't like that film *Les Visiteurs du soir*' he said, loudly enough for his words to carry to Alain Cuny and the girls at the neighbouring table. 'Did you, Dora?'

'Dora didn't quite say that' she said equally loudly, with an apologetic grimace towards the other table. 'I just said it's a pity the German Occupation limits us to watching films about the Middle Ages and minstrels and the Devil.'

'You mean it wasn't 'psychological' enough for you?' laughed Picasso, before turning towards the neighbouring table. 'You hear that, Cuny? It's all about psychology! Is that what you use when you're acting – psychology?'

'Oh, I just follow the script' replied Cuny with a smile.

The two young women, both quite goodlooking, were smiling across expectantly now, as though they had gathered who this demonstrative diner at the neighbouring table was.

'I'd better go and introduce myself' said Picasso.

'Don't you think you already have?!' said Dora.

He picked up a bowl of cherries from the table, took it across, offered it around and stood chatting to the girls and Cuny, with Marie-Laure and Dora rolling their eyes knowingly at each other as they watched the girls respond smilingly while he laughed and gesticulated, dancing from foot to foot.

'Do you think, Charles, that you should go over and help him out?' said Marie-Laure sweetly after a minute or two.

'You think so?' said Charles, getting up and moving off with an apologetic gesture.

'But Picasso didn't look to me as though he needed help!' said Dora, in surprise.

'No, but I fancy Charles would like to ply his charms on Alain Cuny' said Marie-Laure with a grin. 'It's just that he's so deliciously aristocratically polite that you have to give him permission.'

'Oh God!' said Dora with a helpless little laugh. 'You know, Marie-Laure, I wonder if you're not the one with the perfect relationship.'

'No, it's not quite perfect, Dora. Any more than yours is, I imagine.'

'No, that's not perfect either. And I expect it's more draining than yours.'

'Do you ever feel like giving up?'

'Oh I've no intention of giving up. And he's such an enormous part of my life by now, I doubt if I could even if I wanted to.'

Picasso's hand, as Dora noticed discreetly, was shaking slightly.

It had been like walking into another dimension as they left the thin March sunlight behind them and moved into the quieter, other world of this church of Saint Roch in the Rue Saint-Honoré. And, for most of them, unbelievers as they largely were, it was a world in which they felt doubly uneasy. For although an attempt had been made to keep this memorial mass quiet to avoid it being seen as a political provocation by the authorities, there had nevertheless been plainclothes men outside noting the names of those attending. Yet they had come: Eluard, Braque, the

Catholic novelist François Mauriac – forty or fifty of them. To honour a Jew.

There had been the subdued attempts at normal conversation as they arrived, shook hands, said what a terrible end for Max, Louis XIV laid the first stone here, the Marquis de Sade was married here – no escape, apparently, from the Marquis de Sade. But now, apart from the few that were kneeling in prayer, they sat in this solid silence. Waiting. With Picasso's right hand, as he sat beside her resting it on his knee, shaking slightly.

March 1944 and for Dora it was as though the ground was disappearing from beneath her feet. It was not just the sense that the walls were closing in from every direction, but the dreamlike ambiguity of it all, the nagging fear of not knowing just what or who you were up against.

It was all around you, this ambiguity, now that the tide had turned against the Germans. They were being driven back by the Soviets, the Americans were advancing on Rome and the Allies were obviously about to invade France, but the more the vice tightened the more they seemed to need to kill Jews. And, if some of the French collaborators were trying to cover their tracks, others had burnt their boats and were going down in glory. How, in this poisoned atmosphere, with Jews being hunted down all around you, could you begin to feel safe? Especially since the same dark ambiguity had seeped into her relationship with this man sitting beside her with his hand shaking.

For the two young women with Alain Cuny in Le Catalan that evening in May of the previous year had turned out to be art students and one of them – the one with the green eyes and the green turban – had visited Picasso once or twice after that. Dora had not really been concerned, especially since this Françoise had disappeared shortly afterwards. But she had come back on the scene on her bicycle at some point in November and seemed to have been turning up fairly regularly ever since.

Initially, once again, Dora had not been too concerned, since

Picasso joked that she was his first ever student and since she did not quite believe that this girl was yearning for a relationship with a man of sixty-two. But over the past few months she had noticed that her lovemaking with Picasso was tailing off and that Sabartés was not keen on Françoise, a sign that he was afraid this might complicate his life even further. So after seeing Françoise emerging from the Grands-Augustins building on the previous Thursday, and finding her both overdressed and embarrassed, she decided to challenge Picasso.

'Have you been sleeping with that girl Françoise?'

'Of course not! How ridiculous!' he had said angrily.

But perhaps a little too angrily? The trouble was that, whatever her suspicions, she just did not know. And it might be worse than that. For, having said casually that it wasn't fair to keep her from her painting, he was now using Brassaï to photograph his sculptures and she was beginning to feel somewhat marginalised. She only met Picasso at his invitation, and had less and less contact with the regulars who, though now fewer in number, still turned up in the late morning. So could it be that these people knew more about Françoise's comings and goings than she did? That if there was indeed something going on, she could be the last to know about it...?

Yes even that, as was brought home to her by the sight of a priest in a white surplice beginning to speak, was submerged by this greater concern over Picasso's attitude to the plight of one of his oldest friends – the poet and painter Max Jacob, whose death had brought them here today. They had been so impoverished in their early days, it seemed, that they had to share a room and even a bed, with Picasso sleeping in it in the daytime and Max sleeping in it at night. They had drifted apart long since because of Picasso's greater success and because Max, a guilty Jewish homosexual, had converted to become a devout Catholic. But Dora had accompanied Picasso years before for a surprise visit to Max's retreat at Saint-Benoît-sur-Loire, and she remembered his gentleness and the sadness underlying his delight at seeing Picasso again.

But now there was this awful mystery surrounding his capture and death. It seemed that he had been seized about a month ago, taken to Orléans prison and then transferred to the transit camp at Drancy, from where consignments of Jews were despatched by rail to Auschwitz. On the way there, through the kindness of a guard, he managed to smuggle out a brief note appealing to several friends, including Picasso. Since others had already been alerted, a number of people – with Cocteau in the van – were now making strenuous efforts to save him, pleading his age, his reputation as a poet and his longstanding conversion to Catholicism. And it was a close friend of Max – who had in fact organised this memorial mass – who had approached Picasso in Le Catalan to ask for his signature to a petition. And, like Dora, been taken aback by the reply.

'There's no point' he said. 'Max is a crafty little devil who'll wangle his way out of prison without any help from us.'

As soon as they were alone, Dora had challenged him sharply.

'How do you know it wasn't a set-up?' he said. 'You don't approach people with a request like that in a public place like a restaurant. Anyway, I was warned off by Georges Prade.'

'Prade? The Prade from that collaborationist rag *Les Nouveaux Temps*?'

'Yes, they're using him as go-between to the Germans. I did offer, but he said that psychologically my name might not be helpful.'

'Psychologically? You're not normally keen on 'psychology', Picasso.'

'I'm telling you what he said!'

Ironically, it made no difference, for when friends went out to collect Max from Drancy in the mistaken belief that his release had been granted, they found that he had died the day before of bronchial pneumonia. Also, given the confusion and the mixed motives of some of the collaborators involved, it was never clear just what had happened or whether any decision had ever been taken at all. Even so, as another priest began to intone a Latin prayer for the soul of our brother in Christ, Max Jacob, it cast a dark shadow over Picasso in the minds of many here today.

It was the not knowing that was so awful, the ambiguity of everything, the mistrust, the way it diminished those you mistrusted and diminished you for mistrusting them, the dread that resulted, the way you woke up at night in a panic, the way you lost your appetite for certain foods, the way you sometimes heard yourself speak as though you were just pretending, the way you found yourself for trivial reasons ready to hate people. The helplessness of it froze you until you could imagine yourself curled up whimpering in a corner.

And if the distinguished people in this church had not been able to protect Max Jacob, what hope might there be for her if somebody somewhere decided she was Jewish and they came to collect her at dawn one morning to dispatch her to Drancy and beyond? Could she expect this man sitting beside her, whose hand was still shaking as it rested on his knee, to protect her…?

'*Descendez,*'

Not 'would you like to come down?', or 'would you care to come to lunch at Le Catalan?', but just a brusque 'come down'. He obviously suspected that she didn't believe his denial about sleeping with the student Françoise and he resented the fact. He even resented the fact that she had not raised the matter since. Sometimes you could know a man too well, know him better than you knew yourself.

'*Dix minutes.*'

Her reply on the telephone was equally brusque. She could have left at once, with no need to wait for ten minutes. But it was a tense game they were playing, like their own private *drôle de guerre*. And a phoney war within a phoney peace in this year of 1944 for, though Paris itself had been liberated at the end of August, the whole country was not yet free of German forces and the war was still going on.

After the nightmare of the Occupation, the liberation of Paris had been like some surreal dream. There had been the fear that the Germans were laying mines in order to destroy the city, the sudden uprising by the Resistance, the six-day battle for Paris – which imprisoned Picasso in Marie-Thérèse's apartment, and then the triumphal stroll of General de Gaulle down the Champs-Elysées. And after the throwing of flowers, the singing and dancing in the streeets, there was the sudden appearance of new and younger people in authority, the revenge attacks on collaborators, and the sight of women who had slept with German soldiers being paraded with shorn heads in the street. And it was not only for them that life had turned upside down.

For it had turned upside down for Picasso. He had become well known in America in particular but, since the outside world knew little of conditions in France, it was not known how he had fared. So when it was discovered that he was still in Paris, he came to be seen as symbolizing the heroic survival of art against barbarism – indeed Dora was stopped in her tracks one day by a large magazine poster showing the image of 'Picasso the Resister'.

And she was startled to see the studio in the Rue des Grands-Augustins become a place of pilgrimage for a surprising variety of visitors. Not just journalists – some of whom wanted to interview Dora herself – but art critics, officers in foreign uniforms and the odd American GI who occasionally ended up sleeping on the floor of the studio. And of course, assuming that Picasso had suffered appalling privations, they brought a plethora of gifts, ranging from chocolates to the box of grenades thoughtfully offered by the American writer Hemingway, who clearly saw Picasso as a comrade-in-arms. And indeed the legend that was emerging was of an artist who, if not actually leading the charge gun in hand, had nevertheless at a nobler level incarnated the spirit of the Resistance.

If Dora found this comical, Picasso took it all in his stride, charmed his visitors, showed often mystified groups around his studio and retold his now well-worn story of the German officer and the photograph of *Guernica,* with the officer – whose rank tended to fluctuate – asking if Picasso had 'done that' and a defiant Picasso replying with cold contempt 'no, *you* did'. But if Dora could not quite see Picasso as a heroic symbol of the Resistance, Sabartés, who had warmed to her now that it was Françoise and others who threatened to disturb his life, had further concerns. Complaining to Dora about all these callers, he confided that he was especially worried now that Eluard was back on the scene and sending some breathless young female student from the Communist Party to do a series of interviews with Picasso.

'I like Paul' he muttered darkly in Spanish, looking around him surreptitiously 'but you know his views about... sharing.'

'And you think he may be feeding fresh flesh to the Minotaur?' she had said, laughing it off. 'I expect she'll be too busy lecturing him on the dictatorship of the proletariat and trying to get him to join the Party.'

'Oh God!' he had replied in that doom-laden voice. 'That's all we need!'

On entering Le Catalan, she found Picasso and Eluard discussing the forthcoming annual autumn art exhibition, which this year was to be called the Salon de la Libération and would feature those works – 'decadent' or otherwise – that could not be displayed during the war.

'It should be quite exciting' said Eluard. 'Don't you think, Dora?

'Yes, it will be fascinating to see everybody's wartime production.'

'And of course Pablo will have a room to himself.'

'That's if I can fill it' said Picasso with a laugh. 'What do you think, Dora?'

'Of course you can fill it' she said with a smile. 'You've lots of stuff to show. And it will be interesting to see the reception. With people's changed perceptions, I mean.'

'Changed perceptions? What are you getting at?'

'Well, it's just that they won't have seen any of your work since

Guernica, which you remember they found difficult enough, and they might find it hard to grasp how you've developed since then.'

'You're not suggesting that you and Paul concoct some 'explanation', the way you did for the World Fair?'

'Well I wasn't' she said with a smile, 'but it mightn't be such a terrible idea. Especially since your recent work reflects a wartime bleakness that's not quite in tune with the present optimistic, celebratory atmosphere. The general public may not understand it and of course the Communists will hate it.'

'That *could* be a problem' said Eluard with a smile. 'But we're taking care of that with the co-ordination of the announcement...'

'The announcement...?' said Dora.

'Yes, the announcement about Pablo. In *L'Humanité*.'

'What announcement?'

'That he's joining the Communist Party, of course.'

'He's *wha-a -at*...?!' exclaimed Dora with an involuntary laugh.

'Joining the Communist Party' said Picasso with a show of casualness. 'Didn't I mention it?'

'Well, it's the sort of thing just slips your mind, isn't it?' she said, with a sarcastic laugh. 'But I'm sure the Party sees you as a useful addition, doesn't it. Paul?'

'Yes it does' said Paul, obviously embarrassed that Picasso had sprung this on her.

'And of course this solves the problem of the public's understanding' she went on. 'You could have a brief Marxist commentary on the pictures, couldn't you? Perhaps provided by the artist himself?'

Not, needless to say, that this flippant suggestion had been taken up when she visited the Salon in October. But the bafflement of much of the public was obvious and many visitors were outraged to the point of demanding their entrance fee back. Moreover, *L'Humanité* barely mentioned the work, but splashed out with a declaration attributed to Picasso suggesting that, after suffering a lonely enforced exile from his homeland, he had now found a new family in the Communist Party.

The result of all this was that groups of right-wingers threatened to tear the pictures down from the walls, and a group of art students was brought in to guard them. And one of these, when Dora returned with Paul in November to see how this rumpus was developing, was visibly Françoise, who had a friendly exchange with Eluard.

'So you know about Françoise, Paul, do you?' asked Dora.

'Oh, I think it's just an intermittent little thing, Dora. And look at the age difference.'

'That doesn't seem to be stopping either of them.'

'Maybe not, but it's you he admires and wants to be with.'

'Or wants to be *seen* with at least.'

It was true that Picasso hated going out alone and that he needed a partner who would be considered acceptable in the circles he moved in. But for how long?

'You know I love both of you, Dora. I can see that he's hard on you, but I'd hate to see you break up.'

'Well, I won't leave him, Paul, he'll have to leave me. That's if he has the guts to do it, since as you know he can never quite throw anything away – whether it's used fag packets or used people.'

'Yes, but you can be quite hard on him too, Dora. You've got so much pride.'

'Eight years of loving Picasso, Paul, doesn't leave you much else.'

A fine spring morning in 1945 and Dora was just leaving for her solo exhibition at the Jeanne Bucher gallery in the Boulevard du Montparnasse.

She had been working hard for the past few months and had found it a great relief to be kept so busy. Indeed painting had seemed to be the only refuge from the draining experience of living in a world she no longer felt she understood. For, ironically, the Occupation had made life easier in a way. You knew who you were, who other people had decided you were: a Jew or not a Jew – you were held together by fear. And now that the fear had gone, it left a curious unease, the sense of a void.

And what was this new world that was emerging as the war in Europe ground slowly towards its end, with millions being killed, cities reduced to rubble, and details emerging of the senseless industrial murder practised in the concentration camps? She no longer felt that she had the energy to find out.

While she was left with a sense of relief at what she had escaped, the relief was poisoned by an irrational sense of guilt. But the sheer barbarity of what had happened in those camps was something she no longer felt strong enough to confront. It was as though you got up in the morning, you put on clothes and went out into the world as usual, but you no longer quite knew who you were. And in the event, as she saw her reflection in a display panel in the Odéon Metro station, she realised that for no particular reason she had dressed that morning – oddly formally for a visit to the gallery – entirely in black. It was as though she was in mourning – but for what?

And if you were not too sure who you were, neither were you sure, in a France in which everybody was suddenly claiming to have played a role in the Resistance, who other people were. Relationships were changing and people seemed to be drifting. She had just heard from Jacqueline, who was still in America, that she had left André Breton for an American sculptor, while André was with some Chilean woman Elisa and was now declaring himself to be an anarchist – making the innocent days of the Surrealists, the 'Muses' and the solemn debates of Contre-Attaque seem comically far away.

More significantly, her attitude to her parents had changed since the death of her mother. It was not just that she had begun to view her absent father more critically, but that she was more aware than before of mortality, of being next in line as it were. And her paintings seemed to reflect that. Her still-lifes – often of single objects, such as a clock or a loaf of bread – deprived them of context in such a way as to lend them a lonely mystery that seemed to be asking why things existed in the first place. As though she was still looking for the same answers as in her Surrealist photography of years before, but finding only the same questions – and questions beyond the questions. Except that now the search seemed much more presssing.

And all this uncertainty was somehow locked within this long, consuming love affair with Picasso. What was he playing at, this new Comrade Picasso, declaring absurdly that, if it came to it, he would be down there fighting in the streets with the workers? He had certainly been opposed to Franco, but why had he allowed himself, innocent as he was of Marxist or any other political theory, to fall for what – with due respect to Eluard – was really a political publicity stunt?

But above all, she asked herself as the Metro train left the Saint-Sulpice station, was it really all over with this girl Françoise? She had not been seen for the past month or more, according to Nusch, who tended to laugh off the whole affair. Also, Picasso had been spending more time with Dora, had talked of a holiday on the Côte d'Azur, and had not only seen her exhibition but had pronounced himself so impressed that he promised to make a second visit. He was also apparently talking to all and sundry about the good notices she was having. So, as she left the Metro and walked towards the gallery in the Boulevard du Montparnasse, Dora was feeling that she had probably been worrying unduly.

Jeanne Bucher. a lively lady in her seventies who had displayed quite a few of the better known painters, was on station for the morning and was smiling.

'Two more sales yesterday afternoon, Dora. The regulars are supportive and the visitors seem to be saying the right things. It's going well.'

'I'm pleased. By the way, Picasso said he would drop in again.'

'Splendid! That would create interest and help turnover.'

They had been chatting and answering questions from visitors for an hour or so when Dora noticed a young woman in a rather loud multi-coloured striped dress come into the gallery and start quietly looking at the pictures. It was Françoise.

A few minutes later, and rather less quietly, Picasso came in, spoke briefly to Françoise, then advanced towards Dora and Jeanne.

'I thought I'd come for another look, it's so impressive. Isn't it a good thing, Jeanne, that I persuaded Dora to move on to painting from photography?'

He stretched one arm behind him as though to bring forward Françoise to meet them, only to turn and find that she was hurrying back down the gallery and out of the door. He glanced at Dora and Jeanne, then rushed after Françoise, shouting after her in the staircase 'Where do you think you're going?! Come back...!'

Since everyone in the gallery had heard him, there was a certain silence, then a little whispering.

'Well, it was a short visit' said Jeanne with a laugh, 'but I did say he would create interest!'

Dora, however, was so shocked that she almost had to sit down. And, though she managed to leave with some dignity, the feeling persisted. She started to walk home, but found herself walking in the wrong direction. She went into a café, sat down, saw in a mirrored column that her face was stiff and red, and left without ordering. She eventually made her way home, had trouble finding the keys, went in, kicked off her shoes and stared in despair or disgust or hatred at the slightly dishevelled figure in black suit and matching hat in the mirror. She tried to make tea, but knocked over the cup, yelled at it, then just left it. To go and lie fully dressed on the bed, huddled up with a blinding headache.

She woke up some time later, with a dull headache and feeling strangely remote from her surroundings. She discovered that her front door was open, was sure she had closed it, thought she must have been burgled and checked everything feverishly, but couldn't decide whether anything was missing or not. She wondered if she should warn the neighbours, but hesitated and thought it might be safer not to – though it was terrible that you couldn't even trust your neighbours.

She decided to go out, walked around and found herself outside a cinema on the Boulevard Saint-Michel. She went in, had difficulty counting out the money for the ticket, entered the hall, stumbled past complaining people in the darkness, sat down and stared at the uniformed man on the screen walking towards the women cowering in this ruined house with a revolver – until she stood up shouting at him not to do it, that they didn't know they were Jews, that he was a monster. And after that there were complaints and scuffles and somebody shining a light in her face and she was fighting with these people who were dragging her out until she was standing on the pavement shouting that she would set the police on them. And then feeling very alone, and wondering just what had happened, and going back home feeling frightened.

She went to bed sometime before midnight, but twisted and turned and couldn't fall asleep. She got up, feeling hot, and thought she would walk in the cool night air. No point in dressing for the darkness, so she just put on a light raincoat and her shoes and walked towards the Place Saint-Michel. She crossed the bridge and walked on regardless through the late-night stragglers and past a policeman looking curiously at her until a man stepped out of a doorway and said he wouldn't mind fucking her. And she was shouting and hitting blindly at him with her fists, until the man went off and the policeman had come running up and she was telling him excitedly that this man had attacked her.

'But you're on the Boulevard de Sébastopol after midnight, Madame. He assumed you were a prostitute. Are you sure you're all right, Madame?'

She stared at him, realised that top buttons on her raincoat were undone, looked at him a little helplessly and allowed herself to be walked home.

11

'Where the devil is she?' said Picasso. 'I'm starving.'

It was the usual crowd for lunch at Le Catalan – Picasso, the Eluards, Brassaï and one or two others. And in the midst of the banter and the laughter they were getting hungry.

Picasso had not found it so easy to maintain contact with Dora over the past week or so. She hadn't answered her telephone for several days and when he called to see what was wrong he had got no answer. He talked briefly to an obviously nosey neighbour, who told him with some satisfaction that Dora had called the police about the theft of her bicycle, but that it had turned out that she had forgotten where she left it – and that, when the police did come round, they had 'found her sitting naked on the staircase'. But when she phoned him in response to the note he had left, she had laughed the whole thing off, and had seemed perfectly coherent earlier when he phoned her about the lunch. So, since he was looking forward to his steak, where the devil was she...?

It was another few minutes before she came in, looking immaculate if rather tense, went around the table greeting everyone as usual and sat down in her place. Only to get up again suddenly.

'Oh, I've had enough of this!' she said.

And before anyone could react, she was disappearing through the door.

Picasso sat still in surprise for a moment, then jumped up and rushed out after her. He caught up with her further up the street and tried to take her arm, but she fought him off and they were left arguing in the middle of the roadway.

'You may be a great painter' she was shouting, 'but you're a despicable human being, 'Comrade Picasso'. Betraying anybody close to you, treating women like cattle, ruining the lives of anybody you fancy. And thinking all the time that you're clever. Just laughing at it all – you see the way you're laughing?!'

'But I'm not laughing, Dora. What's got into you?!'

'You got into me, Picasso, you're the devil that got into me, and I've got to get you out of me.'

'Well, don't do it here, Dora, we're causing a disturbance. Come along, please…'

He managed to get her to come to the nearby Grands-Augustins, where he asked Sabartés to go and fetch Eluard from the restaurant – but not before Dora had asked a startled Sabartés why he put up with being paid a pittance and being treated like a lackey.

Sabartés rushed off and quickly brought back Eluard, who was shocked and concerned. And whose attempts to calm down Dora appeared to be succeeding until she suddenly turned on him as well.

'You're even worse than he is, Paul Eluard! You know how cruel he is, you know he doesn't care a damn for anybody, not even you…'

'Dora…!'

'But you suck up to him, you would feed him Nusch for breakfast, lunch and dinner if you thought it would get an illustration out of him or get him to join the Party…'

'Dora…!'

'You're each as sinful as each other and you should get down on your knees now, the pair of you – go on, get down! – and ask God for forgiveness while there's still time…!'

And she went on shouting and trying to force them to their

knees for some minutes until she gave up and slumped on to the floor with her back against the wall.

Eluard looked helplessly at Picasso, drew him into a corner and said they clearly needed help – and was there a doctor they could call? Picasso said he would phone Lacan.

Lacan was in and drove over at once, arriving only a few minutes later.

'*Bonjour*, Dora' he said lightly, taking charge masterfully. 'You seem a little bit stressed today. Have you not been sleeping well?'

'What?' she said, surprised both at his presence and at the way he was stroking and kneading her forearm with his thumb.

'Well, we can easily fix that' he said pleasantly, injecting something into the vein with a syringe. 'Just you stay down there for a moment and let that relax you, all right?'

He made sure she was stable against the wall, then drew the others aside and questioned them quietly for some minutes.

'She should go to Sainte-Anne' he said finally. 'I'll drive her there myself. You two had better keep out of this. And don't worry' he added with a smile, 'I'll enter her under a false name.'

And, smilingly raising and supporting the now quiet Dora, he took her out to the car.

This left the others standing awkwardly in silence, with Picasso observing that a white-faced Eluard was avoiding looking at him directly.

'The thing is, Paul…' he began.

'The thing is you have behaved abominably to that beautiful woman!'

'Not so. I'm the one who encouraged her to move from photography to painting. I've built her up…'

'To keep knocking her down and humiliating her!' shouted Paul.

'Don't you see? There was always that weakness there…'

'She's the strongest woman I've ever known. And proud, and dignified. That's what you couldn't stand!'

'I'm saying there was always that mystical tendency in her, that anti-rational nonsense that you and your Surrealist friends are responsible for – *you*, not me!'

'But you're the most anti-rational painter that ever existed! And she gave up Surrealism years ago. No, it's you, Pablo, *you*!'

'It's *life*, Paul! People are either strong enough to survive or they're not.'

'But we're not living in a fucking jungle!' shouted Paul, picking up a chair in frustration.

'You think so?!'

'Even in wartime, when she was at her most vulnerable, you kept trying to test her to destruction. Why did you do it?!' he shouted hoarsely, suddenly smashing the chair against the wall. 'Why are you so hard on women, why?!'

'And why' said Picasso with a mocking smile, 'are you so hard on chairs, Paul?!'

'What are you doing…?!' asked Dora protestingly.

She was in a straitjacket within some box-like structure, they had wiped her temples with ether, so they said, and now they were attaching something to each temple…

'We're just applying the electrodes. It's a brand-new treatment. It will make you forget your troubles. Could you just open your mouth for me?'

The doctor was white-coated, bespectacled and smilingly reassuring. She nodded assent and something like a rubber ball was pushed into her mouth, sufficiently large to prevent her from clenching her teeth – and from doing more than mumble as she asked why a grey-coated man had come from nowhere and was firmly holding her thighs and knees together.

'Don't worry. That's Alain. He's just doing that to keep you safe. I think we're ready. Are you all right?'

She nodded confusedly.

'Good' he said smilingly. 'But I think you've been having a hard time recently, haven't you? You remember?'

As she nodded again, her whole body was convulsed by a shock that arched her back violently and left her legs shuddering within the iron grip of the man in the grey coat.

'You're doing well' the doctor was saying reassuringly, 'very well. But I think somebody may have been treating you badly. You remember?'

As she nodded again, a second shock vibrated through her agonizingly, lasting at least twice as long and leaving her quivering within the straitjacket and the now painful grip of the man holding her legs together.

'Well done!' the doctor was saying reassuringly. 'I wish all patients were like you. Especially when you think of what you've been through. It's not fair what happens to some people, is it? You remember?'

As she nodded once again, rather desperately this time, a tremendous shock ran through her and seemed to go on and on for ever as it carried her into a grey swirling unconsciousness. Which lasted until she woke up in bed some time later, smiling vaguely in surprise at finding the bespectacled reassuring doctor applying his stethoscope to her chest.

'Very good' he was saying smilingly, 'very good indeed. You've done remarkably well. And we'll see how we get on, shall we?'

As to how long all this went on, she had no idea until the dandified Lacan turned up one afternoon – three days later was it?- and said he had come to take her to tea. Did she think La Régence might be a suitable venue?

'Please don't tell anybody or they'll try to analyse me for it, Dora, but I have a tragic weakness for cream pastries. I gather you're well?'

'Yes' she said, smiling. 'I'm not quite sure what happened, but I seem to be feeling all right. Can I go home?'

'Well, that's what we'll talk about over tea and cream pastries.'

So he drove her to La Régence by the Palais Royal, ordered tea and cakes with some panache, chatted lightly about this and that, and then talked seriously to her about her situation. He explained that the electroconvulsive treatment could give a temporary relief, but that it was only a stopgap.

'You've had a real trauma, you know, Dora. We'll have to go on talking for some weeks, if you're willing, to make sure that it never happens again. Are you agreeable to that?'

She watched with some amusement as he took out an elegant Lanvin handkerchief to wave away a fly that was expressing a persistent interest in some crumbs left on his plate and said she was agreeable.

'You may find yourself subject to bouts of depression after this, Dora, so I want to be sure you're all right on your own. Is there a close female friend who could drop in regularly?'

'Yes, there's Nusch Eluard.'

'Well yes, though it might be better not to frequent Picasso or Eluard himself for a week or two, but I'll see you regularly', he said, flipping open a blue-and-gold Hermès diary, 'starting tomorrow morning. Is that agreeable?'

'Yes, I'll be glad to get away from that smiling doctor and his infernal machine.'

'I understand. And now, since I have no psychiatric techniques that would enable me to modify the behaviour of this fly, I suggest I leave you back at Sainte-Anne for tonight, pick you up again in the morning and take you straight to my clinic.'

And over the following weeks, Dora regularly walked the short distance to Lacan's clinic in the Rue de Lille. She came to look forward to these sessions, which were generally relaxed, reflective and sometimes amusing exchanges in which personal reminiscences mingled with references to politics and art. Lacan, sitting back in his armchair and gesturing gently with his large mother of pearl pipe, did not ask directly about Picasso and, if anything, seemed more interested in her friendship with Eluard. But he encouraged her to talk at length about her childhood in Buenos Aires, about her left-handedness, her sense of being watched through the curtained window to her bedroom and her amusing antics with different hats in front of the mirror in her mother's hat shop.

'Do you remember what age you were at that time?'

'Oh I don't know. Perhaps six or seven?'

He was interested in the age at which she had started to use a camera, and in how she viewed her Surrealist activity in particular. And he came back several times to the subject of her parents and the relationship between them.

'Well, my mother was very religious' said Dora with a slight grimace when he first raised the matter.

'And so was mine' he said smilingly, removing the mother of pearl pipe and blowing out a stream of blue smoke. 'My brother even became a Benedictine monk. But it takes all sorts, doesn't it?'

However, it became painful when she talked about her parents and the distance between them – and even more painful when he probed her fear of being treated as Jewish during the Occupation. She cried at times during these sessions, and she had moments of depression, but in the intervals she began to feel more herself. She walked a lot about the city – dropping into Saint-Sulpice one very hot day when she was passing to enjoy the coolness inside – and not only saw Nusch frequently but lunched twice with Lise Deharme. She felt a sharp anger during one session when it dawned on her to ask Lacan about his fee and he told her that it was being paid by Picasso, but she came around to thinking she was being unreasonable and that she ought to be grateful for the treatment.

For Picasso and Eluard, both very solicitous, were gradually coming back on to the scene, dropping in to see her and taking her out once or twice for a quiet meal in unfamiliar restaurants so as not to expose her to the usual crowd. Picasso was also suggesting that they should go down to the Côte d'Azur for a holiday when she was feeling better. But she still felt rather fragile.

And it was a fragility that persuaded Eluard to arrange a private meeting with Lacan at his clinic, to inquire how Dora was coming along.

'Well it's rather unusual, I suppose' said Lacan meditatively,

271

removing his large mother of pearl pipe and blowing a blue smoke ring into the air.

'I know, but I'm a very old friend of hers and I'm deeply concerned.'

'It's a work in progress, you realise. I can only give you the direction of travel.'

'Yes, but that would be very helpful.'

'Well, you won't quote me but, in a nutshell, Dora is a very proud woman of considerable integrity who has been suffering extreme relational stress due to an ongoing clash with a highly narcissistic solar personality who gains near-invulnerability through his celebrity. I make no judgment, of course.'

'That's one hell of a nutshell! You're saying it's Picasso's fault?'

'Oh, I wouldn't give him *all* the credit' said Lacan with a smile. 'There was also the war. More specifically the fear she felt during the Occupation at the possibility of being killed for being Jewish when she didn't feel herself to be Jewish – a fear, significantly, that she saw fit to conceal from Picasso.'

'Really? I didn't realise that. Poor Dora! It must have been terrible for her.'

'Yes, it clearly was.'

'So what do you think you can do for her?'

'She'll have to do it herself, Paul. I just set up the fences for her to jump over.'

'But are you hopeful? Do you see a way forward for her?'

'Yes, I think there's probably enough there to form an emotional bridge.'

'Enough of…?'

'Oh, enough of the usual' said Lacan with a wry grin. 'Of guilt.'

Dora had the ironical, almost amused feeling, as they took their seats in the Sarah-Bernhardt theatre, that she was pretending to be Dora Maar – and indeed that the man sitting beside her was pretending to be Pablo Picasso.

This was their first public appearance, exactly one month after she had stormed out of Le Catalan on May 15, and they were here to attend the premiere of the ballet *Rendez-vous*. Most of their acquaintances seemed to be here as well and of course several were directly involved, including Brassaï for some of the sets and Picasso himself for the drop curtain. In the event, he had not got around to doing the curtain, and they had been forced to do a last-minute enlargement of one of his still-lifes – which produced a few disappointed boos when it appeared. But all of that was beside the point. The point was to be there, to be seen, to keep up appearances – to pretend.

And they were not the only ones who were pretending. It was true that Lacan had done his best to keep Picasso and Eluard out of it, but of course there had been others lunching at Le Catalan that day who would have seen what happened. The fact was that Picasso and indeed Dora herself were too well known for a juicy story like this not to go the rounds. Needless to say, they had all been greeting her on their entrance as though everything was normal. But that simply emphasized that it was not – and that it was unlikely to be normal again.

And she had the same feeling of wry amusement when Marcel – who also seemed initially to be pretending to be Marcel – drove them down to the Côte d'Azur to stay for a couple of weeks at Cap d'Antibes. For Picasso was now displaying a new courtesy and was being solicitous to a fault – suggesting delicately that he would not ask to sleep with her until she felt more like herself. She realised that all this courtesy sprang from his underlying fear of provoking some kind of irrational emotional outburst that he would see as typically feminine. But the arrangement suited both of them in a way. If it established a formal distance between them, it also created the space within which they were able to talk in a fairly relaxed and even humorous fashion as they went along.

And this worked for a while, as they spent time on the beach or made the usual visits along the coast. But after ten days or so, it was

273

clear to both of them that the new formal distance and the new courtesy were all very well, but that they could become mortally boring. And it was at this point that Picasso, with the air of a magician producing a rabbit out of the hat, asked if she would like to go on a mystery tour.

'Well, a little mystery wouldn't come amiss' she said with a smile. 'So where are we going?'

'That's the mystery.'

So off they went, with Marcel – who had apparently not forgiven Marcel Chevalier – treating them to uncertain renderings of Charles Trenet and Yves Montand. And after spending the night in Aix-en-Provence, they drove next morning to the Luberon region in the foothills of the French Alps, a land of mountains and forests dotted with ancient castles and mediaeval fortified hill villages with well-known names like Gordes or Bonnieux or of course Lacoste, with its ruined castle of the Marquis de Sade.

'It's a real story-book land' said Dora, as the car climbed up the steep winding road to the spectacular hilltop fortress village of Ménerbes, famous as a Protestant stronghold during the old Wars of Religion. 'I've never been here before.'

'Neither have I' said Picasso. 'I hope it runs to a decent place for lunch.'

As it happened, it did. And as they started to stroll around the village afterwards, Picasso enhanced the mystery by producing a roughly drawn map, from which he identified the town hall, the narrow streets and the miniature fortress of the Citadelle. Eventually he stopped and stood staring at a tall house built against the rock.

'Let's see if we can get inside' he said mischievously.

'Won't the owner object?'

'But the owner is me' he said with a grin. 'I was given it in exchange for a still-life.'

He produced a large key, opened the nail-studded door, and they went into a large dark hall leading to a simple kitchen and a shower room. They looked around and then climbed an elaborate staircase to the next floor, where they found three rooms with basic furniture decorated rather gloomily in the original Empire style, one of them having been in use as a bedroom. They then went up to the next floor, where the rooms were neglected and empty, but where Dora lingered by the window, looking down across the valley and marvelling at the gradations of colour from ochre through different shades of brown and green to a very deep dark blue.

'What do you think of it?' asked Picasso when they came down again.

'Well, it's not in good shape upstairs and the only running water seems to be on the ground floor, but it's a wonderful village and the whole area is a painter's paradise, especially for one interested in nature.'

'But that's not really me, is it?' he said with a smile.

'Perhaps not' she replied, with an answering smile.

'Well then, would you accept it if I offered it to you?'

She looked at him steadily for what seemed like a long time, aware that the offer in this dark downstairs hall had a significance beyond itself.

'Yes, I would' she said.

And from then on, until they returned to Paris a week later, the tone became even more courteous. Right up to the moment when they finally drew up outside her apartment in the Rue de Savoie and Picasso helped her down and kissed her hand elaborately, almost in an echo of the first time they had met in the Deux Magots.

She knew and he knew – and each knew that the other knew.

It was over.

That victory autumn of 1945, with the celebrations darkened by the dropping of the atomic bomb and further revelations about the concentration camps, formed a confusing backcloth to Dora's sessions with Lacan, which continued at his own suggestion – and which seemed to be getting harder rather than easier.

Dora was not sure why this should be so. For one thing, if the Picasso regulars had mostly drifted off – with the notable exception of

Paul and Nusch Eluard – she was leading quite a busy social life. She was seeing Lise Deharme and Marie-Laure de Noailles, had resumed contact with old friends like the screenwriters Jacques Prévert and Louis Chavance, and had become friendly with the painter Balthus. In fact, as she reflected ironically, she was more socially active and felt less isolated than in the latter stages of the relationship with Picasso. Also, she was working hard on her painting – at this time a series of outdoor scenes of the quays of the Seine – in preparation for a solo exhibition at the Pierre Loeb gallery in the spring of 1946.

However, her life had been complicated to some extent by the return of her father from Buenos Aires. Not that he was in any way a burden – if he was older and a little fussier than before, he was every bit as clearheaded and he was living independently in an apartment facing the Seine. And they had returned to the habit of meeting every Sunday at the Lutétia at Sèvres-Babylone, though it was now for dinner rather than lunch, the waiter Gaston had retired and the atmosphere was somehow not quite the same. Especially since, as she began to notice, she no longer called him *Papa* and spoke to him on quite equal terms.

It was rather that his return inevitably opened up half-buried questions about family life and, in particular, about his flight to Argentina when the war began. This was a painful question for while it was true that this might have saved her life, it was equally true that it had left her mother feeling alone and abandoned in wartime.

'It was the only sensible thing to do' he said, when she raised the matter indirectly. 'She could have come if she had wanted to.'

'But it suited you that she didn't?'

'And it also suited her, Dora. It confirmed her in the belief that she was a victim. With an unfaithful husband and', he smiled, 'a wayward, ungrateful daughter leading a loose life with a lot of immoral Surrealists.'

This was troubling for Dora, especially since it hardly chimed with the image of her mother presented by the priest in Saint-Sulpice. Indeed, she was beginning to feel that she had never really known her mother, that young provincial Catholic woman married to a Croatian Jewish architect and transplanted to Argentina. Had she felt slighted not only by her rakish husband but by her flamboyant, independent daughter? Gradually, and unintentionally, Dora seemed to be trying to enter the world of her mother, dropping into Saint-Sulpice to listen to Marcel Dupré playing the organ, or visiting the mediaeval section in the Louvre to gaze at Christian images and puzzle over the paradox of poor people somehow – like her mother indeed – finding certainty in the very limitations upon their lives.

'I'm beginning to wonder what Lacan is playing at with Dora' said Eluard to Nusch one day. 'I knew she had slightly mystical tendencies, but this sounds rather different.'

'Well, can't you go and talk to Lacan again? And while you're at it' she added with a smile, 'ask him if he has a cure for insomnia.'

After hesitating for a day or two, Eluard did go to see Lacan, who assured him that the analysis was proceeding normally.

'You said last time that there was 'probably enough guilt'...?' said Eluard.

'Well yes, guilt in relation to the mother. Which can be used to form the emotional bridge I may have mentioned, did I?' he asked, starting to light the big mother of pearl pipe.

'Yes, you did.'

'And that's overlaid with this fear instilled during the Occupation of being Jewish. As she begins to identify sympathetically with the mother, who could have been at least subconsciously anti-Semitic to the extent that she resented her treatment by the husband, Dora could be led to internalise those anti-Semitic feelings herself.'

'But she was a potential victim of anti-Semitism, for heaven's sake!'

'Precisely. But that's the problem. At a subconscious level you can feel that, if there weren't all these Jews, you wouldn't have this dread of being seized – that it's they who are causing all the trouble.'

'Which would be totally irrational!'

'But as a poet, Paul' said Lacan, smiling as he removed the great mother of pearl pipe, 'you must know that rationality is just the thin ice we slither about on every day.'

'But this is appalling!'

'Not necessarily. Dora is too intelligent and socially aware not to sense that in the post-war world anti-Semitic remarks are going to sound pretty silly, so it shouldn't be too embarrassing.'

'I can't quite believe this! But what about these apparent religious leanings?'

'Well, in part they reflect the identification with the mother – that's the bridge – but it's much more than that. Dora's problem is that she is a very proud, strong person – I can't think of any other woman who could have stood up to Picasso for ten years. And now that she has hit the wall, she has to go around it or over it. And I don't see her going around it.'

'Why not?'

'Because the relationship with Picasso was obviously extremely intense, not just emotionally but because they worked together, slugged out arguments over *Guernica* and so on. And I don't think her pride would allow her to settle for another relationship that was less intense.'

'So if she can't go around your wall...?'

'She would have to go over it.'

'You mean religion? God?'

'Well, unlike Picasso, God wouldn't let her down, Paul.'

'There's only one problem.'

'And what's that?'

'That God doesn't exist.'

'But isn't that' said Lacan, smiling his wry smile and slowly blowing a blue smoke ring into the air, 'why he wouldn't let her down?'

Was she being stalked by Picasso...?!

In the spring of 1946 Dora hardly knew whether to feel amused or insulted when she suddenly kept running into Picasso, whom she hadn't seen for several months. And it was Picasso with a rather reluctant Françoise in his train.

It began as she was viewing the *Lady and the Unicorn* at an exhibition of tapestries, when he came up behind her, greeted her effusively and said they must have lunch together. It was only when he praised her broad-mindedness that Dora realised she had been lured into a lunch with both of them, and was less than delighted as they were driven by Marcel to a fancy restaurant in the Place de l'Alma. She reacted jokingly by ordering the most expensive dishes on the menu and proceeded to sparkle during the meal, while Picasso kept pressing the embarrassed Françoise to comment and expressed loud admiration every time that she did. And on emerging from the restaurant, he did not offer her a lift home, leaving her wondering just what this clumsy comedy had been about.

The next such occasion was when Dora was sitting with Nusch in the Café de Flore and they noticed Picasso and Françoise, who had clearly seen them, apparently arguing in the street outside. They then came in, with Picasso at his heartiest.

'We just happened to notice you were here!'

'Yes, we noticed that you noticed' said Dora.

'I haven't seen you in such a long time. You know Françoise of course?'

'If you only wanted to see me, you could have walked round the corner to my place.'

'Yes, that's a good idea. It would be better at your place.'

Since the conversation petered out, they soon drifted off, while Dora, who had for months now avoided talking about Picasso, looked questioningly at Nusch.

'What's he playing at, Nusch?'

'I don't know, but they've had their ups and downs, it seems. You saw her cheek?'

'What do you mean?'

'The scar. He apparently held a lit cigarette against her cheek.'

'Oh God! Why on earth did he do that?'

'I think he may be trying to persuade her to move in with him.'

'Well, that's one way, I suppose!'

One evening a week later, he again turned up with the reluctant Françoise in tow to where she was sitting with friends at the Café de Flore. With little pretence this time that the encounter was accidental, he asked if she would agree to talk to him about a very important matter – perhaps at her place in an hour's time? And to avoid embarrassing her friends, she agreed.

She was very composed when Picasso arrived, almost dragging Françoise by the hand. When he suggested awkwardly that they might look at some of Dora's recent paintings, she politely showed them a few still-lifes and Françoise made appreciative comments – though it was noticeable that her eyes kept straying towards the *Dora and the Minotaur* over the mantelpiece.

'But I don't imagine this is why you came?' said Dora.

'No it's not' he said.

Dora waved towards chairs, but they all remained standing.

'So?'

'So I want Françoise to come and live with me, but she's hesitating.'

'I can understand that, since at sixty-four you're old enough to be her grandfather.'

'That's nothing to do with it. I love her.'

'But, Picasso, you've never loved anybody in your life. You're not capable of it.'

'That's not for you to say! Anyway, she doesn't want to feel responsible for the breakdown in our relationship.'

'But none of that' said Dora, glancing at Françoise, who quickly switched her gaze away from *Dora and the Minotaur*, 'has anything whatsoever to do with her.'

'She wants to be quite sure that it's all finished between us.'

'It's finished. Was there anything else?'

She saw them out in a very dignified fashion, came back and sat on a chair. Trembling slightly, but reflecting that at least that was that.

But, mysteriously, it wasn't. For towards the end of June Picasso phoned to ask if she would lend him the house in Ménerbes for the month of July. It was an extraordinary request – at least it would have been from anyone else – and an inconvenient one. However, she decided that she could not easily refuse, gave him the keys when he called and wondered what he was up to.

'So did you get any work done down there?' she asked when he returned the keys at the end of July.

'Just a few drawings' he said, with a glint to his smile. 'Oh, and I've left you something to remember me by.'

What he was up to emerged as soon as she got to Ménerbes. He had left a couple of bedroom drawings of a nude Françoise, to emphasize that they had used the bed that Dora had not yet even slept in. This was a big enough slap in the face, without discovering that he had painted the wooden lavatory seat – with bright blue forget-me-nots. She walked straight out of the house to the café down the street, ordered a cognac. thought angrily of sending him a card with some clever retort – like asking why he should think that she automatically associated him with shit – and then gradually cooled down. For it was so silly it was weirdly flattering in a way. Was it to carry out this coarse schoolboy joke that he had insisted on borrowing the house when they could have stayed in far greater comfort in a hotel? It was so sad, and the sadder for being so predictable.

'Are you staying in the village, Madame?' asked the *patronne*, who had been eyeing her curiously from behind the bar.

'Yes, I've acquired a house up the street and I'm hoping to spend the summers here.'

'Along with that older gentleman and the young girl who were here the other week?'

'Not at all, no. I just lent them the house for the month.'

'Yes, well' the *patronne* said darkly, 'you can't be too careful. Is that young girl all right? We were nearly calling the police, you know.'

Whereupon it turned out that not only had the villagers been shocked by the age gap between Picasso and Françoise, but that she had been seen apparently trying to get away by hitching a lift on the main road below – until Picasso and Marcel caught up with her in the car and brought her back.

'I mean' said the *patronne* severely, 'we don't want to see any kidnapping here.'

'Don't worry, Madame' said Dora, with an involuntary laugh. 'I certainly won't let it happen again.'

And after this unusual welcome to Ménerbes, Dora started methodically to settle in. She threw away the sheets and the lavatory seat, and laid in supplies from the baker, the butcher and the grocer, by which time she seemed to have met about half of the village. But she was anxious to get on with her own painting and for that she needed to be able to get about freely. She thought of a bicycle, but was advised that in this hilly country the proper answer was a motorbike. So next morning she caught a bus to Bonnieux and bought a light motorbike from a slightly mystified young salesman, who explained anxiously how to balance the brake and the throttle. At her first attempt, she sent the machine leaping upwards and ended up in a heap on the ground, but she gradually mastered it and was soon setting off for Ménerbes, cautiously at first and then with increasing confidence until she was sailing along triumphantly with the wind in her hair.

For the painting was everything now. She knew that, even though she had her own circle of friends in Paris, she could still be written off by some as the ex-mistress of Picasso, and that she needed to establish herself on her own terms. Fortunately, she had already in her painting cast off his influence, especially since unlike him she was interested in landscape and abstract art, but she felt she had further to go. It was more than a search to perfect her style, it was a search for a new, perhaps deeper self. And if she had so immediately been drawn to this strange landscape of hills and valleys and ancient homesteads, of eagles and scorpions and every nuance of colour, it was because it felt like a place where you could paint the wind, the silence of the sky, or the whispering of the grass.

It shouldn't have been Nusch. Not Nusch.

And it was so eerily akin to that interrupted phone call from Dora's mother. For she and Nusch had been on the phone that very morning, arranging to have lunch while Paul was away seeing a publisher in Switzerland. Except that Nusch failed to arrive, since she had collapsed with a cerebral haemorrhage, gone into a coma and never regained consciousess.

No, it shouldn't have been Nusch. Because at forty she was too young. Because, for all the mysterious insomnia, there had been no indication that there was anything wrong with her. Because she was innocent, lovable Nusch, so free of pretence or calculation as to put anybody to shame. Because they all died a little that day in late November 1946 when Nusch died.

And it was devastating for Eluard. Returning in haste to Paris, he could hardly be dragged away from the body. And after the funeral he seemed quite lost. It was feared that he might disappear, or kill himself.

'If she had even been ill, Dora! If only there had been time to talk to her, to comfort her. But she was switched off like a light bulb!'

'I know, Paul. It's awful.'

He looked older suddenly and, with the lingering effect of having been gassed in the first World War, he was perhaps not in the best of health. Also the heroic days of the Resistance had gone, he had little taste for the compromises of party politics, and he was not entirely happy with his status as a kind of official poet within a Communist Party formally tied to Moscow's idea of socialist realism.

But above all he was lonely. Unlike Picasso, Paul loved women, had never seen gender difference as a battleground and could not have imagined living separately from Nusch. She had not only been a lover, but a friend, a constant companion. And now that she was suddenly not there, the world around him seemed to be drained of meaning.

Of course, he had many friends in political and literary circles, but he would still go home alone feeling the odd one out. He was falling back on seeing even more of Picasso, to whom he had a longstanding emotional tie and on whom, indeed, he depended for the occasional gift of a drawing or an illustration that would help him to make a living. But there too everything had changed with the arrival of the youthful Françoise, especially since Picasso's predictable response to her attempt to get away had been to give her a child, so that she was now pregnant.

'Wherever I go I feel *de trop*' Paul told Dora as they lunched together on his birthday. 'I'm fifty-one and I no longer feel real.'

'You must write, Paul, and make yourself real.'

'I can't write. I'm supposed to be grief-stricken, but I'm not sure I can even feel grief, let alone express grief. I no longer fit in. Not even into the skin of Paul Eluard.'

'What do you mean?'

'Well it was always a *nom de plume* anyway. And now I can't write except in the guise of this Communist poet Paul Eluard, of whom the Party has certain expectations.'

'Well then' said Dora with a smile. 'If you can't write as Paul Eluard, why don't you write as somebody else?'

'Yet another *nom de plume*?' he said staring at her.

'Why not?'

'It's an idea, Dora' he said with a laugh. 'I'll think about it!

He did indeed think about it, to the extent of sending her a card saying how much the birthday lunch had lightened his heart and how wonderful it was to find her as lively and lovable as always – signed 'your new secret friend Didier Desroches.'

And it was as the unknown Didier Desroches that he produced a sequence of wonderfully direct and moving poems inspired by his love for Nusch. He showed them to Dora as he wrote them and, as he gradually became less downcast, she began to have the unsettling feeling, not just that they were being drawn together at the expense of the dead Nusch, but that he might be moving towards asking her to marry him.

This was a thought that she found oddly disturbing. She had known Paul for so long, she was deeply fond of him and it would be an honour to be married to such an admired figure. But was that what she really wanted? And anyway, quite apart from the shadow that the death of Nusch cast over the whole idea, was Paul driven essentially by his deep need for companionship and the desire to reconstitute his social life, so that he no longer felt the odd one out? It was all quite unsettling.

It was unsettling to the point that she tried to maintain a degree of distance from Paul and that, when he did in fact propose in that late spring following Nusch's death, she found herself quite divided. But as he told her soberly that he loved her and that he had always admired her intelligence and her dignity, she was increasingly swayed towards accepting – until he said that, as a courtesy, he had mentioned his intention to Pablo.

'To Picasso?'

'Yes, he assured me he didn't mind.'

Dora could not suppress a slight laugh. For it was not just the idea that Picasso should be made the arbiter in the matter of a marriage, but that Paul seemed to be imagining a return to the same court life as before.

She told him how honoured she was and how very fond of him she was, but that she needed space and time to find herself again, so that she could not commit to such a close relationship – even with him – at this time.

It was two o'clock in the morning, Ménerbes was dark and silent apart from the odd screech of an owl, and Dora and Jacqueline were on the way to getting drunk.

Slim as ever and still blonde, Jacqueline had not noticeably changed during her seven years in America, despite – or perhaps because of – her typically independent personal life. She had now married her young American sculptor David Hare, and her painting had been influenced by their travels in the American West. She had exhibited in New York and now, on her return to France with David and the eleven-year-old Aube, she was one of the exhibitors in the enormous Surrealist exhibition in Paris organised by Breton.

They had met up with Dora in Paris and gone round the exhibition together, starting with the expensive catalogue featuring a rubber female breast on the cover. And they had not been enchanted by the giant hand made of chicken wire, the room with artificial rain or the nine-foot 'totem of religion' made of railway sleepers.

'It's an embarrassment' said David, a startlingly young thirty year-old with sharp features beneath a great shock of hair, who spoke no French but was not short of opinions in English. 'How can you trot out that Twenties junk to try to shock people who have seen the heaps of false teeth and spectacles left by the gas chambers? We're in 1947 and not 1918, for God's sake, and we're walking into a Cold War.'

'But remember, David' said Jacqueline, 'that we at least lived through the whole shock left by that 1914-18 war, while you were a toddler living safely in America.'

'Still, it does feel like a swansong' Dora had said.

And now they had come down to spend some time with her in Ménerbes. And after making the ritual trips around the area, they had packed David off on a solo trip to sample the charms of the Côte d'Azur, leaving Dora and Jacqueline to catch up after all these years and, with Aube tucked up in bed, to talk their way through a bottle of the unforgiving local red wine.

'He doesn't make you feel old, now that we're pushing forty?' asked Dora with a smile.

'No, he makes me feel young. I don't know how long it will last, but I'm taking it as it comes. Just so long as nobody stops me being me and I can paint.'

'That's exactly how I feel. But I never seemed to be quite as carefree as you.'

'Well you were more intellectual, more political, more serious than me, for a start.'

'For a start?' said Dora, laughing. 'You mean there's more?'

'And you were more socially at ease than me. You're probably still going to those parties I could never stand at Lise Deharme's or Marie-Laure de Noailles's, and meeting intellectual types like Cocteau and Lacan and God knows who else.'

'Yes' said Dora. 'But I suspect I'm now doing it more to keep my end up and show that I'm still around.'

'And I can see why. But, you know, you were never quite what you seemed, Dora. You were all flamboyant and fashionable and had this darkish reputation of having been with Bataille and then Picasso, but at a time when the rest of us were screwing around and playing musical chairs you were the one – admit it – who believed in lasting love.'

'Well, at least I believed in some constancy underlying love, I suppose. And still do.'

'Maybe you should have married André, rather than me. He was big on Love with a capital L.'

'Except that he would have turned me into a Muse with a capital M. Have another splash of this terrible wine.'

'It really is murderous, isn't it?'

'Yes, but you've got to support the local wine, even if it kills you!' said Dora with a grin. 'So here's to us, Jacqueline. What shall we drink to?'

'Let's drink to burying the past and being free.'

'So here's to the blessed memory of Jacqueline, the famous Surrealist Muse. She was a right old fraud, wasn't she?'

'Disgraceful!' said Jacqueline with a great laugh. 'And here's to the memory of that ghastly *Weeping Woman*.'

'She was a fraud as well. The real weeping woman is the one who was kept in a closet and never allowed to become a free woman – poor Marie-Thérèse.'

'So what does that leave to drink to? That's if I can still hold the glass steady!'

'To the present. To being ourselves.'

'To being young again.'

'And still beautiful.'

'Even more beautiful.'

'So here's to the future, Jacqueline.'

'Not that we can know anything about the future.'

'But that's the whole charm of the future. It's open.'

'Wide open. So we can be anything in the future.'

'Of course we can.'

'And we will, Dora – so long as I don't drink any more of this terrible wine.'